Praise for SEEKING SHELTER:

"An absolute page-turner... Howalt expertly balances brisk pacing, a vivid dystopian world, and a humane and subversive cast of characters while simultaneously exploring the complex themes of democracy, governance, and religion, the foundation for the rebuilding of a new society. Readers will be swept away by this fantastic dystopian tale."

— *The Prairies Book Review*

"...Howalt has this amazing ability to write personal topics and feel as if they had devastating world shattering consequences... Like all second books in a trilogy, *Seeking Shelter* is a rebel with a cause, fighting to grow out of its original's shadow, doing so wonderfully. It is an epic of a minute scale, which can cure the lethargic heart of society with empathy and grace."

— Aden Ng, author of *The Chronicles of Tearha* series, and editor at *Ombak Magazine*

"Howalt's brand of sci-fi is my favorite kind—the kind where the characters' depths and growth are equally as important as the sci-fi elements. The world, its history, and its characters are vivid and an absolute joy to read. I'm always happy to escape from our current reality in the pages of anything written by Howalt, and this book is no exception."

— Laura Morrison, author of *Come Back to the Swamp*, the *Chronicles of Fritillary* series, and the *Space Mantis* podcast

"I have to admit that once I started the book, I became a bit obsessed. I latched on to these characters immediately and didn't want to let go."

— Steeven R. Orr, author and host of the *Just Another Fanboy* podcast

"Howalt has created a perfect sequel which builds on everything that made the first book so special and expands on it in organic and meaningful ways. Meeting the previous cast again felt like reuniting with old, dear friends. The themes take on a new life, focusing on things like what makes a society, superstition, and cultural differences. Esmia is a delightful and expertly crafted addition to the cast. Howalt has crafted a beautiful world, and characters you cannot help but love, even when they aren't being their best selves. *Seeking Shelter* is a testament to Howalt's supreme skill in world and character building and is a must-read for anyone who loves dystopian fiction, great characters, and a world you cannot help but sink into."

— Kathy Joy, author of *Last One to the Bridge*

SEEKING SHELTER

MARIE HOWALT

SPACEBOY BOOKS

Denver, Colorado

Published in the United States by:
Spaceboy Books LLC
1627 Vine Street
Denver, CO 80206
www.readspaceboy.com

First printed September 2020

ISBN: 978-1-951393-05-2

For Dorrit
who guided me through magical literary worlds

Prologue:
Marco

The Superior went through the door as if crossing that threshold were the most natural thing for anyone to do. But then, Superiors were so old that they probably had done it hundreds of times before.

One by one, the primary functions maintainers went through. Some carried spools of wire, others buckets or satchels full of tools.

Hurrying after the last of them, Marco glanced back at the door as it closed and breathed purposefully. It wasn't only what they called *the psychological shock of being outside*. It was also the raw, dry wind blowing tiny grains of sand and dust in his face, though it was such a clear day that the Superior had said helmets were not necessary. The ground under Marco's feet was uneven with rocks and dirt. And the light... He felt dizzy and disoriented, could not focus on anything because all around them were sky and mountains and other weird things that he had only seen pictures of before, and the pictures had not conveyed the sheer vastness of everything.

The ground hit Marco's knees. For a moment, he was sure he would faint and no one would notice and he would be left behind. He fought for control and breath and managed to find his feet again, trembling and staggering, and stumbled forward as fast as he could to catch up with the others.

The sensation of vertigo left him. And now... Now he could truly take in his surroundings. They were going up a slope toward the communications array. Behind them lay the Shelter, a flat, grey construction with only the entrance chamber sticking out of the ground. If Marco did not know what hid beneath, he would have assumed it was only a small shack with room for a handful of people.

But what really took him aback was the sight of the crater. He was used to the closed-off sections and the way the Shelter branched out in an L shape in the lower levels, and he rarely considered the reason. From the outside, though, it was clear that almost half of the compound had been crushed.

Instinctively, he glanced up into the blue above, but no rock came hurtling toward him. The catastrophe took place generations ago. It destroyed half of the sleep tanks, crushed some of the crucial systems that kept them working and awakened those sleepers who were still alive. It brought all the Superiors back from their slumber to care for and raise the survivors. Marco's own great-great-grandparents were infants like most of the other human survivors. If not for the Superiors, they would all have died. Starvation would have taken them, or lack of knowledge and survival skills.

Marco turned around again and continued, half running, to catch up with the other maintainers. They had all been outside at least once before and did not appear particularly impressed by the outside world. The Superior strode on, leading them toward their goal.

The array was another thing Marco had only seen pictures of, and it looked a lot more worn and weatherbeaten in reality than in the depictions. But it was still an impressive construction.

As they climbed the hill, Marco found that the ground became more even and much harder. When he looked down, he saw that beneath a shallow layer of sand, a surface much like the walls of the Shelter was visible. He knew the ancient Superiors had built the Shelter and the array many generations ago. But could they also have constructed the hills?

2

At the summit stood the middlemost section of the array. It was the tallest too, reaching into the sky with long, spindly metal fingers mounted on the top. They must have a remarkable flexibility or power to be able to withstand the storms that ravaged the ground above. Marco had seen footage of the storms, sent from that very construction to the viewing screens in the Shelter. The eyes through which the array observed the weather moved, back and forth, sometimes splattered with water or pounded with grit and dirt. That was one of the reasons the maintainers were sent out. To clean the eyes. But that was not all. The metal fingers did not have eyes, but ears. All in all, the communications array had more senses than a human or maybe even a Superior. Marco chided himself for that thought. A human definitely, but surely not a Superior.

"You three, go left and begin from the end of the array," the Superior spoke. Ne had singled out an older woman and two young men, no doubt relying on the woman's expertise. "You know what to look for. If you come across anything you cannot clean or repair on your own, call for me."

The three nodded and began to make their way along the ridge of the hill. It stretched twice the length of the room Marco shared with his sister. And beyond it was a stretch of nothing for... He could not tell how far it went, but the mountains he saw were so tiny that they must be too many Shelter lengths away to count.

"You go right. You know what to do as well," the Superior was saying.

Marco's attention snapped back. That he was outside for the first time was no excuse not to listen to a Superior's every word. Luckily, those particular words were not for him, for two more of the party walked away along the array. Only Marco and a slender woman called Agata David were left with the Superior.

"You two will climb," the Superior said. Ne studied Marco for a moment, nir face as expressionless as ever. Superiors never lied and they did not have the same outbursts of anger or other strong emotions as humans. Therefore they did not need faces capable of showing feelings. When Marco was very small, he thought some people grew up to become Superiors if they behaved well enough and did a lot of good to the Shelter, but of course, it was not so. Humans were born, grew up, became old and died as humans. Superiors lived forever and had never been human. "You know what to do."

"Yes," Agata said and turned to Marco. Her skin was not quite as dark as his, but apparently it was good enough to qualify her for primary function maintainer duties. It was common knowledge that those with fair skin would turn red and boil in the sunlight outside. "Marco, right?"

"Yes," Marco replied, "Marco Osei."

Agata smiled. "Come on. I will show you how to do it."

Marco followed her and saw now that there were rungs at regular intervals like on a ladder, all the way from the base of the construction to the top. She showed him how to place his hands and feet and began to climb ahead of him.

"It's your first time, isn't it?" she called down after a couple of steps.

"Yes," Marco replied, clinging to the rungs. He had practiced climbing in the Shelter in preparation, but there was no wind, no sharp light and no vast world spreading out around him as if he were a fly from the gardens on a pancake.

"You'll learn quickly," she told him. "Come on."

They climbed onto the platform at the top of the array. Standing here, the metal rods were as thick as arms rather than fingers. Agata squatted down and opened the pack of equipment she had brought with her.

Marco stared at the endless landscape below them. He had to sit. He could look right down at the roof of the Shelter and the crater. He had assumed he saw everything the moment he stepped out of the door, but that door was far below him now. The Shelter no longer dominated the view. It was merely one small part of the landscape. He could see more of the mountains surrounding them and the world spreading out in all directions from up here. In the far distance, he could make out green stretches of vegetation and something blue that glittered.

"It's so big," he whispered. "I had no idea the outside was so big."

1:

Esmia

It was curious how the stone stung less than the words. Perhaps it was because it made her resolve easier. The rock only bounced off her shoulder and clattered to the ground.

Esmia had anticipated this. Had feared it would happen for a long time, but now, the fear was gone. It felt like there was a big, gaping hole in her chest where her heart should be. She had cared for her father while he was lying in sweat-soaked blankets coughing up blood and later as he lay motionless and pale, and it felt as if that had drained something from her. As if his death completed the scooping out of what ought to be inside of her. And now she could not cry for him and she could not feel angry with the people who shunned her.

"You brought this on us!" one shouted from a safe distance. He was pale and probably already ill, but the urge to help anyone else had been drained from Esmia's chest too.

"Go away!" another called. She was hefting one more stone, threatening to throw it if Esmia made any move to go back.

Everybody who still could work had helped dig the deep hole for the bodies outside the Covey's campsite. For those who had died and those who were expected to die. It was not the custom to bury several bodies in one grave, but under the circumstances, it would have to do. They would make sure to put enough stones on top afterward. But Esmia would not be there to help with that.

She had dragged her father's body to the grave, and that was the turning point. Without his presence, there was nothing to hold back their anger and fear. Now she would not be allowed back inside the safety of the semi-circle of tents.

"Leave us alone!"

Esmia could not even save her own father. The tolerance the Covey had shown her because she had inherited her mother's knowledge of medicine and soothing teas had turned into the conviction that she had never done them any good and may have been trying to poison them all. How else could she be healthy while such a terrible illness swept over them? How else could she treat its victims and never catch it herself? They all knew the spirits took her time and again, after all.

For her part, Esmia knew she never meant to harm anyone. But she could not explain why she had been spared.

She couldn't say any of this. She couldn't say anything at all. So she shot one last glance at the hole in ground where she had left her father's body and asked Moon to guide him. One last glance at the dusty tents and the well they had so hastily dug when it became apparent that they would have to camp here. One last glance at the mob of people who were spending their remaining strength on casting her out. And then she turned, knowing she would never see any of this again. Knowing she would have to make it as far as she could before the hole in her chest sealed itself and made her waver in her resolve.

And so she began to walk. She was going north because that was her best chance of finding other human beings, be it wanderers or stagnants.

Esmia didn't look back. She didn't see them return to the tents. She kept walking. Ten paces. Fifty. Then she stopped and turned. Not to the camp, but to an outcropping of rocks littering the ground to her right. She veered off her path and made her way around the rocks.

Several days ago, she had bundled up a few useful items that she had brought to her father's tent at intervals. She anticipated what would happen when he died with a strange calculating logic and sneaked out in the middle of the night. Everybody had been too ill, too tired or too worried to notice.

She found the spot again now. It was hidden from view from the camp by a mound flanking the rocks. She removed the stones piled on top of her possessions, relieved to see that no one else, human or animal, appeared to have touched the spot since she was last here.

It wasn't right to take from the Covey. Esmia knew that. Everyone had as much right to food and water and blankets as anyone else. No one should think only of themselves and their own survival. But she had taken a flask and filled it with water, some salted meat and a threadbare blanket, and had made a sack out of hide scraps, which she stuffed these things into. Along with the knife her father used to carry, the pack should keep her alive for a while.

Now she was glad she had done it. And if she thought about it in a harsh, reasonable way, she was stealing from dying people. Some of them would probably survive. She hoped they would. But even so, there would be less mouths to feed with all the deaths, and with her gone as well. She glanced back over her shoulder, but no one followed her. So she dug into the dirt with her hands and tugged the bundle free from the soil and rocks. A beetle was crawling over it. She crushed its head and put it into the sack with the other things. There was no telling how far she would have to go, and it could provide her with valuable nourishment if she found herself without food and water.

And then she hoisted the sack onto her shoulder and began to walk again. Ahead of her was a vast and empty plain. Ahead of her was uncertainty and danger, but behind her was death and blame.

She had wandered since she could walk, alternately going on her own two feet and being carried on her mother's or father's hip or in the arms of another adult. She knew her own capabilities, how far she could walk and how fast. She knew what direction the Covey had been headed.

If only the spirits would leave her alone, she stood a good chance of reaching a stagnant town or finding other wanderers walking the same path.

She walked because it was the best option and the only option and because if she kept moving, perhaps she could keep the heaviness, that would fill her heart sooner or later, at bay.

2:

Teo

Of course Teo had expected hardship and trouble and never-ending lists of practical problems to be solved. But every week, a question would be brought up that needed to be dealt with, and she had quite frankly not considered all the little mechanisms that needed to work for a town to function.

Teo had feared hunger. She had feared lack of water and the whims of the weather. Even clinging to her dear friend Vanni's vision of falling asleep under the stars with no artificial dome obscuring the view, she had been intimidated by the vastness of the world. She had also been intimidated by the fact that many of the others looked to her for comfort when she was probably as lost in this new life as they were.

And yes, in the first days and weeks and even months, the basic needs were all anyone could think of. Everyone was eager to help with digging and building and scavenging. When the first wave of slummers from the outer parts of Florence arrived a month after they began to reclaim Siena from the elements, the newcomers were welcomed and immediately assigned to different tasks.

But now, six months into their exile, the inhabitants of Siena had routines and they felt safe enough to start raising questions that were not connected to their immediate survival.

How did you establish a currency? Was it even a good idea to have money at all? Would it be necessary someday, or could they build a society without it? Renn seemed to be of that opinion. Teo was not entirely certain if he still considered himself a wanderer at heart or truly one of the Sienans. But she knew he was part of all of their lives and she was grateful for his input.

This was the 24th weekly assembly, the kind of direct democracy where everybody was encouraged to speak their minds and suggest ideas. One of the first issues to be brought up, beyond the immediate survival needs, was that of crime. Theft in that first case, which went to show that even if they did not have a currency, people did have a sense of ownership and property. Rules were instated as the need arose, and with those came the question of consequences for breaking them. Law enforcement was still a work in progress, but as a former arbiter, Arsenio was someone they all looked to. He was assembling a group of peacekeepers. He was also Teo's closest friend and confidante and... She tried to stop herself from thinking the word *supporter*. She had never meant to be a leader. She wasn't even sure she believed it was right to have a leader. But the fact of the matter was that others considered her vote to be the final.

Voting was another tricky thing. Should anyone be able to vote? Newcomers who had only been in Siena for one day before an assembly? And children... Should they be able to vote from the moment they could talk or did experience and a fully developed body and mind overrule views based solely on emotions? Well, she thought, at least today's topics were more tangible. And positive.

The assembly hall was almost full. Eventually, they might have to change the venue or expand it. Now, it was situated in one of the first buildings the rebels claimed upon their arrival. It was a safe place for a number of them to huddle up and sleep and had been what Arsenio called the base of operations for the first days. It was from that building they expanded, and while it was not even approximately at the center of the settlement anymore, it held a special place in all of their minds.

Teo and Arsenio had made another part of that building their home.

There was, of course, not a lot of spare chairs in Siena, so the assembly attendees all sat on the floor, some of them on cushions or blankets. When someone wanted to speak, they simply stood up. Except Teo who functioned as the chairperson... without an actual chair. She hoped to delegate the task to someone else soon. Maybe make a roster and switch between a handful of volunteers.

Everybody in the assembly hall had already heard the news that were on the agenda today, but it was still formally announced that Rosa had given birth to the first child in Siena in centuries. Now she and Stefano were showing the baby to the delight of the assembled Sienans... And Teo realized she was only half listening to the proceedings until someone said her name. She blinked.

"If... you don't mind," the new mother said, flushing and looking expectantly at Teo as she stood there holding her baby.

Everybody, Teo saw, was waiting for her to say something.

"Oh, I—" Teo began, desperately trying to guess the question.

Gabriele came to her rescue. "It's overwhelming," the doctor said from his crosslegged position on a blanket. He was smiling, and a number of people laughed. "But I'm sure Teo doesn't mind the little one being named after her."

"Oh. No," Teo gratefully took the cue. "I don't know what to say. I feel honored."

The parents beamed at her. "Thank you," Stefano said.

"Then Teodora will be her name. But we will call her Dora to avoid confusion," Rosa added.

This was met with more laughter and applause.

Teo smiled. She really did feel honored. And having the child named after her was another nail in her leader coffin, she supposed.

"There is the matter of christening," the mother said, shifting the baby in her arms.

When they left Florence behind, everybody was relieved to find an arbiter and a doctor amongst them. They were happy to find a baker and a farmer from the Green Dome. They were content to have someone from the Centre of Rediscovery and Restoration with them. No one had really spared their spiritual lives a thought at the time. But there were no members of the clergy in Siena. Gabriele and, interestingly, the artificial being Mender were often confided in, but there was no religious structure. Teo had privately hoped that there wouldn't have to be one. The religious discussions with her father she had endured were enough for a lifetime.

But a couple of months ago, Clara, one of the rebels, asked Teo if it would be all right to work on repairing one of the buildings at the edge of their current settlement and turning it into a place of prayer. Teo had agreed and hadn't brought it up at assembly because no one was using the building anyway, and Clara was free to do what she wanted. A crude cross made from rusty metal rods welded together was put on the roof. Clara was in possession of the only Bible in Siena, and soon after, she was hosting weekly Bible readings.

Teo sought out Clara in the crowd and raised an eyebrow, hoping the other woman would understand the question.

She did and nodded in return, mouthing, 'yes.'

So here it was, then. Teo's first official speech on religion. "There are those among us," she began, "who have never been religious. There are those who believe in God, although since we are here, I doubt any of us thinks that God meant for us to live inside a domed city." Was that too much? No, people nodded. "I do not think it is right to force anyone to believe." Once more her glance found Renn. She found his moral compass to be very healthy. "But I also don't think it would be right to deny anyone a place for prayer and worship. We don't have a priest. But we have Clara, and I think she is more than capable of taking care of any rites needed. I propose that if she wants to be the person who does this, she should."

Clara stood up. She gave Teo a small smile, then turned, holding out her arms in a welcoming gesture that seemed to encompass everyone in the room. The silver crucifix she always wore on a chain around her neck gleamed. "I would be delighted," she said. "I am no priest, but I will do my best if you will let me."

"All in favor?" Teo asked.

Hands shot up. A lot of them.

"And against?" she continued.

No hands. Some had not voted. Teo wasn't surprised. But those who were religiously inclined had, and that was enough.

"Then Clara is the..." Teo faltered. Acting priest? Spiritual leader?

"May I suggest deacon?" Clara said.

"Yes," Teo replied. She wasn't sure if it were the closest title to what it was they were appointing Clara as, but it had a nice ring to it. "Deacon Clara it is."

Another round of applause. This assembly was turning out to be cheerful. They all deserved it. Needed it. Most of them had left so much behind. Family, friends, jobs, security. They were building everything from scratch here.

She would not have it any other way. Teo was happy to be in Siena. But she too had left something behind. She had lost one home and gained a new. She had lost one family and was, in a way, building a new one. But she had also lost Vanni, and nothing could fill that void. Not yet, if ever.

"All right," Teo said when the applause had died down and their newly appointed deacon was beaming at them all. Teo tried not to look disappointed that so many thought they needed a religious structure. "Does anyone else have a topic that we should all talk about?"

Gabriele's hand shot up. "May Mender and I?" he asked.

"Of course," Teo said and sat down.

"We would like to talk about the importance of boiling water," Mender started in nir pleasant, soothing voice.

3:

Renn

The last rays of sunlight bathed the city below in a warm glow and stretched the shadows deep and dark. Already, there were lights emanating from some of the houses.

From his place in the watchtower, Renn looked at the outline of the wall. It was crude in comparison to Florence's protection against the outer city and organized compared to the walls surrounding stagnant settlements. He watched two figures holding hands in the street below and disappear into the shadows of one of the newly completed houses.

Life in Siena was still new to all of them, but in vastly different ways. The people from the domes were experiencing the rawness of the world for the first time. The people who had lived in the squalor outside Florence were experiencing a kind of equality that Renn assumed was new to them. And Renn...

Renn drew a deep breath, taking in a faint smell of cooking, smoke and... artifice. He was not certain that was the right word for it, but there was an innate scent of buildings and human construction.

The sound of footfalls on the stairs caught Renn's attention.

"Renn," Teo's voice said behind him. "May I join you?"

"Yes," he replied, not looking up. He was used to her accent now and hardly ever spared her pronunciation any thought.

Teo sat down next to him and crossed her legs. She brushed back hair from her forehead and made herself comfortable with her hands in her lap. For a while, none of them spoke.

Renn appreciated this about Teo. Some people took up very little room, while others took up so much that they almost pushed. Mender, once people had gotten used to nem, was one of those who did not impose. Luca was so loud and took up so much space that it was hard to get close to him. But Teo had the ability to fit into the situation she was presented with. When she spoke publicly, she grew so much that one had to listen to her. Yet, in situations like this, she was unintrusive.

The sky grew dark around them, and where there had been wasteland and mountains was now a vast expanse of nothingness. Only the stars betrayed where the ground met the sky.

Teo breathed in. Renn heard the breath catch in her throat. Then she exhaled, slowly, trembling barely enough for him to detect it. He knew she must be thinking of her friend who was killed in the raid shortly before they left the domed city.

Renn leaned back and stared up into the darkness. He had expected to live his entire existence as a wanderer. To migrate when the changes in the weather or the lack of food and water demanded it. To be part of a Covey or a Bevy, reading maps and wayfinders and the wind. To hunt and defend himself and his companions when he had to.

And now he was here. Had been for months. He slept inside a house. They were building, digging wells, expanding, planting crops and trying to raise livestock in this place. They were fortifying the protective wall and meeting to discuss things that had never needed discussing before in Renn's memory.

Restlessness and unease sometimes crept up on him like stealthy scarvhes. When he was listening to the talk of educating more doctors or putting someone in charge of teaching children to read and write and when naming streets was earnestly discussed, he felt a sudden urge to pick up his staff and walk away. To leave all this and meet the hunger and the treacherous terrain and the dust storms and everything else that he knew how to survive.

But alone? He had only traveled alone once after becoming separated from a Covey during a storm. That was days before he met Mender.

Why did wanderers wander? Was it out of necessity, or did their feet possess an innate restlessness that stagnants' did not?

"Thank you for coming to the assemblies," Teo said, her words riding on the gentle breeze.

The first time he met her, Renn had been surprised to find her so ready to accept Mender and so compassionate not only to him, but to those less fortunate than herself. But she looked to others for decisions. Now she was a leader. She listened to others, but she was an authority in Siena.

"I mean," she continued, "I am always happy to hear your opinion, and you are a highly respected member of this community, but I think you give us something more. You give us faith that we can really do this. That we can survive in this world because you have lived in it for longer than any of us. You are the proof we turn to when we start to doubt whether it was a good idea to leave Florence."

"Do you doubt it?" Renn asked.

Teo laughed. "No. I don't think I could have stayed there after what happened. It was the only thing we could do given the circumstances. The only way to be free. And in the end, that's what it's all about, isn't it? Being free."

Renn considered it for a moment. "Being free," he repeated, "and survival."

"Yes, survival too. So we have a deacon now," Teo changed the subject. "I noticed you didn't vote." There was no blame in her voice. Just curiosity.

"It was not for me to decide," he replied. "I don't know what it means."

"Titles are complicated," she said.

Renn almost asked if that was the reason she did not have one like chief or mayor or elder. "It's not only the title," he said. "Your... religion?" That was what they called it, wasn't it? "I find it difficult to understand."

"It is difficult to understand," Teo agreed. Her eyes bore a hint of hardness and disappointment for a moment before she blinked and smiled again. "Do you believe in anything? I mean... a god. A power that's bigger than humans. Something you can't see."

"There are stories. Myths," he said, "about Moon. About her servants. And we know of spirits without bodies of their own who sometimes visit the living."

"I don't know anything about the Moon," Teo said. "I mean, I know it used to be in the sky and circled the world like the Sun, but..." She made a vague gesture toward the heavens. "Will you tell me about the Moon?"

"I am not a very good storyteller," Renn told her. "But I will try." They told stories in Siena too, but they weren't like the myths he had known all his life. "Once," he began, hoping the words would appear on their own to arrange themselves into the right story, "the world was dark and cold and covered by water. Nothing grew and nothing lived in the great ocean. Then Sun found the world and saw that it could be something else. He knew nothing could grow without light and warmth and soil, so he made a round shape with his hands." Renn held up his cupped hands in front of his face to demonstrate. "And he breathed warmth and life and light into them and formed a bright and glowing ball. He put it on the sky above the world and named it Sun because it was part of him."

Teo was listening intently.

Renn was sorry she had to hear the myth from him and not someone who remembered the rhythm and could use the words better. But even so, the story was taking him along too and he could not stop telling it before it was finished.

"Sun shone on the world and made the ocean give way to land. And light and warmth made plants grow. Out of the soil came the first animals and birds, and then finally humans. But there was no night and the world was too hot. So Moon came to Sun and told him she would make his creation better. She sent her servants to help humans and she put Sun's glowing ball into motion to create night and day. But nights were dark and cold and humans felt abandoned without light. So Moon hung her lantern in the sky to show that she was watching over the world and to light the way for night time travelers."

Teo didn't speak for so long that Renn was starting to fear his storytelling skills were so poor that she had lost interest altogether or had fallen asleep. Then she cleared her throat. "That's a beautiful story."

"I have heard others say Moon's Lantern was only a rock in the sky that was destroyed by another rock," Renn said.

"And I think a lot of people don't believe there was ever anything up there besides the stars," Teo replied. "But you know what I think? I think it doesn't change anything either way. If there was a rock or a lantern up there, it's not here now. If there is no practical application of the theory, I'm not going to tell anyone what to believe."

"You don't think there is practical application for a deacon?" Renn asked.

Teo blinked. Perhaps he had seen too much behind her words. "My father told me God intended for us to live inside the domes and for everyone outside to die," she said. "I don't believe that. Clara's God is supposed to be the same God, but she doesn't think God plays favorites. She believes God wants us all to help each other. That's good enough for me."

4:

Luca

'So, when Alexander Graham Bell invented the first telephone back in the 19th century, who did he actually call?' That's the sort of witty joke first year students at the Institute of Robotics and Artificial Intelligence would crack. Now, there was no one to say it because the IRAI was long gone and its only living student was not about to make that joke.

First of all, Bell didn't invent the phone at all; the Italian Antonio Santi Giuseppe Meucci did. And secondly, said student was pretty fucking sure no one would be stupid enough to construct only one communication device. There was no way to check if it worked if you didn't have at least two. Which was why Luca handed his butler Alfredo one of the crude boxes he had spent the past few days building and ran to the other side of the house to test it.

The boxes were not telephones. That wasn't possible now that the world had ended and every satellite and cell tower were either useless junk piles or had been obliterated by remnants of the Moon. Luca, of course, hadn't been around for that. He'd been starring in his own, private production of *Sleeping Beauty* in which he wasn't woken up after a few centuries by the kiss of a handsome prince but instead by the earthquake that killed his family. Being the only human member of civilized society left alive meant he hadn't really thought of communication technology, but now there was a settlement full of people he cared about... Oh, all right, most of them were little more than strangers and some of them were real idiots, but he did care about one or two, and regardless, it would be practical to be able to get in touch with them without having to cross the desert every time.

Luca stopped behind the house, raised the box, flipped the switch on the side of it and paused. This could be a historic moment. He sat down on the ground, retrieved the device he had in his pocket for recording in case anything interesting happened and held it up in a   practiced selfie angle. "Hi, welcome to *Luca's Lab*," he said, grinning at the non-existing audience. "Today we're testing something new. Or old, rather. I have created a dinosaur." He held up the box with his other hand in front of the camera. "It's called a radio. Back before technology like the sexy little gadget recording this for posterity, people used them for cordless communication across fairly big distances. I dug up some schematics and worked out the rest myself, and I'm fairly sure it'll work, but we'll see what happens."

He placed the radio in his lap. It had a built-in transmitter as well as a receiver. For a moment, his hand hovered above the button. He had to come up with something better than, 'Hello, this is Luca,' because who the hell would it be if not him? He pressed the button and held it. "Hey, Alfredo. How's the weather on your side?"

There was a crackling sound as he released the button. And then Alfredo's voice saying, "Not that much different from the other side of the house, I'm sure." The voice came through, but it could definitely use more power. Especially over longer distances.

Luca winked at the camera. "The radio works. It's the dawning of a brave new world," he said and ended the recording. "All right, this is brilliant," he said to Alfredo. "I'm coming back."

"I would compliment you on the construction of this," the sentient said as he handed the device to Luca, "but I have seen you build far more complicated things."

"Yeah," Luca agreed. "But this is for... Aren't you going to ask me what it's for?"

"No," Alfredo said. "That much is obvious. You want to talk to your friends."

Luca bit back a reply that was too snotty even for him. Alfredo and Nanny had both given him hell after the whole rebellion thing in Florence. They weren't his parents. They were his employees. But they were there to take care of him, and that meant scolding him like he was some kid pulling a prank when really he'd heroically gone to Florence, despite knowing that the leaders had it in for him. Okay. Heroically, moronically, whatever. The point was he got out alive, and he did so with a group of people who couldn't be bothered to put up with the asshats in charge of the domed city either.

Regardless of their harsh words about responsibility and taking care of himself, his sentients accepted that Siena was no threat and regularly made comments about it being good for him to talk to other humans. He'd agreed with most of it until Nanny said that she hoped there was someone his own age and Alfredo added that he thought they might have a good influence on him. Luca had reminded them that he was centuries older than anyone in Siena and besides, they were pretty much all illiterate idiots who couldn't work a toaster even if they had a manual.

"What is the range of these radios?" Alfredo asked.

"Theoretically more or less limitless," Luca said, taking the other radio and switching it off, more from habit than necessity since they both had solar powered batteries. "But radio waves travel in a straight line, so the curve of the Earth is a problem over longer distances, and depending on the power and wavelength, they aren't good with obstacles. So..."

Alfredo followed his upwards glance. "You are going to build an amplifier?"

"An antenna," Luca replied. When he was a kid, Alfredo and Nanny had no expertise whatsoever when it came to technology. They knew as little about what made them go as an average human being knew about brain surgery. They were programmed to take care of children, specifically Luca and Leo, and to take care of everything you'd expect a butler and a housemaid to see to. But being sentients, they could learn as well as any other person, and after more than two years alone with Luca, they had picked up a few things. "It'll catch the signal from my radio and send it out there above any obstacles."

"How high do you mean for it to be?" the butler asked.

"High enough?" Luca grinned. "Don't worry, I'll make sure the lightning conductors are in place. I just need to go over the numbers once more and then start building."

"Luca!" called a voice from the front door of the house.

"Yeah?" He shaded his eyes from the sun with his arm.

"It's lunchtime," Nanny informed him.

"It can wait," he called back. "I'm working."

Alfredo made a sound that sounded suspiciously like laughter.

"Your work can wait," Nanny told him. "You didn't bring water out with you."

Luca groaned. He was not a kid. He had a sudden vision of himself as an old man being reprimanded and fussed about by two sentients. But she was right. It was hot, the sun was high in the sky, and he had not had anything but coffee for breakfast. "Okay. I'm coming. And," he added to Alfredo, "what are you laughing at?"

"Nothing, master Luca," Alfredo said, poker-faced. "Is there anything to laugh at?"

Luca rolled his eyes. Semis were easier. You turned them on when you needed them for whatever they were programmed to do and turned them off when you were done. Sentients were persons. Artificial, yes, but still persons. So instead of telling Nanny to shut herself off, he left the radios on the table in the entrance hall, went to wash the dust off his hands and sat down at the kitchen table where, indeed, lunch was waiting for him. It even included fresh vegetables from the garden.

23

"When are you visiting your friends again?" Nanny asked, pouring a tall glass of water from the base's well.

"I expect I'll go to Siena in a couple of days," he replied. "I need to finish something here first."

"Something to do with that communication device you have been working on?" she asked.

Luca smiled. He hadn't actually told her about the radio, but she was smart. "Yeah, I need an antenna here and where it's going to be received."

"In Siena," Nanny concluded. "That sounds very nice. Then you can talk to them more often."

"It'll be practical," Luca agreed and bit into his sandwich.

Nanny nodded. She sat down at the table on the opposite side and studied him. "How is Renn?"

"Last I checked, he was fine," Luca replied around a mouthful.

"Have you invited him to visit?" she asked.

Luca swallowed and chased the sandwich with a gulp of water. Sudden flashback to before the world went to hell. Sitting at the dinner table in their house in Florence with his parents and Leo, talking about school. His dad asking awkward questions like if there were any girls in his class that he liked. Luca, then fifteen, had made out with every gender of attractive people that he could. And he wasn't exactly an antisocial geek, but the truth was that being a top student at IRAI took up most of his time, and none of his friends, not even the ones who had applied when he did, were at the same school.

"He knows he's welcome," he replied. "But I see him when I visit Siena, anyway."

"I like him," Nanny went on. "He's a nice, young man."

"Yeah, super nice," Luca said, not exactly sure that nice was the most accurate word. Nice was what you called an aunt or a painting when you didn't have any strong feelings about it either way. Renn was... Renn was kind of stuck up and had ridiculous hair and no sense of humor, and he was completely badass and stupidly handsome for

24

someone who cared so little about his looks. "Yeah," Luca repeated. "Super nice."

Nanny sent him a look he did not want to interpret. "It would be nice to see Mender again too," she carried on.

"Yeah." Luca stuffed the rest of the sandwich into his mouth and went back outside while chewing it. He had plenty of scrap metal and unused materials for the antenna. All he needed to do was get everything he needed up on the roof and not break his neck.

Making a pulley system wasn't hard. At least, Luca thought as he secured the rope around the materials, he wasn't one of those programmers who couldn't cope if they couldn't code their way out of everything. He had always been as fascinated by the engineering part of robotics as the software part.

He had been on the roof a few times before to replace individual solar panels and to check the connections of the lightning conductors. He balanced for a moment, then tied himself to one of the hooks he had placed the first time he ventured up there as a centuries old sixteen-year-old. He was taller now, though admittedly not much, and maybe he was a little on the wiry side, but he had grown the kind of muscle you didn't get from hitting the gym. The kind you got from actually working because you fucking had to.

The other rope went into another hook and assuming he'd done the math right, he should be able to haul up the materials simply by using his body as a counterweight. But first... He stretched and stood in the middle of the sloping roof for a moment, inspecting his world. Somewhere to the east was Florence with its magnificent domes and ridiculous technology-shunning bigot population. And to the south... Siena. He squinted as if that would make him able to see. Obviously it wouldn't even help to bring a telescope.

"And today's theme is: The curving of the Earth and the distance to the horizon!" Luca announced to no one. He wasn't even as high up as Renn's designated watchtower. He rolled his shoulders and decided to get to work, imagining Renn perched up there, listening to the elements or reading the sand or whatever. "Does he even know the planet is round?" Luca mumbled to himself and then had to take a moment to laugh at the absurdity of it and the demise of science as a whole. Again. He did that a lot. Because really, it was that or crying.

5:

Luca

Every time Luca visited Siena, there would be some kind of progress. A new roof had been laid, the wall had been expanded, rubble had been removed from the ground to reinvent the concept of roads... That sort of thing. Luca had lent the Sienans some stuff to help out, but one of the problems was energy, and Luca couldn't spare enough solar panels to power a whole settlement. And so far, attempts at harnessing wind energy had been on par with the best slapstick comedies Luca had ever seen. But they had started scavenging. That was one thing Teo's boyfriend or whatever was good at, and Teo herself was a quick learner.

Today Luca didn't have any heavy equipment with him. He only had what he could take on his bike. After all, this wasn't an equipment run.

It was another dry day, and he arrived in a cloud of dust that turned his bike and his boots a greyish brown color. There were no sentries, so Luca got off his bike and went straight through what passed for a gate. It simultaneously made him feel good about humanity and exasperated that this portion of it was a bunch of gullible idealists who let anyone enter their town.

It wasn't exactly a buzzing metropolis. It was a village. It reminded him of a small vineyard in the mountains he had visited with his family once, a place so remote and in such a secluded location that there was an eerie sound he hadn't been able to place until he realized it was the absence of noise.

Two kids ran past him further down the main street of the settlement. Yelling, laughing, one chasing the other with a stick. One of them was from the inner city of Florence and was part of the original group of settlers. The other one was from the slums and belonged to a party that arrived only a few months ago. And in this little pothole of socialist equilibrium, no one cared.

Luca decided not to ask anyone where Teo was. Chances were that his visit was public knowledge already. He would stroll through Siena and eventually either find Teo or Renn or be found by them.

Seeing Siena grow, or rather regrow, was weird. Luca studied a woman who was repurposing old slabs of concrete and turning them into a strange mosaic of a wall on a building that had seen better days. He used to have friends here. Classmates. What had happened to them at the time of the impact? How had Siena turned into this pile of rubble? Had they all died immediately, or had the population dwindled gradually over the centuries? In a way, it was a relief that the city was so completely unrecognizable. It made it easier to see it as it was and not imagine how it had been.

A group of people approached him. They were dragging metal poles which would not be half bad for Luca's purpose. All four of them greeted him, one of them by name. Luca had to admit he didn't remember theirs. But that's celebrity life. Or something.

A persistent banging noise caught his attention, and Luca turned left, in the opposite direction of the town hall or whatever they called it. In front of a building that stood a little on its own, a young woman was on her knees, hammering away at a sheet of metal. There was something symbolic about it, Luca mused, probably due to the ominous cross on top of the building behind her.

She noticed him and put the hammer down. "Luca! How are you?"

He shrugged, smiled. "Hey. I'm good. What are you doing?" He was a little curious to see her working on her own. Clara didn't strike him as the engineering type.

She stood up and arched her back to stretch. "I am making a font," she said.

Luca almost made an ironic comeback about it hopefully not being Comic Sans which was such a geeky thing to say that it would have passed under the radar even for most people in his age. "For..?" he said instead.

"A baptismal font. Are you a believer, Luca?" Clara asked.

"We all believe in something," he replied, but she didn't seem super impressed by his philosophical statement. "Christianity is older than the domes of Florence," he tried. There was this thing about religion and science...

Clara grinned at him. "I'm not going to try to convert you," she said. "But some of us were brought up as Christians, and while we may have disagreed with practically everything the elite of Florence stands for, we have not lost our faith in God. And since we need to baptize a child soon, I..."

"Wait," Luca said, "you're the priest?"

"Deacon, actually. We found that more fitting."

He grinned. "But the head of the congregation, right? That's great. I can get one hundred percent behind that." Because that meant they weren't stuck in archaic patterns.

"I thought you weren't religious?" she asked.

Luca scratched the back of his head. "Doesn't mean I can't support what you're doing here," he said. The thing about religion and science was complicated. It would make for a pretty good sitcom, but sadly there was no one around to make it now. But at first they were super tight. Then they had a big fallout and a lot of people thought religion was a load of bullshit, and a bunch of other people thought science was a load of bullshit until at one point someone said, 'Hey, what if I told you you can have both?' It didn't solve the marital crisis of the two, but it made for a whole new set of funny and not so funny complications. And that was just Christianity and science. It got even more complicated when you brought other players on the board, like Islam and Judaism and whatnot. Still, there'd been a truce of a kind for a while. And then someone created a sentient. Wham, bam, everybody up in arms all over again. "What?" Luca asked, realizing he wasn't listening to her.

"I said thank you," Clara repeated.

Someday he'd have a chat with her about AI. Someday he'd explain to her exactly what it was he went to the IRAI to learn and possibly fuck up what positive relationship they had because he absolutely had to poke at things to see what made them tick. "You seen Teo?" he asked.

"She's working on the new well," Clara replied and pointed in the direction he'd already been headed.

"Thanks. Good luck with your bowl," he told her and continued on his way through Siena, marveling a little bit at the fact that he'd just had a conversation with someone on a subject he hadn't talked to anyone about since he found himself in the aftermath of the apocalypse. Hm. He'd have to ask Clara's opinion on that subject too.

Teo was shoveling dirt onto a cart from a hole in the ground which, judging from the fact that Arsenio was a pretty tall man and only his head was sticking up, was almost two meters deep.

Another person was standing by the hole, carrying on the age old tradition of at least one person idly looking at whoever was doing the actual work, whether it was to assess their job, relieve them or hang out because they couldn't do what they needed to do before the others finished. Regardless, Luca recognized the third person as one of the people from the slums who had left only a day or two after the rebels.

"Yo!" he called.

Teo straightened her back and wiped her forehead with her hand. Arsenio's eyebrows did a sarcastic dance and the third person cocked her head slightly at him.

"Hello, Luca," Teo greeted him. "What brings you here?"

He grinned. She assumed it wasn't a social call, and she was right. "I've been working on something I think you'll love."

"Working," Arsenio scoffed from his hole. "You could do some actual work for once and help us dig."

Luca took one step toward the hole, then stopped because kicking someone in the face when said face was at ground level was pretty rude. "Look here, macho man," he retorted, "just leave the jobs that require thinking to me and keep digging your own grave."

"It's not a grave. It's a well," interjected the ex-slummer in the awkward pause that followed.

Teo cleared her throat. "What have you been working on, Luca?" she asked, leaning on her shovel.

"Tech," he replied. "More specifically, a device that will allow us to communicate over great distances. If I have one and you guys have one here in Siena, we can get in touch even when I'm back at the base."

Teo's face lit up in the sort of expression she was the only person besides Luca to ever have. She loved all his gadgets and was as much for technological progress as he was. And she was quick to understand new concepts. "Really?" she asked. "What connects the devices?"

"It's called radio waves," Luca said. "They are invisible, but they can carry sound from one place to another if you have a device called a radio to pick them up and send them. So we can talk to each other."

"But why would we want to talk to you?" Surprisingly, it was not Arsenio talking, but the ex-slummer. There was no malice or mockery in her voice. Just curiosity. "I mean, we can talk to you when you are here."

Well, that was new. Back in Luca's time, people couldn't get enough of being in constant touch with everyone else all over the whole fucking planet. Instant connection and communication were ingrained in daily life, and an hour of downtime caused people irritation and anxiety.

"Yeah, well, I didn't build the radios to chat with you," he said. "Imagine if you need something specific that I might have. It'd be a lot easier if you could just call me and ask."

"Oh, I understand," Teo said. "That is a marvelous idea. And very kind of you."

"What's in it for you?" Arsenio asked, as delicate as a hippo.

"Jesus fucking Christ," Luca groaned. "I guess I'm hoping to hear your lovely voice whenever I feel like it. Look, I made a thing. I'm offering the thing to you guys. Take it or leave it."

"We will happily take it," Teo said. "That is, I will, personally. But I'm sure everybody will agree that it would benefit us all at the next assembly. Perhaps we can be of use to you as well."

"Well, you've got Renn the human weathercock," Luca said. "Like, if there's a storm coming from this area, you can always warn me or something."

Teo's eyes were bright with anticipation. "What do we need to make it work?" she asked.

"I already built the radios. We can test them if you like. I have them here." He patted his bag. "But if we mean to use them over long distances, we need an antenna. A tall mast that takes the radio signals and helps them reach their goal."

"Won't it be really noisy?" asked the ex-slummer. "If it's loud enough to be heard all the way to where you live?"

Luca's mouth opened, but no sound came out. It was really, really hard to wind down to that level of thinking.

"The signal travels through the air, but it needs a device to pick it up to make any sound," Teo said. "Right?"

"Yes!" Luca agreed, gratefully. "Yes, exactly."

"I need to finish this, but will you stay for a while and show me later?" Teo asked.

"Sure." Luca glanced over his shoulder and then back at her. "Any idea where I can find Renn?"

Arsenio planted his hands on the edge of the hole and somehow managed to thrust himself up. "Follow me," he said. "I'm going there anyway."

Teo exchanged a glance with Arsenio, and then she climbed into the hole, and the ex-slummer took over her position at the cart.

6:

Renn

Renn brought up his staff in an arc, holding it one third down the length in one hand. His students mimicked the movement. Some of them were fast, others almost as measured as he was. But no one dropped their staff or accidentally hit someone or themselves anymore. Renn stood with his feet apart, straight back, one hand holding the staff and the other stretched out to the side and behind him to help the balance. Patience was key in a hunting situation, but without the necessary strength, patience was not very useful. So he brought them through these exercises every time they met. To begin with, a few had scoffed at the idea of standing still, but when their muscles seized up and refused to hold the position, they understood.

A staff was a walking aid, a defensive weapon, a tool for hunting, and it could be used as a part of a shelter. A wanderer's companion, yes, but here Renn was teaching a group of stagnants how to wield one.

The classes took place between the ruins south of the settlement. There was no barrier separating the settlement and the wasteland on this side, but it was easy to tell where the town ended. Renn suspected there had been open space between the buildings here because it took hardly any time to clear enough room for the class. The ground here was hard underneath a sparse layer of sand.

Renn transferred the staff to his other hand, and the five students attending today followed suit. One shook the hand that had been gripping the staff. Renn needed to show him that flexing the fingers slowly was more efficient and wouldn't scare away potential prey.

He glanced from one to the other until he heard footsteps behind him. He was expecting one more person to show up, but it sounded like two people. One was, indeed, Arsenio. The other took shorter steps, sounded lighter and Renn would recognize his smell anywhere. It was Luca's approach that made him turn.

Arsenio nodded and shifted his own staff to his left hand as he moved to stand with the rest of the class. He knew an explanation wasn't needed. He did not always have time to train properly with the others, but although the staff was new to him, Arsenio was the only person in Siena who had been trained for multiple types of combat before he left Florence.

"Yo," Luca said, his grin turning into a frown and back into a grin once more as he took in the scene. "What's up, Little John? Or should that be Yangra the Monk?"

These were, Renn had no doubt, references to people from Luca's life centuries ago. He could only assume they used similar weapons. "Luca," he replied. "Will you watch or join?"

"Oh." Luca blinked, quickly assessed the half circle again in the light of this proposition and smiled. "Sure, I'll join. If you have a staff I can borrow..."

Renn did. Despite his conviction that every person should have their own, he had two extra staffs of medium length and weight in order to provide them if someone damaged their own staff and to use them for demonstrating how much it took to break one. He gestured toward the staffs lying on the ground some paces away.

"Awesome. Thanks," Luca said.

Renn turned back to his students. Arsenio stood with his staff now, effortlessly held at a perfectly horizontal angle.

Out of the corner of his eye, Renn saw Luca twirl the staff he had chosen and make his way to the other end of the half circle. He looked from the other students to Renn and then mimicked the stance of the others. This was not as easy as one might think. Most people had a general idea of where their limbs were, but like they would not be able to render a person in drawing, they were unable to copy another person's posture exactly. Perhaps it was due to Luca's frequent use of mirrors that he did it rather well.

He let them balance their staffs for a little longer, and then Renn turned his hand and bent his arm at the same time, bringing his staff in. His other hand closed around it too. His students did the same. Renn launched into a series of slow, deliberate movements that served to stretch the muscles of the whole body and heighten the awareness and control of the staff.

Renn himself had been taught how to properly wield a staff by a hunter shortly after his parents passed away. At the time, Renn was not old enough not to take care of himself, but old enough to be a useful member of the Covey.

Today, Renn's intention had been to pair up the students and let them practise defending themselves. He would then watch them and give them advice and make sure no one was hurt. Normally with an uneven number of students, he would train with the weakest of them, but now Luca was here. It would not be fair to pair him up with anyone. He was too inexperienced to give his partner a challenge.

"I would like you to train defensive stances and defensive moves in pairs," Renn began. "Maybe it would be best if Luca..." He tried to find a polite way to ask Luca to watch while the others practiced.

"I'll take Arsenio," Luca said.

One of the students tried to hide a snicker with a cough. Another laughed out loud.

"What?" Luca bit.

"I don't think that is an even match," Renn said.

"It's fine," Arsenio replied. "I'll be gentle."

"That's okay, macho man," Luca said, "I can take it."

Why would Luca want to be partnered with Arsenio? Unless Renn read them completely wrong, they had a strained relationship bordering on resentment. But maybe that was exactly the reason Luca wanted to train with Arsenio. He was hoping for some kind of retribution. But Arsenio was bigger and stronger. Could Luca not see that? Was he really so certain of himself that he expected to be able to best a person with formal combat training as well as more practice with a staff?

"No," Renn said. "Arsenio, please practise with Miriam." Ignoring Luca for the time being, he quickly divided the others into pairs and told them to begin. He watched them move around and decide who was first to defend themselves against their partner.

"Okay," Luca said, clearly forcing himself to sound cheerful. "I guess I will just watch, then."

"No," Renn said again. "You will fight me."

Luca blinked. "Really? Awesome!"

"The others are practising moves I have taught them already," Renn said by way of explanation. It was not only that Luca would be an inconvenience to the students. No, proof was glaring Renn in the face that the boy from the past thought himself invincible. Confidence was important in most walks of life, but too much of it was dangerous. It was not Renn's responsibility to teach Luca this lesson, but now that the opportunity presented itself, he had to take it. "I will show you defense."

"Of course you will," Luca said in a tone that Renn could not quite place.

"Please attack me using the staff. You don't need to hold back," Renn added.

Luca's grin returned for a moment. But when they stepped away from the other pairs, he wore a serious, concentrated expression. His breathing was good, Renn noticed. And his grip on the staff was strong. And then Luca sprang rather than stepped forward.

Renn brought up his staff to intercept the attack. Luca was putting his weight into the attempt, pushing his staff against Renn's with as much force as he could muster. And of course, he put himself off balance. Renn placed one foot behind the other, turned his upper body and watched Luca stumble past.

Luca managed not to fall. But when he turned, he seemed almost angry, and Renn could not determine if it were at him or Luca himself.

"Okay," Luca said. "All right..."

Renn lowered his staff. It was unlike Luca to give up so soon. Had he realized he was no match already? Renn had barely finished the thought before Luca came at him again, both hands clutching the staff in a white-knuckled grip and bringing it up as he ran the few paces back to Renn, kicking up dust and gritting his teeth against the impact. This time his aim was better, although Renn could not see the purpose of the attack unless it was designed to push him back and make him fall over on his backside. The staffs met with a hard clack, and they stood for a moment. Their eyes met, and Renn was not at all certain what he saw in those green eyes. Defiance, perhaps. But it was not all.

Luca claimed that he spent his time without human company training his physical strength, flexibility and endurance. In a way, it was surprising that a boy who had the many alien conveniences such as a car and servants and masheens to perform demanding tasks for him felt the need to enhance his own capabilities in other areas than the operation and maintenance of his masheens.

Surprise grew on Luca's face when he found that instead of pushing Renn away, he was the one who was forced backward with a sudden thrust. And this time he failed to regain his balance. He let go of the staff to brace for the impact with his elbows and landed much in the way he had intended for Renn to.

Renn took the opportunity to turn to his students to see how they were doing and found that they were not doing at all. They were simply standing, all staring at Renn and Luca. For a brief moment, he wondered why, and was about to tell them to keep practising, but then he understood. They rarely saw him fight. He demonstrated stances and moves and instructed them, but those were carefully arranged and planned sessions. This was something new. A few of the faces turned toward him were focused, intent on learning. Arsenio was smiling. He knew Renn was teaching Luca a lesson, and he clearly appreciated it. But as little as that had been Renn's intention, there was nothing he could do now apart from turning to Luca who was back on his feet and picking up the staff.

Renn had lowered his own staff, signaling that the fight was over if Luca wanted it to be.

Luca did not. When he attacked again, Renn expected a variation of the two first attempts. But as Luca closed in on him, he let go of the staff with his left hand and drew it back with his right. He was going to strike with it like a sword. Renn blocked it, but met no resistance and Luca's staff was knocked aside and out of his hand. But why—

The answer came quickly and in the shape of Luca's left foot aiming for Renn's other side. He had to dodge and still, the tip of Luca's boot actually hit him hard enough to make him stumble back a pace before recovering.

Luca grinned. He had reason to be pleased with himself. He had, however, also discarded his weapon to get in one single hit. And now Renn had two options. Allow Luca to pick up the staff or end it here. He picked the latter.

Closing the distance between them again, Renn brought up his staff with both hands. And Luca leapt forward. Renn almost instinctively jammed the end of the staff into Luca's face which would most likely have resulted in a broken jaw, but he managed to stop himself, and instead Luca took hold of the staff too, ridiculously holding onto it in the middle between Renn's hands, trying to twist it although clearly it would not work.

His fingers were so white with the effort that the fine web of scars was almost invisible. His gaze was steady. Behind the recklessness and impulsiveness was a mind as full of calculations as Renn's own. Still, if

Luca believed he stood a chance, the mind that did intricate calculations when it came to masheens and sentients was failing him now.

Renn turned the staff, effectively locking Luca's arms in an awkward position. Then he struck, not aiming for broken ribs or any other damage, but hard enough to push Luca away, causing him to loose his grip on the staff, skid backward, arms flailing for balance before he finally fell. It hardly took more than a second, and Renn gave him no time to recover before he moved, swinging his staff into position and arriving, perfectly timed as if they had rehearsed this particular sequence of moves, with the tip of his staff a finger's width above Luca's chest before Luca could get to his feet.

Said chest was heaving, dust was clinging to Luca's sweat-slick skin, and for a moment, Renn thought he would refuse the obvious and roll, taking advantage of the fact that Renn would not bring down the staff to crush his breastbone and force him to continue. But then the defiant green eyes closed, and Luca relaxed.

Behind them, cheering broke out.

"Luca?"

No reply. Renn was caught between the fear that he was actually injured, perhaps unconscious, and the suspicion that the moment he bent down to check, Luca would kick or punch him.

"Luca?"

His eyes opened again. "Yeah, yeah. You win. I give up."

"It was never a matter of winning or losing," Renn told him, removing the staff and holding it in one hand while offering Luca the other.

"I guess it wasn't," Luca replied, hesitating, then taking Renn's hand. "You just thought you'd publicly humiliate me."

Renn tried not to scowl or haul Luca to his feet with too much force. Now was not the time to discuss it. Still, could Luca really be so blind to his motive? Was he unable to see that it was exactly to avoid any risk of humiliation that he had decided to practise with Luca instead of pairing up Arsenio with him? There was no shame in being bested by someone more skilled, and the difference in skill between them should be obvious to anyone. "Are you all right?" he asked instead because Luca clearly was suppressing a wince as he stood up.

"Are you?"

The question was redundant at best. "I am," Renn said, regardless, and took a quick assessment of Luca. He did appear not to have been hurt seriously, but his elbows were bleeding through a layer of grit and dust, and he favored his left foot. Renn picked up the discarded staff and tossed it, precisely and unceremoniously, to Luca. It made him smile that Luca caught it.

He turned to face his students again, hoping that they had at least benefited from the brief demonstration.

7:

Renn

Renn half expected Luca to either stalk off in anger or sit out the rest of the lesson, but he joined the others without a word. One half of the students seemed to share Luca's opinion that he had been humiliated and badly concealed their grins and snickers. The other half, however, complimented Luca for having the courage to fight Renn. Only Arsenio appeared indifferent, or perhaps he was merely better at concealing whatever he did feel.

When the lesson ended, Luca handed Renn back the staff.

"Your ankle?" Renn asked.

"I'm fine," Luca said.

Which was true, but did not necessarily mean he had not twisted his ankle and certainly did not mean that his elbows weren't now sporting a dark crust of sand and dried blood. "What brings you here today?" Renn said instead.

"What, I can't just visit my ex-rebel pals in Siena?" Luca's tone was slightly defiant. But then he shrugged, his posture changing into a familiar slouch that set him apart from anyone else Renn had ever met. As if somehow his body language were the most archaic part of him. "Okay, I cooked up a useful something," he conceded.

Renn nodded an encouragement and gestured toward the settlement.

"It's called a radio. You ever heard of those?"

"No," Renn replied as they began to walk, Luca trying, in vain, to hide a limp. Renn prepared himself for an explanation about masheens that he would understand only half of, partly because he had no experience with these things, and partly because Luca never did much to make his tales easily accessible.

"Okay, so say you're in one place and I'm in another. You're here and I'm at the base. And we want to talk. Normally I'd have to come here, right?"

"Yes," Renn agreed. "Though I could also come to you despite my lack of a car." Was this going to turn into a complaint? Everybody appreciated Luca's efforts.

"But," Luca added, "I have found a way for us to talk across the distance. A radio is a nifty little device that can literally take my voice and transport it to you so you can hear me. And it can take your voice all the way to me too."

Renn assumed Luca did not actually mean literally. "So... we would be able to talk over large distances using this device?" he tried.

"Yes! Exactly!" Luca beamed. "If I have one and you guys in Siena have one, we can talk. You can ask me to bring you stuff. And I can... check up on you."

"That sounds useful," Renn agreed.

"I'm glad you agree! Teo's in too," Luca said. "We just need to do a few practical things for it to work. Where are we going?"

"I am headed to the infirmary," Renn said. "Their water storage needs replenishing and I have agreed to get some." He had meant to do a few other things first, but he wanted to make sure someone qualified encountered Luca and assessed whether his ankle needed treatment. He also wanted to avoid suggesting this to Luca since apparently Luca already thought Renn had intended to humiliate him. Who knew if showing concern would be misconstrued to mockery?

"Is there anything you don't do for this bunch?" Luca asked.

"Yes," Renn said. "I do not work with masheenery, teach reading and writing, deliver babies—"

"Yeah, okay," Luca cut him off, shaking his head. "But you are going out of your way to help. Do you ever have any spare time?"

Renn did not know what to reply to that. Spare time was a concept he had only been introduced to recently, and he was not entirely certain how to handle it. The idea of dividing one's time into work and recreation, especially at certain fixed hours of the day, was a strange one. How did you know when you would be needed? Granted, Renn did have fixed appointments with his students and understood that stagnants needed certain things in their daily schedule, but everything he did could be pushed aside to make room for more pressing matters.

"I thought not," Luca sighed.

"Considering you don't live here, you are spending a lot of time helping too," Renn said.

Luca shrugged and kicked a stone, stumbled and winced. "I got it," he said when Renn reached out to steady him. "So... you live here?"

"I—" Renn faltered. "I do currently. I want to contribute while I am here."

Luca studied him for a moment, seemed about to say something, and then he shook his head. "Well, I'm helping out cause I want to. And because..." he hesitated. "I want to piss off Florence."

"They should be happy that Siena is thriving. After all, they wanted the rebels to leave."

"But do they want them to be happy and build an awesome town of their own?" Luca's grin spoke volumes.

Renn did not reply. Instead he opened the door of the infirmary and went inside, closely followed by Luca.

To begin with, the place had been put together in a hurry to have somewhere to treat acute injuries. Now there were several rooms. The one they stepped into was a waiting area. Another room was for storing bandages and medicine, there were two examination rooms and another two for patients to stay overnight. A section of the building had been turned into living quarters for Gabriele and Mender, although the latter had few of the needs humans did.

Renn nodded a silent greeting to the two people in the waiting room. One was a pregnant woman who would be the second to give birth in Siena. The other person was one of the most recent arrivals from the outer city of Florence, a bearded man whose posture suggested he suffered from back pains.

There was space on the bench next to them, and Renn gestured for Luca to take a seat while they waited. Luca ignored it.

A moment later, one of the doors opened and a woman appeared with a bandage wrapped around her wrist. "Thank you," she said to the figure behind her and then hurried through the waiting area to leave.

It was strange that so many people in Siena became ill or suffered injuries which demanded attention by the doctor or the nurse. In all his years wandering, he had never seen a doctor. Yes, his Coveys had people with knowledge of plants with healing properties and how to set a broken bone, and once in a while, a serious injury would slow them down or halt the migration for days, but it was not the same. And yet, he had to remind himself, he had had minor injuries treated by Mender twice already, and here he was with Luca.

Mender stepped into the waiting area, turning nir head to assess the waiting people before focusing on the new arrivals. "Hello, Renn. Luca," ne said with a smile. When Renn had first met nem, nir face was skinless and expressionless. Now ne wore the skin Luca had put in place and could almost pass for a human being.

"Hey," Luca said, "How's my favorite Minder model?"

Mender inclined nir head. "I am well, Luca. Can you wait for a moment before I treat your injuries?"

"Injuries?" Luca echoed. "I don't have any—" He turned to Renn. "You sneaky bastard. We are not here to get a bucket of water at all!"

Renn did not meet his eyes. He was not going to lie, but he also would rather avoid an argument. "I did intend to get water," he said.

45

Luca scowled, then had one of his rapid mood changes and grinned. "You tricked me. I'm impressed. There may be hope for you yet, nomad."

Mender left them to tend to the man with back pains, helping him into the next room before ne closed the door again.

Another door opened, and Gabriele came into the waiting area with a child with a bandage around the thumb of the right hand. Gabriele saw the child out and then turned to Renn and Luca. "Hello," he said. "What can I do for you two?"

"I came for the water containers," Renn said. "Luca is—"

"Fine!" Luca interrupted. "Luca is perfectly fine. Renn makes a fuss over nothing. He's worse than Nanny."

"If Renn thinks we should have a look at you, I am not going to argue," Gabriele said. He ran a hand through his hair and shot the waiting woman a glance. "I will just see to Zenia."

"I can wait," the woman said.

"I'm not exactly dying here!" Luca sighed.

"Neither am I," the woman told him and pointed at her round belly. "And I would rather wait for Mender, if that is all right."

"Oh. Yes, of course," Gabriele said. "Please come inside."

Renn followed them into the examination room, wondering why the woman preferred Mender to Gabriele. Although Mender knew about efficient treatments from the past, Gabriele had studied medicine and health for several years before becoming a doctor.

"Why were you ditched in favor of the sentient?" Luca asked, as tactless as Renn liked to think he was not.

Gabriele patted the examination table invitingly. "Mender is not a man. Some women prefer that when it comes to personal matters. Now, I'll do something about your elbows first and then we'll have a look at your ankle."

Luca sighed, exaggeratedly. He glanced up at Renn. "I'm not gonna run away, you know."

"I did not expect you to." Still, Renn stayed. He felt responsible, minor though the injuries were.

"Although this really doesn't call for professional attention," Luca went on, shrugging in defeat as he sat down.

"Most of the medical supplies in Siena are here," Gabriele told him. "However trivial the matter, I am happy to give you my professional attention."

Renn saw the doctor meet his patient's gaze and there was a moment of silence in which Luca flashed him a predatory grin. Gabriele quickly turned away to open a box with supplies.

Renn watched Gabriele clean Luca's elbows with something that looked like water, but was not. Something that, like the plasters he placed next, originated from Luca himself in the first place.

"Well, aren't I getting something for my tax money?" Luca said, bending and moving his arm to inspect his elbow. "Thanks, doc."

Gabriele smiled. "Now, your ankle."

Luca obediently kicked off his boot. He clearly tried not to wince when Gabriele manipulated the joint. "Will I live?" he asked.

"You've sprained your ankle. I can bandage it, but you should still be careful not to put too much strain on it."

"Guys!" Luca exclaimed. "It's not the first time I sprain something. Why are we even here? I mean, come on. Renn's a fucking nomad used to surviving dust storms and giant, flying skeleton snakes. Gabriele was tortured in prison before being kicked out of Florence to settle down here in the middle of nowhere. The fuck, guys! There is no logic in you two blowing a sprained ankle out of proportions!"

Renn realized that Luca was right. Their concern was disproportionate. Luca lived in his stronghold, surrounded by strange comforts no one else had. He had servants who cooked for him and did his every bidding. He had never starved, never found himself braving a storm with nothing but a blanket to keep the elements at bay. Whenever he wanted to go somewhere, he would use masheen vehicles.

47

But did it mean he was weak? Did it mean he would break easily compared to others?

Gabriele looked a little flushed. "Well, regardless," he muttered while rummaging through a box of medical supplies. "It's better to be on the safe side."

"I will go to the well for water," Renn said.

"And I will find Teo and show her the magical boxes I made," Luca announced.

On his way out of the examination room, Renn heard him ask Gabriele, "So, have you ever heard of a radio?"

8:

Teo

The map spread out across Arsenio's lap was constructed from one provided by Luca as well as Arsenio's recollection of the spotters' map he had followed on his many trips outside the domes. Like the latter, it was a work in progress. Right now, he was scribbling something on it in letters that jumped in accordance with the movement of the car.

Teo changed gears and sped up the vehicle. She enjoyed this. Not only the driving, although controlling this piece of ancient tech was delicious. Getting away from Siena for a little while was nice as well. Oh, she liked most of the people and the town they were building. But although gratifying, it was also demanding. Others noticed what she did. Listened when she talked. Wanted her opinion on things and hoped for her to settle disagreements. Slipping away from all that for a while now and then gave her the energy she needed to do her best the rest of the time. Of course, she wasn't completely alone even now. But that was all right. Arsenio was not everyone else.

"You might want to go back into fourth. The engine doesn't sound happy," he said.

"Who's driving? Me or you?" Teo asked. But he was right. She shifted back to fourth.

"You are. But who taught you?" Arsenio asked.

Teo sighed in mock irritation. "You did. So anything I do wrong can be traced back to you," she added brightly.

Arsenio reached out a hand to rest it on the back of her seat. "I seem to remember you saying you wanted to make your own mistakes."

That was true. She had said that because in the beginning, he was too eager to help. Every time she forgot to release the handbrake or change the gear, he was telling her before she had time to realize something was wrong. And she wanted to learn how to drive properly which meant making mistakes and solving problems with some guidance, not taking orders.

"East when you can," Arsenio said. "That's the fastest way to Bolsena."

She nodded and turned when they passed the crevice that had flanked them for a while. They had gone to Bolsena once before, following Luca's advice to bring something for trading. Back then, they didn't have much. Now at least, they had a forge and could produce tools, so they were bringing a hammer and some nails along with a few handcrafted items, some of them decorative and others useful. And they had a truck.

"We need to find fuel soon if we want to keep using the car," Arsenio said. "But that little rat has probably taken everything in a radius of a few hundred kilometers."

"Luca has been searching abandoned cities for a long time," Teo said.

Arsenio scoffed. "A couple of years maybe. I've been doing it for longer. We could tell when he appeared, you know. Suddenly things would be disturbed before we even got to them, and he would ransack the places for anything of use."

"He was only trying to get by," Teo argued. "I know he's not your cup of tea, but you have to admit he's helpful."

Arsenio removed his hand from her seat and crossed his arms over his chest. "Still, he's giving us things he practically took from right under our noses in the first place."

50

"Before we left Florence," Teo said. "That was another life." A life in which they were friends and Vanni was still alive. A life in which she was safe in Florence, protected by the domes and her father's political importance. Her heart still ached when she thought of Vanni and the way they had to leave city, but they had made it. Were making it. And she got to be a technie and a spotter, things she had only dreamed of before. "We wouldn't have the car if Luca hadn't given it to us."

"To you," Arsenio said, clearly intent on turning every act of kindness into something suspicious. But in this case, he was right.

"I'm glad everyone liked the idea of the radio," she changed the subject.

Arsenio grunted in reply.

Teo shook her head and kept her eyes on the ground in front of them. Everybody who understood the idea liked it. Including Arsenio. It was a rather silly rivalry between him and Luca, tinged with the tragedy of Vanni's death which Arsenio, at least partly, blamed Luca for. "I think it will prove useful."

"Does Renn agree?" Arsenio asked.

"Why wouldn't Renn agree? He doesn't know a lot about tech, but that doesn't mean he can't appreciate it," Teo said.

"It will be on top of his tower."

Teo nodded. "Well, yes. Is there some kind of masculine implication that I am not getting here?"

"What? No!" Arsenio exclaimed.

"I don't think wanderers get particularly territorial," Teo said, hiding a smirk. Apart from the usefulness of the radio, Teo was excited about the theory of it. She had always found practical math wonderful. Luca was the only one she shared that fascination with. That, of course, was also a reason for Arsenio's dislike. She reached out a hand and rested it on Arsenio's thigh, squeezing it in wordless confirmation.

"We're almost there," Arsenio said. His eyes were fixed on something Teo still could not make out, but after only a few moments, she saw the thin smoke rising from distant fires. If the buildings didn't obscure the view, she would have been able to see the lake whose shore the settlement was hugging.

"We should probably walk the last bit," Teo noted. "I don't want to alienate them by arriving in a motorized vehicle."

And so they parked the truck in the shade of a few trees growing on a hill and took everything they needed to bring.

The landscape would change if they went on for long enough in either direction, but Teo had never gone far enough to experience the constant scorching heat to the south or the ever present ice and snow up north. Or the ocean... She would like to see that. Perhaps one day, if they found more vehicles and Siena was prospering. Then she may be able to go away for a while. "How far did you ever go? You and Vanni, I mean?" she asked.

Arsenio didn't answer immediately. "What do you mean?" he finally said.

When she glanced at him, Teo saw defensiveness in his expression. "As spotters," she quickly added. "How far away from Florence did you ever drive?" She hadn't implicated anything else, although...

"Oh." He smiled. "We never went further than it was possible to come back the same day. Except once. We were too far away and only made it back the next day."

"But why?" she asked. "Wouldn't it make more sense to go on longer expeditions to find new places that could hold something useful?"

"Maybe," he conceded. "But those were the rules. It's the way things were done for safety. Besides, combing the area around Florence could take a lifetime, and earth slides and quakes unearth new things on a regular basis... Oh, there is our welcoming committee."

Teo shaded her eyes with her hand. The settlement of Bolsena was not much bigger than Siena, but it had more inhabitants. More children. A handful of them were hiding behind the wall shielding the inhabited part of the old city. Their heads were peeking out to look at the two strangers approaching. Teo lifted her hand and waved at them.

One of the children laughed and waved back. Another promptly pulled them back behind the wall, and Teo could hear some kind of whispered admonishment.

In the beginning, there had been talk among the rebels of going to one of the existing settlements to ask to be let in instead of founding the new Siena. But as Teo saw and learned more of them, she could clearly tell that these people had their own ways and customs, and what the rebels wanted was a fresh start. Besides, the rebels might not have been turned away, but there would not have been enough room in the established settlements, and so they would have been forced to build in any case.

Perhaps it would have been different if the spotters had ever attempted to establish a relationship with them. When Teo lived in the domed city, she was so impressed and so infatuated with the idea of going outside to see the sky and the landscape and find ancient tech that she never questioned all the things the spotters did not do. Now, all she could think of was how much more they could have done. How much more Florence could do.

The children ran down the street and around a corner.

"Looks like we scared them off," Arsenio mumbled.

"You do look a little intimidating," Teo replied. It was true. Even out of uniform, Arsenio had an air of authority, and he was quite a tall, broad shouldered figure.

Before long, a person approached them. Teo remembered her from their last visit. The middle aged woman was called Nayeh. She did not have an official title that she had told them, but Teo was fairly certain she was a leader in the settlement. "Good day to you, travelers," she greeted them.

"Good day," Teo replied.

"What brings you here?" Her way of speaking was closer to Renn's than to anyone else Teo knew, but there were nuances in the accent, something with the vowels, that differed from Renn's speech.

"We hope to trade," Teo said, "and talk."

Nayeh nodded. "Let us talk first, then. Are you thirsty?"

"We would like a drink," Teo said. She didn't need to look at Arsenio to know he was hoping to get better acquainted with the draft of this place.

They were brought to the one public house that served food and drink. Most settlements had one, according to Renn.

The people in the bar room turned and stared. Teo smiled at them. She wanted to make a good impression. Next to her, Arsenio scanned the room for any signs of danger.

"How is your new settlement?" Nayeh asked after seating herself at a table on the opposite side of the visitors.

"We are making progress rebuilding Siena," Teo answered. "More people have arrived from the outskirts of Florence, so we do our best to expand the settlement and accommodate them."

Their host nodded. "Can you feed them?"

"So far yes," Teo replied. "We have luck with the greenhouses." It still felt ironic to have left the domes behind and then pour so much time and energy into building miniature versions of them. But it was the best way to grow anything, and although the crude glass the Sienans produced was no match for the plass of the gigantic domes, many of the principles for using them were the same as in the Green Dome.

"Good." Nayeh raised her cup, and Teo and Arsenio followed suit in a silent toast. "We are used to wanderers coming to our town, but not to new settlements showing up overnight so close to us," she continued. "Some worry that you will take more from the land than you give and that we might all suffer for it."

In this hostile, unsheltered world, more people could deplete the resources as easily as too many people inside the domes of Florence could prove a challenge to the balanced eco systems within the domes. "We understand the concern," Teo said. "But we think that instead of competing for water and food, our settlements may benefit from each other." She put her hands on the table, palms facing upwards. Some things she had learned from being a politician's daughter, and she strove to reverse everything Emilio Terzi employed in his aggressive rhetoric. This was not a time for banging the table with a fist to drive home a point, nor was it the time to display her own certainty and steadfastness by leaning heavily on hands pressed to the table. "We hope to develop our relationship with you to help both of our settlements prosper."

The other woman made a small gesture for her to go on.

"We hope to trade with you regularly. We have recently procured a fast transport vehicle, so we can come to you with fresh wares."

"Yes, I was told you came here today in the belly of a roaring beast," Nayeh said, clearly quoting whoever had told her.

"It is a masheen of old," Teo explained, hoping she didn't insult the woman's intellect while trying to put it in simple terms, "a piece of tech called a car. It travels on wheels and has no will or life of its own. Perhaps we could show it to you? If you would like, we could take you for a ride around this settlement."

"Teo," Arsenio murmured.

Teo put her hand on his thigh and squeezed. She was not going to get into an argument with him now. She didn't necessarily want to make the decisions and be the one to negotiate with other settlements, but she was far more capable than he was.

"I will accompany you to this car of yours when you leave," Nayeh said.

Teo inclined her head. That was good enough for now. Still, it never hurt to push one's luck a little. "We have recently heard of another kind of tech which may interest you. It's called a radio," Teo said. "It allows people to communicate over great distances if they each have a device for it."

"But we have not verified that it works yet," Arsenio cut in.

"No, we have not," Teo admitted, taking it in the stride even as she felt Arsenio's leg nudge hers warningly under the table. "Of course we will test the device before offering it to you, but if you are interested, I will bring it next time we visit."

Nayeh considered it for a moment, then smiled. "You and your new settlement are full of surprises, Teo. Surprises and strange, new ideas."

9:

Esmia

The lines stretched out before her like the traces of giant snakes. But whatever had left them was no snake.

Esmia crouched to examine the print. It was as broad as the width of both of her hands, and an even pattern ran through it almost as if it were decoration. There was another print, identical, next to it. The distance between them was greater than she could reach with both arms outstretched, but they were too perfectly parallel to have been left by two separate creatures. One would veer off, stop, approach the other at intervals, but that was not the case here. What two-bellied snake was this? Despite the heat of the day, Esmia felt a chill run up her spine. Surely this could not be a kind of scarvhe she had not previously heard of?

No, scarvhes left lines in the sand, but they also left traces of their wings, dirt brushed or blown aside. And their tails whipped from side to side, obscuring their prints. Besides, they did not have such a pattern on their bodies. As terrifying as the idea of two scarvhes was, the alternative was even more frightening. She had never seen an Other before. Still, it was an easy conclusion to draw when something defied any other explanation.

She turned as if the monster would suddenly appear behind her. The day was still and no sound, no flicker of movement, no unfamiliar smell reached her. And yet, there was something...

Esmia closed her eyes for a moment. When she opened them again, there was a glint in the air, a shimmer of reflected sunlight. It was not unusual for the light to catch a grain of dust or sand, but as she watched, more glitter rose in the air around her. She glanced back down at the tracks on either side of her. Particles rolled across them, whispering as they began to erase the signs.

For the first time since leaving the Covey, Esmia felt troubled by being alone. Oh, the hole in her chest had begun to fill with memories and pain, but this was different. She had known for a long time that she would end up alone one day. Now the first real test to her mettle was approaching.

She could read the wind, but she was not an efficient reader. It had never been her purpose or sole responsibility. There were those far more adept at understanding the signs who sounded the alarm before she caught the smell of rain or the changing of temperature. The dancing specks around her could be nothing. Or they could be the warning of an approaching storm.

She turned again, stepped across the lines on the ground and resumed walking. If a storm really were coming, she would need to find safety soon. The horizon was littered with lumps that may be mountains or fallen cities or even oases. If she had a map or a wayfinder, it would be easier to discern which way held the best promises of sanctuary, but she would have to trust her instincts instead. And they told her to keep going in the direction she was already headed.

Esmia walked for hours without a pause and only slowed to catch her breath and drink from her flask once. And the lump she was aiming for grew in size to looming proportions. It was angular and jagged in the way of dead cities.

For the first time since the strange lines on the ground, she turned. The sweat grew cold on her back and her brow. A massive wall was forcing its way through the landscape. She could not yet hear it, but she could see it. A mass so dense that nothing would escape.

Esmia turned and began to run. Her breaths were coming in short gasps and she had to force herself to keep moving before she reached the first walls of the dead city. She pressed on, not daring to look back a second time. She had to find a space that would not be filled with sand. Had to hide from the storm somewhere she was certain she could breathe.

Movement on the ground caught her eye. Rats. A handful of the big rodents were scurrying in front of her. Under normal circumstances, the only sane reaction would be to turn the other way. They were carrions, but even so, they would not shy away from attacking a human being if they were hungry enough and numerous enough. Rats were vicious beasts. But they were also smart and expert survivors, and they probably knew these surroundings a lot better than she did.

Esmia ran after the rats, turned a corner when they did and continued in a direction that seemed to be headed for the storm rather than away from it. She almost stopped, but decided to trust the animals. Animals were even more attuned to tremors of the ground, changes in the weather and other signs of the land than wanderers.

They led her to a hole in the side of a half-collapsed building whose sharp edges had long since been tamed by the elements. The rats disappeared through the hole. Esmia flung herself on the ground, wrestled her pack off and pushed it through first. Then her flask. Her arms and head came in too, but before her eyes adjusted to the darkness inside, she found herself stuck. Her shoulders were too wide. She angled herself as well as she could, but to no avail. What would happen if the storm broke over her now? Could she survive by using her own body as a stopper to make sure no sand came through the opening? Could she lie here and breathe unhindered until it was over? Perhaps. Probably. But the sand would pelt the rest of her, and even if she could manage the unpleasantness of that, there was a risk it would cover her and put her in the center of a new dune. Breaking free from that without the use of her hands could prove impossible.

She squeezed back out to the sound of the hysterical howling of the wind and began to dig. The ground was not hard. After all, the upper layers were probably remnants of earlier storms. She pushed dirt and sand aside, dug quickly and furiously, ignoring everything but the job she had to perform. When the indention was deep and broad enough for her to squeeze through, she pushed herself inside, clawing at the ground.

In the darkness, the rats chattered, too close for comfort, but they were not the biggest problem yet. Her eyes were still not used to the darkness. She groped for something to use, found her own pack, then the furry bulk of a rat that made an irritated sound at her. But there... Stones. She began to move them, closing as much of the hole as she could with a pile of fist-sized rocks. The darkness became complete. For the moment, Esmia didn't care. She let herself fall back on the ground, one hand on her pack. She could hear her own heart hammering and blood rushing in her ears.

Her clothes felt sticky with dust. Her fingertips ached. She gingerly moved her hands, tested that each finger could bend. Slowly, her eyes adjusted to the darkness. There was an outline of a staircase in the back of the room she had entered and a still shape near it that could be rubble or the leftovers of others, wanderers or animals who had stayed here. The rats moved about, scraping, sniffing, chattering. She had to do something before they grew too bold.

Finally, she rolled over and opened her pack. There was a tinderbox inside. She opened the container and took out the components, grateful that she had learned to do this blindfolded as a child to make sure she would be able to do it in a situation exactly like this. She struck the flint and ignited one of the small rolls of bark and dried leaves There would only be a few seconds of light. She caught a glimpse of broken nails and bloody fingertips. Turning around, she spotted plants growing on top of the pile of dirt by the stairs. Dead and dry twigs around it.

The light went out. But now she knew where to get materials for a fire.

Once she had used the tinderbox again and lit a modest fire on the ground, Esmia saw that she was sharing the room with five or six rats. As she approached them, they did not back further into their corner, but began to move forward, one of them taking the point and the others fanning out in a formation shaped like an arrowhead. Their beady eyes glinted in the firelight.

Esmia took a deep breath. She couldn't do the sensible thing and leave the rats. But cowering in a corner would make things worse. So she opened her mouth, bared her teeth and spread her arms and screamed at the top of her lungs. It had the desired effect. The rats backed off. She drew a sigh of relief, but moved closer for good measure, flapping her arms in a bad imitation of a scarvhe.

And that's when the storm hit. The noise had been building outside the sanctuary, but there was no mistaking when it transitioned from approaching to engulfing the ruin in its terror. The darkness deepened, the rats fell silent or were drowned out by the noise, everything that could possibly creak cried out, and above it all was a roar of pure, elemental anger.

She arranged her water flask and her pack and sat as comfortably as she could with the fire between herself and the rats. Now there was nothing to do but wait.

10:

Esmia

It was the absence of sound that woke her. The silence was loud in her ears and her body, and Esmia sat up, trying to gauge for how long she had slept.

The fire was down to embers now. She had managed to find a little more vegetation for it before she went to sleep, but she could still not have slept for more than an hour or two. The rats were scuttling in their corner still, as if they were anxiously waiting for something. Then they all stopped.

Esmia barely had time to wonder what was going on before she heard a low rumbling, so deep and lingering that she could feel it in her bones. Thunder. It was not a given, but very often, a dust storm would be followed by a thunderstorm. She rubbed her face with her hands, brushing off sand and grit. If she went back out now, she would be caught in the downpour, and while she could use the water, it was too dangerous.

The rumbling grew in volume and a flash of lightning illuminated the sanctuary for a brief instant. There must be a hole somewhere else for the light to get in, even if the dust hadn't. The rain began to pelt the walls outside. Esmia drew her knees up and sat hugging them, listening for any sign of danger. The rats were quiet too.

As the thunder rolled away and the rain faded a short time later, the rats began to approach the hole to the outside. It sounded as if they were discussing the matter of the rocks blocking the exit. Esmia stood up. This time she did not scream at them, but she flapped her arms a few times. The rats understood and immediately backed away. A larger pack would not have been so compliant.

After pushing the first couple of stones aside, Esmia began to fear that the building may be harder to escape than she had anticipated. Fine dust seeped in through the cracks between the rocks, and as she removed the last of them, sand poured onto the floor. Some of it was damp and clumpy. Looking out, there was no hole to be seen. Just a mass of debris left by the storms.

She wiped her forehead with the back of her hand. From behind her, the rats were peering at the small dune filling the hole. This was not good. How long would it take her to dig through all that? Hours? Days? She did not have days. She would not starve to death. Might not even die from dehydration, but when they all grew desperate enough, there would be a battle between her and the rats.

She moved back and watched the rats inspect the spot where the exit ought to be, making agitated noises and clawing at the wall of debris. Then one of them turned, sniffed the air and scampered away. The others followed a heartbeat later.

Esmia watched them disappear in the darkness, and then all was still again. They must have gone up the stairs. Was there a way out up there? She waited, listening. A faint rustling sound reached her. A squeal. Then silence. If they did not come back, it meant they had found an escape. Didn't it?

She gathered her things and made her way to the stairs. Staying on the ground was always preferable. Ruins of buildings could collapse without warning even if they had stood for centuries, and while this could technically happen at any time, the risk was greater if they suddenly had to carry the weight of humans on upper floors. But what choice did she have?

Carefully, she put one foot on the first step of the staircase, eased her full weight onto it and stood for a moment before taking another step up the stairs that the rats had climbed so effortlessly and carelessly.

As she climbed, Esmia listened for signs that the structure was giving in, but all she heard was her own breathing, her hand scraping along the wall for balance and orientation in the darkness and pebbles and insects slithering away from her feet now and then.

She reached a platform and almost took another step when she saw a shape of deeper black in front of her. A hole. She bent down. How had the rats gotten past it? Running her hand along the floor, she felt a ledge that was definitely broad enough for rats to run across. But could she make it? Perhaps sideways if she abandoned her pack. The remaining floor on the other side of the black chasm was narrower still.

Esmia held her pack in her hands and tried to measure the distance. It landed on the other side of the hole with a comforting thud. She took a deep breath and began to edge past the pit along the wall.

It was not until she reached the other side that she realized she had been holding her breath. She let it out in a shuddering sigh, allowed herself a moment to calm down and then picked up her pack to continue the journey.

Halfway up the next flight of stairs, her surroundings began to grow remarkably brighter. She could see the steps clearly now and didn't have to hold on to the wall as feverishly, but she forced herself to keep the slow pace. Light did not necessarily mean safety.

Finally she reached the end of the stairs and faced what was probably a corridor that should have opened up to rooms on either side. Instead, it ended in nothingness and was flanked only by thin rods in various states of decomposition without a sign of the walls they once stabilized. The floor was wet from the recent rain, and everything smelled like damp soil. There was no sign of the rats. They must have found a safe way off the building.

Esmia stayed in the middle of the corridor, ready to drop flat or take hold of one of the rods for balance if something happened. The water hadn't pooled anywhere, but she could still lose her footing on the slippery surface. She stopped halfway through and moved a little to the side so she could better see beyond the ruined building. On one side, there was a steep drop to the ground. If she jumped or fell, she would probably break her neck. The other side had a more forgiving slope of thick stone-like slabs, rusty rods and soil that ended in a dune of sand. Moving around inside the building had confused Esmia's sense of direction, but judging from the sun's position in the sky, it may very well be the dune that blocked the exit downstairs.

She stood for a moment, staring at the surroundings from this unfamiliar vantage point. She could not see her own footprints or the strange parallel lines she had found outside the city. The storms had erased everything, as was their way. They roamed the land, relentlessly seeking to grind every trace of mankind into a uniform mass of dust and mud. Even the great, old cities were succumbing, every corner and tower growing weaker storm by storm, sand grain by sand grain.

Esmia began the slow descent, crawling with her back to the surroundings so she could better see where to put her hands and feet. The rats had four legs and a tail for balancing and could stand comfortably on ledges where Esmia had to cling to whatever protruding metal bar or piece of stone or hopeful vegetation she could find.

When her feet reached the top of the dune, her legs were shaking. Next to her was a row of paw prints in the damp sand, one last greeting from the rats. The best way to get to the ground from here would be to simply slide. Distributing her bodyweight over a bigger area would make the sand carry her more easily. So she wrapped her face in her scarf, made sure none of her skin was exposed and that her pack was properly closed and pushed off.

She landed hard in a shower of sand and muddy soil a few moments later, rolling twice before coming to rest on the ground. She crawled on all fours, away from the dune in case it began to dislodge itself. She had not come this far to get buried alive.

Finally, she allowed herself to stop, catch her breath and get to her feet. Her heart was drumming still, but her legs were not shaking anymore. She was ready to continue. Ready to make her way through the city, looking for messages left by other wanderers or—

With an overwhelming sucking sensation, the hole inside her returned. While she had fought the elements, the rats and the city, it had mercifully disappeared to be filled by determination and fear. But there was nothing to be done about it. She adjusted her pack and straightened her back. Wanderers only carried with them what they needed, right?

The silent city loomed over her as she traversed its dead streets. She sought out unblocked, broad roads because those were the ones other wanderers would have used before her. There were no footprints, of course, but she watched surfaces that could be scratched. But she saw nothing.

She was hungry and she was thirsty. She still had a little food and enough water to sustain her for a few days if she rationed it, and that was not something she was a stranger to. During droughts, the Covey would keep drinking to a minimum. Esmia didn't remember it very well, but her mother had told her of one particularly bad year when she was very young. They had cut plants apart for the sap inside and dug holes in the middle of dried out lakes to get to the moisture beneath the sand. Esmia stopped, putting the memory aside, and took out her flask.

And then there was nothing. Only a vast, blue sky above her. The ground beneath her was hard, and rocks bit into her shoulder. Her mouth tasted like blood. And there was something wet on her hand. Had it begun to rain again? No, that was not it. Esmia sat up so fast the world spun, but she ignored it, fumbled almost blindly for the source of the water. The flask— She picked it up and heard the hollow sloshing sound inside. Next to her, the ground was not just damp from the rain. There was a shallow pool. She put her lips to the ground, tried to at least get a little of the water back, but she swallowed more dirt and blood than water. Her body convulsed. No. She could not afford to be sick. She could not even afford to spit. She forced herself to swallow again.

Her hands were shaking as she put the stopper back into the flask. There was only a couple of mouthfuls left. Her elbows were bruised. Her hip sore. The back of her head ached. This had happened before. More times than she could remember. But she had never been alone...

Why now? Did this mean the spirits wanted her to thirst? To die? Esmia shook her head to clear it. The spirits never gave a reason for making her their puppet. They never gave her a warning either. She might never know their intention. But she would do what she always did. She would keep fighting. All hope was not lost yet. She could still find water. After all, she could see the clouds far away. The storms must be sweeping across the land, and if she followed them, there was a good chance of coming across pools or crevices or filled with water. Besides, she might find a stagnant settlement or another Covey or Bevy on the way.

Gritting her teeth, Esmia got to her feet. She was a wanderer, so wander she would. It was too soon to give up. It was too soon to die.

11:

Renn

As always, it was a subtle, indescribable change in the air that warned Renn. No one else noticed these shifts. He had tried to teach the Sienans, but he might as well have explained the color of a smell or the sound of a sight. The ones who had lived inside the domes of Florence showed least aptitude. It was not that they were oblivious to the weather; They were often baffled by it or even scared, but they did not sense it. A few of the people who came from outside the domes showed more promise. Dianne, a woman who caught up to the rebels on the way to Siena with her family, said her grandfather used to feel the weather in his bones and joints. Renn was not surprised. Some wanderer elders were exceptional at predicting the weather. He hoped Dianne had inherited the ability herself.

This time, the wind began to whisper of change while Renn was helping Tonino putting up a fence for their precious livestock. Renn excused himself immediately to find out where it was coming from and how soon.

He took the steps two at a time and was at the top of the watchtower only a few minutes later. Surveying the expanse below, he immediately spotted it. From this distance, it looked like a reddish grey cloud of smoke at the horizon. He stood for a moment, counting, staring unblinkingly at the angry ribbon. Then he turned and bounded back down the stairs.

"Dust storm coming our way. We have an hour. Spread the word," he said to Clara, the first person he met.

"I'll sound the alarm," Clara answered. The gong they used to call to assemblies doubled as an alarm for dangerous changes in the weather. Hopefully everybody would remember the signal.

Renn began to run, only slowing down to repeat the news to those he met. He was fairly certain no one was far away from the settlement at the moment... Renn stopped. The radio. This was one of the reasons Luca had shared that masheen with them. Renn turned and raced back toward the tower. They had built a hut for the radio at the base of it, using the ancient ruins as a foundation. He flung the door open. There was no one there.

He could go back out and find Teo or Mender or one of the other few people who operated the masheen. But it would waste time. So Renn carefully eased himself onto the stool in front of the table whereupon the radio sat. Renn picked up the smaller box of the two and put it to his mouth. He had seen Luca and Teo do it. It should not be hard to duplicate the actions, although the mere thought of operating a masheen on his own felt wrong.

Renn pressed the button on the side of the smaller box and lights sprang to life on the larger one. "Luca?" he said into the box. Nothing happened. He thought back. They used to let go of the button after speaking. "Luca?" he said again and lifted his finger from the button.

"Renn?" came Luca's voice from the box on the table. It was tinny and crackled, but it was most definitely Luca's voice.

"Yes," Renn confirmed. "A dust storm is approaching from the south. It will hit Siena in an hour or less. I think you will be in its path too."

"Renn?" Luca said again in a far more amused tone than a storm warning ought to evoke. "I bet you are forgetting to press the button. Hold the button down when you talk and let go of it when you are done.

It's basic mouth-hand coordination." A snort of laughter was cut off, undoubtedly because Luca had let go of the button on his own device.

"Luca," Renn said again, this time holding down the button, "a dust storm is approaching us from the south. It will be here in an hour or less. It is likely to hit you too." He let go of the button.

"Oh. Damn. I should have known you weren't just calling to say hi," Luca said. "I mean, thank you, Renn. That's awesome. Not the storm, of course. You telling me."

"You are welcome," Renn said. "I must go."

He was reaching out to put back the box when Luca spoke again. "Hey, Renn. Be safe, okay?"

Renn nodded. Then he held the box to his mouth again. "You as well, Luca."

The moment he stepped outside the hut, Renn heard the gong. Clara was making staccato sounds, three in quick succession, a pause, and then repetition.

Already people were running, taking in loose objects so they would not be blown away. On Arsenio's insistence, several people had been assigned responsibilities they would need to take care of when the alarm sounded. A handful of the Sienans would be doing their best to keep the greenhouses safe right now, others would be taking care of the livestock or securing loose objects in the streets.

Renn's job was to stay outside for as long as it was safe to see to it that any stragglers were not left in the streets.

"Renn!" came Gabriele's voice.

Renn turned to see the doctor at the door of the infirmary.

"Has anyone alerted Luca?" he asked.

"Yes," Renn called back as he approached the doctor. "I have. Is everything all right?"

Gabriele smiled. "Yes. Thank you." He held out a mask for Renn to take. It was not the one Luca gave him at their first meeting because that one had been taken by the authorities in Florence, but Luca had a few to spare and had let the Sienans have them. They were stored in the

70

infirmary. This one was made to cover the whole face, complete with eye holes covered with a transparent material. "Arsenio already picked up one."

Renn took the mask, thanked him and turned to survey the street again. Windows were being barricaded on both sides. Good. He began to make his way to the protective wall on the eastern side of the settlement.

From one of the smaller streets intersecting the main street, Arsenio came striding toward Renn with his mask dangling around his neck. "How much time do we have?" he asked as he fell into step with Renn.

"Less than an hour. I don't know for sure," Renn replied.

The taller man nodded. He had volunteered for the same duty as Renn. While they rarely enjoyed time alone for social purposes, Renn trusted the former arbiter's competence and dedication completely, whether it came to seeking out scarvhe nests or securing Siena in the event of a storm.

They reached the gap in the wall and stopped. Now it was possible to make out the boiling cloud in the distance.

"Big one," Arsenio said.

"Yes," Renn agreed. "Only a half hour at the most," he corrected his former statement.

As they watched, the chaos crept visibly closer, eating its way through the wasteland.

"Left or right?" Arsenio asked.

"Left," Renn said although he did not have a preference either way. He trusted Arsenio didn't either.

The wind was picking up now. Not dangerously so, yet, but it would make people hurry up their preparations.

"All right. Make sure to get inside before the storm hits," Arsenio said.

Renn nodded. It was a redundant thing to say, but he knew it was Arsenio's way of keeping his own thoughts structured and not meant to suggest that Renn might not do his job well.

They turned almost simultaneously and began to make their way on their respective routes through the settlement. Renn slipped on his mask, not for the first time wondering how many wanderers could have been spared stone lungs if provided with this luxury.

The gong fell silent. Renn steered methodically through the settlement while the wind increased, making sure no one was outside or had forgotten something valuable. He did come across one window without any protection and found that the wind had already pulled off the fabric supposed to protect it. Fabric wasn't a good choice to begin with, but he strung it out quickly and tied it as well as he could so that debris would hit it and hopefully bounce off instead of breaking the windowpane.

As he moved on to the less developed part of the settlement, Renn knew he would not encounter any exposed windows. They had not gotten around to making glass for all the inhabited houses yet, so here they were either boarded up or equipped with primitive shutters.

He glanced up at intervals. Being between buildings made it difficult to see the storm. When he had weaved in and out of streets and was almost at the end of the inhabited part of Siena, Renn was about to turn back. But something caught his eye. A shape huddled up against a ruin.

"Hello?" Renn called, voice muffled into anonymity by the mask.

The figure did not react.

Renn shot another glance at the darkening sky. Now would be a good time to get inside. But this was the reason he was out here. He ran to the figure's side and put a hand on its shoulder.

The figure startled, cried out in alarm and looked up.

Renn recognized him as Nevio, a quiet man who had come with a group of people from the slums. He had left Florence after unfortunate events that he never elaborated on, hoping to find something better. "You need to get inside," Renn told him.

Nevio got to his feet. He looked shaken. It was a mystery to Renn how he had ended up outside like that. Had he been sleeping? An odd place for it.

Before he could ask, Renn felt a tremor in the air, the brief absence of wind or sound as if the world took in one deep breath and held it in anticipation. His back was to the storm, but he clearly saw the terror in the other man's face. He knew exactly what was behind him.

Renn reached out to clutch at Nevio's arm and pull him close. For a brief moment, the idea of giving the unfortunate man his mask occurred to him. But of the two of them, Renn would stand a far better chance of getting them to safety. He could carry the other if need be and he knew how to get to the closest shelter in the fastest possible way. Giving away his mask would be idiotic bravery.

"Keep your mouth closed. If you need my attention, use your hands," he yelled because now the roar of the storm made it impossible to have a normal conversation. The world was a blur of reddish grey. "Close your eyes. I will guide you," he added.

Guide, in this case, translated to roughly dragging and pushing Nevio along. Renn kept himself between the other man and the wind. It would provide a little cover, at least.

The closest inhabited houses had their doors on the wrong side. The infirmary was a longer walk, but they would not be as exposed to the elements. And Nevio may need care that would be easier for Mender and Gabriele to provide him with.

Under normal circumstances, the walk would have taken no time at all, but zigzagging for cover and pulling Nevio to his feet when he stumbled made the trip much longer. At least Renn could breathe and see what little there was to see in the furious storm.

They were almost at their destination when something dark came hurtling through the air. Renn instinctively turned, pushed himself against Nevio and caused them both to stumble. Too late. Something slammed into his back, knocking the wind out of him and almost sending him sprawling on top of Nevio. Renn spotted whatever it was continue on its way through the street and disappear in the soupy mist.

His vision greyed at the edges, and for a moment, all Renn could do was stay on his hands and knees, fighting to get air back into his lungs.

He was all right. It would leave a bruise, but he was all right. He got to his feet again, pulling Nevio with him. But the other man's knees immediately began to buckle under him. Renn gritted his teeth and lifted him since it was the most logical thing to do.

A short hike later, Renn hammered on the infirmary door, rhythmically so they would know it was a person and not debris hitting the building. When the door opened, they both practically fell inside. Renn let go of Nevio, trusting someone else to take over. He allowed himself to collapse on the floor and pulled off the mask.

The air was clear. The sound of the storm was subdued. Next to him, Mender and Gabriele spoke in urgent voices, and Nevio made a half reply before he began to cough and retch.

"Renn! Are you hurt?" Mender's voice. Kind and reassuringly efficient.

"No," Renn replied. "See to Nevio."

"Gabriele is tending to him already," Mender told him. "What do you need?"

Their first meeting had been during a dust storm. Mender had found him in nir home underground and cared for him while he recovered. Since then, Mender had considered Renn nir client, as ne put it.

"A moment," Renn said, hoping it did not come out terse. He was still breathing hard and his back was burning where the debris hit him, but he was certain he had not sustained any injuries to speak of. He pulled himself up into a sitting position. He was drenched with sweat, but the mask had saved him from any real inconveniences.

The sour smell of vomit reached Renn's nostrils. He glanced at the two other humans in the room. Gabriele was talking to Nevio in a low, soothing voice. The latter had been sick on the floor. A messy trail of sand led from the door to the place where the two of them had landed.

"I will get you some water and clean up afterward if my assistance is not needed," Mender informed him, wonderfully practically. Sometimes Renn could not help thinking that of all the people in Siena, Mender was the one who thought most like he did. The sentient had the pragmatic mindset of a wanderer, dealing not with abstractions of society or complicated masheenery but with what was right in front of nem that needed doing.

Gabriele glanced at Mender's retreating form and then at Renn. "He will be all right," he said, gesturing at Nevio. "You probably saved his life."

Renn acknowledged this with a nod. That was what he had been outside for, after all. Even if he had hoped no one needed it.

12:

Luca

"Have I mentioned how much I hate the weather?" Luca asked.

"Yes," Nanny said. "I believe you were four the first time you made that clear."

That was not the reply he had expected. Luca turned to her and leaned on the floor mop he was currently manhandling to take out his frustration. Cleaning while they were stuck inside was his own idea. Nanny and Alfredo were both more than capable of and employed to take care of these things, but they were also flexible and attuned to Luca's state of mind. It was this or getting Sia and Simon to fuck his brains out, and for some reason that idea did not appeal to him today. "I was?"

"Yes," Nanny said, neatly polishing the banister of the staircase and not missing a beat. Luca's parents had insisted on sentients as their employees instead of buying cheaper semis or demis to take care of menial labor. He was grateful to them. Without Nanny and Alfredo to keep him company, he might have grown a long beard, an uncanny fondness for talking to himself and sat around in a cave in a ridiculous loincloth or something. "You wanted to go outside and play with the remote controlled helicopter you built, but there was a thunderstorm and the rain was so heavy we were afraid the Arno would overflow."

"Yeah? Why didn't I play with it inside?" he asked.

"Because you had already knocked over one of your father's antique vases."

"Oh yeah..." The story morphed into a memory in Luca's head. He had wanted to clean up the mess and fix the vase, but Leo ratted on him. Their dad had given Luca one of those Disappointed Looks he was so good at and which were never directed at Leo, either because Leo was a boring kid who never broke anything or because he was better at apologizing. Luca grimaced. For fuck's sake. It was literally centuries since he had seen his parents and Leo. When would it stop feeling like a slap in the face?

"Luca..."

Luca glared at Nanny. He did not need a hug. He did not need to talk about it. That had been all fine when he first found himself in this fucked up world. Now he wanted to get on with life.

"You missed a spot," she said, pointing to a dry place in the corner of the landing he was standing on.

"Right." Luca bore down on the offending bit of floor with the mop.

Outside, the wind was positively howling. Sand and debris rattled against the building. Luca had gone outside during one of these dust storms. Just to see how bad it really was. It was pretty bad. He'd been out for ten minutes and had to remove sand from places on his body where under no circumstances sand had any business being. To think that people like Renn had nomaded their way through it for, presumably, centuries. No wonder Renn was a bit on the badass side. Even if he'd moved in with the most sheltered people Luca had ever met. Or, well, they used to be sheltered, most of them.

Most of the house was clean when the dust storm finally abated. And since it had come from the south, Siena would already be in the clear. Luca was not going to run to the radio to call them up and ask if everyone was okay. That would be ridiculous. So he carefully finished what he was doing, rinsed the mop and poured out the dirty water. He put lotion on his hands. Just because they always got cuts and bruises, it didn't mean he wanted them to end up wrinkled and dry too. He poured himself a cup of coffee and went to the place where he had left the radio at a super casual pace.

Luca did not necessarily expect anyone to pick up immediately. He knew the other radio was located in a shed in Siena and it wasn't like someone was there all the time. But they, or rather Renn, had notified him of the dust storm. It would make sense to expect a follow up report.

"Okay. I'll try again later," he said and went outside to assess any damages to the base done by the storm. A black cloud was hanging ominously low on the horizon. Did he spot a flicker of lightning inside it, or was that his imagination? After all, thunderstorms were often preceded by dust storms. As if the weather went, "Oh, was that too dry for you? Here, have some crazy rain and a bit of electrical charges with that."

One of the solar panels on the roof was not reflecting the light right. He'd have to take a look at that and maybe replace it, but that could wait. Overall, the base was in good shape. Luca and the sentients knew how to minimize the damages by now.

He went back inside and tried getting in touch with Siena once more. Still no answer. His next reinvention would be a goddamn recorder for some kind of voice mail.

When there was only static the third time he tried, Luca began to feel... Not exactly worried. Annoyed. Would it kill them to pick up the damn radio? He sat glaring at the device for a moment. He'd tried to make it fool proof, but the last person to use it was Renn. Not that he was a fool. But the man was practically allergic to technology. "All right, Renn," Luca mumbled, "what did you do to the poor thing?" Surely Teo would be able to fix it. Or Mender, although ne probably didn't know much about ancient communication technology.

There was a chance that Renn had managed to change the frequency. Luca sighed. He reached out to twist the dial manually, ready to go painstakingly through the frequencies. After the first five of them yielded nothing but static and he tried talking to no avail, he was beginning to think it would take less time to jump on his damn bike and just go there. But he could hear the rumbling of thunder now, and if he headed toward Siena, he would probably meet the thunderstorm halfway.

The static changed. Luca almost missed it, but there was something... He slowly turned the dial back again. And there it was: A curious lack of static. Perhaps they really had accidentally switched frequencies.

"Hello?" Luca said.

"Hello," a voice responded.

"Shit, I almost couldn't find you. Everything okay, Teo?"

A pause. During which it occurred to Luca that she sounded different. Maybe it wasn't Teo. Who else knew how to use the radio?

"Everything okay?" he repeated.

"Hello," the voice said again. "Who are you?"

Who was he? Oh, just the only person with a radio. Or— Luca blinked, comprehension dawning on him. "Who are you?" he repeated the question.

Static. Then the voice returned, "I am intern communications maintainer Olivia Bisset. Please identify yourself."

Luca didn't remember anyone by that name in Siena. He might not remember everyone there, but what the hell was an intern communications maintainer anyway? The equation didn't work unless he exchanged Siena for somewhere else. Florence? But long distance radio communication was a new concept to Teo. Still, they could have secret radios. Unless... Luca's heart was hammering in his chest. "I'm Luca Capello," he said, listening hard for any indication that Olivia Bisset knew who he was.

"Capello?" she echoed.

"Where are you?" Luca asked. "What's your location?"

Static.

"Olivia, what is your location?" he repeated around his heart which had jumped into his throat.

"I can't hear you," she said. "What?"

For fuck's sake. "Where are you located?" he asked.

She said something, but the static was drowning out her voice.

"I didn't get that," he almost shouted as if that would make the connection better. "Are you in Italy? What city?"

A giant thunderclap made Luca jump. And there was only static on the radio. "No, no, no!" he hissed. "Hello? Olivia? Ms Bisset? Are you there?" Static. He turned the dial, back and forth, but there was nothing. That was completely unfair. Totally not okay. He closed his eyes and put his face in his hands for a moment. Outside the rain began to lash the roof.

Luca stood up, pushed aside a pile of whatever crap he was building and excavated a tablet. He pulled up a map. He'd math his way out of this. He knew the height of his antenna. He had calculated its range to make sure it could reach Siena. Assuming the signal hadn't bounced off a cloud or been picked up by another radio tower that he didn't know of, Olivia Bisset had to be within a radius of... Luca drew a circle using the compass tool on the tablet. A radius of a few hundred kilometers. He could work with that. And maybe he could narrow it down even further. The bad connection could very well be due to the storm. If that were the case, more than half of the area he'd marked was eliminated already due to the storm's direction.

He paused. The part of his brain that wasn't numbers and equations and programming finally caught up to the situation. "Holy fuck," he breathed. He had just talked to another person with a radio transmitter who was not in Siena and not in Florence. No one else had what it took. Not the nomads, obviously, and definitely not the primitive settlements littered around Italy. Renn called those stagnants for more than one reason. Or, well, if he didn't, he should. Within the circle on the map, there was no town or city apart from Florence who showed any signs of even the most basic technological skills. But that meant— Even stripping away hopeful thinking on Luca's part, that logically implied that there was someone out there like... Well, him.

"Wow," he whispered. He ran his fingers through his hair. The thunder roared outside and a flash of lightning came only a second later.

Luca had been searching for other bases practically since he woke up. He knew his family wasn't the only one who had decided to wait out the catastrophe in stasis and hope for the best. It had taken a lot of planning and preparing and even then, it hadn't worked out for anyone the way they hoped. Not for the Capellos and not for any of the facilities he had located. The cryo pods had all malfunctioned or been left so long ago that there was no determining whether their occupants were the ancestors of some of the stagnants or nomads or even the people living in the slums outside the domes of Florence.

But someone out there had a radio. Luca began to laugh. He laughed so hard that he could hardly stand. For all his searching and all his futile attempts at getting a connection with satellites that were probably not even there anymore, all it took was one simple old-fashioned fucking radio. Why had he not tried that earlier? Why had he not thought of putting together something so simple and trying to find someone that way? Because it had not occurred to him that anyone with an advanced society would backpedal to something like that.

He wiped tears from his eyes. He would try to get in touch with them again as soon as the weather cleared up. They would be interested in talking to him as well. Right? And he'd call Siena... Though he was starting to think their radio or antenna might have been busted. Well, then he'd just go there.

But right now he was too full of energy to do anything productive. He'd tell Nanny and Alfredo, and then he'd get so shit-faced he wouldn't worry about stupid emotional outbursts.

13:

Teo

Arsenio returned too late, of course. He and Renn had taken it upon themselves to guarantee the safety of everyone else, and Teo had to admit that a wanderer and a former spotter were the best qualified for the job. She did want more people on it eventually, but Renn always seemed extremely unimpressed with everyone else when it came to interpreting the weather. Hopefully, everyone would grow to learn from him and from the exposure itself.

She was not particularly worried about Arsenio's absence. He wore a respirator that would filter out the sand, and he could take care of himself. Still, it was a relief when he returned and made a mess of the floor as he shook particles out of his hair and clothes.

"Did you heroically save anyone?" Teo asked him as he stripped in order not to sprinkle the whole place with dust.

Arsenio pulled off his respirator. "No. It seems everyone got the message," he replied, taking off his shoes. They were getting worn out and would need replacement soon. Just one of the luxuries they had all taken for granted while they lived inside the domes. "I helped Miriam board up the last window."

"Good," Teo said. He was now standing in his underwear. She made an impatient beckoning gesture. She was not going to wade into the debris on the floor.

Arsenio grinned and approached her, shaking his feet with every step to get rid of the last grains of sand. "Did you worry about me?"

Teo scoffed. "If you wanted someone who'd sit around worrying about you, you should have found someone else," she said, putting her hand on his neck and pulling him in for a quick kiss. "Come on, let me show you the only good thing about the storm."

She led him to her work table. There were a stack of papers and a pen on it next to a tray with fine sand in it and a thin stick resting on its edge. She didn't want to waste paper, so Teo did most of her calculations in the tray. The ones she hadn't written on the wall above the table, at least.

She was quite proud of her new project. Solar energy was all very well. Like Florence, Luca swore by it, but Teo knew it was not the only possible source of power that could be harnessed. So she had begun experimenting with what she had and what she could build. Right now she was testing a crude contraption mounted on top of the building that Luca called a windmill. He had provided her with schematics that she copied by hand.

Arsenio stared at their new lamp, a glass jar with copper wire inside it that glowed nicely. Wires ran from the side of it to the window where Teo had pulled it through a small gap a few days earlier. "That's the wind powering it?" he asked.

"Yes," Teo said. "It's very efficient in this weather. But it's not able to generate any power when there is no wind, so we need a way to store the energy. Like solar powered batteries. You know, like Mender doesn't power down during the night and doesn't have to be in direct sunlight all the time."

"Hm," Arsenio commented, noncommittally.

Teo kept from sighing at him. Everybody knew Mender was not human. They knew ne was a creature called a sentient that had been made by humans hundreds of years ago. But Arsenio was probably the only one in Siena besides Teo, Renn and Gabriele who knew the details of how ne was powered. Renn took the information in stride although he made no attempts to understand how the technology worked. Gabriele was fascinated and asked the practical questions like how long without sunlight Mender could function and what to do to restore nem in the event of a power failure. Arsenio was the reason Teo found it best not to discuss the matter with others. He was thoroughly uncomfortable with it. Not with Mender nemself, but with the way ne worked. He had confided to Teo that he found it unnatural and off-putting that a person didn't eat and sleep.

The dust storm had barely ended before dark clouds began to amass. Teo didn't need Renn to tell her a thunderstorm was coming. She went outside to make sure everyone else knew too and was happy to see that some of her neighbours were already putting out as many containers for the rainwater as possible. The wells provided enough water right now, but in order to expand the settlement, everyone needed to push for more.

Teo knocked on a few doors and told those she met to spread the message. A thunderstorm was nowhere near as dangerous as a dust storm if someone was outside, and everything that could be ruined by the water had already been secured, so there was no alarm this time.

Next, Teo headed for the infirmary. She was not qualified to treat anyone, of course, but she wanted to keep up with everyone.

A long metal beam with three severed ropes and cords attached to it lay across the street in front of her. Teo looked up. Yes, it was the radio antenna. The storm must have snapped it off the tower. But it would have to wait, she decided as she stepped over it. Climbing up there with a thunderstorm on the way was an unnecessary risk. Hopefully, Luca wouldn't try to call and worry when he couldn't get through. Teo shook her head. No, Luca was not likely to worry about anyone in Siena. Well, except one or two people, but he was a smart kid and could probably guess what had happened.

As Teo entered the infirmary, she almost collided with Renn.

"All well?" he asked.

"Are you all right?" she asked at the same time. Knowing he would prioritize her answer over his own, she added, "No serious damage to the town. A broken antenna seem to be the worst of it. Are you all right?"

Renn nodded. "Yes. I sought shelter here."

Teo smiled at him and moved aside to let him out, but she still scrutinized him as he went. Was there a stiffness to his shoulders? She turned again and went inside.

Mender came bustling through the waiting room where two people were sitting. One looked pale and slightly shaken up, another had clearly injured her hand.

"Teo?" Mender inquired.

"I'm fine," she said. "I wanted to see how you were doing before the next storm hits."

"No serious injuries," Mender replied. "Gabriele is seeing to Zenia. She had a fright during the storm, and the baby felt very agitated, but I'm sure they are both all right."

"Good. Why was Renn here?" Teo asked. "Was he hurt?"

"Not seriously. Only a few bruises," Mender said. "He encountered Nevio outside at the onset of the dust storm."

Teo turned to the pale man in the waiting room.

"He was not seriously injured either, thanks to Renn," Mender added. "Excuse me." Ne motioned for the woman to follow nem.

Teo went over to Nevio. "Are you all right?" she asked. She trusted Mender's assessment, but she could also imagine that having to be saved during a dust storm must be a frightening experience.

Nevio looked up at her. He made a shrug. "Yeah..."

"Why were you outside?" she asked.

His shoulders tensed. "I thought... there was more time," he said.

85

Teo realized he was probably thinking she was reprimanding him for it. She lowered herself to her haunches and put her hands on his shoulders. "I'm glad you are safe," she said. "It must have been scary. Take all the time you need, all right?"

He met her eyes for a brief moment before nodding and looking away again.

A low, threatening rumble rolled across the sky in the distance.

"There is going to be a thunderstorm very soon," Teo said. Whatever had happened during the dust storm, Nevio seemed shaken up, and he didn't have close family to wait out the next storm with. She smiled at him. "It's just rain, but I think you should stay here until it's over, all right?"

He nodded again.

Lightning flashed across the sky when Teo stepped outside. She counted ten seconds before the thunderclap. She was halfway home when the raindrops began to fall.

The downpour sounded like a relentless roar, deafening thunder overhead and water pounding on the roofs for a couple of hours before the black clouds moved on.

Most of the streets were flooded, and some of the buildings with basements had suffered, but luckily most of the dried goods and food storages had been spared. But although Siena had withstood the storms well, there was a lot of cleaning up to do. Teo soon found herself directing the efforts and helping out where needed. She really wanted to fix the antenna, not only because she wanted to call Luca, but because she hated the sight of broken tech and knew that unlike during her time working at the R&R, she now had the tools to fix things and no one to tell her off for it.

"Teo," said Arsenio behind her as she was bent over to pick up some pieces of broken glass.

She straightened up and faced him. "Yes?" While their relationship was no secret, they both agreed that it simplified things and kept them focused on their work if they refrained from doing or saying anything intimate while in public.

"I don't seem to be needed here at the moment," he said. "Now would be a good time to go for a booze run."

Teo nodded. He was right. The spotters used to go out after quakes and storms to see if something of use to Florence had been uncovered. On occasion, there would be treasures to be found. Sometimes preserved foodstuffs or tools. Often alcohol in a forgotten wine cellar or in the back of an otherwise empty warehouse. Hence the nickname. "Good point," she said, shot the shards on the ground a glance and bit her lip.

"You are needed here," he said with an emphasis on the pronoun. "Not just to pick up broken glass. To bolster morale."

The morale seemed to be doing well on its own, but Teo understood what he meant. Like it or not, it was part of what she was to Siena now. "You should not go alone, though," she said.

"No, I'll bring someone else whose time is better spent out there than picking up litter," Arsenio said so readily that Teo knew he had planned on it before she brought it up.

"Renn?" she asked.

"Yes." Arsenio paused, then added, "He's spotter material. And he's not too useful here right now anyway."

Teo narrowed her eyes at him. "Why not?"

"He'll never admit it, but he pulled a muscle or something when he saved Nevio. It's obvious when he lifts." Arsenio shrugged. "Don't look at me like that. He might be heroic, but he's not stupid. If he's not saying anything, it's because it's nothing serious."

"All right. Take Renn and go. Bring us back something nice," Teo said.

Arsenio made a mock salute at her and turned on his heel.

Teo sighed. She would have liked to go adventuring again. But Arsenio was right. She was more useful here.

14:

Esmia

The dark clouds on the horizon were taunting her. Esmia thought she could even make out a ribbon of water falling from them, but it might only be her imagination or perhaps a mirage.

It was ridiculous that a thunderstorm had passed right over her head, and she still had no water. The ground had soaked up most of the water before she emerged from the ruins, and the little water she did find in crevices and holes tasted foul. There was hardly any vegetation in the ancient city, either, so it might be one of those places where the very ground was unclean. She was upset that the spirits had caused her to spill her water in a place like that, but anger was as futile as praying for Moon to come back. Still, it kept her focused and the focus kept her from giving in to self-pity or exhaustion.

The ruins of the city lay behind her now. She had changed her course from its original intent in order to chase the thunderstorm. It was her best hope. She wouldn't catch up to it, but it must have left pools of clean water somewhere.

Esmia crushed a beetle between her teeth. It tasted sour and not very pleasant at all, but she swallowed it. Not a lot of moisture in it by now. She had a few more in her pack that she would eat later. She wiped a hand across her forehead. Then she licked her hand. Dust and salt. She had known this would not be easy. She had known she might not make it. But scarvhes and scavengers if she was going to sit around and wait for death to come.

If only she could get to water. There would be animals too and plants she could eat. That would buy her time. And after that? Did she mean to spend the remainder of her days by a pool of water all alone? No wanderer should be alone. That was why they formed Coveys and Bevies. But her Covey had cast her out. When she thought of it now, she discovered that the hole inside her chest had raw edges that stung when she prodded them. Suppose she could find another Covey or a stagnant settlement. What then? Would they take her in? Even if they did, would they not reject her when they found out?

Esmia pushed the doubt away. It would not do her any good to think of that now.

The dark clouds dissipated. And Esmia still had not reached any water. She had tried filtering wet sand to get some moisture out of it, but that was hours ago now, and the few drops only covered the bottom of her flask. Her mouth and throat were so dry that her tongue stuck to the roof of her mouth and she couldn't swallow. She was lightheaded and tired, but she could not allow herself to stop. If she sat down to rest, she may not have the strength or conviction to get back up. She altered her course slightly to find some shelter from the sun. It would not slow her down much, and a structure in the distance promised shade. It turned out to be a ruin of some kind, a grey bulk with stubborn yellow-green vines crawling over it.

When she reached it, Esmia paused for a moment to yank one of the vines free. It was leathery to the touch, but she had seen these before and knew they were not poisonous. Whether they tasted good was another matter, but perhaps they had enough sap for her to suck some out. She retrieved her knife and made an incision.

She never discovered whether the sap was palatable because in that moment, a rumbling growl came from somewhere on the other side of the ruins. That was not thunder. And it wasn't the wind, either. Esmia dropped the vine and crouched with her knife at the ready. It sounded like a huge predator. Definitely not a wolf or a scarvhe, but what then? She would rather not find out.

The noise kept increasing. Esmia wanted to slap her hands over her ears, but she could not risk deafening herself to indications of its movement. So she clutched her knife and gritted her teeth and tried to breathe silently while she pressed herself against the almost cool side of the ruin.

The predator rounded a corner. And several things happened at once. Esmia gasped when she saw it. A horrible monster, legless like a scarvhe and with some sort of carapace, sunlight glinting off its surface as it slid forward, not propelled by wings, but by something that looked oddly like broad wheels. It was black and even bigger than she had imagined.

Despite her previous resolve to shrink into the shadows, Esmia jumped to her feet, shoved her knife into her belt and turned away from the monster. It would gobble her up in one mouthful if given the chance. But it did not have wings, and it must have an incredible weight. She had to go somewhere it could not follow. She gripped at the vines as the roar grew deafening behind her and began to scale the ruin. One vine broke the moment she pulled at it and she almost fell, but she managed to find a stronger one and haul herself upwards.

She did not dare to look back. What was that animal? It did not look natural at all... Esmia clutched the vines and pushed herself to continue although she was dizzy with thirst and panic. The only thing that came to mind was an Other. Although she had never seen one before, it reminded her of something. As she finally reached the top of the ruin and lifted herself onto the roof, she realized what it was. The tracks she had found in the dust before the storms...

And then the predator stopped roaring. Esmia allowed herself to look down. It had ceased moving in almost the same spot where she pulled herself up into the vines. Its carapace glinted maliciously in the sunlight. An unfamiliar stench rose from it. It reminded her of the taste of the foul water in the city, but she had little time to consider it before its belly opened and spilled... people. Or something that looked like people. Could an Other nest inside a bigger Other?

Esmia turned and fled. Vines threatened to trip her, and the roof was strewn with rocks and pockmarked with holes. She thought she heard someone shout behind her, but she didn't stop and didn't look back over her shoulder. Why were they chasing her? She knew the spirits played with her, but she was certain the beast and the figures it released from its maw were not spirits. What had she done that was so terrible that monsters hunted her?

One of her feet slipped into a crevice in the roof, and she barely managed to throw up her hands to brace herself for the fall before she lay sprawled on her stomach. She gasped, tried to push herself up, but her foot was stuck. She twisted herself so she could see what she was doing and picked up her knife again to sever any vine that held her.

A voice called out, clear and with a comfortably familiar lilt. "We are not going to hurt you," it said.

An Other that spoke like a wanderer? Esmia looked up. Two figures stood between her and the place where she had climbed up to the roof. Were they going to kill her and eat her?

She focused on the one in front. He was standing like someone used to the dangers of climbing a ruin. He wore his dark hair long, most of it gathered with a ribbon. His skin was brown like hers and he wore what looked a lot like a wanderer's garments.

Esmia blinked and looked away from him. Even if he resembled a wanderer, it did not mean he wasn't dangerous. Why would a wanderer be inside the belly of an Other, after all? She would have to cut off her shoe. It was too stuck to get her foot out in a hurry otherwise.

Then the man who looked like a wanderer moved. She glanced up again. He sat down with his legs crossed. But why?

"What are you doing?" his companion asked. His voice had a hard edge, and although Esmia understood him, the words sounded mangled.

"We are not in a hurry," the brown-skinned man said, keeping his gaze on Esmia.

The other one reluctantly sat down too, adjusting his belt in a careful way that suggested the tool attached to it may be a weapon.

"You don't need to ruin your shoe." It was the wanderer talking again. "I can help you. If you will let me."

Esmia didn't reply. Instead she brought up her knife to show him she was not afraid of using it on an Other. Or a human.

"We are not going to hurt you."

"Why are you hunting me?" Esmia asked, keeping her voice calm.

"Not hunting. I was only wondering why you are not with a Covey. You are a wanderer too, aren't you?"

Too? So perhaps he was really one, after all. "What is that monster?" Esmia asked instead.

"It is called a car," the man said, glancing toward the edge of the roof, indicating that he knew she was referring to the roaring thing below. "It is a tool with no will of its own. My friend uses it to transport us quicker than one can walk. It does no harm. I am Renn," he added. "My friend is called Arsenio."

Renn was a decent enough name. Arsenio had even more syllables than Esmia's, which was silly.

"I was separated from my Covey a year ago," Renn said. "I would have died if not for the kindness of strangers."

"Will you go away if I ask you to?" she asked.

"Yes," Renn said, dipping his chin. "You are likely to die, but I will honor your wish. I have no claims to your future."

"We can't just leave her here! She's a little girl!" the man with the absurd name said.

"She is a wanderer," Renn said. "I will do nothing against her will." He looked at her again. "We have water. I will give you some even if you choose not to come with us."

Esmia considered this. Despite the difficulty making out what the man who controlled the car beast was saying, he sounded genuinely worried. And Renn did seem sincere as well.

"I give you my word," Renn said. "Let me give you water and then you can decide if you want to go on alone or come with us."

"To your Covey?" Esmia asked.

"To a settlement called Siena," Renn explained. "You will be allowed to stay there if you wish and to leave as well. Those are the same terms as I am currently living there on."

She wanted to decline the offer. How did she know they were not luring her into a trap? How did she know they were not doing the car's bidding and wanted to feed her to it? Then again, they had emerged unscathed from its belly. Esmia studied the pair for a while. She did need water. Could she really take it and leave? She would not be able to fight them and win if it came to that. But she was stuck right now, and they could easily have overpowered her already.

Esmia tugged at her foot again, without much conviction. Trusting them would be a risk, yes, but if she did not take the chance, she was likely to die. Maybe not today. Maybe not for a while. But... "Thank you for the offer," she finally said. "If you have water to spare, I would have some."

The tall man clapped his hands once. "Good!" he said. "Now we're getting somewhere."

Renn made a gesture in his direction, then began to stand up. Slowly, deliberately. As if she were a frightened animal. Esmia almost cringed. What was she thinking? She was exposing herself to them, reacting to what they did instead of asserting herself. She was no animal. She drew in a long breath and put her knife back in her belt. "Will you help me up?" she asked, just as Renn opened his mouth to ask her if he could.

"Yes," he said. Esmia thought she saw a smile flicker across his face. He approached her, crouched and stuck his hands into the hole. "I need to cut the vine down there," he said. Their eyes met.

Wordlessly, Esmia handed him her knife. If he had any designs on her life, he wouldn't need a blade to take it. She could smell him this close. Sweat, dust, and a strange cleanness underneath those scents.

Renn severed the vine and handed her back the knife. "Try now."

Esmia slid backward. Her foot came free. "Thank you," she said.

15:

Esmia

Esmia was never quite sure what convinced her to actually get into the car with the two strangers. They gave her water as promised and never made any attempt to force her to do anything. It was tempting to trust them. Perhaps the tipping point was when Arsenio explained something about the car using words like *enjin* and *masheen* and Esmia glanced at Renn and saw him looking entirely as lost as she felt. That was comforting, somehow.

Eventually, she found herself inside the roaring beast, behind the two men, on a seat where space was cleared for her. Flasks with water, metal tools and strange objects that looked like they had been excavated recently were scattered on the floor and the seat next to her.

Renn had not lied when he said traveling in the car was much faster than on foot. Esmia stared out of a windowpane in the side of the masheen and saw the landscape whisk by. It was strange and oddly disheartening to know that it was possible to travel like that. What was migration without the ground under your feet? The car felt like something that should not exist. An artifact from the distant past that had no place in the world.

Yet, she did not ask them to stop it. She did not attempt to open the door to escape. She allowed the car to carry her to an unknown settlement. If the spirits had meant for her to thirst, surely they had not meant for this to happen. Part of her entertained a fragile hope that perhaps they would not follow her when she moved this quickly. And maybe, if they did, a stagnant town made up of masheens and wanderers and strange, tall men would be different from her own Covey. Her old Covey.

Their destination was a wall behind which the ruins of an ancient city reached for the sky. The wall was a new construct, made from chunks of old buildings and clay. The car slowed and went through an opening in the barrier. It turned to align itself with the wall and stopped.

Outside the window, Esmia saw people. They were not wanderers. They were stagnants removing debris from the ground and carrying buckets. But they did not resemble the stagnants she was used to either. Not quite.

"Here we are," Arsenio said. "Will you show her around while I unload the car?"

"Yes," Renn said. He pushed open the door next to his seat, stepped out and opened the one closest to Esmia. "We are in Siena now," he explained as if she had not figured that out. He held a wanderer's staff now. The sight of it was comforting. "I would like to introduce you to a few people. Is that all right?"

Esmia wondered what he would do if she said no. But she nodded and slid out of the car, setting her feet on solid ground very carefully.

All the buildings around them were either new or had been restored. They did not look like most stagnant settlements, worn down by years of usage and patched up layer upon layer over the generations. There was something too even about the angles, something deliberate and practical and new that she had never seen on buildings before. Wanderer camps had the same practicality to them, but they were not constructed from stone and clay.

The streets were broad and could easily accommodate cars, but she did not see others beyond the one they had arrived in. Instead there were people hurrying along in clothes that were certainly not wanderers' garments. Some of them glanced curiously her way, but Renn kept them from asking questions or approaching her. Or she thought he did. He did not exactly tell them to mind their own business, but something about his posture and the way he moved discreetly into their line of sight made Esmia feel that he did.

"It is different," Renn offered.

Esmia was not certain what he referred to, but it was applicable to anything surrounding them. The houses, the people, the smells, the sounds. She could just make out a low humming noise that she could not place at all.

A woman came striding toward them. She was carrying a bucket and was clad in comfortable trousers held up with a belt around her waist. A shirt with rolled up sleeves was tucked into it, and her hair was gathered in a practical knot on top of her head, spilling strands into her face. Her skin was not as dark as a wanderer's and something about her reminded Esmia of Arsenio although they looked nothing alike. Her face was alert and curious, but not unkind, as she approached them.

"Hello," the woman said to Renn. "All well?"

Renn inclined his head.

"Nothing much in the car," Arsenio called from behind them. "But Renn found a girl."

"So I see," the woman said, stopping in front of Esmia, smiling. "Hello, and welcome to Siena."

"Thank you," Esmia said because what else was she supposed to say?

"My name is Teo." The woman stretched out her hand.

Esmia shook it. "I'm Esmia," she said. She was hoping for Renn's help, but he said nothing.

"Are you hungry?" the woman asked.

"A little," Esmia admitted although it was quite the understatement.

Teo smiled at her. "I think we should talk over food, then. Renn?"

For a moment, Esmia was afraid he would decline, but then he nodded in acceptance of the invitation.

97

"Come with me, please. It's not far," Teo said and beckoned them to follow her. She led Esmia down the street. The ground was muddy and pools had gathered here and there. Esmia was glad the two men had given her water or she might not have been able to keep herself from scooping some up into her flask to boil later. She kept pace with the two others, walking between them. She couldn't quite tell if it made her feel safer or like cattle being herded. Perhaps a bit of both.

The woman smelled strange. Esmia could discern sweat and dirt, but like Renn, she had an underlying scent that could best be described as clean. And her hair was shiny and healthy. She must have access to plenty of food and water.

"Here we are," Teo said and pushed open a door to a house that looked patched up with bits of other buildings. She went inside, and Renn held the door, nodding in encouragement to Esmia.

The inside of the house was dry and cooler than the outside. There was a mat on the floor and pegs on the wall where two pieces of clothing hung. The place smelled of people, but not like a tent did. She followed her host's example and took off her shoes. When she saw that Renn leaned his staff against the wall and left it there, Esmia placed her pack next to it, although it felt like a risk.

This was the first house Esmia had ever seen from the inside. She had seen the stagnants' homes from the outside, but she only visited their marketplaces and animal pens. She always wondered what it would be like to live surrounded by thick walls and have a solid roof over your head. Would it feel protective or would it be impossible to really breathe inside them?

The floor kept drawing her eyes to it. It wasn't tightly packed earth, but the same material as the walls. Whatever she had expected, she had not thought that the ground would be different from inside a tent. She also had not expected that there would be so many walls inside. The house was divided into several smaller sections and, Esmia surmised, they probably had different functions.

"We haven't done much with the interior decoration," Teo said, an apologetic note sneaking into her cheerful tone. "But make yourselves comfortable. I'll be right back." She disappeared through an opening in a wall to another room.

Esmia looked up at Renn.

He made a half shrug. "In there," he said, gesturing. "That is the living room."

The living room was some sort of communal space. It had a low table and pillows around it. There was a higher table with a chair in front of it too, but it appeared to be some sort of workspace although the bits and pieces on it were all unfamiliar to Esmia. One of the walls was almost covered with drawings, some on papers while others were made directly on the wall. There were patterns on them and words with arrows pointing to different parts. And lots of numbers and signs. The writing was probably in the old script, but Esmia had never learned anything but the numbers because they were still in use when wanderers traded with stagnants.

A window with a transparent pane of glass like the ones in the car took up a lot of space on one wall. It was smooth and made Esmia want to touch it. Through it, she could see the street outside.

They sat down on the pillows around the table. This at least Esmia knew how to do. She and Renn both crossed their legs and rested their hands in their laps.

A few moments later, Teo joined them. She was carrying a pitcher and three clay cups and removed a tray with sand and a stick in it from the table. She told them to help themselves and disappeared again.

Renn carefully poured water for all three of them.

"Here we go," Teo said, returning once more. She put down a plate with slices of bread and a bowl with something greasy and red in it.

Esmia watched as Teo took a slice and put some of the red stuff on top of it with a spoon. Her stomach growled, and she gratefully replicated Teo's actions. The bread was cold and a little hard, but it tasted well enough. The red stuff was unfamiliar to Esmia, but it had herbs and vegetables in it.

"So," Teo said, "I assume you are a wanderer like Renn. Have you been separated from your Covey?"

Esmia used the mouthful of bread she was chewing as an excuse to think before answering. "Yes," she said. "I was on my own in the dust storm. I was following the rain when Renn and Arsenio met me."

"I'm sorry," Teo said. "Were you close to the members of your Covey?"

"No," Esmia said, maybe a little too quickly. "My father died not so long ago. He was my only family."

"May Moon guide him," Renn said.

"I'm sorry for your loss," Teo added. "As Renn no doubt has told you, you are welcome here."

But how did a wanderer stay in a settlement? And one as strange and new as this one, at that. Renn managed... Esmia would have to ask him if he had decided to become a stagnant. She smiled at Teo. Regardless of what she decided, being so readily invited was a rare and precious feeling.

16:

Luca

The day after the storms was a bike day. Luca knew it would be more sensible to take the Rover, a sturdy thing with tires made for off-roading and space for everything he imagined Siena might need since he couldn't reach them via the radio. But the ground was already dry enough for it not to be completely insane to take the bike. And he had too many emotions all scrambling about inside to be cooped up in a car for even a few hours.

So he stuffed what he needed into a backpack, put on his helmet and was on his way. He would have preferred to go the night before, but he wasn't that stupid, so he'd gone to bed and been so completely awake despite the pills he'd popped that he ended up in his workshop anyway. He'd tried getting in touch with Siena again to no avail and checked the frequency where the other signal had appeared, but nothing there either. Eventually, he'd fallen asleep at his work table. Oh well. He'd gotten a few hours of sleep.

It was a beautiful morning if you were into cloudless skies and bright sunlight and a landscape that had been so ruffled by the elements the day before that it looked all crisp and new.

Siena grew on the horizon from a speck that might be anything to the unmistakable shapes of straight lines and manmade angles. And as

Luca approached it, he spotted the reason for their lack of communication. The antenna was gone. He groaned. Would it have killed them to put it back up the moment they got the chance?

But their lack of communication had given him something else. He could not wait to tell them of his discovery. Teo would be thrilled to hear that someone else out there had a radio. She'd understand the implications of it right away.

Luca slowed down and followed the protective wall around the settlement. It looked intact. And someone had already been outside in the car, judging from the tire trails. He went through the gate and stopped, parking his bike near the wall although he supposed he could theoretically just go down the street on it and park it anywhere he pleased. Designated parking areas were a thing of the past. Speeding tickets too, thankfully.

The place was quiet. All right, it was always pretty quiet even when Siena was at its busiest because how hectic could a village of maybe fifty people get, after all? But even by those standards, it was almost eerily silent.

Luca stood for a moment with his helmet in his hand. No sound but the whisper of the wind and the rattling of a broken shutter on a window somewhere in the vicinity. It wasn't exactly creepy, but he was standing in a ghost town. He used to have friends here. Classmates... What had happened to them when the world went to hell? Had they managed to get into Florence? Had they gone somewhere else? Had they tried to get by in Siena and simply died, or were the nomads their descendants? Shit, there was so much he didn't know. So much lost...

He shook himself. The hell. What was he thinking, letting himself get spooked by a quiet settlement? It wasn't like everyone had vanished. They were probably just at one of their weekly meetings. Luca scoffed. He was here to deliver exciting news, not to dwell on the shitty past.

The building housing the assembly hall and Teo's home was the hub of the settlement, and Luca headed straight for it. He stopped in front of the door. A helpful sign above it informed him that this was the right place, as if anyone would be in doubt, but he supposed it was healthy of the Sienans to anticipate the settlement's growth.

He would most likely arrive in the middle of a wonderful socialist discussion about distribution of wealth or a vote on what subjects should be taught in school. Not that Luca wasn't a bit of an idealist himself, but Siena was incredibly optimistic about human nature.

How to best make his entrance? The door opened to the venue itself. He should probably sneak the door open and tiptoe in as quietly as possible and sit down near the wall without attracting too much attention.

The door groaned and Luca almost tripped over the doorstep that he could swear was a new installation. He suppressed a string of profanities and regained his balance and dignity, but his entrance had not gone unnoticed. Teo at the head of the assembly paused mid-sentence, and faces turned toward him. Luca grinned and spread out his arms theatrically. "Here you all are!" he shouted. "I'm so happy you all made it through the storms! So did I, in case anyone was wondering."

Teo, with her unnatural power of adaption, smiled. "Hello, Luca," she said. "We're glad to see you. Our antenna broke, as you probably guessed, but we are fine. You are here in time for the exciting news."

Wait, what? Wasn't he the one with exciting news?

"Sit down," a low voice next to him ordered rather than suggested.

"I'm so glad you weren't struck by lightning or something," Luca muttered, not even looking at Arsenio. He sat down, scanning the crowd for a few particular heads.

Gabriele turned and smiled at him and by the doctor's side was the unmistakable bald head of Mender. Check. Clara's blond hair, Tonino's dark mop that always looked like he'd just pulled off his baker's hat... Luca kept searching and spotted another familiar and ridiculous hairdo in the middle of the room. But who was that girl next to Renn? Even if Luca couldn't be bothered to learn the names of every single person in Siena, he was pretty damn sure he hadn't seen this one before. As he watched, she looked at Renn, and Renn smiled at her. Her skintone was pretty close to Renn's. Her hair was shorter and darker, but it was tied back in a way that suggested that either Renn had become a hairdresser overnight or else they used the same stylist.

"As I was saying," Teo picked up whatever she had been talking about when Luca entered, "a lot of you have already met our newest arrival, but let's all welcome her properly."

Teo turned to the girl next to Renn with a trademark Teo smile. As Luca watched, the girl said something to Renn, and he nodded at her and made a gesture. The girl stood up.

"Welcome to Siena, Esmia," Teo said.

And people actually broke out in welcoming phrases and even applause. Luca had to wonder what it was about the girl that was so goddamn awesome, apart from her name nearly being an anagram of Siena.

"Thank you," the girl said, barely loudly enough for Luca to hear. She quickly sat down again and Luca saw Renn smile reassuringly at her.

"Esmia is a wanderer like Renn," Teo continued.

Luca listened to her go on about housing arrangements for almost-anagram girl, an empty room in the building Renn was in, and then move on to various other announcements about water supplies and damages done by the storms. He didn't really pay attention. Didn't seem like anyone had died or anything. Should he announce his discovery at the assembly? Half of them probably wouldn't understand the technical details. But he'd do it anyway.

"I think that's all for today," Teo said, standing up after having sat down for a few minutes while someone else went on about greenhouses. "Unless anyone—"

"Yeah, hi," Luca said, getting to his feet. His ass was numb. That's what he got for not bringing a pillow to this bring-your-own-cushion party. "I've got something to share with the group today."

No one laughed. But they did look at him.

"So after the dust storm, I tried to call you guys on the radio." He ignored Teo's worried glance. Honestly, she ought to have more faith in him. It wasn't like he was going to make a scene about them not getting their shit together and fixing the antenna. "But I couldn't get through cause your antenna was busted. I didn't know that, so I tried out other frequencies."

Blank stares. Teo understood, but Luca wasn't sure anyone else did.

"Like if you turn around and call out to someone in a different direction to see if anyone's there." Not at all like that, but he wasn't here to give them a science lesson. "And someone responded."

Teo's mouth opened slightly. No one else reacted.

"So ladies, gentlemen, nonbinaries and sentient," Luca continued, "to put it simply: It means that someone out there is using radio technology too. Someone we've never met before."

"Florence?" Tonino asked.

"No," Gabriele said, "we would know if they did."

Luca flashed him a grin. "Exactly. It's not Florence. I talked to a woman from somewhere else. Another preserved city or base with old technology from the sound of it."

"Luca," Teo said with a tremor of excitement in her voice, "Do you know where this person is located?"

"The connection died before I could find out," he admitted, "but she can't be far away. And if I could get in touch once, I can do it again. It's just a matter of time."

"Did you share your own location or ours with her?" Arsenio asked.

Luca rolled his eyes. Someone was taking their job as head of village security very seriously. "No, I didn't tell her where you are."

"Well, it certainly is interesting," Gabriele chimed in. "In Florence, we believed we were the only ones living in a technologically advanced society. But there is no reason others couldn't have fortified a city."

"Except we never saw them," Arsenio said.

"We don't know if this is a large city or a small settlement with a single functioning radio," Teo mused, "but if they have a radio, it stands to reason that they communicate with others."

"I'll find out," Luca said because he would. If he had to comb Tuscany for signs of them, he would.

The majority of people were starting to look bored or restless. Why couldn't they see how huge this was?

"Good. Thank you for keeping us informed," Teo said, dismissing the discussion. Luca almost protested, but he wouldn't get much out of talking to the average Sienan about this anyway. So he waited while they all stood up and began to file out.

Renn and almost-anagram girl went up to Teo along with Arsenio. Clara smiled and waved at Luca as she headed out, and Mender was talking to a man Luca didn't know about something relating to wrist pain. Tonino nodded at Luca as he went, and Gabriele approached to save Luca from impatient boredom.

"Luca," the doctor said, "how is your ankle?"

"Fine," Luca replied, demonstrating the point by shifting to stand on one leg. "You probably saved my life," he added mock-earnestly.

Gabriele's expression was somewhere between annoyed and flustered.

"Thank you," Luca added.

Gabriele smiled and shook his head. Then he joined Mender, and Luca stubbornly waited until Renn and the girl were ready to leave. He nonchalantly joined them at the door. "Hey," he said.

"Hello, Luca," Renn greeted him, his glance immediately flickering to the girl.

"Esmia, right?" Luca said and held out his hand. "I'm Luca. Obviously."

"Yes," the girl said, answering both points in a manner that made Luca suspect all wanderers were silent, stoic types. "It's nice to meet you."

"So, did you just wander into Siena? Aren't you supposed to be living with a tribe?"

Renn's face changed a little, and he subtly moved closer to Esmia. Good grief. Luca wasn't going to eat her.

"I was separated from my Covey," she explained. "I met Renn and Arsenio in their car."

Their car? Luca decided not to be petty about that. "That's funny," he said instead, "That's pretty much how I met Renn. We've known each other for a while now. But seriously, does that happen a lot? You people getting lost, I mean."

"No," Renn replied, a bit on the terse side. "But it does happen."

"Yeah, you're both living proof of that," Luca agreed, wondering why Renn seemed upset by that question and why he even bothered to worry about it. "Oh, Teo's free now. I need to talk to her about the antenna. But nice to meet you, Esmia. I bet you'll fit right in here. Siena's a cool place." He grinned at Renn. "I'll get out of your hair and leave you to your new girlfriend. Catch you later."

Before Renn could make a retort, Luca was already jogging toward Teo.

17:

Renn

Renn had always considered stagnants rigid in their ways, but the Sienans were different. They did favor a permanent residence and needed more rules and regulations than wanderers, and yet, Esmia was treated with hospitality and friendliness in exchange for her future contribution to the settlement. It was a pragmatic mindset. It was probably the reason Renn had stayed for so long. That and the lack of a Covey.

"No one has asked me to work," Esmia cut into his thoughts. They were walking away from the assembly hall together.

"They are giving you time to get used to Siena," Renn said. She had only been there for a few days and had been quite exhausted when she arrived. "You are also very young," he added.

Esmia frowned at him. "Why does my age matter?"

Renn swallowed a smile. She was sixteen. Wanderers would not have hesitated to make use of her skills right away and teach her how to be better at them. "Where they come from, children are..." He faltered. "They are taught to read and write and count until they are around your age."

"I'm not a child," she said.

"No, but you are young," Renn replied.

"Do they do nothing but learn to read and write and count?" Esmia wondered.

"Well, yes," Renn said. He was not the right person to explain this. But he was glad she was asking questions. It meant she was adapting to the new situation. This process was going even quicker than he had expected. "They also help their families with cleaning their homes and cooking," he added.

"But they all learn the same skills? Why don't they learn what they are good at?"

"I think they learn what they are good at later." Renn cleared his throat. He couldn't really defend why a cook or an arbiter should learn to read long and complicated books. "But you will have to ask someone who knows more about their ways than I," he added.

A perfect candidate for it would be Mender. Renn felt a little strange for not telling Esmia that ne was, but no one ever explained nem to newcomers before they asked. That was Teo's idea. Renn was surprised at first since she was usually very honest, but he could see the sense of it. If people were told Mender was an Other, an artificial human, they may get scared. If they saw nem working and talking like the rest of the inhabitants, they may take the revelation better.

"Your friend," she continued, broaching another subject that had not been explained to her, "with the odd clothes and the yellow hair. Who is he? He said he has a car too."

"Luca," Renn said. He was doing his best to pronounce it like its owner did although it clung oddly to the tip of his tongue when he did. "He does not live here. He is an ally of Siena. He once saved me and Mender from a pack of scarvhes, and he helped Teo and her friends when they decided to leave the city they lived in before." It was a highly abbreviated version of the events, but Renn did not know how to tell the story without raising more questions than he answered.

"I see. Then... where does he live?" Esmia asked. "He is not a wanderer."

"No, he is not," Renn said. The idea of Luca migrating, traversing the land on foot instead of comfortably resting inside a car or on a bike, was almost unimaginable. The thought of Luca leaving behind the strange luxuries of his home with servants and endless amounts of food and soap and lights that turned on when he walked into a room was laughable. "He lives by himself with two others." Renn shot Esmia a quick glance. He hadn't thought of it as double speak when he said the word, but she did not seem to take it at such, either. "He knows a lot about old tech. Masheens. Like cars and..." Renn made an indistinct gesture.

Esmia considered it for a moment. "How?" she asked. "How does he know all that?"

Luca had explained to Renn how he was alive hundreds of years ago, how he worked with masheens and artificials back then. How he had lived when Moon's Lantern shone in the sky every night. How he had somehow been asleep for centuries before waking up only a few years ago. If Renn had not seen him give Mender new skin, if he had not seen the cupboard where Luca kept cooled food or any of the other wonders in his home, he would find it hard to believe. "He claims he was alive in the ancient times," Renn said, not surprised to see disbelief spreading on Esmia's face. "He says masheens made him sleep and not age until he woke up."

"Do you believe him?" she asked, earnestly.

"I do," Renn replied. "I can see no other explanation. He surrounds himself with working masheens, and others who know more about it than I believe he is telling the truth. In any case, I don't see any reason why he would lie about something like that."

Esmia quietly accepted this, but she was not convinced, Renn could tell. They continued through Siena to Clara's church. Another mystery. Clara had explained to Renn about a great man who performed miracles and died in order to save people thousands of years ago. The part that had stuck most vividly in Renn's mind was the story of how a boulder on top of the grave could not keep the man's body underground. There was something strange about the whole thing because the body and the spirit seemed to have been reunited.

Renn was used to being the only one with no knowledge of churches and stories like that, but now another wanderer separated from her Covey was here. Luca's way of putting it had been exasperating, but he did have a point. Wanderers did not migrate alone. They were part of Coveys or Bevies, and if they were on their own, they rarely lived for long.

Renn was hoping she would fit in with the other Sienans. But another small bit of him was entertaining the thought that she might not. That she may wish to leave in search of a new Covey... And if she did, that he may wish to go with her.

Granted, Esmia was not volunteering a lot of information about herself. She would say that she and her father were part of the same Covey and that her father recently died. She had survived the dust storm alone by hiding in ruins with a small pack of rats. She said she had followed the thunderstorm in order to find water when Arsenio and Renn came upon her, but apart from that, Renn knew almost nothing about her. But she was a wanderer who shared his accent and his way of thinking. And he did quite like her, although that was not a necessity to form a Covey.

"If you want to work, have you thought what you have to offer Siena?" Renn asked, circling back to the previous topic of their conversation.

Esmia nodded. Her mouth formed a determined line as she thought. "Gabriele and Mender are healers, aren't they?"

"Yes," Renn confirmed. They used different words, but that was what they were.

"I can gather firewood and move rocks as well as anyone else," Esmia continued, "but I was taught to make soothing teas and medicine by my mother. I know how to deliver babies and set broken bones. Perhaps I could be of use to them."

Did that mean she intended to stay? Renn didn't ask. "Perhaps we should pay them a visit today," he agreed.

Esmia smiled. "I don't want to be a burden to this settlement," she said. "I want to do what I can to help for as long as I am here."

"Of course." Renn resumed walking. He glanced up at the sky. It was as clear and bright as it only became after downpours when the ground was still drinking and there was little dust whirling in the air.

Renn stopped and turned to see why Esmia was no longer walking beside him. She was standing a few paces back, staring at something. Renn couldn't tell what. "Is something the matter?" he asked.

Esmia's knees buckled. She collapsed on the ground without a word, her eyes empty and blind. Renn took one step toward her, instinctively, before he faltered. He watched her begin to shake, thrash about in the cracked mud on the ground. She spasmed violently and without any control of her own being.

And Renn understood. He knew why she was alone. He knew why she had not explained the circumstances of her separation from her Covey.

On the ground, Esmia was helplessly being jerked from side to side, her teeth clattering, and her eyes only showing white.

18:

Luca

There was only static. Again. Luca had run out of fingers to count how many times he had tried reaching the mysterious strangers. He put the gear down. He'd try again later. For now, he'd do some repair work on a robot he'd found a while back.

"Still no luck?" Nanny asked from the door to his workshop.

Luca didn't turn. "No," he said, picking up a tiny screwdriver.

There was a very loud silence. Luca ignored it.

"Are you going to talk about it?" Nanny asked.

"About what?" he said. Okay, snapped if he was honest.

Nanny moved closer, completely not taking the hint. Or, her model's sensitivity taken into consideration, taking the hint and choosing to ignore it. "About whatever happened when you visited your friends in Siena."

"They are allies," he said. "And nothing happened. I helped fix their antenna."

"Did Arsenio not treat you well?"

Luca jabbed the screwdriver way too hard into the fine mechanics he was performing surgery on. "You can't spell Arsenio without arse," he said in a fake posh British accent. "But no, he didn't do anything."

"What did Renn do?"

Luca finally looked at her. "Who the fuck says Renn did anything?"

Nanny smiled, way too knowingly for comfort. "I don't think anyone else could make you that upset."

The hell was that even supposed to mean? Luca opened his mouth, but nothing came out. He shook his head.

All right, he was upset. And it was because of Renn. Because Renn was a goddamn scientific imbecile. A fucking caveman sometimes. "There's this new girl in Siena," Luca said. "A nomad like Renn."

Nanny's face set into a sympathetic expression. "Oh, I see. I'm sorry, Luca..."

"For what?" he asked and continued before she could elaborate, "I haven't told you about the problem with her yet." It was super simple, really. Or ought to be.

Luca was talking to Teo about radios and giving her a crash course in the history of communication devices while they worked when they heard people shouting and running. Something was going on with the new girl, someone said, and of course Teo set off to see what it was, and Luca went with her.

They arrived at the scene with a bunch of other people. Renn was standing a little to one side. At first Luca wasn't sure what to make of his expression because it was one he'd never seen before. It was fear. It sort of made Luca want to hug him and tell him everything was going to be fine. But Renn was not the person with the problem, that was easy to see. The new girl, Esmia, was on the ground, seizing and cramping and obviously having a fit of some sort. Epilepsy, Luca was pretty sure, although he'd only seen it in movies and fucked up videos by people whose friend had neglected taking their meds so they could make a fucked up video.

From the look of it, no one else had watched those videos or movies or even heard about it before. "Get Mender!" Luca yelled at no one in particular because even if Mender happened not to have treated anyone with epilepsy before, ne would have everything ne needed to know stored in nir database.

114

Luca pushed past one of the uselessly gawking Sienans and kneeled. He was pretty sure the important bit was making sure the person having a seizure didn't injure themselves by banging their head on something. He had a vague recollection of being told that putting something in their mouth to prevent them from biting their tongue could cause suffocation, so he wasn't going to risk that. Whether he was doing this right, he had no idea, but he pulled the thrashing girl to him, placing her head in his lap. It only took a few moments before the seizure stopped.

Luca held his hand above her face. She was breathing. Irregularly, but who wouldn't be?

"Excuse me. May I?" a polite and calm voice asked.

Thank fuck. Luca smiled up at Mender. Someone qualified, yay!

Mender folded nemself and transferred Esmia's head from Luca's lap to the ground and began to talk to her.

Luca stood up. "All right, show's over," he said to the assembled audience. "Give her some space, okay? Mender's taking care of her, and she will be fine."

Most of the others began to leave. Teo smiled at him. "Thank you," she said. Then, "What can I do?" to Mender.

"We are fine, thank you," Mender replied. "She needs to recover a little, and then I will take her back for examination."

Teo nodded and seemed to decide going after the others was the best option.

Luca shot Renn a grin. "Don't worry," he said. "Your girlfriend will be fine."

Renn stared at him. "She is not," he said.

"Hey," Luca said and stepped closer, "don't worry, man."

Renn backed away from him, and Luca barely had time to explore why that felt like a slap in the face before he realized that there was more to Renn's behavior than fear for Esmia's well-being. There was disbelief and hatred in there too, and the fear was for himself.

"The fuck is going on?" Luca asked, looking back over his shoulder to see Mender helping Esmia to her feet before giving Renn his full attention again.

"You touched her," Renn said as if that explained everything.

"Yes, I did," Luca agreed, "because unlike some people I don't freeze in a crisis."

"You should not have interfered," Renn insisted.

"What?" Luca said with as many exclamation points and question marks attached to the word as he could figuratively put there.

"That girl," Renn said in a low voice with an edge that Luca had never heard before, "is a plaything of the spirits."

"What?" Luca repeated. "Is this some kind of nomad hoodoo? She suffers from epilepsy. It's a fucking illness."

Renn shook his head, dismissively. "The spirits haunt her. She isn't safe."

"She isn't safe if she knocks herself half dead on a rock because of some fucked up idiot superstition!" Luca told him.

For a moment, Renn only stared at him.

Luca was beginning to wonder if he'd talked too fast for Renn to keep up with his accent, but that usually wasn't a problem. "I said—" he began.

Renn held up his hand in the universal stop-right-there gesture. "You don't understand. She is not safe. For others."

"She's not gonna bite you and turn you into a werewolf," Luca said.

This Renn ignored, which was probably for the better. "The girl is haunted by the spirits. She is not to be touched. The spirits can come through her to others. And she brings bad luck."

It was Luca's turn to stare. "Are you for real right now?" he asked. But he could see the answer burning with bright earnestness in Renn's eyes and stupidly handsome face. Yes, Renn was completely serious. "I tell you, that is an illness. Not spirits. It's not contagious. You can't catch epilepsy. That's ridiculous. Like, you don't catch a dislocated kneecap from someone sneezing on you."

The discussion was absurd. Yeah, okay, so Renn was from a less advanced society, but he was normally calm and reasonable and kind of badass... "That's just a dick move," Luca summed it up to Nanny. "Esmia's ill. I know I'm not always mister sensitive 2217 here, but I'm not an asshole to people with a medical condition."

Nanny said nothing. She just studied him.

"What?" he snapped.

"Renn is from a culture very different from yours, Luca..."

"Yeah. Culture," Luca repeated. "Awesome."

Nanny sighed which was kind of annoying because she didn't need to breathe. It was only a mannerism that could be removed. If only he could download a sensibility patch to Renn's brain or replace the caveman OS with a civilized OS. "I'm sure he'll understand it if it is explained to him."

"I did!" Luca almost shouted. "That's what I'm telling you!"

"In a calm and friendly way that made him feel safe? It sounds like a taboo that is embedded in his culture." Nanny said, ignoring Luca's emotional outburst.

"Yeah, whatever. I'll start by explaining to him that the world is round and the sun doesn't actually move around it on a string attached to the sky filament above."

"Luca."

He managed not to throw his screwdriver at something. He knew he was more upset than he should be. What did he care if the nomads had some fucked up taboos? Luca didn't even know the girl. He'd talked to her for five seconds. But Renn cared. And then he didn't. And all it took was one epileptic seizure for him to turn 180 degrees and that was creepy as fuck. Especially for someone whose moral compass was usually so straight it probably had a stick up its ass.

"Do we have something that can prevent epileptic seizures?" Luca asked.

"I don't know. Would you like me to check?" Nanny asked.

"Yeah. I kind of promised Mender and Gabriele I would." And considering how the base had been well-stocked to begin with and he had raided every sealed medicine cabinet he'd been able to find for the past two years, just in case, the odds were pretty good. "Thanks," he added.

Nanny left, and Luca turned back to the radio. One more attempt. Just one more and he'd call it a day. Go for a run. Punch a sandbag. Practice his aim with a gun. Something.

He slowly turned the dial, listening for anything but static. Maybe he was wrong. The signal could have bounced and come from somewhere too far away to be able to reach normally. It wasn't like Luca believed he was the only one with any technology to speak of. There were others out there. Cities who had been protected like Florence, some of which may not have gone old-fashioned. Bases with surviving cryo pods. Communities full of people who'd weathered out the climate changes and the meteor showers. It was only a matter of where. They could be overseas. They could be somewhere in what had once been Russia or whatever.

But the one he'd reached spoke Italian. She had a bit of an accent, but he'd understood her fine. It wasn't worse than Renn's...

Luca scoffed at the thought of Renn. He focused on the dial again, turned... and the static changed. "Hello?" he said.

"Hello?" a voice replied.

Oh shit, it was happening! It was real. Luca swallowed. "This is Luca Capello. We talked a few days ago."

"Hello, Luca Capello," the voice said, and it sounded so different. Not nearly as much interference as last time. "You talked to my colleague, not me. I am Andrea."

Okay, so not different because of the signal alone. He was dealing with at least two people. "Where are you located?" he asked.

"Our Superior finds it appropriate to learn more about you before revealing our exact location," came the reply a short while later. "We are in Italy, not far from Terni."

Luca's heart was positively pounding. "Fair enough," he said, dragging the tablet closer and pulling up the map and his notes. Terni was almost halfway between Siena and Rome. "What do you want to know?" Stop yourself, Luca Capello. He'd tell them things, of course, but not everything. For all he knew, they could be some kind of evil mega corporation who'd come riding in tanks with an army of artificials to gun him down and take everything he owned.

"How many are you?" the voice asked.

It occurred to Luca that he should be recording this. He opened the appropriate tool on his tablet. "Me and my staff and occasionally some friends," he replied, which wasn't a complete lie. "How many are you?"

"At the present time, 417 all included," the voice said.

Luca tried not to hyperventilate. More than four hundred fucking people living right under his nose and he had no idea. "That's a lot," he said, lamely. A lot more than the Sienans who would have to rely on wanderers passing through or visits to other settlements if they didn't want some serious in-breeding problems in a few generations. Four hundred might have the same problem, but it didn't take a genius to come up with a handful of solutions if they had access to the right technology. "I'm surprised I haven't run into any of you. I like to explore," he said.

"We live in the Shelter," she told him. Luca was certain he heard a capital S.

"Is that what you call your town?" he asked. "Is it like Florence? Do you know Florence?"

"We know of Florence," she told him. "Florence probably doesn't know about us. Luca Capello... Why did you contact us?"

"By accident the first time. But I have been trying to contact you again ever since," he said.

"Why?"

Why? What kind of question was that? "As you may have noticed, there aren't a lot of people around who have any kind of technology. I was hoping we could... form an alliance. You know, help each other out.

I am in contact with another settlement, and we use radio communication to alert each other of dust storms," he added.

"Dust storms," the voice echoed. "On the surface, you mean?"

Okay. So this Shelter was not on the surface. That would explain a few things. And it told him something about their technological level. Living underground took ventilation, the ability to grow plants in artificial conditions, that sort of thing. These guys really were a whole new level of sheltered, even compared to the people Luca normally gave that label. "Yeah," he said, "on the surface. You don't go out much, then?"

"Only the primary function maintainers who are trained for it," she replied, "And they don't stray far from the communications array."

Luca smiled. Here was his first bargaining chip presenting itself. "Okay," he said. "So there's probably a lot you don't know about the lay of the land, so to speak. Maybe I can help you out there."

19:

Teo

"How can I help?" Arsenio asked.

He didn't ask if he could help or ask what was the matter. Sometimes Teo had doubted his emotional capacity, but that was before. That was when he'd worn an arbiter's uniform and worked in Florence to enforce laws, some of which he didn't believe in. The move to Siena had changed him.

It had changed all of them. Mostly for the better.

"I don't know," Teo sighed. She had sought out the sanctuary of her home to vent, but what she really wanted was to take the car and go. Go somewhere to clear her mind and get distance. Or go to the top of the watchtower, but she was pretty sure Renn was there. She would have to talk to him, of course, but not while she felt like punching something. "Everybody expects—" What? That she had the answers to everything?

Arsenio turned on his heel. For a moment, Teo thought he was leaving. But he only went to pick up one of the pillows they used to sit on. "Sometimes," he said, "when we had a particularly bad day, Vanni would get like that."

"Like what?" She wasn't denying that she was upset. But Vanni was always the voice of reason.

"Like that," Arsenio said, gesturing with the pillow. "Wound up. He didn't know where to put his anger. He was too nice for that."

She smiled. "All right. What's the pillow for?" She had a pretty good guess.

"Up to you. I just hold it."

"And did that work for Vanni?" It was difficult to imagine him punching and kicking a pillow.

"Yes," Arsenio said.

"All right." Teo held up her fists. She could throw a pretty decent punch. Still, she wasn't entirely convinced that beating up a pillow was going to help.

She pulled back for a punch that would have landed square in the middle of the pillow and which she imagined would have made Arsenio take a step back from the force. None of this happened because he sidestepped, and she staggered forward, barely keeping herself from falling over. She turned. "What the—"

Arsenio was smiling at her. He held up the pillow once more.

Teo almost sneered at him. She charged again, feigning a jab at the right side of the pillow in the hope that he would move to the left and into her actual attack.

He didn't. He avoided the attack again.

That was so annoying. He was doing it on purpose. And it was working. She attacked... and this time, her fist connected with the pillow, and it did indeed make Arsenio step back. Teo followed up with a kick that sent him back a few more paces.

"So?" Arsenio said.

"All right." Teo nodded. "It helped. But only because you annoyed me. And you knew that," she added.

Arsenio tossed the pillow back where it belonged, doing a poor job of hiding a smug grin.

"I don't know what to do about the Renn situation," Teo said, making the pillow company on the floor.

"I thought the problem was Esmia," Arsenio said.

"No, Esmia has the problem," Teo corrected him. "It's an illness and we may be able to get medication against it. The problem is Renn. He thinks she's possessed by evil spirits. To him, she is dangerous. He doesn't even want to talk to her."

"That's ridiculous," Arsenio said.

"Well, there's one thing you and Luca agree on," Teo mumbled.

"That's a first," Arsenio scoffed. The scoff turned into a cough, and he covered his mouth with his hand.

"Everything all right?" she asked.

"Just dust," he replied, clearing his throat. "You stirred it up."

"The point is that it's real to Renn," Teo continued. "You can't just dismiss it as ridiculous. He was brought up to think like that."

"Well, can't you explain it to him? You or Mender or Gabriele?" Arsenio asked.

Teo shook her head. "I'm going to try. I just... I feel bad about it. I don't want to tell people what to believe. But I'm going to have to because it's not only Renn. Everybody respects him and looks up to him. We're used to asking him for advice, used to his knowing more about the weather and the animals and the plants than any of us. It's like everyone in this town has a feeling that Renn just may be right because he usually is." She sighed. "No one told me it was going to be so complicated."

"Does it matter?" Arsenio asked. "What would you have done differently? I personally prefer this to a life in prison."

"Me too." Teo smiled at him. "I'll talk to him. I only hope it's not going to be a choice between them. What if he threatens to leave?"

"You'll make him see reason. And if not, Esmia will have to go."

He was right. Renn was more important to the settlement at this point. They could take her to another settlement in the car. Provide her with plenty of food and water... But it was not going to come to that.

The reattached antenna perched above Renn as he sat there, crosslegged with his staff leaning against the wall behind him and the light wind toying with his hair.

Teo placed herself next to him. Not too close to make him uncomfortable, she hoped. "We have to talk," she said.

"You have come to tell me there is no such thing as spirits," he said.

Teo cleared her throat. No beating around the bush. Well, good. She wasn't one for too much smalltalk either. "No," she said, "I have no idea if spirits exist. I have no idea what happens to us after we die or what is roaming out there that we can't see."

Out of the corner of her eye, she saw him look at her. Surprised?

"That's the point." She folded her hands in her lap and looked up at the sky. "I don't think Esmia is haunted by evil spirits. I don't think she can spread bad luck to other people." This was a gamble, and she hoped dearly that it would work. "But I'm not going to tell you what to believe. I am, however, going to ask you to trust me. To trust my judgment in this matter, specifically."

He nodded. Not a confirmation that he would trust her, but an indication that he was listening and open to what she said next. So far so good.

"Luca has technological wonders that we can hardly imagine. I worked with tech— with masheens before we left Florence and I never saw anything as amazing as what Luca has in his home. And he says he has medicine that can help Esmia."

"Yes. So he claims," Renn agreed. There was an undertone in his voice that Teo could not quite determine.

"I suggest we let him give it to her," Teo said. "If it works, I don't care whether it's an illness inside her that the medicine can cure or spirits that the medicine keeps away. It doesn't matter to me."

"I see," Renn said. His voice was very quiet.

"Will you believe that the medicine can possibly cleanse her? Will you give it a chance?"

124

He was silent for a while. "I don't want to have to shun her," he finally said. "But as long as she is here, she is a danger. Letting her stay here is your choice. I have warned you, but the decision is not up to me. If Luca can truly cure her... Well, that is good. There is no way of knowing if the medicine works."

"Apart from waiting to see what happens," Teo finished for him. "Will you wait with me?"

"Yes," Renn said.

Teo drew in a slow breath. "Thank you, Renn." There was nothing more to say. She had convinced him without forcing her beliefs on him, and for once she felt that perhaps the faith the Sienans had in her was justified.

Renn was gazing at the horizon. Teo followed his glance, but there was nothing for her to see apart from wasteland and mountains. She looked down instead. Siena was still a small settlement. Perhaps in time it would grow into a city, but she was happy not to be handling thousands of people now. Children didn't grow up overnight, and perhaps a society was a bit like a child. It had to be raised and to develop over time, learning for itself, having rules and regulations put in place as it grew.

She saw Gabriele and Esmia walk across the street below. As fond as he and Mender were of Renn, they had both firmly rejected the idea that Esmia should bring bad luck. In fact, Gabriele was encouraging Esmia to learn more about medicine since she showed an interest. He hadn't said that he wanted to formally train her, but Teo suspected he was thinking it already.

Gabriele stopped and pointed, clearly explaining something to Esmia. She nodded. Teo could not see Gabriele's face, but she could tell from his posture that he was smiling. Then he slapped a hand across his mouth and coughed. Esmia took a startled step backward. The doctor gestured at her, calming her down.

Renn was observing the scene as well. Teo almost said something, but hammering home the fact that Gabriele wasn't scared of Esmia would not make anything better.

Teo stretched. "I'd better—" She was abruptly cut off by a scream from somewhere below.

Renn was on his feet immediately.

"What was that?" she asked.

"I don't know," Renn replied, brushing past her toward the staircase with his staff clutched in his hand.

Teo stood up too. The scream sounded so heart-wrenchingly urgent. She could not help feeling that it was going to be bad. Really bad.

20:

Teo

Teo and Renn dashed around the house in time to see Gabriele on his knees trying to revive the body on the ground. It was Nevio. The man Renn saved in the dust storm. But how... Teo saw Esmia standing a little to the side, holding what looked like a noose in her hands. She was turning it over, studying the frayed fibers.

Glancing up, Teo saw the telltale rope hung from the window on the upstairs floor. Miriam was leaning out of it, watching what was going on below. There was a knife clutched in her hand.

Teo knew better than to interfere with Gabriele's work. She tried not to look at Nevio's face. Tried not to look at the angry, red marks on his neck. "If you are not helping, please give the doctor space," she said to the crowd that was forming. She searched the faces around her, saw Renn almost glaring at Esmia, and then located the person she knew would be there. It was a boy called Adam, no more than ten years old. Teo wished it weren't him. But it clearly was.

"Hey," she said, placing herself in front of the pale boy. His eyes were wide and his hands were clenched into tight fists at his sides. "How do you feel?"

The boy's stiff gaze moved to Teo's face. He didn't reply.

Teo smiled her best confident, compassionate smile. "You did well," she said, allowing the rest of the world to fade into a background murmur for a while. Gabriele was working, and Renn was more than capable of keeping the crowd under control. This was the thing she could do. "You found him, didn't you?"

Adam nodded.

"Well done," she said. "You alerted the doctor and everyone. There was nothing else you could do."

"Is he dead?" the boy asked in a voice that made something inside Teo clench up.

"I don't know," she said. "The doctor is doing his best just like you."

Behind her, she heard Renn speak. His voice was perfectly calm. It was part of what made people trust his judgment so wholeheartedly.

"I don't know how long..." the boy began, then swallowed.

"You got here right away," Teo said. "He was not there for long at all." That had to be true. Gabriele would not be taking his time trying to revive the man if he had been dead for long.

"But what if I didn't get here in time?" Adam argued.

Teo opened her mouth to say something else when Gabriele spoke.

"I'm terribly sorry," he was saying as Teo turned. "There is nothing I can do. He is dead."

Teo found herself reaching out for the boy's hand. It was better than running away which was what she really wanted to do right now.

The crowd were in various states of disbelief and shock. One person started crying, another began to ask questions.

"Esmia, will you get a blanket from the infirmary?" Gabriele asked. Then he turned to the person asking questions and continued, "Yes, Arsenio and I will investigate the matter, but I doubt there was foul play involved."

Teo had to say something. She had to do something. "We will have an extraordinary assembly tomorrow," she heard herself say. "Anyone who would like clarity on the matter or an influence on the proceedings can attend." What did that even mean? She wasn't sure. That they

128

would talk about suicides? That they would plan a funeral? Teo looked at Gabriele, unable to hide her desperation.

The doctor nodded. "I will inform his next of kin," he said.

Teo smiled in ill-placed relief before she could stop herself. He was a doctor. He must have done it before.

"If anyone wants to talk about this," Gabriele continued, mild-mannered and reasonable, "you know where to find me or Mender."

Teo was grateful for that too. It crossed her mind that some may prefer to talk to a clergy person, but she decided not to say that now. Probably that was part of what Clara had signed up for in her new role as deacon, but she should be the one to suggest it. Teo realized she had no idea what Clara's religious stance on suicides was, and this filled her with dread.

"Thank you, doctor," Teo said. She squeezed Adam's hand and gave him a sad smile before disengaging herself from him. She was glad to see the boy's father pushing through the crowd toward him. "And thank you all for your concern," she added, hoping people would disperse because she felt she could not stand staying here for much longer.

Renn stepped forward as others began to leave. "I will help with the body," he offered.

Gabriele nodded his thanks and turned to Teo. "We will handle it," he said.

She mouthed a sincere thank you that did not want to venture beyond her lips. Remembering that Renn had carried Nevio once before, saved him from the storm only few days ago, made the confused pain stab her harder. She needed to get away. She needed to be alone and she needed to sort out her emotions.

It was not that she had been close to Nevio. It was rather the opposite if anything. That she hadn't seen it. That she hadn't known. That she and everybody else had been too busy building their new home to see that something was so very wrong. It was the fact that this was the first death in Siena, and it felt so utterly amiss.

The assembly was every bit as excruciating as Teo expected. Gabriele confirmed the cause of death, and Tonino asked what they should do with the body. Clara seemed every bit as troubled as everyone else, and she did not say anything to condemn the suicide. Instead, she suggested establishing a graveyard outside the settlement. This was a relief, at least. Teo would not have been able to keep her temper if anyone viewed what had happened as some kind of religious sin. No one knew what Nevio would have wanted. His closest connection was the people with whom he had left the slums of Florence, and while they were upset, it was clear that they had not been close.

Teo's hands hurt from clenching them to keep from storming out instead of listening to people talking about coffins versus wrapping the corpse in a blanket or maybe cremating the body and burying an urn with the ashes instead. Instead of watching Renn earnestly explain how wanderers disposed of their dead and that it was important to put a stone on the grave.

When finally all was said, Teo headed out of the settlement to sit down with her back against the wall. It poked her with its uneven surface, but she didn't mind.. She closed her eyes. Unwelcome tears burned behind her eyelids.

She heard familiar footsteps approaching. Then a cough.

"It's not your fault," Arsenio said.

Teo shook her head as if that would put the words into the right order. "Isn't it?" she asked and opened her eyes. She wiped the back of her hand across her cheek. "Everybody expects me to be a leader, and a good leader should— should see..."

"You can't keep track of everyone," Arsenio said. "And besides, if you want to think like that, shouldn't Gabriele have noticed? Or Renn for that matter? To me, it looks like Nevio was outside during that storm to get himself killed."

Teo shook her head again. "I only wish I or someone else had seen it. Maybe we could have made a difference. But it's not only that. Arsenio, that was the first death here. That should not be the first death!"

A roar of an engine interrupted Arsenio before he could reply.

Teo took a deep breath and stood up.

"Oh, that's just what we need," Arsenio murmured.

"If he has medication for Esmia, it is what we need," Teo said. She watched the motorcycle approach and stop a few paces away.

Luca turned off the engine and took off his helmet. When he approached them, he was practically sauntering.

"If it isn't the welcoming committee!" he called, grinning. "I've got great news and greater news!"

Teo tried for a smile.

"Is one of them that you can't stay long?" Arsenio asked.

"Fuck off," Luca told him, but it didn't sound like he was really offended. He was studying Teo's face. "Okay... Who died?"

"Nevio," Teo said.

"Who?" Luca asked. "And how?"

"He took his own life," Teo said. It didn't get easier to say with practice.

"Oh. That sucks," Luca said, fidgeting with a loose thread on the sleeve of his jacket. "But why is it that every time I have major news, something here completely overshadows it?"

Teo felt rather than saw Arsenio tense. "Don't you have any manners?" he asked.

"And this from you," Luca said flatly.

Arsenio was about to make a retort, but it was cut off by a fit of coughing. Teo wondered if he had caught a cold, or if he had neglected protection when working where the dust was bad.

"Look," Luca said, ignoring Arsenio, "It's totally tragic, but these things happen. I know you guys want to built a utopia here, but there isn't such a thing as a perfect world. There will be trauma and mental illnesses in your community, and some of those lead to suicide if not treated properly. You will have crime too, eventually. Like theft and murder and rape. It fucking sucks, but that's how it is."

His gaze was steady and serious. He was right. He was right, and it broke Teo's heart. They left a lot of things behind in Florence, but the Sienans were human, and more bad things were bound to happen in their settlement. Maybe not now. Maybe not even in her lifetime. But what bothered Teo as much was Luca himself. He was not even twenty years old. He had only lived for fifteen or sixteen years in the company of other humans, and yet he was so convinced. It felt wrong that she was almost ten years his senior and yet, his outlook on people was that bleak. What had society been like in his time to do this to him? She was afraid to ask.

Luca kicked at the dirt with the tip of his boot and studied the ground deliberately. "Anyway," he said in a tone full of forced cheerfulness, "I found the medication for Esmia. It's not exactly a lifetime supply, but it's a start, and there's probably more out there if you know what you're looking for."

Teo had an impulse to pull Luca into a hug, to thank him and to protect him, but she had a feeling now was not the time. "That is wonderful news," she said instead, "Thank you."

Luca lifted his head again, a grin spreading on his face. "Yeah? Well, that's not all. I got through to our mystery settlement again."

21:

Esmia

Esmia stared at the small container in her hand. She was in the infirmary with Gabriele and Luca. And Renn, but he was standing by the door as if keeping watch. Esmia didn't need to ask on whom. She knew he thought she was somehow at fault for the man who took his own life.

She couldn't meet his eyes. For some reason, the stagnants of Siena did not seem particularly worried about her affliction. On the contrary, they had attempted to explain to her that she was suffering from an illness. But Renn knew better. Esmia had never deliberately done anything to hurt other people. She had never even been used by the spirits to cause anyone any harm, but merely been jerked around at their whim, sometimes bruising and scraping her face and body. Once she had woken up to find her tongue bleeding and swollen. But that didn't mean she didn't bring bad luck to those who touched her.

And she hadn't told Renn. She had not told him because she was scared. Yes, she hoped the spirits would leave her alone, but she had not really believed it. Not telling Renn was a breach of trust.

The strange boy was talking, and Esmia shifted her attention to him. "So if you take one pill every day, there should be enough for almost a year. But there has to be more out there waiting to be found."

Only a few hours ago, before the assembly, Esmia had seen Gabriele bury his face in his hands, his shoulders tense and shaking when he thought nobody was looking. Esmia had longed to hug him, but she had not dared. Now he nodded enthusiastically and smiled at Luca. Gabriele was a healer, and he put his own grief aside as soon as others needed him. He read the symbols on the container carefully before giving it to Esmia and appeared to be as convinced as Luca that it would work. He explained that it was medicine, like the remedies she knew how to make, only compressed into a small pebble-like shape and for the very specific illness that she suffered from.

Esmia swallowed and looked up. "So... it will keep the spirits away from me?" she asked to be certain that they were talking about the same thing.

Luca snorted and rolled his eyes. "Yes, it'll keep the goddamn fucking spirits away," he said, half turning toward Renn. "Are you happy now?"

Esmia wished he wouldn't do that. Renn, of course, did not reply. But Teo said he was willing to accept Esmia's presence if she took the medication, so he must believe in it too. "Thank you," she said to all of them.

"No problem," Luca replied.

"Arsenio is always on the lookout for more medical equipment, but I will tell him to look for this in particular," Gabriele said.

"If he can beat me to it," Luca added, grinning.

"Well, that is—" Gabriele began, but he cut himself off coughing.

Esmia's fingers tightened around the container.

"You okay, man?" Luca asked as the doctor turned away from them to cough into the crook of his elbow. "Don't cough up your own lungs or anything."

Gabriele managed to stop and cleared his throat. "I'm sorry," he said. "I'm fine."

Esmia and Luca both studied him. "You sure? You look a bit..." Luca told him.

"I'll just have a glass of water, but I believe we were done anyway," the doctor said, smiling first at Esmia and then at Luca. His gaze lingered for a moment on the boy before he left them in search of water.

Esmia had to talk to Renn. She didn't want to, but she had to. She took a deep breath and a step toward the other wanderer. "Renn," she said.

"Hey," Luca said at the same time.

They both stopped and looked at each other.

Esmia smiled apologetically.

From his place in the doorway, Renn was regarding them both. Esmia had a feeling she knew what was going on inside his head.

"I can wait," she said to Luca, feeling simultaneously cowardly and like it was the polite thing to do. Luca was clearly very close to Renn.

Luca quirked an eyebrow and looked from her to Renn and back again. "We should catch up sometime, Esmia," he said.

Esmia blinked. "Yes," she replied because there wasn't really anything else to say. He made her a little uncomfortable with his blunt behavior and strangeness, but he was friendly, and that was rare. And besides, she was indebted to him now.

Luca clapped his hands once, visibly pulling himself into motion as he approached Renn. "Okay then. Wanna show me your watchtower or something?" he said.

Esmia watched them go.

Gabriele entered again with his glass of water. He looked pale. "Did they leave?" he asked although they obviously had. "I need to find Clara... Could you stay until Mender gets here with the laundry?"

Esmia nodded. "Of course. I can help with the laundry if Mender needs it," she added. She still wasn't sure what gender to use when speaking about Mender. It felt impolite to ask, and everybody else either did not use pronouns or used one Esmia didn't know.

"Good idea," Gabriele said, a little distracted as he stuffed a few things into a cloth bag. "I'll be back soon."

The infirmary fell silent. Esmia held up the container to examine it again. The signs on it had not begun to make sense since the last time. If she was going to stay here, perhaps she should ask someone to teach her to read.

If she was going to stay here... Her heart fluttered at the thought. She realized she had never really believed in it before. She had expected the spirits to visit her sooner or later and to be cast out again without anyone to speak for her or take the responsibility for her like her father did when he was alive. But now... If even Renn believed in the medicine. If even Renn was willing to let her stay... Perhaps she could.

She truly did want to work with the doctor. It was not only something she was good at. She also enjoyed helping people. The only reason she had not been the Covey's primary healer already was simply that people were afraid of her touch. If the Sienans weren't scared, then maybe this could truly be her life.

Renn looked at the horizon sometimes in a way that suggested he longed to be out there, wandering the wasteland, following the rain and the migration of animals and exploring dead cities. So far, Esmia had not missed it at all. Staying in Siena felt like the thing she wanted the most. It felt like the raw edges of the hole in her chest might begin to contract.

The door opened again, and Mender appeared with a basket full of newly laundered sheets. "Can I help you?" Mender said, turning to Esmia with that enigmatic face. Always kind and smiling, but somehow too symmetric and perfect without being extremely beautiful. Mender's skin was light, and although Gabriele's assistant could not be older than Teo, Mender was completely bald.

"I wanted to help you," Esmia replied. "Gabriele said you were doing the laundry?"

"That is very kind of you," Mender said, smiling. "Thank you. Was Luca here?"

Esmia held up the small container, nodding. "Yes. He gave me this."

Mender stepped closer, inspecting the container. "Oh, that is great news. I'm certain it will help you."

"I hope so," Esmia said.

They began to take laundry out of the basket and fold the sheets. They smelled wonderfully clean and a little like flowers, but not any that Esmia could identify.

"How do you feel? I realize you did not know him, but Nevio's death affects everyone," Mender said.

"It is sad," Esmia agreed and almost added that she hoped no one besides Renn blamed her for it. But it would be selfish to say that now.

"If anyone is to be blamed, it is me," Mender continued. "I am the only one here with professional psychological training, but I didn't recognize the signs. I thought Nevio was merely shocked because he was caught outside during the storm. I didn't register it as a suicide attempt."

Esmia studied Mender. There were several words in that explanation she was unfamiliar with, but she could clearly see Mender's regret. "In a Covey," she offered, "the members look after each other, but everyone is responsible for their own lives."

"Thank you," Mender said. "Yet, he suffered from an illness that could have been treated. I believe it was an error of judgment on my part. Sadly, the only one who would be able to adjust my programming is Luca, and I doubt he would have the expertise or the right software for something that specific."

The room fell silent. Mender continued folding up laundry. "I... assume no one has told you where I come from?"

"No," Esmia replied. When she looked up, she saw Mender had stopped folding sheets and was studying her as if trying to make a decision.

"I came here with Renn," Mender said. "We met under the ruins of an old city. I was in the basement where I used to work. I took care of people. Very ill and very old people. Renn fell through the upstairs floor. I found him and helped him because he was hurt in the fall. At first he was scared of me."

Esmia's eyebrows shot up. Renn? Scared of someone like Mender? That seemed very unlikely. Unless Mender was telling her about helping people and saving Renn to soften the blow of something truly frightening. She took a step back, instinctively putting more space between them.

"But he decided to form a Covey with me," Mender continued. "We traveled together. We were attacked by humans and scarvhes and defended ourselves together before joining the people who founded this settlement."

"I see," Esmia said. She was growing increasingly certain that Mender was telling her all this in anticipation of a strong reaction to something else. But whatever it was, she had not told anyone in Siena about the spirits, either.

"People tend to be afraid of those who are different. You know that better than anyone else here," Mender said.

Esmia nodded, although that wasn't entirely accurate.

"I am not human," Mender said.

"You look human." Esmia blinked. "I don't know any creature that looks like you do if not human."

"I was created to resemble humans as closely as possible. But I am different. I was in that basement for many years before Renn encountered me. Earlier, I was called a sentient. I was created to help humans. I believe your people refers to me as an Other."

Esmia thought this over. She had heard the stories about Moon's servants going mad. She knew Others were to be feared. But if the spirits weren't spirits at all but an illness... Then perhaps Others weren't as dangerous as people made them out to be, either. "I see," she said. It certainly explained why Mender looked different from anyone else.

"I am sorry for not telling you right away," Mender continued, "but I did not want to scare you. I thought it better to wait until you knew me. I imagine perhaps that was your reason for not telling Renn about your epilepsy as well."

Esmia couldn't help smiling. No, that wasn't it at all. But it was a nice thought. "I understand," she said.

"And you are not scared of me?" Mender asked. "You can ask me anything."

"Does Renn trust you?" Esmia asked.

"Yes, I believe he does," Mender replied with no hesitation.

Esmia nodded. "Others are supposed to be dangerous. Have you ever hurt a human?"

"Yes," Mender said again, just as readily. "On three occasions. Once to prevent a client from harming himself. Once because a client attacked me and I needed to stop her. And once to save Renn from an attack."

Esmia nodded again. No one could be that precise and calm and lie. And she had seen Renn as well as Gabriele and several other Sienans with Mender, all completely relaxed. If trusting Mender was a mistake, so was trusting anyone in Siena, and who was she to distrust the people who took her in and allowed her to stay despite her condition? She smiled. "I don't have any other questions."

22:

Renn

Perhaps it was a life surrounded by sentients to care for him, a steady supply of water and food and a clean, soft bed that gave Luca time to make things more complicated than they really were, Renn mused as he ascended the stairs of the watchtower. If one never had to worry about surviving a dust storm and had medicine to cure all sorts of ailments, maybe one had so much time to waste that it was easy to construct problems in one's own head.

It really was no more complicated than a simple apology. But he would listen because Luca had asked him to. That alone should be enough to tell Luca that although Renn was angry, he did not wish to permanently end their... Renn hesitated and decided the most adequate word was friendship.

"Wow," Luca breathed as they stepped out onto the platform. "Nice view."

Renn did not reply. The good thing about being up here, he thought, was that any impulse to walk away quickly or shove the other person was bound not to be brought to fruition. Even Luca would stop himself before he pushed someone off a tower.

"Okay," Luca said, "I think we should talk."

Renn nodded once. It was that or agreeing that yes, Luca clearly did think so.

"You know, like reasonable people," Luca continued. "Cause moping about it is stupid."

Renn almost sighed. So many words. And the strange implication that he was moping.

"Right. So I didn't mean to imply that you're a primitive, ignorant caveman."

Renn turned to stare at Luca. It was hard to imagine what he had meant to imply then.

"But I guess... I get that it could be interpreted that way." Luca studied his fingernails for a moment. "It's just that I know epilepsy is a medical condition and not spirits or whatever. It's not her fault. Look, are you going to take part in this conversation or should I keep talking?" The last part sounded almost desperate.

"I never said it is her fault," Renn replied. "I feel for her."

Luca frowned. "You do? Cause that's not the vibe I was getting."

"I feel for her," Renn repeated a little more pointedly than he meant to because despite Luca's attempt at making him talk, Luca clearly found it hard to be quiet for even a few seconds. "But she chose not to tell me. And whether I feel for her or not makes no difference. She is dangerous."

Luca stood looking into the distance, for once thinking before he spoke. "But now that she is basically cured, whether you believe me or think it's spirits... It's okay, right?"

Renn had promised Teo. And Mender and Gabriele who knew so much about illnesses and injuries agreed with her and Luca. Renn would not be surprised if they were wrong after all, but for now there was not really anything to do but accept things the way they were. "I have said what I had to in the matter," Renn told Luca. "I only hope the medicine works and no one has to suffer any consequences."

Luca nodded. "Okay. That's fair enough." His face changed, taking on a vulnerable quality that Renn would have entirely missed if he had not been studying him. "So... we're okay?"

It was in that moment that Renn understood two things about Luca. First of all, this was Luca's backward way of apologizing. And secondly, it was never about Esmia. He regarded Luca for a long moment. "Yes," he finally said. "We are okay."

Luca grinned and held out his hand. "Shake on it? Or are you still afraid of touching me?"

Renn decided not to take the obvious bait. He grasped Luca's hand and shook it. It was cool and dry and felt rough with the scars crisscrossing the skin. It also had a new bruise. Strange, really, considering how well-groomed and polished Luca generally presented himself. The skin of his face was smooth and clean and his hair and clothes always smelled slightly like the soaps he used.

"You've never asked," Luca said.

Renn released Luca's hand, a little surprised. Under normal circumstances he did not seem that observant. But since Luca was practically encouraging it, there was no reason to deny his curiosity. "What is wrong with your hands?" he asked.

"Jesus Christ," Luca breathed. "Could you be more blunt?"

Renn held back another sigh.

"Something happened either during the cryo or when the whole thing malfunctioned and woke me up," Luca said, studying his own hand. "I think some nerves were damaged. I can't feel my hands like I used to, so I end up... well, like this." He held up both of his hands so Renn could clearly see the white lines and a scar that was still red. "I'm damaged goods, but it looks worse than it feels."

"That must be limiting," Renn said, thinking that it probably wasn't that limiting because if Luca took proper care, his hands wouldn't look like that.

Luca shrugged and flexed his fingers. "Well, the good news is that despite the limited sensation, they work perfectly." He grinned.

"Good. But perhaps," Renn suggested, "you should try not to injure yourself before you end up with more serious damages."

Luca opened his mouth, but closed it again quickly, realizing perhaps that Renn was genuinely worried. "I try," he said instead. He turned and stepped toward the edge of the platform. Renn joined him to look at the settlement spreading out below them.

"I'm sorry that guy killed himself," Luca said.

"I as well," Renn replied. "He tried once before, I think, but I didn't realize it." In a Covey, members took care of each other, but Renn was used to groups formed for convenience. They weren't close friends or family and while they sought to help each other if the need arose, every person was responsible for themselves. How did it work for stagnants?

"It's not your fault," Luca said.

"No," Renn agreed, hoping that Luca could see the difference between guilt and regret. "I do not believe I caused him to do it. But perhaps there was a way to prevent it that I did not see."

"Just don't let the what ifs eat you up," Luca muttered. Then he visibly straightened up. "Hey, I've got some pretty cool news. I got through to the mystery settlement on the radio."

"Did you find out where they are located?" Renn asked. Despite his migrations through these lands, he had failed to know of Florence's existence until recently. It wouldn't be strange if he had missed another settlement as well, especially one that Arsenio and Luca with their cars had not managed to discover.

"Approximately, yes. They want to chat more before I get their exact coordinates. Which is fair, I guess," Luca said. "It's so weird, though. Knowing that they are out there. You know? I thought I was alone, but from what I can tell, they are a lot like me. There are more than 400 people there. And they live underground."

A lot less obvious than domes, then. Though how someone lived underground was almost unimaginable. "I see. Do you want to go there?"

Luca frowned. "What makes you say that?"

"You have been looking for others," Renn said, omitting that Luca had begun to radiate a restless kind of excitement the moment he mentioned the other settlement.

"I guess," Luca said. "Yeah." He craned his head back and stared at the sky.

Renn waited. There was clearly more he wanted to say.

"What about you?"

"What about me?" Renn asked.

Luca bit his lip. He shot Renn a quick glance. "I don't know. Do you want to..." He cut himself off with a shake of his head. "We'll see. I might go visit them sometime."

"I hope they will be more friendly than the people of Florence," Renn said.

"They will. I mean, they already are. I think." Luca shrugged. If the movement was meant to make him appear not to care one way or the other, it failed.

"Please let me know if you go," Renn said, wondering exactly why he said it.

"Right back at you," Luca replied with an ease that was not reflected in the way his hands suddenly clenched and unclenched.

"I will," Renn replied.

"Good," Luca said. He smiled. "But hey, you can always come with me to the other settlement if you're worried."

23

Teo

"I don't care," Teo told Arsenio.

"It's just a cold," he said for the umpteenth time.

"I still don't care," Teo said. "You can barely get out of bed. You have two options. Either we go see Gabriele, or I get him to come here. It's up to you."

She folded her arms over her chest, determined to glare at him until he agreed. As keen she normally was on voting and listening to the opinions of others, she was going to assert her will now. It had indeed begun as sneezing and coughing like a common cold, but now Arsenio was paler than she had ever seen him and his skin much too hot.

"Fine," he grunted. "If it makes you happy."

Teo nodded. "Let's go."

The waiting room of the infirmary was packed and there was nowhere to sit. Teo watched a mother with her daughter dozing off in her arms. The mother was peering nervously at the girl's face. Around them, people were coughing and looking as haggard as Arsenio.

Teo had thought it was only Arsenio, but this... Hopefully it really was only a cold. Hopefully Gabriele and Mender had a way of treating it.

A door opened and Mender saw another coughing Sienan out of the examination room. "I am terribly sorry for the wait," ne said to the assembled patients. "We are doing our best." Ne glanced at Teo and Arsenio, then excused nemself to go to the other examination room. When ne returned, ne beckoned the woman with the little girl to enter.

Teo sized up Arsenio and decided he was fit to stand. She gestured for another man to take the free seat.

The door to the other examination room opened, and Gabriele appeared. He was wearing a white cloth mask over his nose and mouth that muffled his voice. "Teo," he called out.

"It's Arsenio," she said quickly. "But the others have waited for longer, so..."

Gabriele shook his head. "Nevertheless, I would like to talk to you for a moment."

Teo patted Arsenio's arm and went with Gabriele with a sinking feeling in the pit of her stomach.

He closed the door and stood leaning against it for a moment before joining her in the middle of the room. He must be exhausted with so many patients.

"We appear to have an epidemic," he said, still muffled because of the mask.

Teo tried not to look alarmed. "It's only a bad cold or maybe the flu, isn't it?"

Gabriele took off his glasses and rubbed his eyes. "I hope so."

"But?" Teo asked.

"But," the doctor said reluctantly, "a lot of the patients have high fevers. Some have violent coughing fits and nosebleeds and cough up blood. So far twelve are ill that I know of."

"But we have antibiotics, right?" Teo asked. "If there's some kind of pneumonia going around..."

He shook his head. "Pneumonia is bacterial and doesn't really go around, as you say. So far, it looks like a virus that affects the patients' breathing. Not entirely unlike a flu, but..." Gabriele seemed to have to force himself to look her in the eyes. "Well, I'm afraid our antibiotics are not helping. I have been administering them to one of the first cases for some days now, and he is only getting worse."

Teo nodded and leaned against the examination table, then almost sprang away from it before she could stop herself. It was ridiculous to be scared of that when she shared her bed with someone who was most definitely ill. "All right," she said. "What are our options? How bad will it get?"

"I wish I knew," Gabriele sighed. "I don't..." He stopped and took a step back. He collapsed rather than sat down in his chair.

"Gabriele?" Teo asked.

The doctor rested his elbows on his knees. Teo could hear his breath hitching as if he were having trouble breathing behind the mask.

"Gabriele?" she repeated. "I'll get Mender."

"No!" he managed.

She crouched in front of him. "Are you getting enough sleep? You can't work twenty-four hours a day, doctor."

Gabriele shook his head. "That's not it," he croaked before a fit of coughing shook him.

"Oh," Teo breathed as it dawned on her. "You are ill too."

He nodded. "I'm not wearing this for my own benefit," he murmured, gesturing to the mask. "But I'm letting Mender care for the patients who are not here because of the epidemic. Hopefully..." He trailed off.

"When did it start?" Teo asked.

"I am the test subject for the antibiotics," he said with a cough that might have been an attempt at laughter. "Mender and Esmia know, but I have been reluctant to tell anyone else. Esmia isn't ill, but I think she is scared of it."

"How bad do you think it will get?" Teo asked again although part of her would rather not hear the reply.

Gabriele heaved a shuddering sigh. "At the moment, it appears to be getting worse. Individual cases are likely to differ according to the patients' general health and pre-existing conditions. We have no elderly

147

among us, so at the moment I'm most concerned about young children and pregnant women. I recommend asking Luca if he has any knowledge or medication..."

"I will do that right away," Teo said, glad that there was at least one thing she could do. "I also think we have to call for an assembly. People need to know what is going on. Need to know what to do if they get ill." She closed her eyes and tilted back her head. Everything had gone so well to begin with...

"Teo," Gabriele said. Something in his voice made Teo's attention snap back. He was slumped back in the chair.

"Gabriele?" she asked.

He didn't react when she shook his shoulders gently.

Teo almost took off to call for Mender. But panic was going to solve nothing and only make matters worse. She carefully pried off Gabriele's mask. The fabric stuck a little to his stubble, which in itself was a sign that something was wrong. Gabriele De Felice was meticulous about his appearance and perfectly shaved under normal circumstances. But the beard was nothing compared to the dark red crust at the corners of his mouth and the fresh blood staining his lips and the mask. "Goddamn it," Teo whispered, resorting to Luca's vocabulary because her own didn't begin to cover what the situation called for.

She put down the mask. She couldn't get him onto the examination table and much less to his bed on her own. So she carefully pulled him out of the chair and laid him on the floor on his side which, if she remembered correctly, was what you were supposed to do. But she had no idea what to do next. Why had she never insisted on basic first aid training? Arsenio had rudimentary training as a former arbiter. And although he was ill too, he was the closest remotely qualified person. If she left Gabriele in his care, she could go get Mender in a composed manner.

Teo opened the door. "Arsenio, the doctor would like to see you now," she called out in a tone of voice that sounded too cheerful to be genuine. She hoped nobody noticed.

148

"Hiya," Luca's voice said. It sounded crisp and carefree, and Teo knew she was about to ruin that. "Hang on a moment, I need to turn off this thing."

Teo waited. She had no idea what thing he was referring to, but undoubtedly one of his many experiments. For once she didn't feel the urge to ask.

Mender put nir hand on her shoulder, and Teo reached up to squeeze it, thankful for nir company. What would any of them do without nem in Siena?

"Okay, what's up?" Luca asked.

"We have a problem," Teo said.

"Shit," Luca replied. "That sounds bad."

"We don't know how bad it is yet," Teo began. "We have an outbreak of an illness."

"What kind of illness?" Luca asked. "I swear to god, if Esmia's epilepsy is contagious after all—"

"No, not that. It's a lot like a cold or flu. A virus of some kind. Only... bad. Coughing, fever, exhaustion. No one has died." She bit the inside of her cheek to keep herself from adding, 'yet'.

"Renn?" Luca said.

Teo felt herself smile despite the situation. "Renn has not caught it. I'm fine too. And Esmia and Clara," she added since those were the people Luca was closest to as far as she knew. "But I think a third of us are ill now. Arsenio isn't doing so well. And Gabriele..." She tried not to think of his limp form in her arms and the blood in the mask. "He collapsed earlier today. He's awake now, but..."

"Shit," Luca said again. "Okay. What do you need? What does Mender say?"

"Ne is here with me," Teo said and handed the transmitter to the sentient.

"Hello, Luca," Mender said. "I'm afraid, I can't do much at the moment apart from keeping the patients as comfortable as possible.

Gabriele tried to cure himself with antibiotics, but they had no effect. We believe it is a viral infection that attacks the respiratory system to varying degrees. Is it possible that you have any useful medication to spare?"

"Give me a list and I'll see what I can find," Luca replied.

Teo gestured for Mender to hand her back the transmitter. "Luca," she said, "I don't want you to come here. Maybe if you could leave supplies somewhere outside Siena, we could get them after you leave."

Luca snorted. "Fuck of, Teo. I'll be fine."

"Luca!" she snapped. "I don't want you to get ill too."

"Okay, look," he replied, "I'm not stupid, and I'm not being heroic. You guys did not exactly invent epidemics. What you are experiencing now is probably a reboot of the shitshow the world starred in during the twenty-first century or whatever. I will be fine because I take immune boosters at regular intervals like everybody else back in my time. I haven't even had a cold in forever, and I'll take extra shots before going anywhere near Siena."

Teo nodded although he couldn't see her. There was a lump in her throat and she was pretty sure it was not a symptom of the illness. "Thank you, Luca," she said.

"So what are we talking? Painkillers? Immune boosters?"

Teo handed the transmitter back to Mender.

"Yes, any pain relievers, paracetamol and dacterotyl are highest priority. Cough medication and immune boosters would be useful. If you have access to sterile masks or gloves, that may help contain the illness. And there is a chance we could get results with a different kind of antibiotics," Mender said. "And perhaps corticosteroids." Ne began to list what sounded like brand names, carefully and slowly to give Luca time to write them down. Nir voice was so calm and careful, worried, but not panicked. Teo wondered how ne would sound if this got worse. If people started dying. Probably not very different. She envied nem a little.

"Yes, I believe I would," Mender was saying, noticed Teo's frown and added for her benefit, "If I had antibodies and the right equipment, I would probably be able to make an antidote. But I have neither."

Teo rubbed her neck. She wanted to get back to Arsenio. Check up on Gabriele. Call for an assembly. There was so much to do. But it was better to wait so she could at least give her people some hope.

"I'm bringing Nanny," Luca stated. "And maybe a couple of others if I can make it work."

"Other sentients?" Teo asked when Mender handed her the transmitter again. Just how many sentients did Luca surround himself with that she didn't know of?

"Erh," Luca replied, hesitating. "Semis. They look human, but they aren't as autonomous as Mender or Nanny and Alfredo. I just need to see if they have anything... useful in their programming."

"All right," Teo agreed. "Thank you."

24:

Esmia

Her feet were sore and her back was stiff and she hardly had time to sit down and eat. She was doing everything she could to care for the ill, but no matter how much she did, it was not enough.

It was never going to be enough. It was happening all over again.

Esmia held out a cup of water to the patient in front of her. He was called Tonino. The bread Teo had offered her when she arrived had been his work. Before he came to Siena, he had made his living baking bread and cakes, he'd told her. When she looked surprised, he had grinned and told her she would understand why people would pay a lot for his cakes when she tasted them. Now he wasn't making any such claims. He was too weak and shaking too much with fever to hold the cup on his own.

Only the most ill were in the infirmary. It was happening so fast. A day ago, there were not nearly this many. Now they had moved beds and mattresses in so Mender could care for the ones who needed it. The worst part was that Gabriele was amongst them. No, that was not true. The worst part was that it was all Esmia's fault.

The door to the infirmary opened. Esmia turned to see Mender and Teo return. There had just been an assembly to discuss the crisis, but Esmia offered to stay in the infirmary and care for the patients. When she did, Mender said it was a good idea since ne was already concerned about gathering too many people in the same place due to the danger of infection. And Teo thanked her for her help. It was all wrong. Esmia stayed in the infirmary out of cowardice, not compassion or helpfulness.

"Any changes?" Mender asked.

Esmia cleared her throat. "Dianne's coughing is worse. And Tonino's fever is rising," she added, quietly, in the hope that her patient didn't hear it. "Gabriele wanted to get up, but I told him not to. I don't think he could have. His breathing is still bad."

"Very well," Mender said. "Thank you, Esmia."

She nodded and stole a glance at Teo. Teo who had been kind enough to take her in, to make her feel welcome in Siena, to explain away the spirits as an illness. And this was the reward. This was how Esmia repaid Teo and everyone else. All of a sudden, she had to get out of the infirmary. She needed air. She needed not to look at any of them.

"Esmia?"

Esmia ran past Teo, pushed the door open and stumbled into the street. It was so quiet, so empty. Even after nightfall there were usually people. Now everyone was ill or caring for the ill or staying away from others because they were afraid of getting ill.

She couldn't breathe. She couldn't see. Tears stung her eyes. She had to leave.

"Esmia!" Teo said, gripping her arm tightly. "What is it?"

Esmia turned with tears streaming down her face. She tried to shake Teo off, but the grip around her arm was firm.

"Are you getting ill?" Teo asked, her voice so full of compassion that the shame was more than Esmia could bear.

"No," she sobbed. "No, I'm not. I'm not ill. I'm not ill, but I wish I were! It's my fault and everybody is going to die! Everybody..."

Teo yanked at her arm. "Esmia! Stop!" she shouted.

Esmia closed her mouth, tried not to cry, but she couldn't stop.

"I'm sorry," Teo said, softer and too kindly. "But we need to stay calm. I don't want anyone to hear you talk like that. I'm scared too. But we will get through this. Nobody is going to die. All right? And it's not your fault. You are doing everything you can to help."

"No!" Esmia hiccuped. "No, no no! You don't understand. It is my fault!"

Teo was going to reply, but Esmia couldn't let her. She could not let Teo or anyone else go on like that. "It is my fault!" she repeated, balling her fists so hard it hurt. "All the others were ill. My old Covey. My father couldn't breathe and he died and everybody had a fever and they cast me out because they thought I made them all ill because of the spirits! And you use a lot of words like epilepsy, but it does not change what is happening!"

Teo gaped at her. Trying to make sense of the story. Maybe even trying to find more excuses for Esmia.

"So you see," Esmia said, "it is my fault. And I am sorry." She felt better now that she had said it. It didn't change the fact that a lot of them were going to die. It didn't change the fact that she would have to leave Siena too. But at least she had told someone the truth.

"You—" Teo stuttered. "Your Covey. Did they have the same illness as Gabriele and the others?"

Esmia nodded. She was used to being shunned. It wasn't nice, but it was familiar.

"You brought it here..." Teo looked like she was going to cry. That was all wrong. She was supposed to get angry. Supposed to shout and shove Esmia away. She was supposed to tell her to go away and never come back. Instead she looked so, so sad and disappointed, and Esmia found that it was worse. "Why? Why didn't you—"

"I didn't get ill. I thought... I hoped." Esmia forced herself to meet Teo's eyes. "I hoped the spirits would leave me alone and I wouldn't bring you bad luck. And you all believed I wouldn't."

"But—" Teo began. Then she hid her face in her hands, and Esmia couldn't tell if she was laughing or crying. "It's not bad luck. It's not because of your epilepsy or evil spirits," she muttered. When she looked at Esmia again, she was smiling, but it was not a happy smile at all. "It's a contagious illness and it wasn't your fault that your Covey got ill. But you must have carried it here."

"Without getting ill myself?" Esmia said, trying to understand Teo's way of seeing the situation. Trying to comprehend how she could not be the cause of the illness in some but still carry it with her to others. "I'm sorry," she whispered. "I will do whatever you ask of me. I will leave…"

"Oh no, Esmia." Teo's eyes grew hard. "You didn't know, and I can't blame you. But I will ask you to stay and help care for the ill and work as hard as you can along with me and Mender and everybody else who are able to. And I will ask you to stop crying and go straight back in there and tell Mender everything you know about this illness and answer all nir questions completely truthfully. Will you do this?"

"Yes," Esmia said.

"Good. And one more thing," Teo added. "You will not talk to anyone else about this. Not Renn and not anyone else in Siena. Not unless Mender or I tell you to. Understand?"

"Yes," said Esmia again. "I understand."

"All right. Go back in and speak to Mender. If we are lucky, your knowledge will give nem some new insight into this."

Esmia wanted to apologize again. But she didn't. It wouldn't change the situation. The only thing she could do now was to follow Teo's orders.

Mender reluctantly left nir patients and brought Esmia into the room where ne lived. It did not look like Gabriele's room. There was no bed, but there were two chairs and a table. They both sat. And Esmia talked. She told Mender everything she could think of. How the illness had spread through the Covey while they were migrating and how they had to stop because many were too weak to continue. She described the symptoms of the illness, how they treated the ill, how long it had been before the first died, how many were unaffected and how many were still well enough to care for the others when she left.

"Have you ever had an illness like it?" Mender asked when she was done.

Esmia bit her lip and thought. "I can't remember it, but my father told me I was very ill at one point when I was small. He said I had a high fever and was coughing so much my face turned blue and no one in the tent could sleep."

"Perhaps..."

Esmia waited while Mender thought. She hoped that despite everything, the strange creature would have a solution. Any kind of solution.

"Esmia, Siena is not like your Covey. What I mean," ne continued, "is that we have resources here that were not available to your people. Gabriele and I have medical knowledge which surpasses that of wanderers as far as I know. I need no rest and cannot contract the disease, and tomorrow, Luca will be here with others like me."

Esmia nodded. Mender was right. If any place could get through this, it was Siena. Still, it did not make her guilt any smaller.

Mender reached out to put a hand on her shoulder. "And I think that with your help, we will find a solution."

"I already promised Teo to do everything I can," Esmia said. "I will work and do everything you ask me to."

"Yes," Mender said, softly and so calmly that Esmia could almost believe there was no reason to worry. "I have something slightly different in mind. But I need to consult Gabriele."

25:

Luca

Luca pushed open the door of his car to a soundtrack of crickets and tumbleweed. He stood looking at the deserted street and forced a confident grin onto his face. If he had thought Siena looked abandoned the last time he was here, it was nothing compared to this.

"Okay," he said, turning to the three artificials getting out of the Rover, "this is Siena. Grab your gear and let's get going."

Nanny, at least, looked perfectly cast for her new role as nurse. She was wearing a sensible, grey outfit, and her hair was in a tight bun on her head. She studied their surroundings with polite curiosity as she retrieved the provisions she was in charge of from the car's trunk. She was programmed to care for children and had perfect bedside manners. And Luca had a brilliant plan that would give her a crash course in nursing.

He was a bit more worried about the others. He hadn't wanted to leave the base completely unattended by someone sentient, so Alfredo had stayed behind. The army in the storage unit was... well, an army, and although Luca could do some reprogramming, bringing armored warriors into Siena felt like it would be more trouble than it was worth at this point. Sia and Simon looked completely out of place with their beautiful faces and bodies although Luca had tried to tone down the perfection by dressing them in baggy, comfortable clothes. They both had a program for people who liked to play doctor, and Luca had tried to tweak the commands to remove the sexual aspects and leave the caring bit in place. He really hoped they understood his orders and wouldn't start hitting on the patients. He also hoped no one was going to ask what they usually did. Not that he was embarrassed or anything, but he couldn't shake the feeling that he was basically bringing out sex toys to help with a potentially fatal disease.

"They have rebuilt so much already," Nanny remarked.

"Yeah," Luca agreed. "Let's find the infirmary."

"Okay, Luca," Sia and Simon purred in perfect sync.

"Could you maybe not do that?" Luca said.

Renn came to greet them halfway through the town. He looked like Renn should. Serious and healthy.

"Hey!" Luca called out. "The cavalry is here!"

Renn, of course, seemed a little confused, but he got the point. "I am glad to see you," he replied.

"Hello, Renn," Nanny said. "It's very nice to see you again. How are you?"

Renn inclined his head. "I am well. Thank you for coming."

Luca saw him glance at the twins. "Yeah, so this is Sia and Simon. They're artificials too."

"Hello," Renn greeted them.

"Hello, Renn," they trilled in unison.

Luca glared at them. "All right," he said and clapped his hands. "Let's do some damage control around here."

Renn nodded and made a vague gesture in the direction of the infirmary.

"How many are down for the count now?" Luca asked.

"A third of the Sienans are too ill to work. More are showing early signs of the illness."

"You're okay, though. Right?" Luca asked, wishing his voice would sound more casual.

"Yes. I appear not to have caught it. Esmia is healthy too," Renn added as an afterthought. "Perhaps wanderers don't succumb so easily to the illness."

"Good point," Luca agreed. "You outdoorsy types are probably more resistant."

The small procession made it to the infirmary and went in. The place smelled wrong. It smelled ill. It wasn't enough to make Luca gag, but there was an unmistakable stench of sour sweat and bad breath and blood. And there were beds and mattresses everywhere. He tried not to look at anyone as they went through to the door in the back of the clinic to Gabriele's personal quarters.

Inside, Gabriele was propped up in his bed, and he looked like he would collapse if someone snatched the pillows away from his back. Teo was standing by the window looking just fine, and Arsenio was sitting on a stool wrapped in a blanket and clearly shivering. He was looking so ill that Luca didn't even feel like poking fun at him.

"Luca," Teo said, smiling thinly. She might not look ill, but she did look exhausted. "Thank you for coming. Thank you too, Nanny. And..?"

"Sia and Simon," Luca finished for her. "Just put the bags there," he added to the artificials, "and let's get this shithole in shipshape, okay?"

Arsenio opened his mouth to make a retort. All that came out was a coughing fit.

Gabriele was smiling weakly and Luca flashed him what he hoped came across as a confident, friendly grin.

"I got you some face masks and gloves, but they won't last long. So I'm thinking you should only give them to people that you know are at high risk when they need to interact with others. But Mender can work that one out."

"Yes," Teo said. "Mender will be here in a moment. Ne has some ideas." Luca saw her look at Renn with a worried crease between her eyebrows. What was that all about?

"Cool. In the meantime," Luca said, crouching next to the bags and opening one of them, "we might as well get started with step one. Luca

Capello's viral epidemic guide says you all need to have your immune systems boosted stat." He unwrapped a number of ready-made shots. They were manufactured like medication for diabetics and were pretty fool proof to administer. Just place on naked skin and push the button. "Nanny, will you swab our subjects?"

"Of course," she said, taking disinfectant and approaching Teo first.

Teo pulled up her tunic and let Nanny wipe a small area on her abdomen which was, Luca casually noticed, rather nice. Probably she was getting a lot of workout in Siena.

"You don't need a vein?" Gabriele wheezed.

"Nope," Luca confirmed. "And it's perfectly safe. Back in my day, everybody used to take these. There were some pretty nasty pandemics going on before my time that made medical innovations a priority. Sucks that they aren't readily available anymore. Anyway, I take these shots regularly and have no side effects."

Gabriele nodded and whispered his thanks to Nanny as she swabbed him too.

Luca put on rubber gloves and got started. This was a tough crowd, so obviously no one flinched or complained about the prick of the needle. Renn did look suspicious, though.

"Don't worry," Luca told him. "It doesn't hurt." He wrapped an arm around Renn's waist for good measure as he kneeled in front of him and focused on the nicely chiseled, brown skin. He jabbed the needle into the wanderer, suppressing a sigh of relief. He had been worried that Renn would throw a fit and think the needle sucked out his soul or something.

"How many of those do you have?" Teo asked when Luca was pulling off his gloves again.

"Just one," he replied.

"What?" Arsenio exclaimed.

"One more," Luca said, holding up a finger to illustrate the number.

The room grew very, very quiet.

"What?" Luca said, turning from one to the other and settling his gaze on Teo. "Did you think I had enough for the whole damn town?" He had done some serious math before leaving the base. Sure, he had a nice stash, but it was from the supplies in his home. He had never found any on his treasure hunts. He wanted to be able to take regular shots for the rest of his life. He wanted to have enough to help out his friends again in a similar crisis. It all added up to having only a few spare shots. His first priorities were Renn, Teo and Gabriele, not only because he liked them, but because they were vital to Siena. That left him with two spare shots. Arsenio had already gotten one because Teo would probably insist on that anyway and besides, he was almost as useful as the others.

"No," Teo said, trying not to look disappointed and failing hard. "No, we are grateful for anything you can spare."

"Who gets the last one?" Renn asked.

The door opened and Mender entered. "I am sorry for being late," ne said although it was completely unnecessary. Everybody knew ne had been attending to patients. "Oh," ne replied, seeing the three other artificials. "It's a pleasure to see you again, Nanny. Hello," ne added to Sia and Simon, "I am Minder 3431-B, but I answer to Mender."

"Hello, Mender," they replied together.

"I'm Sia," said Sia.

"And I'm Simon," said Simon.

Mender assessed them for a moment.

"These two and Nanny are here to help out," Luca explained. When Mender met his eyes, he could swear the sentient knew. Knew and was puzzled and slightly judgmental to boot. At least ne didn't say anything about it. "We've just given these guys an immune boost," Luca went on, "and now we're about to decide who gets the last one I brought."

Gabriele waved at them for attention. "Esmia," he breathed. "She is good with the patients."

"But she only just got here!" Arsenio argued. "Giving her special treatment..."

Luca rolled his eyes. "Yeah, okay, you guys need to sort out your immigration policies."

"We think Esmia might be immune," Teo said. That got everyone's attention. She and Mender proceeded to explain the worst dumbfuckery Luca had heard in a few hundred years.

Gabriele listened to the story, looking like a particularly sad puppy. Arsenio was fuming, but he didn't say much. Renn was silent in the way that meant he had Opinions and Luca had a feeling he knew exactly what they were.

"That's ridiculous," Luca groaned when Mender and Teo stopped talking.

"But," Mender interjected, "I believe it is possible to use antibodies in her blood to make a cure for the illness. I was going to speak to you about it yesterday, Gabriele, but you were..."

Gabriele nodded. "Yes. I think you are right. But," he added after taking as deep a breath as he appeared able to, "we don't have the facilities here."

Mender inclined nir head. "I am afraid I did not in the home either."

"Florence does," Teo piped up.

"No!" Arsenio said.

"I'm with your boyfriend for a change," Luca said. "You can't ask Florence for help."

Teo planted her hands on her hips. "I don't want to, but if it's between that and risking the lives of everybody here, I'll go myself. Ask to talk to my father. Surely they don't want us to die and—"

"Haven't we had this conversation before?" Luca interrupted.

For once, Teo looked positively angry with him. "Do you have a better idea?" she spat.

"As of matter of fact, I do!" Luca almost shouted. "The Shelter probably has the means!"

Teo closed her mouth to consider it. "All right," she said. "Ask them."

"Are they just going to help us out of compassion?" Arsenio asked.

"I don't know, I haven't asked them yet," Luca told him. "But everybody always wants something, and these people are living in a hole in the ground. I'm sure we have bargaining chips. We still need to decide who gets the last shot, though."

Teo rubbed her eyes. "Don't ask me to make that decision."

"All right," Luca said. "I won't. I'll make it." Teo and the others might be emotionally compromised in their little socialist haven, but Luca didn't mind making a tough call. "Clara."

"Clara?" Teo echoed.

"Yes," Renn said.

"Oh hi, I didn't know you were part of the discussion," Luca said, winking at him.

"Why Clara?" Arsenio asked.

Luca gestured for Renn to explain because he was pretty sure the nomad's practical mind had reached the same conclusion as he had.

"She has the function of our elders," Renn said. "She helps people believe in hope. As far as I can understand, the belief she embodies encourages helping others."

"What he said," Luca agreed. "Clara's Christianity done right. And she's the only religious leader we have here, so you need her to boost morale and take care of funerals if that becomes relevant."

"Let's hope not," Gabriele croaked.

"Just trying to be realistic," Luca said. "But don't worry, you'll be fine," he added lamely.

"Thank you for the confidence," Gabriele managed.

26:

Marco

As dangerous and honorable it was to be a primary functions maintainer who went outside the Shelter to feel the wind and the sun on his skin and breathe the unfiltered, dusty air, Marco had to admit there was nothing glorious about the work itself. What felt like an adventure when carried out on the communications array was tedious cleaning work at all other times. He did get to do light repairs too, but it was a matter of screwing on a loose bolt or connecting a wire to a connector it had fallen out of.

Apart from going outside, the only exhilarating thing someone in the primary functions department did was visiting the Heart from time to time. Never alone, of course, and never unprotected.

Marco stood in the second cleaning chamber watching vapor gather on the visor of his helmet and turn into droplets. He glanced to the left. The Superior was not wearing protection. Nir smooth surface was completely resistant to the poisonous bi-products of the Heart. Superiors could go anywhere they pleased. They were practically immortal. Marco turned away his gaze when the Superior began to move. The doors slid open in front of them in a pattern of horizontal and vertical lines.

At this point, Marco's suit and the Superior's sleek form ought to be sterilized. They marched through the narrow corridor to the next chamber, waited until the doors behind them closed and let the last step of the cleaning wash over them.

When they left the chamber, it was time for Marco to take off the bulky suit. Although it had cooling and was made so he could move freely in it, he always felt awkward. He turned the head piece slightly until the catch loosened and lifted it off. He placed it on the bench in the changing room and began to undo the closing on the rest of the suit until it peeled away from his body and he could step out of it, taking off the boots last.

The Superior stood watching him while he folded the suit and put the helmet on top of it before sitting down to put on his own shoes again.

"You did well," the Superior remarked.

"Thank you," Marco said, almost unable to keep himself from grinning with pleasure at the rare compliment. They had only carried out routine inspection, but Marco paid attention to details. He had a good memory and immediately noticed if anything looked out of place.

"I relieve you of duty for today," the Superior informed him.

Marco nodded. His job was done, but leave it to a Superior to point it out so it seemed like nir benevolence. Marco's eyes darted back up to the Superior, but ne was already on nir way out of the room. It was ungrateful to think ill of the Superiors who cared for the Shelter and made sure everyone was happy and fed. He knew that. He knew ungratefulness only led to greed and selfishness and other evils. Chiding himself, he stood up and followed the Superior.

Nir tall form was already far down the corridor. Marco didn't go after nem. Instead, he went in the opposite direction toward the elevator. A couple of light skinned maintainers from the technical and computers departments came toward him, talking about what sounded like hypothetical computer failures. They broke off when they saw Marco, greeted him and stepped aside so he could pass. The hallways this far down were not as wide as above, simply because few people were allowed to access levels this close to the Heart. Sometimes Marco wondered what it would be like to be a maintainer in the technical and computer department or in intern communications. Or to work with the hydroponics or educate children or take care of the ill. But he had been appointed to be a maintainer in primary functions, and the Superiors were never wrong in their assessment of a person's qualifications.

The elevator took a while to get to Marco's level. He idly watched the lights leap from one number to the next on the panel. When it arrived, another Superior stepped out. Ne was only distinguishable from the one Marco had just worked with by the color of nir coating. This one was not in maintainer silver, but security blue. Marco nodded in greeting and waited for nem to pass before he entered the elevator. Then he pressed the button marked with the number ten and waited while he watched the countdown.

No one else got into the elevator, but it was not so strange. He was often working odd shifts compared to the majority of the Shelter's inhabitants because his job depended on the conditions outside and what the Superiors deemed urgent work.

The elevator stopped with an almost imperceptible jerk. The doors slid open, and Marco stepped out. The smell of food was wafting toward him from the dining hall on this level. His stomach growled and Marco tried to clench the muscles of his abdomen to make it stay quiet when two women around the age of his parents passed him. They smiled respectfully at him. He was wearing a maintainer's colors. Until he became one less than a year ago, he was only a student like every other teenager. Now he worked directly with the Superiors and that earned him particular attention.

Marco entered the dining hall. It was, as he had expected, almost empty. An older maintainer Marco only knew from briefings sat in a corner reading something on a slate while sipping at a cup at intervals. Marco went to the serving station, grabbed a plate and a cup. One of the kitchen staff was manning the station, but he only greeted Marco and let him pile food onto the plate on his own. Today's lunch, or what was left from it, was protein steak and vegetables. Some of the algae-based garnish was a bit more slippery than Marco preferred, but he took some anyway. Once his plate was full, he poured juice, carrot with something spicy by the smell of it.

The other maintainer was still reading. He took a sip of his cup and thumbed the screen on his slate. There was no indication he'd even seen Marco, and Marco made his way to one of the empty tables. But the moment he pulled out the chair to sit, the other maintainer spoke. "You can join me."

Marco glanced around. But the man was still looking at the slate in his hand. Still, there was no one else. Marco had the immediate impression that the maintainer had an air of superiority that only suited... well, an actual Superior. But it would be rude to ignore him, so Marco picked up his plate and moved to the other man's table. He sat down opposite him.

"Hello, Marco," the man said, finally looking up. His skin was a lot paler than any primary functions maintainer's. He had jet black, straight hair and cool, brown eyes set in a face that Marco's history lessons had taught him to think of as East Asian whereas his own was considered West African, whatever any of those terms meant to the Shelter's population.

"Hello," Marco replied, wishing he remembered the other man's name.

"Giuliano Ahn," the maintainer said and placed his slate on the table. The screen was blank. He must have closed the book he was reading. "Heart work?" he asked.

"Yes," Marco said although he could not guess how the other maintainer had reached that conclusion.

"Mm," Giuliano said. "I suppose you would not have been around to hear the news, then. It seems we finally have contact."

Marco chewed and washed the mouthful down with juice. "With who?" he asked.

"Whom," the other maintainer said and continued before Marco could figure out exactly how annoying he found it, "Communications picked up a signal from outside. A radio signal."

"Really?" Marco blurted, forgetting his irritation. "Who is it?"

"Well, it's interesting, really," Giuliano said. "Apparently there are several towns on the surface, practically on top of the Shelter."

Marco frowned. That was not entirely true. If it were, he would be able to see them when he was at the communications array.

"Not literally," Giuliano said. "But it would seem that several of those towns have radio equipment. One of them contacted the Shelter a few weeks back. Not that anyone outside communications was told about it. But I expect it will get out soon," he added with a feigned casualness that made Marco want to roll his eyes. "After all, they are coming here."

"What?" Marco exclaimed. "Who is coming here? From the surface?"

Giuliano smiled. "Well, I happened to be up at intern communications earlier and heard them talking about it. There were two Superiors as well. Apparently, someone from one of those towns called yesterday and asked for something, and communications called them back this morning after the Superiors made a decision.

"What did they ask for?" Marco asked.

"From what I heard, their town is in trouble because of some illness. People are dying left and right. They can make medication, but they don't have the facilities. We do." Giuliano leaned back in his chair and folded his hands behind his head. "The Superiors decided to let them come here."

"Really?" Marco exclaimed. The communications array had to be kept in good condition in the hope that someday someone would contact the Shelter and report that the surface was habitable again, but it had never happened. Not before now.

"Oh yes," Giuliano said.

"But…" Marco paused, not sure which question he wanted to ask first. "Is it safe? I mean, if they are ill…"

"I don't know everything," Giuliano said loftily. "But from what the Superiors were saying, there are security protocols. They will have to go through decontamination and such."

Marco could tell that despite his nonchalance, Giuliano was intrigued and as curious about it as he was.

"They also have Superiors with them," he added.

"That makes sense," Marco said. "I mean, if there are settlements out there with advanced enough technology to contact us, they must be supervised by Superiors."

Giuliano's eyes searched Marco's face for a moment. "None of this is common knowledge, of course. I only know because I happened to be there."

"I'm not going to start any rumors," Marco replied, although if Giuliano was so terribly concerned about that, he might have chosen not to tell someone he hardly knew. "But like you said, people will know when the strangers get here."

But until then, it was too big not to imagine all sort of things. What would the strangers look like? If they lived on the surface, they would have to be dark skinned. But how did they talk? What did they wear? Where were they from? And how many of them were there? The idea of Superiors traveling was odd. The idea of anyone traveling was, really. It wasn't safe out there.

"Enjoy your meal," Giuliano said abruptly and stood up, leaving Marco with more questions than he had answered.

27:

Renn

The world moved past the car in a blur. Walled in by the metal frame and windows, with the artificial smells and the unnatural noise, Renn felt no connection to the land around him. He needed the ground beneath his feet and the air on his skin to be able to read the wind and tell which direction he was going. Inside the car, he was deaf and blind. But it was fast. He had to admit that.

"I can't believe they've been right there all this time! Right under my nose," Luca was saying from the front of the car. Renn had opted for the backseat. It may not be logical, but he felt marginally safer there. "I can't wait to see what sort of place it is."

Renn glanced at the equipment on the seat next to him. Right now Luca sounded more excited about the prospect of this new old settlement than worried about the reason they were going in the first place.

"Are you feeling all right?" Luca asked, but he was not talking to Renn.

"I'm quite fine, master Luca," Nanny replied.

"No glitches or anything? I mean, it's not like I expect Mender to carry a Trojan or anything."

"It was only a small download. I feel fine," she reassured him.

The wonder of the car was nothing compared to how Luca's plan to help Siena had unfolded so far. Teo and Luca called the procedure technology, but to Renn, it seemed like Luca performed deliberate, advanced witchcraft. Somehow, Luca had taken contents from Mender's mind and put them into Nanny's. He used words like laptop and data package and upload, but in essence, it appeared that Mender's knowledge of creating a cure to the illness that plagued Siena was shared with Nanny. If that were possible, Renn couldn't quite understand why the same method was not applied to share all knowledge between the sentients. Luca had tried to explain it using a very simplified metaphor about how full a box was.

After the procedure, Luca, Nanny and Renn left Siena. Mender was needed to care for the ill, which was the whole point of imparting some of nir knowledge to Nanny. Teo wanted to go, but everybody agreed that she was needed in Siena. Esmia stayed too. Renn was still not sure if he thought that was a good idea.

Renn had not offered to go immediately. He was not a doctor or a healer, but he was not ill and could help the settlement better by being there. But part of him had not wanted Luca to go alone, although Luca was capable of taking care of himself, mostly. Besides, he had Nanny. Still, Renn had felt uneasy, so when Luca returned after using Siena's radio to arrange matters and told Renn and Teo the outcome, part of him was relieved.

The occupants of the place called the Shelter agreed to help them, but on certain conditions. Renn had expected no less, but the price was twofold. First of all, the Shelter wanted some of Luca's treasures. This didn't surprise Renn and didn't appear to deter Luca in the least. For someone who chose to live in solitude, guarding his belongings from the past for so long, he was extraordinarily willing to share. He explained that some of the things the Shelter wanted were only copies of information held in objects so small that it was almost unbelievable that anything should fit in there.

The second condition was Renn. How exactly that came about was a bit of a mystery, but it seemed the Shelter was very interested in the geography around their secluded habitat. They did not venture far away themselves, but they were keen to talk to someone who did and who might be able to help them understand the difference between their ancient maps and the real world. And, in Luca's words, who could possibly be a better choice to educate them than a nomad? It did occur to Renn that Luca himself could probably provide much of the same information, but he agreed to the terms. If nothing else, the arrangement relieved Renn of his concern of Luca and Nanny going alone.

Instead of going straight to the Shelter, the small party went back to Luca's home first to gather the items Luca had promised the Shelter. Even prepared for it, the place was as strange as that first night when Luca had brought Renn and Mender home after the scarvhe attack.

Now they were finally headed for the Shelter. It was already afternoon, but Luca said they should be there before nightfall. Studying the map, Renn agreed.

"Renn?" Luca asked from the front seat. "Are you moping?"

"No," Renn replied and met Luca's gaze in the mirror. His green eyes were positively radiant with anticipation. "I hope the Shelter can help us," he added, trying to bring Luca's focus back to the reason they were doing this.

"They will. We've got a nice sample of Esmia's blood and with Nanny's new medical upgrade, we just need to use their lab to mass produce the cure." Luca sounded perfectly confident.

Esmia's blood... It was strange that the cause of this peril could be turned into the salvation.

"You're still blaming Esmia, aren't you?" Luca asked, briefly looking away from the mirror and then back again.

"Yes," Renn said. "I know you claim the spirits have nothing to do with it..."

"Enough with the spirits!" Luca exclaimed and rolled his eyes. "And you don't need to get defensive. It totally is Esmia's fault, just not because of some nomad mumbo jumbo. She carried the illness with her and didn't even mention it so you guys could take precautions. It's a dumb ass move."

Renn decided not to be goaded into another argument about that. It was in the past now.

"Oh, for fuck's sake," Luca muttered. He began to decelerate the car. "That was not on the maps."

"Oh dear," Nanny said.

Renn leaned forward to peer out of the front window between them.

The terrain ahead promised trouble. At first, there was a crevice, a wound sliced into the ground by, most likely, a quake. Although it wasn't broad, its length stretched as far as Renn could see. Beyond it, the ground rose in a jagged pattern of rocks and clumps of trees. Renn did not recognize this area, but migration never took him this far west. "I assume the car can't go across the gorge?" he asked.

Luca struck the steering wheel with the heel of his hand. "Even if it could—" he began, cut himself off and opened the door.

Nanny and Renn followed him outside.

"We'll never make it up the mountain even if we could get the Rover across that," Luca sighed. He moved closer to the edge.

Renn stood next to him. The gorge was not very deep. He would probably be able to reach the ground standing on the bottom of it.

"We could go around it," Nanny suggested. "Or perhaps build a bridge..."

Luca shook his head. "Let's do the math. If we could drive the whole way, we'd be at the Shelter in maybe an hour. What's faster, finding a way around that and only maybe a way up the mountain, or just going on foot?"

It was hardly a mountain. "That is a difficult question when we don't know how far we would have to go in the wrong direction in the car," Renn said.

"How fast can we do the hike you think?" Luca asked.

"Four hours at a reasonable pace. For me," Renn added, knowing already as he said it that Luca would think of it as a challenge.

"Nanny's a sentient," Luca said, "and I'm not your average Sienan. We'll match your pace."

"So we build a bridge?" Nanny asked.

"Waste of time. We jump," Luca said.

"With everything we will need to carry? Is that wise?" Nanny asked.

"Your hydraulics will be fine," Luca said and went back to the car. "Let's gear up."

"It was not myself I was worried about," Nanny said. There was a note of exasperation in her otherwise calm voice that Renn could sympathize with.

"He can make the jump," Renn told her. He had seen enough of Luca's physical capabilities to know that. "And if he fails, the fall will not kill him," he added.

"Chop, chop, guys!" Luca called from the vehicle. "We need to get going if we want to get there before nightfall."

Like Mender had carried most of their belongings when Renn traveled with nem, Nanny took the heavier burden to allow Renn and Luca to move faster and more unhindered.

Leaving the car was, despite the speed it was capable of, a relief. Renn felt a lot better with the ground beneath his feet. He also felt better knowing that Luca was not ultimately in charge of the route they took.

Nanny leapt across the rift first. She tested the edge on the other side, but it was as compact and solid as it looked. They threw their backpacks across to her. Then Luca stepped back toward the car and approached the pit, running faster than was strictly needed to make the jump. When he landed on the other side, he yelled out in victory and turned back to Renn with his arms in the air. "Beat that, nomad!" he called.

"I was not aware we were competing," Renn replied.

"You are not," Nanny said, looking at Luca sternly. "All that matters is getting across safely."

"Sure," Luca said, ignoring her, "but I bet you won't beat me anyway."

Renn waited for the wind to be in his favor. Luca was smaller and lighter, and the footprints near the edge of the gorge showed that he had gone closer than advisable before leaping. But Renn's own jump landed him almost in exactly the same place.

"Sweet," Luca said, nodding in approval.

There was a small part of Renn, a part he would never admit to anyone else, that was curious to see how Luca would tackle the hike. But as they ascended the hill, Luca's pace surprised him. It was not as brisk as he had assumed. Clearly the boy from the past did know how to set a reasonable, steady pace. And his feet found even, safe ground with almost every step. And, perhaps most surprisingly of all, he did not talk very much. Renn thought the only time he had seen Luca this quiet was when he performed repairs on Mender.

When they made a halt two hours later, Nanny handed them both bottles. Renn was carrying a flask of his own because it was never good to rely on one person for vital provisions, but he accepted the drink regardless. It was not water. Renn almost spit the beverage back out in surprise.

"Electrolytes," Luca said with a grin. "To keep from dehydrating." He wiped his forehead with the back of his hand and then poured the strange concoction into his mouth.

"It is more efficient than water," Nanny explained. "In the past, it was administered to people who needed rehydration as well as a precaution to people who were very physically active."

"It tastes a bit like sweat," Luca added. He handed the bottle back to Nanny and stretched.

As the last rays of the sun faded and the landscape was bathed in warm light and long shadows, the three hikers stood on the highest point of the hills. Luca was breathing hard now and stood with his hands on his knees. Renn was next to him. His own pulse was elevated and he took deep, purposeful breaths.

"Something tells me we made it," Luca said, straightening up again. "Holy fuck."

Renn would not have chosen those exact words, but he agreed with the sentiment. Even without directions and a map, he would have known they were looking at something besides ancient ruins. The Shelter may be located underground, but there were clear signs of its existence on the surface. The ridge of another hill was topped with a wall adorned with several strange contraptions. Renn thought a couple of them looked like bigger, more elaborate versions of the radio antenna in Siena.

"They have fucking satellite dishes," Luca laughed. "That is the most comprehensive communication center I've seen in... centuries. See," he added, grinning. "I told you guys they are advanced!"

Sunlight gleamed off the objects of Luca's adoration. Renn had worried that this settlement would be hostile to Luca's ways in the same way that Florence was. But if Renn understood the meaning of the different kinds of masheens and technologies correctly, the Shelter was indeed equipped with contraptions closer to Luca's own home than Florence.

Beyond the masheens, a crater was marring the ground. Renn shuddered to think of the size of the rock that must have caused it as it plummeted from the sky. It might as well have hit the masheens or flattened the hill they were standing atop.

"I hope it was as deserted as it looks now," Nanny said softly. She was looking at the giant crater as well.

"Well, the Shelter is still there," Luca replied. "Let's go knock on the door."

Door? Renn spotted the place he was talking about as they began to make their way down the sloping hill with dislodged pebbles skittering along. Nanny's gait reminded Renn of Mender's. Measured and calculated. Luca balanced himself with his arms stretched out, dust whirling around his feet.

They approached a foreign-looking monolith sticking out of the ground. It looked like a small house that had been left intact despite the destruction around it. As they got closer, Renn saw it did indeed have a door. There was no handle, but panels the size and shape of a door were inserted into the wall facing them.

"Look!" Luca exclaimed, pointing at the ground.

"A path," Renn acknowledged. "Not a wanderer route."

"Probably one used by the people in there," Luca said. Then he stopped and turned to the masheens that were now nearly right above them. He waved his arms. "Heya!" he shouted. "I'm Luca Capello, and these are my friends! We have an appointment. What?" he continued to Renn and Nanny. "I bet they are keeping an eye on their surroundings with that camera up there. Oh look. It moves."

Renn squinted. Yes, some kind of device was indeed rotating toward them. He reached for his staff.

"A camera!" Luca intoned. "It's not a gun."

Renn tried to look like he was not ready to take action in case Luca was wrong.

The contraption stopped its rotation, and Luca waved again. "Hello!" he shouted, articulating his words so carefully that his ancient accent was almost lost, "We are here to visit the Shelter. I am Luca."

For a while, nothing happened.

"Should we knock?" Nanny asked.

"Nah. They've seen us," Luca replied. His voice was calm and casual, but his shoulders were tense. "It's probably just taking them a while to get out of their hole in the ground and greet us. Let's give it a few more minutes."

28:

Renn

It turned out that Luca was right. They waited for no more than ten minutes in the twilight before the door slid open to reveal a figure. It was shaped like a human or a sentient, but it was impossible to determine anything further because it was wearing what looked like a suit of bulging, grey fabric and a helmet a little like the one Luca wore when riding his motorcycle.

Luca's breath hitched, but when Renn tried to read his face, there was nothing but a bright smile.

"Hello," the figure called out.

The trio stepped closer to the door. "Hi," Luca said. "I'm Luca, this is Renn, and that is Nanny. Thanks for meeting us."

"My name is Marco Osei. I'm a maintainer," the figure said. His voice was muffled, but Renn could tell that his accent was close to Mender's. "The Superiors sent me to greet you and go through the procedure with you. I..." he faltered. "We were not expecting you all to be human."

"We aren't," Luca replied, grinning. "Nanny's a sentient."

"A sentient?"

"An artificial. Android. Manmade person," Luca said.

"Oh, I see." The voice sounded flustered. When Marco turned toward Nanny, Renn saw that inside the strange attire, their guide was a dark-skinned boy probably around Esmia's age. "Please accept my apologies," he continued, bending at the waist to bow in Nanny's direction. "I— I didn't realize. Our Superiors aren't so—"

"I took no offense, Marco," Nanny said, smiling.

"Thank you." Marco gestured toward the door. "I'll take you all through the decontamination process. If you'll follow me into the first chamber."

"Jesus fucking Christ," Luca muttered under his breath. "Hazmat suit and everything. You'd think we were radioactive."

"That is how you got in touch with them," Renn reminded him.

"What?" Luca blinked. "What are you— Oh. I meant poisonous. They're treating us as if we're super poisonous."

Renn nodded. He could sympathize with it. After all, they may well be carrying the illness they were here to make a cure for.

They stepped into an almost cubic room, and the door closed behind them. Luca's breath shuddered as he drew it in.

"You will go through two phases. It helps if you close your eyes and hold your breath," a disembodied voice rang out from somewhere near the ceiling. "Please stand by for decontamination. Process begins in three... two... one..."

Zero was drowned out by the sudden onset of what felt like the brunt of a dust storm. Renn barely managed to breathe in and hold his breath. He shut his eyes tightly against the force of the air whirling around them. It was a cold blast, but it was dry.

A hand clamped down on Renn's arm. Luca. Whether it was for Luca's own comfort or to make sure Renn stayed in place, he did not know. The grip was released the moment the wind stopped.

Opening his eyes again, Renn saw the wall in front of them slide apart.

"Are you all right?" Nanny was asking Luca.

"Yeah, I'm fine," he replied. He sounded shaky, which was strange since he probably knew more about the nature of this process than Renn.

"We aren't trapped," Nanny murmured soothingly.

"I know!" Luca said. "I said I'm fine."

They all followed Marco into the next room, and the wall closed again behind them. This compartment was as small and empty as the first one, giving Renn no clues of what lay beyond.

"This part will take a little longer," Marco said. He was still wearing the bulky suit. "And I have to ask you to take off the outer layers of clothing."

"You've done this before, I take it," Luca said. "It's pretty extensive for a standard procedure."

"We usually skip this part," Marco admitted. "But we can't risk anything."

"Cristoforo Colombo could have learned a thing or two from you," Luca said.

Renn put his staff on the floor and began to undress. Next to him, Luca was already stripping.

Renn glanced up at Marco and saw him turn away from Nanny as she took off her clothes. Because she was a sentient or one specifically created to look female?

They put the equipment they had brought on the floor so whatever was coming next would be able to cleanse it.

"Luca Capello," said the disembodied voice suddenly.

"Yes?" Luca replied. He was now wearing only his socks and undergarments and stood gazing up at the ceiling as if he could see the person who spoke.

"You will leave your projectile weapons in this room."

Luca was about to argue, but then he shook his head. "Fine. We come in peace and all that."

"You really want to keep your eyes and mouth closed for this too," Marco said. His back was still turned to Nanny.

"Please stand by for decontamination. Process begins in three..." the voice said.

A moment later, they were enveloped in a new kind of whirlwind. This time, it was wet and cold and stung every little scratch on Renn's body. At some point, the wetness disappeared and when the air grew still again, Renn found himself dry and shivering.

Luca was on his hands and knees, and his breath came in shallow gasps.

Nanny and Renn began to approach him at the same time, but to Renn's surprise, Nanny stepped back and gestured for him to go on.

"Are you all right?" Renn asked, bending to touch Luca's shoulder. His pale skin felt like ice, but his trembling was disproportionate even to the drop in temperature.

Luca reached out one unsteady hand and grabbed the first thing he touched which happened to be a strand of Renn's hair. Renn didn't object to the tug. "Luca?" he said instead. "What is wrong?" No answer. Not knowing what else to do, Renn moved closer to at least shield him from Marco's stare.

"Fucking fuck shitfuck!" Luca finally choked out. "I can't—"

Was he crying? Renn dropped to one knee and pushed a lock of hair away from Luca's face. "You are not alone," he murmured.

For a moment, Luca didn't react. Then he seemed to realize he was clutching Renn's hair. He slowly let go. "S— Sorry," he muttered.

"No need," Renn replied. His hand was still resting on Luca's shoulder.

Luca took a deep, shaky breath, the effort audible. He released it, and Renn felt some of the tension go out of him. "I swallowed a bucketful of disinfectant or something," Luca said.

While his voice was hoarse, Renn was not at all convinced. He may not know the exact reason for it, but panic wore many faces, and this was one of them.

"I'm fine," Luca said as he pushed himself back up with Renn's support. "I'm okay. I'm fine." He sounded more like he was trying to convince himself than Renn. "Of all the fucking moments my latent

PTSD decides to fuck me over, this is it. I'm fine, Renn, and we will not talk about this, like ever again, okay?"

Renn hesitated, then let go. Luca was clearly clawing his way back to his usual self.

Marco told them not to dress again, but to gather what they needed to bring down to the Shelter and leave the rest. He assured them their belongings would be safe and returned to them when they departed. Luca left two guns behind, one of which Renn had not been aware he was carrying. Renn considered leaving his staff, but it was not a weapon as such, and he felt safer bringing it. No one objected.

The next room was lined with benches and closets built into the walls. The temperature was warm here, and it was bigger than the previous chambers.

Marco opened a closet and pulled out piles of light grey fabric that turned out to be clothes for Renn and Luca. Nanny's clothes were stored in another closet and had a very different texture. Marco was still refusing to look at Nanny when he handed her the garments.

The clothes were quite comfortable, Renn found, but probably not very practical. The upper part was attached to the trousers and instead of buttons, the front was closed all the way to his neck with what Luca called a zipper. In such an attire, one would have to take off the whole thing if part of it was torn or soaked, and the small metal teeth of the zipper did not appear to be able to stand much duress.

Renn turned to Luca. He had dressed quickly and was putting on his boots again. Dressed, he didn't look quite as vulnerable as he had a moment ago, but his suit was as loose as Renn's felt, and it was so plain and anonymous that Renn had to wonder how much conscious effort Luca usually put into his clothing.

"What?" Luca asked. "We look like fucking inmates."

"We are asking you to wear those clothes to minimize the risk of contamination," Marco said. He twisted the domed helmet he was wearing. It made a small click, and then he took it off. "I'm sorry to put you through all this," he said. "But the Superiors say that despite the air filtering in the Shelter, we can't risk spreading disease among ourselves."

"That is wise," Nanny said. Her new clothes were not in one piece but consisted of a tightly fitted top and trousers in white. Renn was not familiar with the material, but it looked smooth and shiny.

"We did not know which colors to present you with, Superior," Marco told Nanny.

"This will do nicely," she replied.

Marco was taking off the suit he wore on the surface. Underneath it, he wore a white undershirt and a kind of tunic and trousers of a darker grey than the garments he had presented Renn and Luca with. There were stripes around the sleeves and collar in shiny silver. His hair was cropped short, but what was left on his head was black and curly. "Ready?" Marco asked them.

"Can't wait to get going," Luca said, grinning. There was still tension in his voice and movements, but Renn could tell he was leaving the previous chamber behind in more than one sense. Renn couldn't help wondering, but he would respect Luca's wish not to talk about it.

29:
Teo

The number of assembled Sienans was staggeringly low. And not only because Mender had advised that only one person from each house should attend in an attempt to limit contagion. They were even fewer here now than when they held their first assembly months ago. If Teo were religious, she might have shouted at the heavens to give them a break and let them build their new home in peace. Then again, if she were, she might exactly not have done that.

"Thank you for coming," she said, forcing a smile onto her lips. "We will do this quickly so we can all get back to work. As you know, Luca left with Renn yesterday to go to the settlement where they can work on a cure for us. With a little luck, they will return tomorrow, so we really just need to keep up spirits until then."

Teo's eyes met Clara's. Somehow, the deacon was radiating hope and confidence. There was no sign she was ill. Yet. Teo was fairly certain half of the gathered people were, although they could clearly still function. Esmia was somewhere else working with Mender and Luca's two superhumanly beautiful artificials. Despite the injection Luca had given Arsenio, he was still so weak that Teo flat out told him to stay in bed and not go anywhere until she returned. He had, of course, whined about that. By some stroke of luck, or maybe due to the injection, Teo was fine herself.

"Let us go over the situation," Teo said. "Who can work, and what do we need to get done now?"

They went over the chores and the numbers, and the list was not encouraging. But it was Teo's job to be, so she tried to keep a brave face.

Afterward, Teo went back to the infirmary. Gone were the days when it smelled clean and sterile. Now a stench of vomit and sweat met her as she entered. Simon was mopping the floor, frowning and wrinkling his nose in a way that looked cuter than it ought to. Teo caught sight of phlegmy, bloody puke on the rag he was using and had to turn away.

Sia was leaning on one of the beds they had moved into the waiting room. She was talking to its occupant and handing them a cup. Before she could stop herself, Teo's eyes fell on the artificial's curves and extremely well-shaped backside that seemed to be posed deliberately for anyone's viewing pleasure. Teo wanted to berate herself for thinking like that, but... What exactly had these artificials' purpose been before the fall?

The door to one of the examination rooms, now also housing beds, opened, and Esmia came out carrying a bucket with a towel covering it. She smiled up at Teo, but it looked more like a grimace than a smile. Her eyes were ringed with dark, and her hands were trembling.

"Let me take that," Teo said, closing the distance between them with a few quick steps.

Esmia held on to the bucket and opened her mouth.

"Please," Teo insisted, placing her own hand on the handle. Hopefully she wouldn't have to wrestle it out of Esmia's grasp. That could get messy. "You look exhausted."

"No, I—"

"Esmia," Teo said. "Please. You are working harder than anyone."

"As I should be," the wanderer retorted. She looked almost as exhausted as the ill.

"I never meant for you to," Teo almost whispered. Sia turned and was studying them in a way Teo couldn't quite decipher. "Please. Go rest. Stay in the infirmary if you must, but try to get a nap at least. I promise I will wake you up if you are needed."

They stood for a moment longer. Then Esmia let go. "I will be in Mender's room. There are some blankets," she said. "Please don't let me sleep for more than an hour."

"All right," Teo lied. She would let Esmia sleep for at least three if she could.

As the wanderer retreated, Teo went outside with the bucket. The streets were deserted and the air was still and dry. It felt like the whole world was holding its breath.

She made her way out of the settlement to the waste disposal site. To think a clogged toilet had been her worst concern of the sanitary kind less than a year ago. They were planning on engineering a better system, but it had not been the most pressing matter so far and certainly wasn't now.

Holding her breath, Teo emptied the waste into the designated hole in the ground and then tossed a few shovelfuls of sand on top of it.

When she returned to the infirmary, Simon had finished cleaning the floor, and the air smelled considerably better. Teo put the bucket where it belonged, washed her hands thoroughly and decided to see if she could help with anything else. She knocked softly on the door to Gabriele's room, and although no one replied, it creaked open. She slipped inside and peered at the figure in the bed. The doctor was so pale and still that for a moment, she feared— But no. When she approached him, she could tell his chest was heaving and could hear the rattling sound of labored breathing. His forehead was slick with sweat and the bed linen had damp patches.

If they were still in Florence, there would be more doctors to care for the ill. There would be medication. There would be a proper waste disposal system. There would be someone else... Someone who was not Teodora Terzi in charge. If they were still in Florence, none of this would have happened. But Gabriele would be in prison. All of the rebels would. And Esmia would probably be dead. And... And there was no use speculating. They were here, now.

"Please get better soon," Teo whispered, not expecting Gabriele to hear. Not wanting him to.

Outside the room, there were suddenly other voices, much louder than Teo's. Someone shouted Mender's name and a reply came, calm and measured. Feet moving quickly through the infirmary.

Teo did not want to step out of the relative sanctuary of Gabriele's room. She did not want to hear and did not want to know. But she had to. So she took a deep breath, straightened up and left the doctor.

"Do you know where Mender is?" she asked the first person she met. It was better than to ask what was going on in case that alarmed anyone more.

"Ne went into that room," answered Sia, pointing.

"Thank you," Teo replied. She quickly followed the direction. The door was open. Inside were more beds than ought to be crammed into one room. Mender was bending over one of them. Nir back was to Teo, but she could tell ne was doing something, moving nir shoulders and arms.

The occupants of the other beds, the ones who were awake and aware at least, were craning their necks to see what was going on. The curtains partitioning the room did give some privacy, but they were far from sufficient with this many beds. Next to Mender was the pregnant Zenia. She was leaning on the bed and holding out something to assist nem, but she looked like she ought to rest.

"Teo, would you please take over for Zenia?" Mender's voice called out, still so calm that it was impossible to tell if anything serious was wrong.

"Yes," Teo replied, "What do you need me to do?"

"Take the mask. Keep it in place over the patient's nose and mouth and press the air container at five second intervals," Mender explained.

Zenia stepped aside to make room for Teo, and as she moved in, she realized the patient was Tonino. He was one of the members of the rebellion who took her in as part of their group along with Arsenio and Clara and Gabriele and those whose names were still painful to say. She also realized exactly what they were doing. They were trying to save his life.

They worked in silence, Mender pressing on Tonino's chest with both of nir hands in a steady rhythm, pausing once in a while to check for a pulse, Teo doing what she was ordered to. She wanted to ask what had happened and she wanted most of all for Mender to tell her to remove the mask and for Tonino to breathe on his own again.

But as the seconds stretched into minutes and Mender's hands left Tonino's chest once again and ne shook nir head, she knew.

Teo removed the mask, and Mender reached out to close the staring eyes. Teo had no idea what to say. No idea what to do. She wanted to ask Mender for reassurance that she hadn't been doing it wrong, that there was nothing anyone could have done differently, but this wasn't about her.

"I'm very sorry," Mender said softly.

"Me too," Teo whispered, weighed down not only by the loss, but the fear as well. Fear that this was only the beginning. Fear for Arsenio. Fear that everything they had worked for would turn to dust.

Mender drew a sheet over the body, leaving a human-shaped topography as the only clear sign of the tragedy. "Did you, by any chance, see Esmia?" ne asked in a low voice.

"Yes. She was exhausted. I told her to sleep. She is in your room," Teo said, trying in vain to strangle the idea that perhaps if she had allowed Esmia to keep working, she would have done a better job of keeping Tonino alive.

"Good. She needed it. I will wake her up later," Mender said, meeting Teo's eyes. "You probably have other obligations," ne added. "I will take care of things here for now."

Teo nodded. "Thank you," she said. She had never wished she were an artificial and quite frankly, she was unsure how deep their emotions ran, but what she saw in Mender's face was blissfully simple. There was sadness and regret and sympathy. But no doubt, no fear and no pain. She turned, trying not to look at anyone else in the room.

30:

Luca

It was all Luca could do to keep his cool. The Shelter was bigger on the inside, huge and magnificent and if he was honest, practically everything he had searched for all this time. Fuck Florence and fuck Pontedera and fuck Siena. Okay, maybe not Siena, but the rest of the primitive settlements and the technologically stunted domes were bland imitations of how a society should look.

They rode an elevator from the top level, several floors into the ground, reminding Luca slightly of a dystopian classic, just better. "How deep does this go?" he asked their guide.

"Twenty-four habitable levels," the cute black kid replied. "And then a few more before the Heart."

"The Heart?" Luca echoed. He swallowed, then held his nose and breathed out. They were going down so rapidly his ears were popping. From the look of it, Renn was experiencing the same thing.

"It's our source of energy," Marco said. "Only maintainers supervised by Superiors go there, and we have to wear protection. More thorough than what I wore outside."

"Really? No solar power? Wind turbines?" Luca asked. It made sense in a way because weather and climate changes could mess up outside sources of energy. But every base he knew of, and even Florence, harvested natural energy. The alternative— "Don't tell me you're sitting on a fucking nuclear reactor?" he exclaimed.

The elevator stopped and the door slid open to reveal a hallway that curved enough in both directions to obscure its length. What they stepped into looked like a broad corridor in a school or a public building. There was something slightly stilted about it, something deliberate that was not found in settlements that sprang up and grew organically. The walls were painted in muted colors and the lighting was not the yellowish of old fashioned light bulbs that Luca had seen in Florence on the few occasions he had been there. Strips were lining the ceiling, creating an even, slightly blue tinted illumination that mimicked daylight well.

Luca filed the question in the back of his head because now they were among people. Locals. A passerby glanced at Marco and nodded and completely ignored the guests. Another stared at them in surprise. A group of three stopped and pretended not to gawk, badly. Everybody was wearing synthetic materials as far as Luca could tell. The air smelled clean, but a little bit too dry and stale to be anything but heavily filtered and possibly recycled. And the people... They came in all ages and shapes and colors and genders. Sure, the gene pool was pretty diverse in Florence and Siena and the primitive settlements too, but they were all a bit more muddled than in the Shelter.

A tall, slim figure stepped up to them, and Luca almost whimpered. "Oh, you are beautiful," he breathed before he could clamp his mouth shut.

"Thank you, Luca Capello," the beauty replied courteously. Clearly nir hearing was in as good condition as the rest of nem. Ne was not beautiful in the way that Simon and Sia were. Ne was not endowed with traits to sexually attract humans, but ne was the first properly functioning, pristine condition sentient apart from Nanny and Alfredo that Luca had encountered in forever. Every other artificial had been damaged in some way, even Mender. This one was androgynous and sleek, not meant to be mistaken for a human being. Ne wore the same kind of clothes that Nanny had been given, and nir skin was almost translucent, a pale, smooth surface that made nem look like a mixture of an elf from a game like *EverMist Isles* and an outdated depiction of an alien.

The sentient inclined nir head to Nanny. "Welcome to the Shelter," ne said.

"Thank you," Nanny replied. "We are grateful for your willingness to help. I am Nanny, Caregiver Model 7114141."

"I am Superior," the sentient said.

"Is that your model name?" Luca asked, fingers twitching to touch that wonderful piece of machinery.

The sentient fixed nir gaze on him. Oh, those perfect, inhuman eyes, taking in so much more than normal sight. "I am Superior," ne said again.

"Okay," Luca said, frowning. An artificial who did not willingly list nir full model name and serial number and also did not have a nickname? That was a first. Mender was a spin on the Minder model's name, Alfredo was a geeky in-joke in the Capello household, and Nanny was named by Leo and Luca when they were small. Mom was mom, dad was dad, and the nanny was Nanny.

"Please come with me," the sentient said and turned.

"Superior?" Marco chirped up.

"You will accompany us," came the answer. The sentient was already gliding down the hallway.

Luca pursed his lips and blew out air, barely managing not to whistle. He shot Renn a glance to see how the nomad was taking being only the second most desirable person around for once. But Renn, of course, was as unimpressed with the sentient as he was with everything else. His eyes were roaming the place, probably mapping it or mourning the fact that he could not feel the wind on his face down here.

Luca wanted to tell him that this was how the world ought to look. Well, maybe not the whole underground thing, but functioning sentients, working electricity, technology discreetly peering out, from the touch panels next to doors to the tablet in someone's hand as they hurried past.

Another artificial passed them. This one was wearing different colors, but otherwise, ne was almost identical to the one leading them. Ne threw them all a cursory glance, then cocked nir head a little at the sight of Nanny before continuing on nir way.

Their destination was a lab. Not the kind from the title of Luca's vlog, but medical, biological kind. It looked a lot like a hospital from the good old, futuristic days. Although Luca was clueless when it came to operating any of the equipment, he knew a microscope when he saw one. And those machines for speeding up the culture of samples and a centrifugal contraption for vials. There was just one chair here, white and sterile-looking like everything else in the room apart from a few chrome or steel surfaces.

"Will this do, Superior?" the Shelter artificial asked Nanny.

"Yes," she replied. "Thank you."

"Doesn't it get annoying?" Luca asked. "That you're all just called Superior. Like, if someone calls for you and there are more than one Superior present?"

The Superior only regarded him coolly. "No," ne said.

Well, damn. They had not been programmed with particularly good manners or a sense of humor. Luca refrained from saying that since it might be considered in poor taste.

"Please use whatever equipment and materials you need," the Superior told Nanny.

"Thank you. We all appreciate it very much," she replied graciously and warmly. See, that's what a sentient should sound like. Otherwise they may as well be semis or demis.

"You appear to lack a communication link," ne continued. "If you need assistance, please ask. The communication device in this room is voice activated. I will be alerted by the Superior in communications."

Communication link? Luca wasn't exactly a stranger to the technology. A lot of artificials used to have something similar back in his day, but most civilian sentients did not get instant, wireless data transfer or communication links installed as a default. They had to rely on the same means as humans after the augmentation disaster in 2130-something.

"Renn," the Superior addressed the nomad. "Your presence is requested to confirm the geographical changes we have mapped and any other information you can offer."

"Of course. I will do my best," Renn said.

Or, they could get their asses out of the Shelter and take a look for themselves, Luca thought, but kept from saying it. He had been the one to offer Renn as a bargaining chip, after all.

"Take him to the surface research department," the artificial told Marco. Luca was starting to think Superior was not just their name, but also their view of themselves. No *please* or *thanks* or polite smiles here.

"As for you, Luca Capello," the artificial continued, "I will escort you to my peers who will take the equipment you have brought." Again no indication of gratitude. But maybe this Superior had a superiorly shitty day.

"That okay with you?" Luca asked Renn. Nanny would be fine on her own. She had the software to do the job and appeared to be perfectly at ease with the artificials here. But Renn was a fucking fish climbing a tree. Luca tried to make a similar metaphor involving wanderers and underground, but couldn't come up with anything catchy.

"Yes," Renn replied. And then he added. "I will bring my staff although the terrain here appears to render it unnecessary. And I am sure Marco will explain to me what I need to know. I'm certain you will be fine as well as long as you listen to what the revered Superiors tell you." His dark eyes were serious and imploring.

"Yeah," Luca said, slowly, trying to decipher what the hell Renn meant. He had a sudden sinking feeling in his stomach, partly because whatever Renn was getting at, there was some sinister implications, and partly because it seemed that for once, something was eluding Luca of all people and he did not like not being on top of things. But, he rationalized, what did Renn really know? He was probably freaked out by the artificials because they were different from Mender.

Luca nodded, deciding that must be it. He picked up the bag of equipment they had brought. The artificial did not offer to carry it for him. "Okay. Let's get to it, then," he said. Beaming up at the artificial, he added, "Please lead the way, Superior."

The sentient made a measured gesture toward the door, and Luca saluted Renn, Marco and Nanny before following nem.

"So," he said as the door slid close and the artificial began to make nir way down the corridor. "Were you here from the beginning when the Shelter was made?"

"Yes," the artificial replied.

"Awesome. Me too, actually," Luca added. "It's rare I get to hang out with anyone around my own age. I don't think I'm familiar with your particular model, though."

At this, the sentient turned nir head to gaze at him. "No," ne said. "I think you are not. Your Superior seems very different from us."

"Well, I know other kinds," Luca argued. "Anyway, Marco said something about the power source of this whole place being underground too. I practically only use solar power. My arti— Superiors too."

"Everything here is powered by the Heart. That includes the Superiors."

"The Heart. I'm going to take it that's not some kind of magical item. It's a nuclear reactor, isn't it?"

"Yes," the artificial said.

"Thought so. But I have a million questions," Luca continued. "Like, what do you do with the waste? How long will it power this place for? And what about safety? I mean, with earthquakes and everything..."

"I assure you, our reactor was constructed with the most advanced and safe technology. There is no danger."

"Just out of curiosity, though," Luca persisted, although he was admittedly thinking more about his own ass than the Shelter, "if something completely unlikely happened and you had a meltdown, how far would the radiation spread?"

"It would not likely reach the ground," the Superior said. "You need not worry about your own home."

Luca opened his mouth, but he couldn't deny that was exactly what he had been thinking. "Great," he said. "I'm still curious about the waste disposal, though."

"Do you always make demands of your Superiors?" the artificial asked, so smoothly that it was easy to miss the note of irritation.

"You ain't seen nothing yet," Luca replied, grinning. "Just wait til we start talking robotics and AI."

31:

Renn

The Shelter was even more alien than Florence. Living underground, confined inside walls, including ceilings and floors that defined the inhabitants' very world... It was off-putting, but Renn did not see any signs that the people here felt the oppression of the Shelter like he did. Perhaps because they had never known anything else. But some of them had, Renn reminded himself. His guide, Marco, was used to going outside.

"We are going up two floors," Marco was saying. "But we'll take another elevator."

Renn nodded. It made sense that there were more of those. Perhaps the ability to traverse the ceilings and floors made them feel less trapped.

"Do you not run out of air this far down?" Renn wondered.

"No, we have great ventilation systems," Marco said. "And the gardens provide us with a lot of air."

"Gardens?" Renn echoed. He knew the term, but plants needed sunlight and soil to grow.

Marco chewed his lip for a moment as if he were trying to make up his mind about something. "Do you want to see?" he then asked.

"If it is no trouble," Renn replied. Marco did not make him feel the least uneasy. But the Superiors put him on edge. There was no doubt the Shelter and its technology were what Luca had searched for ever since he emerged from his hibernation. No settlement on the surface rivaled this place. It was an inverted version of what Renn imagined the towering ruins above must once have looked like.

"It's on the way to the surface research department. The Superiors won't mind if I show you," Marco explained.

And that, Renn thought, was a perfect example of why he felt uneasy. His experience with sentients was limited, but according to Mender as well as Luca's testimony, artificials were servants of mankind. They were highly independent and very intelligent, but they were somehow subordinate to humans because humans had created them. Whether this was how it ought to be, Renn was not certain, but it was an issue of a time far gone. In the present, the Sienans treated Mender as an equal, and Luca acted almost as if Alfredo and Nanny were his parents.

But in the Shelter, the sentients were regarded not as inferiors or equals, but as Superiors indeed. For Renn himself, this was not a big problem. He was only here to help Siena. His concern was Luca. He was so eager for this place to be like his lost past that he ignored the differences. If he strayed too far from the norms here, there was no telling what consequences it may have. Renn had tried to warn him, but with Luca, he never knew if his warnings were heeded or willfully trampled and ignored.

Marco showed Renn to another elevator. Renn clenched the muscles in his abdomen as the masheen shot upwards. He had quickly discovered how unpleasant the vertical movement was on the way down. Instead of going up the two promised floors, they only went up one. Renn was about to ask when the doors slid open. Moist, warm air welcomed them, and there was the unmistakable smell of soil and decaying leaves. It was like stepping into an oasis.

Another hallway stretched out ahead of them, but unlike the level below, this one only had a few doors, and large sections of the walls were transparent.

"This way," Marco said.

Renn followed his guide through transparent panes that slid apart when Marco touched a rectangular panel at one of the seams. Renn gasped. The humidity of the warm air and the smell overwhelmed his senses. The staff was dead wood in his hand, comfortable and familiar, carefully taken from the sparse vegetation above. But here was nothing but damp greenery.

The panes closed behind them.

"Surprised?" Marco asked.

Renn nodded. They were standing on a hard floor that stretched out ahead of them like a well-trampled path. Two people could walk abreast, but not more. To either side were long containers with an abundance of plants spilling over their sides and rising halfway to the high ceiling where— Renn winced and looked down again, dark spots dancing before his eyes. It was too bright. Like the high sun of a cloudless noon. Once his vision cleared, he attempted to take in the surroundings again.

A woman with dark stains on the knees of her trousers and a set of large shears passed ahead of them, and Renn realized there were paths crisscrossing the one they were on. How big was this room? Big enough that the room felt like a wholly inadequate word.

"This is one of the gardens. I am not a gardener, so I don't know a lot about what goes on here. But as you can see, the plants are growing in these tanks. They provide breathable air and most of our food supply," Marco said.

Renn took a step forward. "May I?" he asked, gesturing at the nearest plant.

"Touch it? I don't see why not," Marco replied, smiling.

Renn leaned closer and stroked a leaf. Then grew bolder and closed his hand around the end of one light green twig, careful as not to crush the miracle he was holding. Peering into the tank, as Marco called the container, Renn saw dark water and what appeared to be a system of tubes or wires running all along the tank. He let go of the plant again. "I have never seen anything like this," he said. Thinking of the struggling greenhouses the Sienans constructed, the dusty vegetation and the clumps of trees around lakes he was used to seeing, this place was a wonder.

The woman in the soil stained clothes crossed the path again. This time, she was going slower, stooping to assess certain plants on the way.

"Thank you for showing me," Renn said, smiling at Marco. It occurred to him that he had plunged into the fantasy of this place almost to the same degree as Luca, forgetting for a moment to be alert. But perhaps he was too suspicious. After all, the Shelter had allowed them to come, had promised to help them in exchange for only a few pieces of masheenery that Luca could easily spare and Renn's knowledge. Maybe... Just maybe this visit could be the beginning of something else.

Renn wiped a frown from his face before it could manifest too clearly. He was beginning to think like Teo. She always sought ways to trade with other settlements, negotiated everything at assemblies, thought of ways that her people could flourish and grow. Renn felt a little of that weight now. He might be a wanderer, but right now, he was also an emissary from Siena. He was responsible for the impression they made here as much as Luca and Nanny.

"You're welcome," Marco said. "I should probably get you to the surface research department now."

Once they were back in the corridor, Marco continued, "They say the surface once was green."

Renn nodded. "Yes."

"But now it is all dead," Marco continued, sending Renn an inquiring look.

"It's not dead," Renn replied. Though people around him kept saying so. It was a constant refrain from Luca and the Sienans. Only

Renn and Esmia were wanderers and had been born into the world as it was now. Esmia... The thought of her brought him back to the task at hand.

"No, you have seen a lot of it. I mean, more than anyone here," Marco went on.

"I have. But while there is plenty of life, it is not as green as that," Renn replied, indicating the panes on each side of them.

"The Superiors say it is not fit for human habitation out there," Marco said, placing his hand on a panel next to the elevator door.

An arrow lit up, signifying, Renn surmised, that the contraption was on its way down to them. He felt he had to contradict that statement, but whenever the Superiors were involved, he felt unsure how much it was safe for him to say. "Yet," he settled on, "there are humans on the surface. Wanderers and stagnants alike. And Luca."

If Marco was offended, he didn't show it. The elevator arrived and they went inside, Marco studying Renn. "He is not like you at all, is he?"

"No," Renn said, a little too quickly perhaps. "I am a wanderer. He is... Luca has a lot of masheens like you."

"And he has Superiors looking after him," Marco said as they exited the elevator once more. This floor was bustling with so much activity that it took most of Renn's attention to keep an eye on every person passing them, coming out of doors and turning around corners. There was one group in particular who caught his eye; a family, he assumed, of two adult women holding hands and two small children playfully circling them. "I... can't imagine what it must be like not to have them."

Renn's focus snapped back to Marco. This was an opening to ask more questions. "And I can't imagine what it must be like to have them."

"Do wanderers not have Superiors at all?" Marco asked.

"No."

"So there is no one to guide you," Marco concluded, his face going through expressions of worry and a little bit of wistfulness. "No one to help you or tell you what to do."

"We rely on ourselves and our own abilities," Renn offered. "I do, however, know one Superior," he added, reluctantly slipping into the vernacular of the Shelter. "Ne saved my life once, and I consider nem a friend."

Marco's eyebrows rose almost to his hairline. "Friend?" he echoed.

"Yes," Renn insisted. "We traveled together for a while and got to know each other quite well."

"I didn't know one could be friends with Superiors," Marco murmured, his gaze darting to the ceiling and back at Renn. "Is Luca friends with his Superiors as well?" The question was simple, but it was asked too carefully.

"Luca used to work with Superiors. I think perhaps what he did is close to your job as maintainers. He cares for Superiors if they break. I have seen him do this."

As reassuring as this explanation was intended to be, Marco looked crestfallen. "But Superiors don't break. They can't die."

Renn cleared his throat. Trying not to overstep some invisible boundaries of the Shelter's taboos was proving more difficult than expected. "But sometimes they need maintenance," he said. "The Superior who is my friend was injured in a scarvhe attack and needed help."

"What is a scarvhe attack?" Marco asked.

"Scarvhes are predators," Renn said. "They are very dangerous. They are like big snakes, but they fly and carry their skeleton on the outside."

"Oh, a wyvern!" Marco said. "I have seen pictures of them. The Superiors say they evolved from reptiles created to eat insects."

It was Renn's turn to be surprised. "They eat more than insects," he said. "They attack humans if they get the chance. Sometimes they lie in wait for days and when a small Covey goes by, they strike. They are quite clever. They take children and weakened people because they are easiest, but they can kill healthy adults too. They wounded my Superior friend quite seriously."

"Oh." Marco bit his lip. "The surface really is dangerous. Well, things like that never happen to our Superiors. And they care for us. Not the other way around," Marco said, satisfied.

32:

Teo

The urge to run away had reared its ugly head after Nevio's death, and Teo had managed, barely, to suppress it. She had told herself she needed to be strong. She needed to be what everybody else thought she should be. But she had felt its breath on the back of her neck for longer than that. Just once in a while. Lately, though, it was never far away.

Teo left the infirmary. She was not running. Only walking briskly, half wondering where her feet were taking her. But only half.

The building adjacent to Tonino's home had become a storage space over the months. It was here they piled up useful objects found on the so-called booze runs and stored anything the Sienans produced for future use.

There was no one inside when Teo entered. She went through to the back room, found a crate and reached into it. Refusing to ponder her own actions, she pulled out the first object she found.

She avoided the main street on her way through the settlement. The only person she met only greeted her in a friendly tone, and Teo hoped her own grimace resembled a smile.

And then everything was behind her. The inhabited houses, the even streets, the eyes and the voices that would plead her for comfort and answers. The dead man in the infirmary, the grave outside the wall,

Arsenio, Gabriele, Mender, Esmia, everybody. For a while, she kept walking through broken pieces of lives lived centuries ago. When finally she stopped between the crumpled buildings and sat down on a corroded length of rebar the circumference of a human thigh, everything was so silent that the noise of the cork popping out of the bottleneck felt alien.

Teo brought the bottle to her lips. Red wine, by the taste of it. Old with a dusty, bitter aftertaste. There was a cruel irony to sitting alone with her father's favored drink. That she was clutching the neck of the bottle and gulping down the contents that would be poured for her in a brightly lit dining room by a servant while the elite of Florence were basking in their own leadership in another life.

"I can't do this," Teo said. Her voice was small and weak, exactly the way she felt. Everybody thought she could. Everybody asked her for advice and counted on her to fix things all the time. But she couldn't fix this. She was as helpless as everybody else, just waiting for Renn and Luca to return.

Maybe she should not have left Florence in the first place. Maybe she should not have gone outside with Arsenio and Vanni. If she hadn't, maybe Vanni would still be alive.

A sob burst out of her. It was followed by more that shook her so thoroughly she could hardly keep hold of the bottle. She kept telling herself she wasn't the Sienans' leader, but who was she kidding? Everybody thought she was. She thought so too, didn't she? But Teodora Terzi was not cut out for this. What the hell had she thought would happen? She couldn't save Vanni. Or Patrizia. Or Nevio. Or Tonino. Or the next person to die, or the one after that. She was only pretending to be something she had never even wanted to be.

She took a long swig of the wine, savoring its bitter, burning passage from her mouth and down her throat. Siena was supposed to be a good place. A refuge. Was Luca right that there was no such thing as a perfect society? That there would be crimes and tragedies no matter what she did? Or was it simply that she didn't do her job well enough?

The sharp edges of her emotions began to blur a little and she sat staring at nothing, feeling blissfully numb. She was not sure how much time passed. Minutes? Hours? After a while, she began to wonder what to do next. Go back to the settlement? Pretend to be that competent leader? She didn't want to deal with everybody's demands. Besides, it didn't matter when she did such a bad job anyway.

Teo stood up. The world swayed. Maybe she should just go. But where? She couldn't run back to Florence. That wasn't what she wanted. She had lost sight of what she did want. She took an experimental step forward, hoping her feet would know where to take her. But they didn't. They faltered after only a couple of steps.

She stood in the middle of what might once have been a busy street, surrounded by husks of buildings and the ghosts of the past. Siena's and the world's, which she could handle, and her own, which she could not.

"What the hell am I supposed to do?" she shouted. Before she could question the action, she pulled back her arm and flung the bottle as hard as she could. The remaining wine went flying in a red arc, and the bottle struck the ground and smashed into tiny pieces.

"Teo?"

She blinked.

"Teo?"

Her first impulse was to hide. But no. "I'm tired of hiding," she mumbled.

Coughing somewhere behind her. Then the voice again. "Teo!"

She turned. Arsenio.

"What are you doing here?" she asked. Her voice sounded drunk.

"Looking for you!" he replied, breathing hard. "Why the hell didn't you reply?" His forehead was creased in a frown, and his hair and forehead were slick with sweat.

"Why should I?" she said.

"What is going on?" he asked, reaching out for her. When she twisted out of his grasp, he stumbled. "Are you drunk? Nobody knew where you went! People need you—" More coughing.

"Maybe they are better off without me!" she retorted. "I can't do anything right. I'm not a sentient who can just carry on like nothing is wrong! It would be easier if I were, but I am not." Arsenio gaped at her. And it occurred to her that this side of her was new even to him. He had seen her frustration, sure. Even her fear. But not this. "Tonino is dead. Did you know that? I couldn't save him! I never wanted—"

"Stop!" Arsenio shouted. And coughed again. He spat on the ground and wiped his mouth. His lips were stained with blood.

"You should be in bed," Teo said.

"I was. But then they told me Tonino died, and you were gone," he replied. "We needed you. I needed you. And here you are—"

Teo held up a hand to stop him. "Everybody expects me to take charge and be responsible, but I can't do this!" she shouted. "I can't go on like this!"

"So instead you just run away and wallow in self-pity?" Arsenio asked. "Is that it?"

"I'm not wallowing—" her voice broke.

"Nobody expects you to be perfect," Arsenio said, so quietly that the rasping of his breath was painfully clear. "Responsible, yes, for yourself, but not for everyone else. We all do our best with what we have. You can't carry this whole settlement alone. Stop trying."

Teo didn't know what to reply.

"Tonino was my friend," Arsenio added.

Something inside Teo twisted. She had been so preoccupied with feeling she should be able to save everyone that she had lost sight of this one human thing. Arsenio had lost Vanni just like she had. He had lost Patrizia. And now he had lost Tonino too. They had been friends, known each other for years and fought for a better Florence together. "I'm sorry," she whispered, feeling like a deflated balloon. "I'm so sorry for your loss." She took a step forward and pulled him into an embrace.

Arsenio was trembling, from his fever or from crying, or both. Teo held him tight. This was a thing she could do, she realized. And maybe it was really all that was expected of her. Not fixing every problem that arose. Just being there, doing her best.

33:

Luca

If he were the sentimental type, Luca might have sobbed a little over the beauty of the Shelter. He might have hugged the closest person, artificial or human, and bawled, "Finally! You're my kind of people! I've been looking for you for almost three years!" He wasn't that type. Instead, his face threatened to grow a huge grin that he only barely managed to turn into a confident smirk.

He felt slightly like a creep for hanging back a moment to look at the sentient from behind, but it wasn't like he was checking out nir ass or anything. He was simply appreciating the beautiful, sleek figure. The ease with which ne moved, the silence and seamlessness of it all. Unlike Nanny and Alfredo and Mender, this gorgeous piece of machinery was not made to look human. Humanoid, sure, but not human. Which was kind of an interesting turn in artificial history, Luca thought. To begin with, it had been all about making them as human as possible. That was the way to make humans think of them as sentient people and not as mindless robots. Some even had a small bit of software that made them randomize unnecessary movements like scratching their cheek, rolling their shoulders or shuffling their feet. That the artificials here did not strive to look and behave as much like humans as possible struck Luca as an evolutionary step. Probably they were designed somewhen in the period after the Capello family went to sleep and before the world as a whole went down the drain. Probably they had already been under development in the latter days before the Moon exploded.

Luca wanted to write a fucking dissertation on the subject. He wanted to do field studies on human reactions to the different types of sentients. He wanted to be back at IRAI. But the institute was gone, and although he didn't have exams and a graduation ceremony to look back on, his work in the past few years made him the world's leading expert on robotics and AI. Or one of them. There had to be engineers in the Shelter too.

The sentient stopped for a moment. "Luca Capello," ne said, "staring at a Superior is not polite."

He snorted in a charmless attempt at not laughing. "I'm sorry," he said. "I'm sorry, but what was your original purpose?"

"This," the artificial said levelly.

"Walking strangers to a place where they can dump the equipment they brought upon request as a trade for medication against a virus in a nearby settlement?" He couldn't resist. Just to see the reaction.

"You are being deliberately obstinate. Stop it."

Shit, he wanted to see what was under nir hood so bad he was practically getting a hard-on. Wanted to plug nem into his laptop to study nir software as well. "Sorry," he said.

They had gone down another couple of floors by elevator, and there was almost no one else here. Luca only saw one person in the same grey outfit with silver decorations that Marco wore and glimpsed one sentient crossing their path far ahead.

The sentient came to a halt outside a door, and it opened to nem. Luca had noticed Marco had to put his hand on a touch panel, but the sentients just stepped up to the doors to make them open. Interesting design choice to let the motion sensors react to sentients and not humans. Or maybe it wasn't that at all. They could be broadcasting a signal—

210

Luca cut his own thought stream off. They stepped into a particularly gorgeous part of this utopia. This time he couldn't hold back a low whistle. They were in a big, spacious hall that Luca hadn't imagined would fit in here. It was partitioned by transparent plass walls, effectively creating a kind of office cubicle environment. People sat at desks in each room, all of them human, Luca was pretty sure. One was wearing a headset and was sitting at a device that looked a lot like some kind of radio relay.

"Is that..?" he asked, making a gesture.

"Yes, that is one of the monitoring stations," the sentient told him. Ne didn't slow down, so Luca had to hurry along, past the people at work at their respective desks. He wanted to see what they were doing. A few of them were looking at screens, and he managed to see that one of them showed the area outside the Shelter as seen from the entrance.

The sentient led him to an area beyond the cubicles. It was a storage room. The transparent walls were lined with shelving units, and there were all sorts of tech here. Luca shook his head at himself for thinking of it collectively as tech. That was such a Teo term. Next he'd be going on about masheens. He had a brief pang of worry at that thought, but Renn would be fine. Marco was a good kid. He'd take care of the nomad. And Renn was more than capable of giving the researchers an account of the world above.

"Giuliano Ahn," the sentient said to the occupant of the room whom, admittedly, Luca had given no thought until now.

"Superior," the man said with a polite nod and a sidelong glance at Luca.

Giuliano was, Luca estimated, somewhere in his mid thirties. He was around Renn's height, but leaner and of a different ethnicity. He was wearing a maintainer uniform and was holding a tablet of anonymous design.

"This is Luca Capello," the sentient said in a blunt and not very fancy introduction. "He is here to deposit spare parts for us. Assist him. I will be back presently."

"Yes, Superior," Giuliano replied deferentially. "You are one of the people whose radio signal we picked up," he added as the door closed behind the sentient.

"No," Luca corrected him, "I am the person who built a radio and picked up your frequency."

Giuliano raised one eyebrow. "All right," he said. "Let's see what you have."

Their eyes locked for a moment. Despite looking older, he reminded Luca of a rival at IRAI who competed with Luca for top marks at every given moment. If the world hadn't ended, Luca was pretty sure they'd have ended up fucking. "How about I show you mine if you show me yours?" Luca suggested.

"I was under the impression all of that already is ours," Giuliano replied, not missing a beat. He gestured at Luca's pack.

"All right. But I am dying to learn more about this place. Your artificials aren't exactly forthcoming with information," Luca explained as he began to unload the contents of his pack onto a black plass table in the middle of the room. "Are you in charge of this place? I mean this department or whatever?"

Giuliano picked up a battery from the table and inspected it. "I'm just a maintainer," he replied.

"Like Marco," Luca said. "So what does that mean? You keep things going, but you don't design or build new stuff?"

"I suppose you could say that," Giuliano admitted.

"Area of expertise?"

"This," Giuliano said, making a sweeping motion to encompass everything in the room. "Mostly computers. I don't go outside like Marco."

"Would you like to?" Luca asked.

There was a small pause. "No," Giuliano then said. "No one wants to go out. Marco and his team only do it out of necessity."

"I don't know about that," Luca replied. "I have a friend who's all about that outdoorsy life. And except for the fucked up weather sometimes, I'm pretty hooked on it myself too." He could feel the maintainer studying him carefully as he continued to extract items and put them in a neat row on the table. "I'm thinking we could give you some advice. Help you get a foothold upstairs, if you know what I mean."

"I'm afraid I don't," Giuliano said.

Luca was pretty sure he did. "I'm saying," he tried, "that this doesn't have to be a one-off thing. Now that we are aware of each other's existence, we can benefit mutually from the contact. We can trade. Learn from each other. That sort of thing."

"That is not up to me," the maintainer said levelly.

"Well then, take me to your leader," Luca deadpanned.

"Ne will summon you if ne wants to see you."

It was Luca's turn to raise an eyebrow, and not only because Giuliano completely missed the joke. Ne? He was cool with the non-binary talk, of course, but in Luca's time, that pronoun was only used for advanced artificials. Humans would be ze or they. Maybe that had changed? "I wish they would do that, then," he said. "Do they have a name or a title or something?"

"The Supreme. But you are likely only to talk to nir agents. The Superiors," Giuliano clarified.

"I see," Luca said, not seeing at all. The Supreme acting through artificials made it sound like whoever it was was a sentient too. But that made no sense. "About that. Does your maintaining include Superiors?"

Giuliano cleared his throat. "Of course not. If they have needs, they take care of them themselves."

"Do they, now?" Luca asked. "Artificials repairing artificials, then." Not that there was anything wrong with it, necessarily. Of course an artificial could perform much of the same labor as a human, but there was always human quality control somewhere along the line. "So your sentients, sorry, Superiors, are basically equals to humans, yeah?"

Giuliano physically took a step back from him at that. He looked startled. "No!" he said. There was something off about the whole thing.

213

As if it were scripted. But Luca didn't have a copy of the manuscript. "What gave you that idea?" he asked, then quickly added, "I'm curious, Luca. What exactly do you do with your Superiors?"

"Um," Luca said, "does that include semis as well as sentients?"

"I'm unfamiliar with those terms."

"Okay. Where I'm from... Or when I'm from, we called all robots, excuse the term, with some degree of autonomy artificials. Sentients are the most advanced ones. Semis are pretty advanced too, but you can turn them off when you don't need them." That was simplified, but he wasn't sure how much technobabble he could get away with.

"Turn them off," Giuliano echoed.

"You can turn off sentients as well, but only if you need to do repairs."

"And you have done that?" Giuliano asked.

"Yeah," Luca said, shrugging. "All the time. I've salvaged a few sentients out there. Had to shut them down and reprogram them before they could be of any use."

"Reprogram?" Giuliano said. He sounded kind of impressed.

"Yeah, sure," Luca said. He was on a roll now. This was good. Sharing knowledge, building a relationship with someone in the Shelter. "That's kind of my thing. I studied robotics and artificial intelligence back in the day. Before the Moon was destroyed and all that. So I can remove parts of their personalities or change their objectives. Stuff like that."

A shadow of something Luca couldn't place crossed Giuliano's face. It didn't quite look like admiration. "And how many are there now? Like you? Does everybody in Siena know how to do that sort of thing?"

"Oh, as far as I know, I'm the only one left," Luca said. "The only one who knows how to deal with artificials."

And then all hell broke loose.

The door opened and Luca saw Giuliano take another step backward. Away from Luca and away from the door. As he spun around, two artificials entered. One was probably the one who had taken him here in

214

the first place. The other wore identical clothing, but with red stripes instead of silver. Instantly, Luca knew we was in trouble. He did not know why and he did not know how exactly he knew unless it was some reptilian brain sort of crap kicking in, but he knew. The sentients had it in for him. Instantly, Luca found himself looking for a weapon and some sort of leverage. He snatched up a screwdriver and before he even knew what the hell he was doing, he was standing next to Giuliano, an arm around his neck and the point of the screwdriver resting at his jugular.

"One wrong move and I will fucking kill him!" Luca shouted.

Giuliano made a strangled noise.

Luca wanted to apologize to him for this, but now was not the time. He'd send him a box of chocolate or something later.

The two sentients stood motionless in front of them. They didn't do anything. Just stood there. But they had come to attack him, right?

Luca's brain did a quick replay of the whole time he'd been in the Shelter, connecting hints and events and even Renn's cryptic monologue. Shit, Renn knew. He'd tried to warn Luca. For fuck's sake. But now was not the time to kick himself for not seeing it coming. Right now, damage control was vital.

"Release him," one of the sentients said as if ne was used to being unquestioningly obeyed which, Luca admitted, ne probably was.

"Now, this is what is going to happen," Luca growled, hoping he sounded more imposing than he felt. How fast were these sentients? What kind of weaponry were they equipped with? If he was lucky, maybe they weren't armed at all and only relied on everybody doing what they wanted. "You guys are going to back off, and I'm taking Giuliano with me. I'm not going to harm him if you let me go."

"And where do you want to go?" asked the other sentient, the one who had brought Luca here. Nir voice sounded almost amused.

Luca scowled. He had a sudden flashback to that time when he was twelve and his dearly departed older brother Leo and he had kept one-upping each other with stupid dares. One would think Luca had learned something about quitting while ahead from almost falling off the school's roof, but the point had always been to get better at whatever he set out to do, not back down from it. "I'm going to pick up Nanny and Renn, and we are leaving with the cure, and everybody walks away from this unharmed."

Giuliano made another noise. For a moment, Luca thought it was a scared whimper or a sob, but the man was laughing.

"Shut the fuck up!" Luca told him.

"I'm sorry, but do you actually think this is going to work?" his hostage asked.

Luca tightened his grip. Truth be told, he didn't. There were a million ways this could go wrong, starting with them taking Renn and Nanny as hostages which would leave Luca short one hostage to exchange. But he didn't have a choice but to try now. "Are you actively trying to commit suicide?" he hissed at Giuliano.

"Are you?" Giuliano returned with the level of sass that ought to be reserved only for Luca himself and possibly, on rare occasions, Teo.

For the first time since picking up the screwdriver, Luca wanted to use it. He didn't, though, because he was the good guy here. "We're going now!" he told the sentients. "Move aside."

They moved.

Luca barely had time to react before they were on each side of him. He stepped backward, keeping his hold on Giuliano, effectively using him as a human shield which wasn't playing by the good guy rules, but what choice did he have? He didn't stab his hostage's neck, partly because he didn't want to, and partly because he wouldn't have any leverage if he did. Instead he brandished the screwdriver like a puny, little sword.

The red sentient was fast. And strong. Ne clasped nir fingers around Luca's wrist and twisted, and while Luca's attention was momentarily on the bright pain in his arm, Giuliano managed to wrestle himself out of Luca's grasp.

Luca screamed and kicked at the artificial, but although his foot connected, it had little effect. The screwdriver clattered to the floor, and the artificial twisted his arm, forcing him toward the black table in a manner that suggested ne was programmed for this exact thing. The side of Luca's face hit the cool, smooth surface of the table and its contents spilled noisily to the floor. Luca was mentally screaming at himself to keep fighting even as he tasted blood.

Then something sharp pricked the back if his neck, a mockery of the threat he made moments ago. But it was not the screwdriver.

The sentient let go of him and stepped back.

Luca grabbed hold of the edge of the table, pushed himself up and turned to face them again. Someone outside the storage room must have seen this and would alarm the authorities. Right? His wrist and his face hurt, but that was the least of his worries.

"Now you come with us," the silver sentient said.

"What did you do?" Luca asked, running his fingers over the back of his neck. If there was something there, his hand didn't have the sensitivity to discern it. But then he felt it. The room looked like someone had poured half a bottle of vodka down his throat. One of the sentients said something, but it was woolly babbling to Luca's ears. He stumbled forward, and someone caught his arm.

He had a vague sense that someone was holding him up. That his feet were moving. They were taking him somewhere. He wanted to protest, to call for help, but he wasn't sure if he he managed to get anything coherent out.

34:

Esmia

She tried not to think she might have been able to save him. She tried not to blame herself for not being there when it happened, and she tried not to blame Teo for making her sleep. Esmia knew Mender was second only to Gabriele when it came to medical knowledge, and ne had done everything in nir power.

The body was laid out on the table in front of her, still and white and already with the blotches of the dead. The man— No, Tonino, that was his name, was already rigid with the loss of his spirit.

Esmia had other patients to see, but she could not rush this. She had already undressed the body and put his clothes aside. Singing softly, she soaked a cloth in a bucket of water and began to work. The stench of death had to be cleaned away.

A knock on the door stopped her singing as she called out a confirmation.

"May I come in?" Clara asked as she opened the door.

Esmia nodded and returned to her work.

"I brought clothes," Clara explained as she slipped inside and stood behind Esmia.

Esmia frowned. She was wearing a sleeveless tunic, perfectly suitable for the task before her.

"They are plain and nice. Obviously, very few of us have family here, and we haven't discussed these matters, but I think he— I think he would agree they are suitable."

"For being buried in?" Esmia asked. The idea was strange. Usually people were buried in what they wore when they died, stripped of any valuable or useful objects.

"Yes." Clara stepped up beside her. Breath caught in her throat. She reached out and placed a hand on the cold, dead flesh, then withdrew it quickly as if she had needed to confirm that he really was dead.

"Did you know him well?" Esmia asked, not knowing what else to say and rather wanting not to speak at all.

"In a way. I met him four years ago. We joined the movement in Florence at practically the same time." Clara breathed deeply. "It's funny, really. We never saw each other privately while we lived in Florence. I think he and Arsenio did, but I hardly know anything about Tonino's life before we came here. And yet, he's one of the people I've known the longest."

Esmia did not find that funny at all. She nodded and continued her work, carefully and methodically.

"I'm sorry, I didn't mean to interrupt your work," Clara said. "I— We all appreciate this. What you do."

"I do what I can," Esmia mumbled. She wasn't used to being appreciated. It was a nice change, but not one she knew how to handle. Especially not since she was technically the cause of Tonino's death. It made it hard to appreciate being appreciated.

"Can I stay for a while?" Clara asked.

"Yes," Esmia agreed. She kept silent for a moment, but Clara did not say anything else. She just stood there, quiet and with her hands clasped tight in front of her chest. So Esmia resumed singing. Her voice wasn't fit for entertaining, but she wasn't entertaining. She was addressing Moon, asking her to guide Tonino's spirit so it would find peace with her.

"Thank you," Clara whispered when Esmia's song ended. "That was beautiful."

Esmia looked over her shoulder. Clara's eyes were brimming with tears. Esmia smiled and bent down to dip the cloth in the bucket. She concentrated more than necessary on wringing it just right.

"I'm sorry," Clara said when Esmia's job was almost done. "I came here for another reason too. Tonino was a Christian."

Esmia blinked. "I don't know what that means," she admitted.

Clara smiled and shook her head. "It's the most common faith in Florence. And I was elected to take care of rituals and such in Siena. So I've been doing that. You know the church with the cross on the roof?"

"Yes," Esmia replied.

"We meet there to pray. To baptize babies. Eventually I will probably get to marry couples too." Clara sighed. "I am also the one who needs to take care of the rituals when a person dies. So I— I also came to see what you..." she trailed off, flustered.

"Am I doing wrong by your ways?" Esmia asked. Stagnants had traditions and beliefs that were different from wanderers. And even wanderers had their differences. Esmia had heard that somewhere to the North, Bevies and Coveys built pyres and burned their dead rather than burying them.

"No!" Clara exclaimed. "No," she repeated, more softly. "I think you are doing everything right, Esmia. What does your people think happens to the soul when a person dies?"

"The spirit?" Esmia asked.

"Yes, you can call it that. What is invisible inside a person and makes them that person."

"The spirits are meant to go to Moon," Esmia said. "We tell Moon to guide them. When they go, they are at peace." Some spirits, of course, lingered, maliciously or simply because they could not find peace. But there was no reason to bring that up.

Clara ran a hand through her short hair. It had the look of dry, yellow grass. "We believe the spirits go to Heaven," she offered. "And I

220

think… it sounds to me like being with Moon and being in Heaven are very similar." She faltered, stared at the ceiling for a moment as if conferring with the heavens beyond it. When she spoke again, her words were slow and deliberate as if she were tasting them for the first time. "I think it doesn't matter if we prefer to bury our dead in new clothes or not, or if we sing one hymn to them or another. I think Siena is young and we come from different worlds, and because of that, we can accept differences. We can even start to think differently now. I think we have to."

Esmia searched her face. She was not sure she understood the depth of Clara's realization, but she understood that it mattered to the other woman. And whatever it was, it included acceptance. "Everything is new here," she said.

"Yes," Clara agreed. "Everything is new here."

The burial itself was new too. Esmia had attended several before. Attended and partaken in, both by preparing the bodies, singing, digging the holes and shoveling earth into them. She had put stones on graves and asked Moon to guide the spirit of the departed. But the people in Siena were not wanderers, and their rituals were different. At first there was an observance in Clara's church as they called it. Clara and Teo both spoke, and Arsenio tried to as well, but his voice was a croak, and he was trembling with fever. Mender and Luca's two beautiful servants were not present. Neither were Gabriele or any of the patients Esmia needed to return to.

They went in a small procession from the church to the burial area outside the settlement. There was only one grave there already, the man who had taken his own life.

Someone Esmia didn't know was carrying Tonino's body, swathed in a white blanket. This was a breach of tradition, as far as Esmia understood, but Clara had decided they could do without a wooden box for the body. Esmia couldn't quite understand why they would want to waste wood on that, anyway.

Tonino was lowered into the ground. And they began to fill the grave with earth. It was a lot deeper than a shallow wanderer grave.

Clara was holding a cross. It was made of metal like the one on her church and the grave next to Tonino's. Esmia studied the people around her. Clara looked sad, but well. Arsenio was stricken, with grief and with fever. The man who had carried Tonino and a couple of others seemed well enough. Esmia couldn't quite make out if Teo's pallor was only due to grief and exhaustion.

No one spoke as the grave was finally filled and the long end of the cross plunged into the soil like a particularly dry and fruitless plant. Someone, probably Clara, had written Tonino's name on it.

"May Moon guide you," Esmia said as each person made some private statement of farewell.

They turned back to the settlement and began to walk. Teo wrapped her arm around Arsenio and he returned the gesture. Most of the others formed a group that quickly pulled ahead, talking in low voices amongst themselves.

Esmia longed to be back in the infirmary. Not because she liked the stench of vomit and blood or the sound of rattling breath and violent coughing, but there she had a purpose. Out here, what she had caused was staring her in the face.

Something touched her hand. Esmia looked up to see Clara beside her. The other woman tried to smile, but it came out as pathetic as Esmia's own grimace felt. Then Clara's hand slid into hers and squeezed it. Esmia wasn't sure of the significance, but there was comfort in the gesture. She tested it and held on tight, and Clara's smile began to resemble a real smile. Esmia hadn't held anyone's hand since she had comforted her father on his deathbed. She had no memory of anyone ever taking hers like this. But it felt good. She hoped Clara wouldn't let go before they reached the infirmary.

But they were only halfway when Esmia detected a faint sound that could be the wind picking up. It could be sand whirling, perhaps heralding a dust storm. Oh, please let it be a storm.

"What is it?" Clara asked.

Esmia realized she had stopped walking, and at the sound of Clara's question, everybody turned to her. "Be quiet!" Esmia said. And there was silence, almost too much of it. Except for that high pitched noise growing ever louder. And Esmia knew it was not the wind.

35:

Marco

"Mind if I join you?" Giuliano asked.

Marco jumped. He was so deep in thought he hadn't noticed anyone around him or tasted the food he was eating. He had been trying to make sense of a story one of his friends told him when he crossed paths with her on the way to the dining hall. A story that Giuliano himself starred in. "Go ahead," Marco said.

Giuliano pulled out a chair and sat. He deposited a cup of coffee on the table between them.

"Are you all right?" Marco asked.

Giuliano cocked his head. "Yes, I'm fine. Shouldn't I be?"

Marco leaned across the table. "I heard you were attacked," he said in a low voice. He had a feeling this wasn't public knowledge yet. His friend Sophia worked at one of the monitoring stations, and the incident had taken place right in front of her.

"Oh." Giuliano touched his neck, then let his hand drop to the cup again. "I... was a little shaken, yes," he said, although he did not look it at all. "What else did you hear?" he asked.

"Not much." Marco shrugged. "Just that Luca was delivering the equipment to you and—" He faltered. Sophia had said that she saw the Superior leave and Luca and Giuliano talking. Not long after, two

Superiors had rushed in to save Giuliano from Luca who was trying to strangle him. But it made no sense. If Luca found Giuliano annoying, Marco tended to agree, but that was no reason to bodily assault him. "And then he just attacked?"

"Whom did you say you talked to about it?" Giuliano asked.

"I didn't," Marco said, trying not to get irritated at the questioning and wondering how it were possible to go from concerned and asking about the man's well-being to being interrogated about what other people saw or said or did. "It was Sophia Romano from intern communications. She said the Superiors rescued you and led Luca out of there."

One of Giuliano's eyebrows twitched. "Hm," he said and sipped his drink.

"But what really happened?" Marco asked.

"What do you mean?"

Marco made a vague gesture. "Well, he can't have tried to strangle you out of nowhere." No one in the Shelter knew the outsiders particularly well, but from his brief time with Luca, Marco found it hard to believe that he would attack without any kind of provocation. He seemed so eager to establish a relationship between his own people and the Shelter. And unlike Renn, he also knew a lot about technology and Superiors. In that case, he ought to know the Superiors would be watching. Ought to know that he wouldn't get away with something like that.

Giuliano shook his head. "Yet he did, almost," he sighed. "I was showing him where we keep things and trying to be helpful and answer his questions about the Shelter, but all of a sudden, he started saying a lot of weird things about our Superiors. And I—" He looked up at Marco, smiling. At first Marco thought he looked sad, but then he realized Giuliano's smile just didn't reach his eyes. "I suppose it was stupid of me, but I tried to argue with him. I couldn't let him talk like that. And then he jumped me. I'm glad his friend didn't try anything with you. I mean," Giuliano added, "He didn't, right?"

"Renn? Oh no," Marco said. "He was very polite and interested in our ways. I showed him the gardens and he looked like a child playing there for the first time."

"That's a relief," Giuliano said. "I would have hated for you to go through what I did."

There was something odd about that sentence. It was trying to pull Marco into a closer relationship than they really had. "Well, nothing bad happened," he said.

"What about Luca? You talked to him as well. Did he say anything to you about Superiors?"

"He called them something else. Sentients," Marco said. "But that's only a word."

"But words," Giuliano interjected, "can be the instigators for something dangerous." He smiled again. "I'm merely worried. Because the things he said to me were appalling, frankly."

Marco didn't want to sound nosy, but he had to ask, "What did he say?"

"He talked about making them do what he wanted. Something he called reprogramming." Giuliano wrapped his arms around his own body as if the temperature had dropped. "As if he were their leader."

"But they are the Superiors," Marco said. "They take care of us and guide us. Why would anyone want to change that?"

"That's exactly what I said," Giuliano replied. "But he didn't want to listen to reason."

Marco frowned. Something didn't add quite up, but he wasn't sure what. There was something odd about Giuliano taking such an interest in his opinions… But maybe Giuliano didn't have anyone else to talk to about this. After all, very few people had had anything to do with Luca and Renn.

"Are you all right?" Giuliano asked.

"Am I all right?" Marco exclaimed, perhaps a little too incredulously. "You are the one he attacked!"

Giuliano smiled weakly. "I'm fine. I mean... I'm fine," he repeated with a bit more conviction.

There was something vaguely studied to his responses. But nothing Marco couldn't blame on the shock of being attacked. "What happens now, though?" Marco asked. "Did the Superiors tell you?"

Giuliano sighed. "They are going to let Renn go when their Superior finishes making the medicine they came for, I think. The Superior should stay here. What is there for nem out there?"

"And Luca?" Marco asked.

"I don't know." Giuliano made a face. "I suppose it depends on how dangerous the Superiors think he is. How serious his threats are. Don't get me wrong, I know he was serious," he added, shuddering, "but it all comes down to what he is capable of, doesn't it? If he really can do those things— Well, he can't just be released from custody, can he?"

Marco found himself looking away from Giuliano's face. It felt horribly like a test. But Giuliano was probably only looking for comfort and making sure Marco hadn't suffered any abuse from the strangers. "I suppose that would be problematic," he said. "But what is the alternative?"

"Keeping him locked up," Giuliano said.

"You mean keeping him in a cell forever?" Marco asked. He knew they were there, the cells. Once in a while, someone was confined, but only as a precaution for a short period of time. Everybody knew the Superiors had to be trusted and respected and acted accordingly most of the time. "But that's..."

"It's what?" Giuliano asked, kindly but with a hard edge to his voice.

Marco shrugged. He had no idea where that sentence had been headed. "Don't you think the Superiors can talk some sense into him?" he asked.

"We can only hope," Giuliano sighed. "We can only hope." He sipped his coffee again, then leaned forward with his elbows on the table. "Marco, I need to make a request of you."

Marco blinked. "A request?"

"Yes. I assume Renn is still with the surface research department, and it will be a while before his Superior finishes nir work with the medicine. Someone needs to keep a close eye on Renn. Someone who is capable of alarming our Superiors if his behavior begins to deviate." Giuliano tapped his cup, thoughtfully. Then he pointed at Marco. "That someone is you."

"Me?" Marco echoed. "Why? If the Superiors are worried, wouldn't it be better if one of them—"

"No," Giuliano practically cut him off. "We don't want Renn to feel he is being observed. We don't want him to ask questions, either. As far as he is concerned, Luca Capello is spending time learning about the Shelter's practices and technology. Presumably, he trusts you, and it will seem natural that you offer to show him more of the Shelter. You have already gone a bit beyond your duties to show him the gardens, after all. Keep him entertained. Show him whatever you want apart from the restricted levels. Take him home with you if you want. We just want him not to make trouble while the Superiors sort out the situation with Luca and their own Superior finishes nir work."

Marco nodded. It sounded a bit like betrayal. But how could he betray someone he hardly knew? And why was Giuliano talking to him about this and not a Superior? "Why are you the one asking me?" Marco said.

"To make matters seem more casual than if a Superior gave you the orders. I was instructed to request your help. We don't want gossip," Giuliano immediately replied.

Marco supposed that made sense, but he took orders from Superiors all the time. Perhaps the reason was that the responsibility for the outsiders' visit had moved from the maintainers to security, and unless there was an emergency, security never issued orders.

"Can I— Can the Superiors rely on you to take care of this?" Giuliano asked.

"Yes. Of course," Marco replied. Giuliano suddenly acting as a liaison between the Superiors and him, and the whole thing about keeping the truth from Renn... It felt wrong. But it couldn't possibly be. Not when the Superiors were involved. They always acted in the Shelter's best interest. It was just that now, there were people involved who did not belong to the Shelter, and that complicated matters.

36:

Renn

Renn did not mind sharing what he knew with the so-called surface research department. It was not that different from coming across another Bevy or Covey and exchanging information about the respective routes they had traveled. While the Shelter did not have any geographical knowledge that he could benefit from, it was a small price to pay for the cure.

Still, the sheer lack of insight into the conditions above ground that he was met with was unsettling. There were three people at work in the archive, as they called the place. It was a big room with shelves lining the walls and three tables arranged in the middle. They were littered with masheens of the sort Luca called computers and other pieces of equipment that Renn did not recognize. One of the researchers present was constantly working with a computer. She glanced up once in a while to see what Renn and the other two were doing, but her own tasks took up most of her time.

There were no Superiors in the archive. Renn felt more relaxed when they were not around. As comfortable as he was with Mender and Nanny, he could not shake the feeling that the Superiors were watching him differently. Where Mender was observant in order to be able to help if the need arose, the Shelter sentients' presence felt restrictive.

The researchers arranged chairs so they and Renn could sit around a table. One of them put a small, round object in the middle of the table and asked Renn if he minded, and his confusion must have been obvious because before he could ask, she explained that the object recorded his voice so that they may later write down what he said or listen to it if they needed to. Renn didn't mind. But he did wonder if such a device was entirely useful as one may start paying less attention if everything could be recalled from a masheen later.

The researchers had maps on a shiny slate of the sort Luca called a tablet. The maps were extraordinary. When one touched them, a text would appear with the name of a city or a landmark, and the scale of the maps changed when the researchers made certain movements with their fingers.

Renn found himself disagreeing with the maps quite a few times, and the researchers clearly took his testimony seriously and tapped the maps to create tiny depictions of red flags when he pointed out differences between his memory and the maps.

It was odd that they did not venture outside the Shelter when they were clearly so interested in learning what was out there. Apparently, they did have eyes outside attached to the wall of masheenery, but their other means of surveying the landscape did not work anymore. Renn was told why, but he did not know what a satellite was, nor why its demise had such an impact on the Shelter's methods of observation.

After talking and looking at maps all afternoon, he was starting to feel that there was very little left to contribute with. So it was a bit of a relief when Marco returned. But something was not right. Renn did not know Marco well, but the boy had a different posture, as if he tried to make up for insecurity by squaring his shoulders and setting his jaw. It might be a personal matter irrelevant to Renn, but somehow Renn doubted that was it.

"We are going back to Luca and Nanny now, I assume?" Renn asked the moment they were alone again.

"Well, yes, but not right now," Marco replied. "Your Superior is still working on the cure, and Luca is occupied elsewhere with some computer stuff."

This sounded perfectly plausible, but Renn could not shake the feeling that there was something he was not being told.

"I was assigned to escort you around. I told the Superiors you liked the gardens," Marco continued. "So they thought maybe there are other parts of the Shelter you may want to see."

"Thank you," Renn said. "But I don't mind going back to the others. I can wait while Luca does... computer stuff."

"Yes, but—" Marco swallowed. "It's just that I have orders to keep you entertained. The Superiors feel it's important for our relationship to your settlement. So I thought maybe you would like to see our water tanks or recycling facilities."

Admittedly, Renn was curious to see more of the Shelter. And if Teo were here, she would agree that understanding and building a relationship to the Shelter was vital. Renn knew he was not the most qualified person, but he would not waste time by suggesting waiting for Luca and Nanny. They needed to leave as soon as Nanny had the cure. "Thank you," he settled for. "I should like to see how you manage your water supplies."

"Yes!" Marco said, grinning. "We'll go to one of the the water units, then."

They went down one of those endless hallways that Renn was beginning to think of as roads connecting vastly different houses rather than corridors inside a single dwelling. Marco explained that there were three water units in the Shelter, placed far apart and connected to three different underground water reservoirs. But most of the water was recycled inside the Shelter, he added.

Renn was good at sensing danger, and he could imagine possible outcomes of situations as well as the next person, but his imagination had been severely tested in the past year. He had never expected to meet anyone like Mender or Luca. Nor had he imagined seeing working masheens or anything like the domes of Florence. This underground society with sentients as peacekeepers and guardians and plants growing under artificial lights was even stranger.

As Renn and Marco stepped through one of those sliding doorways to the water unit, Renn's perception of reality was challenged yet again. The facility took up at least two stories, judging from the high ceiling. It was a clean-looking place with smooth surfaces and pipes adorning the walls.

Renn had always thought of his knowledge of water purification as adequate. He knew how to sift it and boil it, but clearly there was more to the Shelter's ways. Towering before them was a row of tanks the size of small houses, each with thick hoses and pipes coming out of them. A low, monotonous humming filled the space, so low that Renn thought he felt it rather than heard it. How much water was there? The tanks were not transparent, but their white exterior was translucent enough to show the water level of one giant tank just above head level and the adjacent tank practically full from floor to high ceiling.

"This is where our water comes from," Marco was saying.

Renn blinked and looked back at him. "How much water is in each of those tanks?" he asked.

"I don't actually know," Marco admitted, "but we can find someone who works here and ask."

Renn nodded. So much water. Surely enough to fill a lake... And there were three such places in the Shelter. The land above was dry and thirsty, and here they grew plants in water and had the luxury of those giant reserves... Could it be that the Shelter sucked the moisture out of the ground? For a moment Renn almost believed it could. But he had migrated enough to know everywhere was as dry as the Shelter's immediate surroundings. Only moments ago he had been describing the dried up lakes several days' wandering away.

"Are you okay?" Marco asked.

"Yes..." Renn cleared his throat. "Yes. It is overwhelming. I am glad you showed me," he added when Marco began to look worried. "I still don't understand where it comes from. There is so much, but over the years, I would think the storage gets depleted."

"We recycle," Marco said, beckoning for Renn to follow him further into the water unit. "There is clean water in some of the tanks waiting to be used for cooking, bathing, drinking and so on all over the Shelter. The rest of the tanks have dirty water in them that gets cleaned down here. So whenever we pour water in the drains, it goes down here to be cleaned. I think maybe even urine, though that could just be a rumor, really, because—"

"Maintainer."

Renn did not manage to stop himself from whirling around and bringing his staff up to defend himself. He did succeed in not actually slamming it into the face of the Superior who stood right behind him and Marco, though.

A startled yelp escaped Marco, which did make Renn feel a little better about his own reaction.

"Superior!" Marco said. "I didn't hear you. I'm sorry."

"Are you here to carry out work?" the Superior said. Ne was wearing blue stripes instead of the silver Renn had seen on others, but apart from that, ne was practically identical to them.

"No," Marco replied, "I am showing Renn around. He is from the outside. I do have permission."

The Superior's answer came a little delayed, and Renn had the distinct feeling that ne was somehow verifying Marco's statement. Was ne using the communication link that the other Superior mentioned earlier? "Yes," ne said. "Carry on, Marco."

"Thank you, Superior," Marco replied.

"Do you have proper license to own a weapon?" ne continued to Renn.

"This is a walking stick," he replied. "I was not asked to leave it behind on the surface."

Another brief pause. "Very well," ne said. "Do be careful with it when close to others."

Renn gritted his teeth. He would easily admit his lack of knowledge of masheens and radios and water recycling, but he had carried a staff since a hunter showed him how to defend himself when he was a child. He knew how to handle a staff. "I will," he said.

The Superior left them without another word in the direction of the door.

Marco shrugged and smiled apologetically. "The Superiors take good care of us," he said, and Renn wasn't entirely certain whom he was trying to convince.

"Did you want to talk to one of the workers?" he added.

"Yes," Renn said. He had not paid much attention to anything apart from the giant tanks until the Superior appeared, but there were people in here. One was walking around with a tablet, raising it occasionally to point it at a tank and then tapping it rapidly with the tips of her fingers. Two others were discussing something intently. One of them pointed to a contraption fastened to a tank.

"Hi," Marco said to the one with the tablet as they approached her.

"Hello," the woman replied with a bob of her head. "And..."

"This is Renn. He is visiting us."

"Okay," the woman replied, sizing up Renn with a frown. "Are you... training to be a maintainer?"

"No," Renn answered. "I am a wanderer. From outside."

The woman laughed. "Oh, come on," she said. "I'm not that gullible."

"It's true," Marco said. "He lives on the surface."

"But how?" she asked. "That's not possible. Did you go up there and decide to live there?"

"No. I was born on the surface." Renn watched her expression change as she looked from him to Marco and back again, apparently deciding they were not joking.

"Renn is visiting with his friend and their Superior," Marco said. He sounded like he was beginning to think it might have been a mistake to introduce Renn as an outsider. Renn partially agreed.

"Lana," one of the workers by the tank called.

"Excuse me," the woman, Lana, said. She stared at Renn even as she joined the two others.

"I'm sorry," Marco said. "Maybe I shouldn't have..."

Renn shook his head. "It's fine. Perhaps we should go back to Luca and Nanny now," he added.

"No!" Marco cleared his throat. "I mean, there is so much more to see. I can show you how we live. Or a waste processing unit if you are more interested in that. Or a gym so you can see how we work out."

Something was not right. Marco was deliberately keeping him from the others, and Renn was about to insist on going back when a klaxon rang out, loud and insistent. "What is that?" he shouted instead.

"I don't know. It's an alarm," Marco replied, looking around.

The three workers stood frozen. One of them was covering his mouth with his hands, and another was pointing up. Renn followed her gaze. And somewhere half up one of the tanks, he saw it. Water was pouring out from a crack.

"We have to get out!" one of the workers shouted, starting to make his way toward the door.

"It's too late!" Lana yelled back.

"Attention all personnel. Tank number three has been breached," a calm, clear voice came from somewhere high above. There was no one there, but a Superior had spoken from out of the ceiling in the decontamination rooms too. "Please stay calm and go through the emergency procedure."

"No! Let us out!" The worker was now banging furiously at the door with his fists, but it did not open.

236

Renn looked down. Already, water was spreading from the base of the tank. How long would it take for the floor to be flooded? Was the hole in the tank low enough to make the water drown them all? As he was trying to figure it out, Renn saw the crack widen. It traveled downward, and as it did, the flow of the water turned from a trickle to a forceful downpour.

37:

Teo

Esmia's voice was more urgent than Teo had ever heard her before. "Scarvhes!" she shouted.

Teo had seen their tracks in the dust, and she had seen them from afar when she was outside Siena and safe in the car. And even though Renn, Arsenio and Luca had gone hunting for scarvhes and allegedly obliterated a nest of them in the early days of the settlement, they had always felt like an alien, almost mythological danger.

Teo was curious, but she would rather stay curious and oblivious than learn firsthand what scarvhes were like.

"Shit!" Arsenio voiced what they were probably all thinking. "We need weapons."

And now Teo could hear them too. Screeching was the best word she could think of to describe the sound although it didn't quite cover it.

"We need to get to safety!" Esmia told them. "Now!"

"Where are they coming from?" Teo asked.

"From the ruins," Esmia said. "But I think they are fanning out."

"Your house, Teo," Clara suggested, already tugging at Esmia's hand.

"Our house," Teo agreed. It was the closest place where they knew they could barricade themselves and find weapons. "Go!"

Esmia and Clara were already running.

Under normal circumstances, Arsenio's long legs could outrun Teo any day, but he had not even gone twenty paces before he stumbled, coughing.

"You keep going, Arsenio Sabbadin!" Teo shouted at him, putting her arm around his waist and practically dragging him along.

He didn't reply. Only made a grimace and draped his arm around her shoulder for support. At least there was no one else in the streets. The other funeral attendees should be safe by now. It was only the four of them.

Ahead of them, Clara and Esmia turned around a corner, but before Teo and Arsenio reached it, they came bolting back.

"The other way!" Clara yelled. Her voice was almost as high-pitched as the whirring screech that came from several sides now, one of them the path she and Esmia had abandoned.

"Check if it's clear!" Esmia shouted. She had stopped in her tracks and was looking around wildly. There was a stack of metal barrels they used for collecting rainwater and a ladder propped against the closest building. Esmia kicked at the ladder, and Teo understood. She heard the barrels toppling, clanging, and rolling behind her as she and Arsenio made slow progress in the direction Clara had fled.

"It's safe!" Clara called out from around the next corner. Good. It wasn't much of a detour. They could make it.

Esmia caught up to them and put her arm around Arsenio from the other side. They rounded the corner. So close.

Clara had reached the door and was pushing it open. At least locks hadn't been a priority, Teo thought.

Teo's heart was beating out a rapid rhythm. How close were the scarvhes now? She turned around as they reached the door and almost wished she hadn't. They came from the paths between the houses, claiming the space the Sienans had presumed theirs for months. The logical, detached part of Teo's brain noted that they must be quite advanced predators, being able to fan out to cover a large territory. She supposed the screeching was a sort of communication. If the rest of her mind hadn't been a panicking mess, she would have marveled at the absurdity of the creatures. They did indeed look like improbable snakes covered not in hide but exoskeletons. She counted four individuals. They propelled themselves forward by lashing their tails and beating their powerful wings, never lifting far from the ground.

Teo followed the others, stumbled through the door and barely had time to turn around before Clara banged it shut.

A few seconds later, something heavy smashed against it on the other side, and Clara cried out in surprise or terror. Teo saw the door opening a fraction despite Clara's weight against it. She let go of Arsenio and threw herself at the door too, effectively shutting it again. The door wasn't moving, but Teo could hear claws or fangs or beaks, she didn't know which, scraping and tapping against it.

"Hold it!" Esmia shouted. She was pushing the table from the next room toward them, and together they managed to prop it up against the door.

"We're all right," Teo gasped. "We made it." Her knees wanted to buckle, but she refused to let them. The scraping from outside subsided.

Arsenio, she saw, had let his. He was crouched on the floor, heaving for breath and looking like he might faint at any moment.

"We're safe," Teo said, kneeling next to him. "Just breathe."

He made an annoyed groan. She knew exactly what he meant. He was feeling weak and useless and passive, and he was used to neither.

"What now?" Clara asked.

"Now we plan," Teo said.

Between them, they got Arsenio to the bedroom and made him lie down. Teo found herself in the absurd role of the hostess, handing them all a cup of water, partly because they needed it and partly because doing something calmed her.

"Do you think anyone else—" Clara's voice broke. "Do you think anyone was out there? Do you think everybody is safe?"

"Most people are inside because of the illness," Teo said, hoping she was right, dreading what they would find once they ventured outside if she was not. "I suppose that is one good thing about it."

"No," Esmia said flatly, reminding Teo for a moment of Luca when he was stripped of his attitude; too young to be so grim. "The illness is the reason the scarvhes are attacking the settlement. There are no masheens or fires to keep them away, and they can smell disease from far away. They think we are easy prey."

Teo nodded. She reached out for Arsenio's hand. It was clammy and far too hot. "All right. You are our expert, Esmia. What do we need to do?"

"I've killed scarvhes," Arsenio croaked.

"We know," Teo said, squeezing his hand. "But you are going to have to let us take care of things." She smiled at Esmia. "Please."

For a moment, Esmia hesitated. At first, Teo thought perhaps she was insecure, but then she understood. Esmia grew up with scarvhes as a real and present threat to her Covey, just like Renn. To Esmia, the Sienans were impossibly, or at least improbably, ignorant. She must be wondering where to even begin.

"You can't outrun a scarvhe for long," Esmia started. "They are smart predators, but you can outwit them. The best way to kill them is a blow to the top of their head. They prefer to hunt slow and weak animals and to catch them alone, but when they are in packs, they will take more challenging prey."

Teo nodded. "So how do we do this?" she asked. "Do we wait for them to leave?"

Esmia cocked her head from side to side, weighing their options. "No," she said, slowly. "We can, but... they are patient. They can wait for days."

"And someone will make a mistake or need to leave the safety of their house sooner or later," Teo sighed.

"What about Renn and Luca?" Clara asked. "Cars scare scarvhes, right? They should be back soon."

"Yes," Esmia agreed. "But we can't know exactly when they will return."

"We need to get rid of the creeps," Arsenio wheezed. "We have a car. And guns scare them too. You can kill them with bullets. I can—"

The three of them rounded on him. "No!" Teo said. Esmia shook her head, and Clara sighed in exasperation. If the situation were less dire, Teo would have laughed. "You will have to sit this one out."

"The only thing we could use you for is bait," Esmia said with startling ease. "But that is too risky," she added.

"How many guns do we have?" Clara asked.

"Two," Teo said. One was Arsenio's, and the other had belonged to Vanni.

"But none of you—" Arsenio tried again.

He was going to have to work on that arbiter's attitude and let someone else take responsibility once in a while, even after all this was over. The irony of this thought was not lost on Teo. It was what he had told her only a few days ago. And he had been right, of course. She was working on it. "I can shoot well enough to scare them," she said.

"I'm a fairly good shot," Clara said. When the others stared at her, she added, "Vanni taught me."

Gratitude and sadness tugged at Teo. "All right. Good," she said. "Esmia?"

"I can use fire," the wanderer said. "I need torches."

Teo wanted to tell her not to set fire to the whole settlement, but Esmia knew what she was doing. If her cynicism reminded Teo of Luca, her levelheadedness and directness reminded her of Renn. Perhaps it was a wanderer trait. If Esmia said she could use fire to fight the scarvhes, there was no doubt that she could. "Then you'll get torches," Teo said.

"You also need a plan," Arsenio said, pushing himself up on his elbows. "Give me the tray."

As much as she wanted him not to exhaust himself, Teo knew his former profession would give him and edge in planning the tactics that she did not have herself. Esmia had never fought scarvhes in a settlement, and despite Clara's unexpected prowess with firearms, Teo didn't think she had any experience with this either. She went to get the tray and put it in Arsenio's lap.

He picked up the writing stick and began sketching their surroundings. "How many do we think are out there?"

Esmia bit her lip. "I'm not sure. I think I saw six, but there were more in other places... Maybe around ten?"

"Too many to kill," Arsenio said. "Your priority should be scaring them away. You can shoot to kill, but the important thing is the noise." The map he was drawing in the sand was a simplified version of Siena, but the location of the roads were fairly accurate. "You want to lead them in the same direction," he said.

"Herding scarvhes," Esmia said. "It's not easy. But I have an idea."

38:

Luca

When the world came into focus, Luca was lying curled up on the cool, hard floor and trying to make sense of it. He remembered being coerced through endless corridors and seeing everything through a thick haze. Voices babbling nonsense around him and possibly at him. He even had a vague recollection of explaining something, but he had no idea what or to whom. They had drugged him, and it was humiliating as fuck. Sure, it was better than killing him or beating him up. He supposed they might have liked to give the impression that he was going with them willingly, but it was still embarrassing.

He pushed himself up to a sitting position with his back against the wall, wincing as his right wrist and the socket of his arm protested loudly. The side of his face felt like someone had slapped him with an iron rod. What the hell were they thinking? Forcing him in here and throwing him on the floor... He blinked. Next to him was a cot. Okay. So maybe he had fallen off it at some point. Still didn't make it all right, though.

The cot took up the whole length of the tiny room. Luca followed the seam between the walls and the ceiling all the way round. Where was the camera? There had to be one. The walls were smooth, but a discreet box was mounted above the door. Luca tried to ignore the door.

It ought to have made him feel better, but there was no handle or scanner and no motion detector that he could make out. Not even a window or a peephole in it.

Where were Renn and Nanny? He'd apparently upset the artificials to no end and been thrown in prison, but what about the others? He supposed it was good news that they weren't here with him, but still. Did they even know he was here? Well, Nanny would never leave the Shelter without him. And Renn totally owed him a prison break, even if that would be more difficult here than in Florence. It was only a matter of time before they came to get him. Right?

Windows, he decided, would have made a world of a difference. What the hell was it with people putting him in tiny rooms anyway? The decontamination chambers at ground level had taken him completely by surprise. It wasn't just the confined space, though. Combined with procedures that resembled waking up from cryo, it had been a nightmare. He'd freaked out enough for Renn to notice the panic. Well, this prison cell wasn't half as bad as that. He could totally deal with this.

Luca closed his eyes and leaned his head against the wall, trying to visualize something more spacious. Something that didn't feel like the walls were creeping up on him. Something that didn't feel like he may be left in here to suffocate to death.

He stood up, hoping that moving would make his heart rate chill the fuck out. He felt lightheaded, but it was impossible to tell if that was the aftermath of the drugs or the confines of this space. How long had he been here already? An hour? A day? No, not a day. Then he would have been suffocating already due to the CO_2 levels. He paced the room, filling his head with numbers, calculating how long he was likely to survive in an airtight room of this size. He'd done these calculations before, last time in a fucking wine cellar in Florence, and although the results weren't accurate, the stream of numbers did calm him down a little.

He stopped pacing. Glared up at what had to be the camera. "Okay," he said, concealing the tremor in his voice with a super fake chuckle. He spread out his arms. "What happens now? Are you planning on letting me live out the rest of my life in here? Don't I at least get a fair trial or something?"

He hadn't expected an answer. Didn't get one either. There were just him and the six sides of the box that threatened to creep closer if he didn't keep an eye on them. "What happened was a mistake. It was a clusterfuck of mistakes," he said. It felt better to talk. It was an illusion of agency, he knew, but it still felt better. *The Illusion of Agency on the Intersection of Human and AI Psychology.* It was the title of a PhD dissertation he vaguely recalled reading a few chapters of in preparation for an exam. He groped around his memory in search of a good quotation to throw at whoever was eating donuts and watching the surveillance feed from this place. Or not eating donuts if it was an artificial. He refused to believe no one was watching.

"I feel we need to talk about this," he told the camera. "Like civilized people. I am not going to pull a screwdriver out of my ass and attack anyone, and if you just let me explain, I am sure we can reach a peaceful solution that we'll all be happy with."

Nothing happened. Eventually, he retreated to the back of the room and sat down on the cot. He studied his wrist. It was bruised and swollen, but it didn't seem to be broken. He flexed his fingers, one at a time. Everything was in perfect working condition. Experimentally, he reached up to touch his face. The tips of his fingers told him nothing, but his jaw and cheek ached when he probed them. He should sue those artificials for police brutality. In fact, Luca thought, he could not think of one single encounter with law enforcement in the post-apocalypse that hadn't consisted of someone attacking him. There was the artificial in Pistoria a few years back and every police officer in Florence he'd ever met, with the exception of Teo's friend who died. And now the sentients here. Fucked up.

There was literally nothing he could do. And he hated doing nothing. The only thing that was worse than doing nothing was doing nothing in a confined space. If only he had something to keep him occupied. Take his mind off this teeny tiny room. But at this point, his best option was to spit on the floor and draw or write something with his own saliva, and he wasn't quite there yet. He willed his eyed closed and began to solve equations in his head.

Luca didn't know how much time passed before a noise snapped him out of an attempt at meditation. It wasn't a loud noise at all, but this place was so silent he couldn't have missed it even if he'd managed to fall asleep. He held his breath, waiting.

The door opened, and the sleek shape of a Shelter artificial stood there. This one wore red like the one that accosted him. "Come," ne said.

Yep, someone clearly left out smalltalk from the software of these guys. Luca didn't say that. He also didn't say how relieved he was to finally see someone. Anyone. "Okay," he said instead and got to his feet.

"Hold out your arms," the sentient said.

Luca complied because right now the important thing was getting out of the cell.

The sentient produced zip ties and slipped them over his hands. With   practiced or well-programmed ease, ne tightened them and motioned for him to follow as ne turned.

Luca flexed his fingers. The zip ties cut into his wrists. The bruises complained. But damn if he was going to whine about that now. Still, if this had been back in his time and some artificial had manhandled him like that, there'd been ramifications coming down so fast the fucking robot wouldn't know what hit it.

Outside the cell was a sterile-looking room with a number of doors. Luca'd wager a guess there was a cell like his behind each of them. He wondered if they were occupied. He wondered what kind of offense usually called for imprisonment in this place.

The room itself was empty. The sentient proceeded to one of the doors, and it slid open. And behind door number one... was Giuliano.

247

"Do you need further assistance, maintainer?" the red sentient asked him.

Giuliano shook his head. "I am sure I will be fine. Thank you, Superior."

And with that, Luca was handed over like a parcel in a mail distribution hub.

Giuliano looked perfectly unruffled and well-groomed. He could be the poster child in a commercial for life in the Shelter, shining silver lining on the sleeves and collar of his shirt.

"Come with me," Giuliano said.

"Just out of curiosity—" Luca began.

"You would only get to the end of this corridor, and security would step in before you even reached that far," Giuliano said. "Now, come on."

"Jesus Christ," Luca muttered, "who said that's what I was going to ask?" But he had to admit he had been wondering. "Your artificials are acting like I'm super dangerous."

Giuliano beckoned for him to follow, and they began to make their way through the bland corridor, side by side. "Well, aren't you?" Giuliano asked.

Luca suppressed sigh. "Not really. I swear I'm not going to suddenly rip an artificial open and reset nir personality or anything."

This earned him a long, calculating stare.

"I said I'm not. It's not even how it works. And we've all seen how efficient your security is in this place. But anyway, where are Renn and Nanny?" He went for a casual tone.

"Your Superior and your partner are fine," Giuliano said.

Luca blinked, taking a moment to digest that statement. "That's awesome," he then said. "Do they know I'm here? Can I see them?"

"Not right now," Giuliano said.

"Okay, when can I see them, then?"

"That," Giuliano said, smoothly, "is not up to me. I am only here to escort you."

Luca had half a mind to pursue the matter, but probably Giuliano was telling the truth. If the artificials ran the show in the Shelter, a random maintainer couldn't make any promises or decisions. "Where are we going, then?" he asked

"I have instructions to transfer you," Giuliano said.

Luca had been so relieved to get out of the cell he hadn't even considered it, but it was kind of weird. It would make more sense for security personnel to pick him up. Giuliano could not possibly be the random maintainer Luca had assumed he was. "Yeah? From whom?"

Giuliano sent him an almost-glare. When Luca was about to continue talking, Giuliano held up his hand. "Not now," he said, and Luca saw his glance flicker to the ceiling. Surveillance? Was there something this guy didn't want to say on record? That was interesting.

They reached the end of the nondescript corridor that Luca allegedly would not have reached if he'd tried to run. It was an elevator. They stepped in, and Giuliano put his hand on a panel next to the level indicator before he pressed an unmarked button. Unmarked buttons were, Luca thought, probably not good news.

The elevator sped down what felt like two or three levels before coming to a halt. The doors slid open, and they stepped out into, you guessed it, the umpteenth damn, bland corridor Luca saw in the Shelter. Maybe the meteor that had struck the ground wiped out their department of interior decoration.

Giuliano turned to face Luca. "I am taking you to the Supreme," he said.

"The Supreme," Luca repeated. So he was going to meet this mysterious person, after all. "And you couldn't say that before, which means... This is not standard procedure. And you didn't want others to hear, and there isn't surveillance here," he ventured.

Luca thought he saw an impressed expression cross Giuliano's face. But it was gone almost instantly.

"So, who is this Supreme of yours?" Luca asked. "No, let me take a wild guess. It's an artificial, isn't it?"

"What I don't understand," Giuliano offered, "is that you are supposedly quite gifted, and yet you sound like I should be impressed that you know the Supreme is akin to the Superiors. Whatever else would ne be?"

Luca's mouth opened. Then closed again. Whatever else, indeed. This place had an unhealthy obsession with artificials, and this was coming from someone who dedicated a considerable amount of time to studying them, repairing them and fucking them.

39:

Renn

The worker at the door was still hammering on it, begging to be let out, screaming for help, panicking despite the disembodied voice's orders to stay calm. No one made a move to console him. They would all be in far more trouble if they took the time to do so.

"The doors lock automatically in the event of a leak," Lana shouted over the sound of the alarm. "We need to fix it ourselves!"

"How can I help?" Marco replied.

Lana beckoned for him to follow to the corner of the room where the third worker had opened a panel in the wall and was pulling out equipment.

Water sloshed over Renn's feet. A moment ago, there was only a pool around the tanks. But the crack was longer now, and the deluge was coming fast and hard. Whatever they wanted to do, they had better do it quickly.

Lana handed a box with a handle and straps to Marco. "Spray it from the edges of the crack toward the middle and don't get anything on your skin," she was saying when Renn reached them. "It dries immediately and is very sturdy."

"Okay," Marco replied.

"The ladder is on the side of the tank," Lana continued, pointing at the nearest tank. "There is equipment for abseiling on top of each of them. If you go down, I'll manage the rope. Are you sure you want to do this?"

"Yes," Marco said without hesitation.

"Lana!" her colleague called out.

"I can't help you!" she shouted back. "I need to go up!"

"Have you done it before?" Renn asked.

Lana made a face. "No. I've seen a leak once before, but the pumps took care of it. Our big pump is away for repair right now and the small one isn't going to cut it."

"I'll go with him," Renn said.

"You shouldn't even be here," Marco said.

"Neither should you," Renn replied.

Lana sent her colleague a nervous glance. "Are you sure?" she asked Renn.

"I am used to climbing," Renn said. "And I can't swim," he added.

Lana nodded at both of them, accepting the offer. "Good luck." Then she began to jog toward the other worker who was pulling out a long, thick hose from the wall.

Marco strapped the box to his back and began to stride through the water toward the tanks. It was now nearly at his knees.

"What is in the bag?" Renn asked, following him.

"Some kind of sealant. I'm going to spray it on the leak. I'm sorry about all this," he added although he really was not at fault.

The ladder was fastened to the side of the tank all the way up, so it was a steady climb, one solid rung after another. Marco was keeping a fast pace. The soles of his shoes, Renn had ample opportunity to see, were made for giving traction. While the Shelter's floors were smooth, they weren't slippery. Perhaps it was because he went outside.

Renn looked down, thankful that heights didn't bother him like they did some people. They were already halfway up the tank, but the water was still rising. Lana and her colleague were up to their waists in water

252

now. The one who panicked had given up pounding on the door. He was now standing on the table in the corner, as out of harm's way as possible.

Marco reached the top of the tank and crawled onto it. Renn followed him a few moments later. There was a fine layer of dust up here, and Renn brushed his hands on his trousers as he stood up. The surface was a little too smooth for comfort and curved toward the edge.

"So far, so good," Marco breathed. "Now we just have to make it across to the other tank." He began to walk briskly across the top of the tank.

"Marco," Renn said, reaching for his staff, "Maybe I should—"

Marco's foot slipped, despite the soles, and he cried out as he fell, frantically clawing at anything to hold on to.

Renn threw himself flat and managed to grab hold of Marco's wrist before he slid too close to the edge of the tank. The boy's eyes were round and scared when they met his. "You are fine," Renn said. "You are not going to fall. Move slowly toward me. Use your feet to push yourself."

Marco gritted his teeth and did exactly what Renn said. Good. Panic or reluctance to follow orders were disastrous in a crisis.

"Thank you," Marco panted as they were both on their feet again, now closer to the middle of the tank than before.

"Do you want me to take the pack?" Renn asked. "It may interfere with your balance."

Marco looked like he was going to argue, but then he took off the pack and handed it to Renn. It was heavier than it looked. Renn quickly retrieved his staff, put on the pack and began to walk across the tank.

They reached the leaking tank without any further incidents. Maybe it was only because he knew it was damaged, but it felt different.

"Here it is," Marco said. He was tugging at the end of a thick rope on a spool near the back of the tank. "Let me have the sealant again so I can go down."

Marco was undoubtedly the lighter of them, and Renn knew how to hold his weight when he descended, so he did not object to this.

A few seconds later, Marco was standing on the edge, clutching the rope. He nodded to Renn, and Renn let a bit of rope slide through his hands before gripping it tightly again. His feet were solidly planted behind the spool so he wouldn't slip. Over the edge Marco went, and Renn had to lean back to make sure the descent was not too quick.

"I'm there now!" Marco's voice called out, barely audible over the alarm and the gushing water.

Renn waited. He could feel Marco's weight shift.

"There's too much water!" the boy shouted. "The sealant won't stick! I spray it on, but—It's not working!"

Renn made a face. They had already wasted time slipping and shifting the pack around. He didn't know how much water was down there now, but they needed a solution quickly. The sealant shouldn't get on skin. It stiffened quickly. Renn frowned. He had an idea, but it was...

"Stay where you are!" he yelled. "I am going to join you!"

"But the rope!" Marco called.

"I will fix it!" Renn shouted back. He needed something to wedge under the spool... He awkwardly pulled off his boots, the ones that Luca gave him and that got him into so much trouble in Florence, and pushed them under the spool. When he tentatively loosened his grip on the rope, it did not move. Hopefully the makeshift lock would be able to carry his weight as well as Marco's.

"Renn?" Marco shouted. "The water is rising!"

"Stay where you are!" Renn repeated. He pulled down the zipper and pulled off his clothes. It really would have been easier if he were wearing two separate pieces, he thought as he pulled his feet out of the legs of the suit. He tied the suit to his staff like a kind of banner and approached the edge.

"What are you doing?" Marco asked.

"I'm coming down to help," Renn replied. Carefully stepping backward over the edge, he began to scale the tank. His feet slipped on

254

the surface of the tank, but he managed to get a few meters down, placing himself right above Marco and the leak. Water was still pouring out, and when Renn studied the crack, he could see that a strange substance was lining it. "Put sealant on my clothes," he told Marco.

"Oh," Marco said, understanding at once, "that's a good idea. Hold the suit out to me."

Renn wrapped the rope around one arm and held out his staff with his clothes dangling from it. His muscles were already complaining.

Marco reached up. The handle of the sealant was attached to the box with a tube, and as he squeezed it, a cloud of foam burst forth. Within seconds, Renn's suit was heavy and stiff. "There!" Marco called.

Renn leaned over as far as he could and pressed the clothes to the crack. The staff was almost wrenched out of his hand by the water flow, but he managed to keep it in place. It didn't stop the water, but the deluge did quiet down a little. Immediately, Marco was spraying again, and this time it appeared to work. The suit was locked in place by the foam, and the downpour turned into little more than a trickle.

"Yes!" Marco shouted. "We did it!"

Renn tugged at his staff, for a moment irrationally worried that it might be stuck and he would lose his second staff in less than a year. But the sealant hadn't reached the wood, and it came away without too much pulling and wrenching.

"Can you climb back up?" Marco called.

Renn was about to reply when he felt something give. "No!" he shouted instead. Before he could elaborate, something broke. It might be the rope itself or the spool or simply the boots slipping out from under it. Regardless, they were falling.

Beneath him, Marco screamed.

Renn had survived a fall more severe than this, but it was not much of a consolation when he was plunging toward the floor.

There was a loud splash that he barely registered before his back hit a solid wall of water. And then he was completely submerged, water filling his ears and nose and mouth. The second impact was not as hard.

It felt like he almost bounced off the floor. Renn flailed. He knew how swimming looked, and he knew he had to head for the surface, but he could hardly tell which way to go, and his arms and legs refused to cooperate in the dense water. Despite his efforts, his body tried to breathe in. He thrashed, desperate, heart pounding so loudly in his ears that he could hear nothing else, a surge of panic making any rational thought impossible.

Something pulled at his hair. Then a hand closed around his arm. And a moment later, his head broke the surface. He was coughing, gasping, retching.

"Hold on to the rope!" Marco yelled and pushed it into Renn's hands. "Just hold until the water level falls enough to stand again."

Renn clutched at the rope, shaking wet hair out of his face, water streaming from his eyes and nose. When the panic subsided, he saw Marco next to him, also holding the rope. So it didn't break, after all. Probably the whole length had just been unspooled. "Thank you," he managed.

Marco smiled weakly. "Thank you for helping."

After the pump cleared away most of the water, the door opened again. Two Superiors and three people Marco called medics were waiting for them and immediately began to fuss over the five of them, though Renn told them he would be fine if he could just get dry and have some footwear and clothes, if someone could spare them.

This proved to be no problem. The Superiors detained Marco and the three workers from the water unit to question them about the accident, and Renn felt he had at least some leverage now to demand seeing Luca and Nanny again.

There were no objections to the request this time. Indeed, he was promptly taken to another level of the Shelter to meet them.

"Wait here for further instructions," The Superior escorting him told Renn and gestured for him to enter the room ne had taken him to.

Renn thanked nem and complied. The room was void of furniture or decoration except for an oblong table in the middle with six chairs arranged around it. Luca was nowhere to be seen, but Nanny sat in one of the chairs.

"Renn!" she exclaimed and rose the moment she saw him.

The door closed behind him. The Superior had not followed him in.

"Where is Luca?" Renn asked. He didn't like the expression on her face one bit.

40:

Luca

The zip ties were making Luca's hands numb. Well, more numb than they usually were. But fuck it if he was going to beg. Especially for that smug bastard's mercy.

"I was going to apologize for pulling that stunt earlier," Luca said.

"Oh, do feel free," Giuliano replied. There was a hint of a smirk on his face.

"But," Luca continued, "You were in on it all along, weren't you? You meant for that to happen. You manipulated me."

"Perhaps. But you are still welcome to apologize," Giuliano said. "I wasn't expecting you to be desperate enough to attack me."

"Gee, thanks. That's so nice of you," Luca muttered. He had wandered into a mad world where artificials were gods. And Giuliano was some kind of intermediary, it seemed. It felt needlessly complicated. "So what is it your boss artificial wants from me?"

"The Supreme," Giuliano intoned in an annoyingly correcting voice, "is going to make use of your particular skills."

"My brilliant sense of humor?" Luca asked.

"Your knowledge of Superiors. If," Giuliano added, "you can actually do what you claim."

"Oh yeah, cause I'd lie about the very thing that got you all up in arms," Luca grumbled. "Of course I can. You're welcome to watch my vlog if you don't believe me. But what I don't get is why we had to go through all this." He held up his zip tied hands to make the point. "Why couldn't you just ask for my help straight away?"

Giuliano arched an eyebrow. But conveniently for him, they had reached the end of the nondescript hallway and a set of doors slightly more elaborate than what Luca had seen in the Shelter so far. They parted when the two of them were a few paces away.

"The Supreme will see us now," Giuliano announced. He took a few long strides to bring himself in front of Luca and stepped through the doors.

The Supreme—Holy fuck, Luca couldn't even think the term without cringing. Superiors were bad enough, but he'd assumed from the beginning that they were superior compared to artificials with less autonomy and not to humans. Well, the Supreme was sitting in the middle of an almost circular room on something that Luca tried not to think of as a throne. He failed. The thing was mounted on a sort of plinth, surrounded by what looked like screens, all facing the throne, and cables spreading out from the center of the room to the wall where they disappeared into sockets. The Supreme nemself stood up as they entered. Ne did not look at all like the rest of the artificials in the Shelter. Sure, they looked more artificial than most sentients Luca had met, but this one took the prize. Ne was not dressed, but what was visible was not skin or any suggestion of human anatomy.

Ne was bipedal, had hands and feet and a head like a human being, but ne was so tall ne would find normal doors a nuisance. Unlike other tall artificials, ne was not bulky at all, but sleek and metallic. Nir face was just detailed enough to pass for a face in the same way that emojis did, but there was absolutely nothing human about it. It looked like CerEvolv's design team went, "Hmm, what if high elf, but android from outer space?" and came up with this.

Giuliano stood next to Luca and then seemed to disappear. When Luca turned, he saw the man kneeling. Giuliano glanced up at him and nodded toward the floor.

Were they fucking kidding him? Luca swallowed his pride and kneeled, resting his tied hands on his knee and hoping that sometime soon someone would remove the damn zip ties.

"You may stand," the artificial said in the most self-important tone Luca had ever heard from a sentient. Nir voice did not originate only from a voice box inside nem, but surrounded them in the circular room. A cheap trick, but Luca didn't doubt for one moment that it worked on the people who lived in the Shelter and had grown up to revere artificials.

They got to their feet again.

"I have brought the outsider as you requested, Supreme," Giuliano said. His voice had lost its sarcastic edge.

"Well done," the sentient replied as if ne were a kindergarten teacher complimenting a lousy drawing. Ne stepped closer, and Luca studied nir movements. The other Shelter artificials were not of a model he'd worked on before, but they appeared to be fairly standard ungendered workers like Mender, only stripped of individuality. But the Supreme was something else all right.

"Thank you," Giuliano said.

"I have been watching you, Luca Capello," the Supreme said.

"I'm flattered. Did you like what you saw?" Luca asked.

Giuliano glared at him as if Luca had insulted this god complex robot. Maybe he had. His heart was racing. But he had a hunch that the best way to deal with this was being himself. He was not going to grovel and not only because because of his pride. If the so-called Supreme wanted ass kissers, there was a bunch of those around already.

"Quite. Apart from your poor manners," the artificial said. "Hold out your hands."

Luca thrust his hands forward. Before he could brace himself, the Supreme reached out and there was a sharp pain around his wrists. The zip ties broke. "Thanks," he said.

"You can leave," the Supreme told Giuliano.

Giuliano shot Luca a glance, then turned on his heel without a word.

"Come with me, Luca Capello," the Supreme said without waiting for the doors to close behind Giuliano. Ne turned and began to move in the opposite direction.

There was something odd about the way ne moved, Luca thought as he followed. As if ne glided rather than walked.

"What I am about to show you, only a select few have seen before," the Supreme said.

"I'm flattered, again?" Luca replied.

The Supreme didn't look at him, but Luca rather suspected ne didn't need to. Ne probably had cameras everywhere in this room and was patched into the feed. "I expect your utmost discretion, of course."

"Of course," Luca said. He had to admit he was pretty damn curious. If this artificial wanted something from him, he automatically had a bargaining chip.

Almost seamless doors slid apart in front of them and the Supreme stepped through.

Luca found himself in a long, rectangular room with the same smooth overall design as the hallways in the Shelter. There wasn't much by way of furniture apart from a row of steel tables spanning the length of the room. Half of them were empty, but four of them had sheets draped over something that lay on them. Luca blinked. Bodies? Was this some kind of morgue?

"What exactly is it you need me to do?" Luca asked, hoping his voice didn't betray him.

The Supreme approached the closest occupied table and pulled back the sheet.

Luca breathed out. It was an artificial. One identical to the Superiors.

"I want you to help them," the Supreme told him.

"What seems to be the problem? Apart from obviously being deactivated?"

"That is not the issue in itself," the Supreme said. "I deactivated them because they malfunctioned."

Luca frowned. "Malfunctioned? Are we talking a software error? Corrupted OS?"

"I don't know."

Well, there was a sentence this artificial probably didn't say very often. Luca cleared his throat. "Okay, so this might be a dumb question or super taboo, but don't you have any engineers? Anyone with a degree in AI or programming or anything?"

"The Superiors were not given the skill to meddle with their own programming. And the learning centers were destroyed a long time ago while the Shelter's human inhabitants were still asleep."

Luca nodded slowly. He was beginning to piece all this together, but it felt a bit like being thrown into the sequel of a sim and not know what happened in part one. Sequels were far-fetched money machines most of the time anyway. "Okay," he said. "So you want me to boot them up and fix them?"

"Yes. That is what I want."

"Just out of curiosity, how long have they been here?"

"This one malfunctioned a month ago." The Supreme indicated the artificial on the table in front of them. Then ne moved further into the room. "This one has been here for three years," ne said, gesturing at each occupied table in turn. "That one for 67 years. And this one for 105 years."

"105?" Luca echoed. "That's a long time. Seems like the malfunctions are getting more frequent."

"There is not enough data to formulate a theory," the Supreme replied. "And they did not malfunction in the same way. The three latest ones started behaving erratically and there was nothing I could do to convince them to stop. The first one... Please have a look."

That sounded ominous. Luca peeled back the sheet as carefully as if he were removing the protective film from a delicate component. "Shitfuck," he breathed. "Something corrupted all right. Right in nir face." The artificial on the table was marred by a dent on the left side of nir head and a hole with melted edges in the temple. "What happened to nem?"

"Ne was shot by a powerful projectile weapon."

"No shit," Luca muttered. "I meant the circumstances."

"That is not necessary information for your work."

Luca straightened up and crossed his arms over his chest. "You've already shown me all this and you intend to let me mess about with their programming. How is any information you can give me going to compromise your situation further?"

"There was a revolt. It was quelled quickly, and only a small amount of humans were involved. A handful of people who were under the delusion that the Superiors were not acting in their best interest. One of them had come into possession of illegal weapons. This Superior was in the line of fire. Ne ceased to function immediately after being hit. No attempt to reactivate nem has been successful."

Luca nodded. Wonderful utopia they had built for themselves here. If he were more into social science and anthropology, he might have found it interesting to view everything this broken world had in store in terms of capitalism and socialism and how everything would dissolve into anarchy eventually. "This is going to take more than poking around the software," he said. "Do you have any spare parts? A new shell?"

"No, sadly we do not."

"Let me guess, they were destroyed by the meteorite that smashed half of the Shelter including the learning center?" When the Supreme nodded, Luca made a face. "That's going to be a problem. First of all, vital parts in nir brain might have been destroyed, so I can't promise anything. And secondly, I can't just pull spare parts out of my ass."

"I understand. Do you have access to spare parts elsewhere?" the Supreme asked.

Luca bit his lip, considering his options. "Can I ask you a question?" he said.

"I am certain you can."

"Why are you keeping all this so secret?" he asked. "The way I see it, and do correct me if I'm wrong here, you set me up to get in trouble with your own law enforcing sentients. You let them drug me and humiliate me and lock me up and probably worry the hell out of my friends, whom, by the way, I have not been allowed to see, only to drag me down here and ask me for a favor. How is that logical? Couldn't you have asked me when we arrived? Actually, couldn't you have asked me on the radio so I could have brought the right equipment and spare parts with me?"

The Supreme studied him. Luca refused to cower under nir stare. Now that he knew the Supreme needed him, he was so done with nir shit. "The Shelter's social structure depends on us," the artificial finally said. "The humans in our charge trust us to care for them and they consider us indestructible."

Luca glanced at the busted artificial on the table and back at the Supreme. "Oh?"

"That," the Supreme said, nodding at the artificial, "is one of the things we must avoid ever happening again. My analyses show that the best way to keep everyone happy is to keep certain unpleasant facts from them. Furthermore, I did not know of your engineering skills before you arrived. And yes, Giuliano was indeed asked to confirm certain facts because of the way you speak to your own Superior. Once that happened, security would step in. You complicated matters by attacking Giuliano and leaving the Superiors no choice but to detain you. But given your actions, you can rest assured that everyone who hears of the incident will view you as the perpetrator. While you were in detention and your human companion was occupied elsewhere, I had your own Superior interviewed to confirm matters before I summoned you here."

Luca nodded, trying to fit every new piece of information into the jigsaw puzzle and trying not to wonder what Renn had been so occupied with. "Okay," he said. "So Giuliano is basically your secret agent? Hold on," he added, eyes widening in surprise, "The other sentients didn't know! He works for you personally!" That explained why the bastard didn't want to discuss things before they were out of reach of the security cameras.

The Supreme did not reply. That was answer enough.

"So basically," Luca continued, "you're asking me to help uphold this whole illusion not only to the general population, but to the sentients as well?" He whistled softly. "That's morally grey." He ran his fingers through his hair. Rubbed his temples. "Just out of curiosity, what happens if I refuse?"

"Then, sadly, you are a dangerous individual who needs to be kept from harming other humans and Superiors as well. Your own Superior and your human companion will be free to go."

Luca scoffed. The Supreme had done a good job of painting him as the antagonist in all this, and he had a feeling no one would listen to him if he decided to tell people what was really going on. "And if I agree?"

"Then you will be free to go when you have finished."

Not much of a choice, then. He wasn't going to stick to a moral code that would get him locked up down here forever. "Fine. Let me have some tools and I'll get started. Oh, but one more thing."

"Yes?" the Supreme intoned.

"I am agreeing to your terms, but there is one thing I insist on. I want to see Renn and Nanny. I've been told they are safe, but I need to see them. If you won't let me, I am going to assume they are not safe at all, and if that is the case, I'm not going to work for you. You can do whatever you want to me." This sounded melodramatic even to Luca, but the Supreme considered it and then nodded in agreement.

41:

Teo

Teo did not want to go out. She wanted to stay in the safety of her own home and wait for the creatures to leave. But that was not an option. Esmia had explained it in no uncertain terms, and although this was the girl who brought the illness to Siena and neglected to tell anyone she might be a carrier, Teo completely trusted her on this matter.

Clara was muttering something under her breath. Her eyes were closed and she was holding her crucifix between the palms of her hands. Then she opened her eyes, put the chain into her shirt and pulled the gun out of its holster at her hip.

Esmia came up to them with two unlit torches. They were practically household stables in Siena. Tightly wound plant fibers from dried clumps of a certain plant that Renn had pointed out in the early days. An extra layer of cloth dipped in whatever available inflammable substance they had. These ones were oil. Esmia assessed Clara and Teo grimly as though she were the only one here who really knew what she was doing. She was.

"Everybody ready?" Teo asked, more cheerfully than the situation warranted.

Esmia nodded.

"As ready as we will ever be," Clara said, forcing herself to smile.

Arsenio was leaning against the wall behind them. He had insisted on at least closing the door behind them. He brought out his lighter and lit the torches. They whooshed as they flared to life.

Teo pulled out the gun from her own holster and opened the door.

If everything went according to plan, she wouldn't have to use the gun for anything but scaring off the scarvhes after she did her bit. She backed up against the wall to let out Esmia. The wanderer spread her arms wide, a flickering, crackling torch in each hand. Teo couldn't see her face, but she knew it must be as tense as her own.

Clara followed Esmia, giving Teo a nod on the way.

And then it began. The flock of scarvhes must have heard them or smelled them. They came weaving through the street, tails lashing up dust and gravel, elongated heads baring their teeth in what Teo tried not to think of as a skeletal grin. They were letting out constant high-pitched whines.

Esmia waved her arms like wings, making sparks fly. She screamed and began to run toward the approaching predators. Clara followed her closely, training her weapon on the scarvhes, ready to fire if they began to move the wrong way. Esmia and Clara were going to attempt pushing the scarvhes away from the center of the settlement while Teo made her way to the one place they were sure people would be gathered in sufficient numbers.

She waited long enough to see the scarvhes hesitate and fervently hoped it would be enough. That the fire and the noise of the gun would frighten them and they wouldn't attack. Scarvhes were smart, Esmia said, and when they discovered there were only two humans chasing them, they may very well regroup and attack.

Teo ran. Her heart pounding, she sprinted down the street, away from the scarvhes, away from Esmia and Clara. She was not the scarvhes' target, but everything depended on her doing this quickly. Originally, she had offered to be the bait and let Clara do this, but Clara and Arsenio had argued that Teo would be better suited for the plan since she could drive. Teo had also detected a bit of reluctance in Clara when it came to leaving Esmia. She hadn't noticed them becoming so close, but her mind had been on other things.

She rounded a corner at break-neck speed, then skidded to a halt. "Damn," she whispered. Plan A was for her to get the car, but that would only work if she could actually get to it. There were two scarvhes circling it, curiously pecking at the windows with their long beaks. Teo wondered what had attracted them. Perhaps they had seen or heard a car before and thought this one was dead.

Plan B then. Teo turned as silently as she could, hoping they wouldn't hear her or catch her scent. She walked a few paces, then broke into a run back the way she had come until the street forked. She darted right, almost tripping over a pile of metal rods in the middle of the street. Metal rods. Teo filed their location for later use, swerved around them and continued.

The infirmary was right in front of her. The door was closed, which was a good thing, and there was no sign of people outside. Did they even know what was going on? Had they heard the scarvhes? Seen them glide through the streets? They must have. In which case, they were sensible and stayed inside. And here she was to ask them to do this foolish thing along with her...

Teo was only a few paces from the infirmary when the tense air broke into a scream. A scarvhe tore out from behind the infirmary, heading directly for her, screeching its intent with such force that the sound alone caused Teo to stumble to a halt.

It could not be one of the scarvhes examining the car. The direction was wrong for that. But regardless, it was not supposed to be here. Esmia and Clara were meant to push them away from the infirmary. But what was supposed to happen didn't matter. Reality did.

The scarvhe came straight at Teo so fast that there was no time to take aim. Teo flung herself to the side. The smell of rotted flesh and dust in her nostrils, the sound of powerful wings tearing at the air. Then sharp, stinging pain and added momentum as she rolled on the ground, instinctively trying to protect her head with her arm. Forcing herself to hold on to the gun.

Teo scrambled back to her feet in time to see the scarvhe abruptly stop and turn sharply with an accomplished predator's speed and grace. She began to suspect that it had not meant to take her down in that first pass. That it was toying with her before going for the kill. Her legs were shaking and her hip and thigh hurt where the scarvhe's tail had hit her. A quick glance down her side revealed a dark stain spreading on the torn fabric of her trousers. It wasn't important. She could stand. That was what mattered. Already, the skeletal snake was closing in on her again.

She brought up the gun and held it with both hands to get a steady aim. She forced herself to draw in a deep breath, aimed at the impossibly swerving and bobbing shape and pulled the trigger.

The crack of thunder was deafening, and Teo staggered back a pace at the recoil. The scarvhe screamed. As if a vicious gust of wind had hit it, the creature was thrown off course. It smashed into the wall of the nearest building. Broke the windowpane in a shower of shards, drew out its pain in long, deep gashes in the dirt.

She had wounded it. But it wasn't dead. Teo brought up the gun again, cautiously moving closer to the predator. The top of its head. Or, she suspected, a sufficient amount of bullets anywhere to shred it. It was thrashing, rising up, but one wing was not working properly. Good. Teo gritted her teeth. She did not like how quick she was at becoming a calculated killer. But it was her or the scarvhe, right?

She fired once more. She did not hit the right spot. But she did hit its head, and she was close enough for the projectile to burrow through the skeletal armor, to exit in a spray of blood and grey goo and embed itself in the wall behind the scarvhe. The creature convulsed and screamed, but it was dying. It must be dying.

Another loud clatter behind her. Teo whirled around, gun at the ready to fire at another attacker. But there was no scarvhe. Only a familiar figure rushing out of the infirmary.

Teo found that her legs were made of pudding. Her vision swam, and she crashed to her knees.

"Teo!"

"I'm all right," she said, fighting the bile rising in her throat because of the pain or what she had just done or both. "We need everybody who can go outside with whatever they have that can make a lot of noise," she said.

Mender was at her side, gently reaching down for her. Nir face was concerned and comfortingly composed. But ne was holding a long knife. The nurse had come to fight, Teo realized. To save her.

Ne hesitated. The look on nir face was one Teo had come to understand as a battle of priorities. She could not begin to fathom the complex programming that entailed, but she knew what it meant. Mender was torn between nir concern for her and the willingness to comply with her request. Artificials weren't much different from humans when you thought about it. "I am fine," she said and took the offered hand.

"You are injured," Mender said as if she might not have noticed the burning pain in her left leg.

"Later," she told nem. "Esmia and Clara risk far worse if we don't act now." She was not in the habit of giving orders, but this was one. She began to stride toward the infirmary, limping and breathing hard, but still with the gun clutched in her hand, and Mender followed without any further argument. Ne opened the door for her.

"Siena is being attacked by scarvhes," she said to the room at large. Loudly, but not trusting herself to shout. "We have a plan, but I need the help of anyone who is well enough to run or walk and make noise."

The waiting room was silent for a moment but for the sound of labored breathing. People on mattresses or beds made of blankets on the floor. A few were too deep in their fever to even look at Teo. People standing or sitting next to their ill friends or family members. Sia pausing her feeding soup or broth into the mouth of one man.

Then a boy stood up. It was Adam.

270

Teo frowned. He was too young for this. "Adults—" she began.

"I want to help," Adam said. And the look on his face told Teo everything. He had found Nevio. He had been holding his sleeping or unconscious father's hand when Teo entered. He felt helpless and he wanted that to change. Needed it to.

"All right," Teo told him although it should be a parent making the decision. "Stay close to me."

Mender had disappeared from her side, but now ne reappeared with a stack of empty bedpans. Three others followed nem. One was Simon, looking as pristine and untroubled as ever. The others were, Teo gratefully realized, one of Renn's students and one of Arsenio's peacekeepers in training.

There was no time for discussing. "Come with me," Teo said. And then, as she was limping back out into the street followed closely by Adam and Mender, "Should you not stay here?"

"My analysis of the situation," Mender explained as if describing the process of picking a color to paint a chair, "suggests that Simon and Sia can take care of the patients until I return, and in case of injuries, my immediate presence will be more useful to you."

Teo nodded. "Let's hope there won't be any," she said. She didn't stop to wait for anyone, but looking over her shoulder, she could tell that five others were already in the street and more were coming. "Follow my lead, everyone!" she shouted as she picked up the pace. "We are going to help Clara and Esmia press the scarvhes out of Siena. Don't get too close to the scarvhes if you can help it. Make a lot of noise, throw stones at them, but let Clara, Esmia and me stay in front. If Esmia gives you an order, follow it." Feeling the need to say something else, she added, "Let's chase the bastards out of our town!"

There was sporadic cheering at this.

As it died down, they all heard the sound of Clara's gun.

42:

Esmia

Sparks flew from the torches as Esmia swung them. She had never willingly walked toward a pack of scarvhes before. Had never even slain one. There were always others, better hunters and better fighters. Renn would have hefted his staff and gone to battle. But Renn was not here, and most of the Sienans were helpless.

At first, Esmia thought that was the reason for doing this. That she was attempting to make amends, trying to atone for everything she had brought on this settlement.

The scarvhes hesitated in the empty street. There were eight of them here, and Esmia hoped her first estimate was wrong and there were no more. But it would not surprise her to learn that this was the main hunting force, and a handful of others were scouting the settlement.

Teo had taken off in the direction of the car. If she succeeded, she would drive it to the infirmary to rally more people. Then she would push the predators away with the masheen and a mob of noisy people.

The plan relied on Esmia keeping the main pack away from Teo for a while. The scarvhes did not advance. Instead, they did exactly what Esmia hoped for. They began to slither away, crouched low on the ground, wings whispering as they beat them. But at some point they would understand that although Esmia was wielding fire, she was no real threat against so many.

Behind her, Clara walked with the projectile weapon, ready to use it, but holding back because it did not contain endless ammunition and because it might cause the scarvhes to disperse in all directions. "I can't hear the car," she said.

"We have to trust Teo," Esmia replied. Trust that she was alive. Trust that if she had not been able to get to the car, she would find another way.

Clara did not reply. Instead, Esmia heard her singing, so softly that Esmia could not make out the words over the hissing and spitting flames.

"Louder, please," Esmia called out. Clara's voice may help confuse the scarvhes.

As Clara's voice rose, Esmia smiled. Not only because it was clear and powerful, but also because Esmia realized with startling clarity that she was not only here to make up for the bad luck she had brought. She was fighting for Siena because it felt like she belonged here. Because the Sienans had welcomed her and helped her fight the spirits in their own strange ways. Because she wanted Clara and Teo and all the others to be safe.

Sweat was running down her face, pooling above her upper lip and dripping off her brow. But the plan was working... At least until one of the scarvhes broke off from the group. It did not charge at Esmia as she would have expected but tore down an intersecting street.

Clara stopped singing. "I can't hit it from here!" she shouted.

Esmia turned her head. Clara was aiming the gun, but Esmia was in the way, the pack of scarvhes were in the way, and after only a few seconds, the scarvhe had vanished from sight.

"We keep going for the pack," Esmia told her. There was no other option. They could only hope the scarvhe wasn't going to meet anyone else or, if it did, that it was Teo.

Esmia pressed on, walking, swinging the torches, hoping.

273

Clara resumed singing. It was a different song now, one with a faster pace, a determined tone, or perhaps that was only the way she sang it.

A loud bang rang out some somewhere in the settlement. It startled Esmia and nearly caused her to drop the torches. The scarvhes flinched too, one of them breaking away and hurtling away from them, but in the direction they were hoping for this time.

"What was that?" Esmia asked.

"A gunshot. Must be Teo," Clara replied.

A gunshot. They had told her it would be loud, but Esmia had not realized exactly how deafening.

"I hope she's all right," Clara added.

"Yes," Esmia agreed. But there was nothing they could do now.

Another shot. Hopefully Teo had hit her target or targets. But even if she were dead and no one was coming to help them drive out the scarvhes, there was nothing to do but this.

One scarvhe soared up from the pack. They usually stayed low, and Esmia knew what it meant when one of them rose like that. It was going to dive, beak first toward prey on the ground.

"It's attacking!" Esmia yelled.

"Keep going!" Clara shouted back.

Esmia knew Clara was right. The scarvhe would be aiming for Clara because Esmia was wielding fire and Clara looked less menacing. And if Esmia turned her attention away from the pack, they might all come rushing. Besides, Clara had the gun. Esmia knew the logic of all this, and yet, she wanted to step in front of Clara to protect her. It was a strange feeling.

The pack was in turmoil. Esmia gritted her teeth and moved on, swinging the torches as fiercely and threateningly as she could. She felt the rush of wings above her and then another shot, even louder than Teo's, tore through the air and made Esmia's ears ring. Out of the corner of her eye, she saw the scarvhe tumble to the ground. It screamed and nearly clipped her head with one desperately beating wing before it crashed.

Clara shouted something, and Esmia turned her head in time to see her stumble as she tried to avoid the falling scarvhe. It missed her at first, but then its tail lashed out and caught her legs.

"Clara!" Esmia shouted.

Clara threw herself to the side. She had dropped the gun, Esmia realized. And the scarvhe was flapping in angry agony, trying to take off although one of its wings was nothing more than splinters of broken bone.

"Watch out!" Clara yelled.

Esmia whipped around again. She had taken her eye off the pack for too long and now they were charging at her. All of them. She took the rising panic inside of her and turned it into a roar, a battlecry that matched the screeching of the scarvhes. It was louder and more desperate than the scream she had aimed at the pack of rats in another life. She held out the torches in front of her, bent her knees a little, ready to stand her ground.

Could the first scarvhe have been a diversion? They may have understood that the fire was no real threat to them at a distance and that the two humans would be no match for their greater numbers.

Esmia thrust one of the torches at the scarvhe that reached her first. Drove it into its face. It cried out, blinded, and fell away in a stench of burned bone and flesh and a sizzling noise like dry leaves catching fire. It tumbled into the closest building, shattering the windowpane in a shower of glass before it hit the ground.

The next scarvhe was just as unlucky. Esmia caught its open mouth with one torch and hit a wing with the other. But as it fell aside, the torch somehow got stuck in the gaping jaws and was wrenched out of Esmia's hand.

Clara shouted again and fired the gun once more, but the flock of predators was upon them now. Esmia landed another blow of the torch, but it only singed the side of the attacker's head, and she had to dodge the bulk of it as it came hurtling toward her. Something hit her from behind, and she fell, refusing to let go of the torch and paying the price for it when flames licked her hand.

"Esmia!" Clara yelled.

Esmia hoped it was a warning and not a plea for help. She turned in time to see white teeth and bony wings and rolled to the side. Pain lashed across her back and the force of the blow made her roll again. This time, she did lose the torch. And all she could do was curling up around herself, shielding her head with her arms and hope. She could hear Clara shouting, then another shot and the cries and screams of the scarvhes. She knew it was only a matter of time before Clara would be unable to protect her, before they would both be overpowered by the vicious predators.

And then, through the din of everything that was happening, new sounds appeared. Voices. And above them clanging, metallic noises. A scarvhe screamed and something hit Esmia's shoulder and for a moment, she could not understand why her skin didn't break, why there were no more stabs at her body. As the voices grew louder, the new noises rolling over her, she unfolded herself and saw. Clara was breathing hard, but she was standing, still with the weapon in her hand, and she was not alone. Teo and Mender and a small boy had arrived, followed by a handful others. Some smashing metal bowls together, some stomping their feet and shouting.

And best of all, the scarvhes were retreating.

Teo was shouting orders, saying something about two more scarvhes by the car, and people ran past Esmia as she sat up. A man picked up one of the torches. They were going to follow the scarvhes. Finish what she and Clara had begun.

"Are you hurt?" Clara asked, kneeling next to her.

"No," Esmia said, although she felt sore all over and her burned hand was pulsing with pain. "Are you?"

"I'm fine," Clara said. She did look all right, Esmia thought. Sweaty and scared, but all right. "I'm going with the others."

Esmia nodded. "I'm coming," she said.

276

"No, you're not," said Teo. She was standing in front of them now, dirty and with blood soaking one of her trouser legs. "Mender!" she called out and then, to Clara, "We will be fine. Go."

Clara squeezed Esmia's shoulder, then stood and hurried after the others.

"Adam, will you take that and stay with us? In case one of the scarvhes come back here."

The boy nodded and picked up the extinguished torch from the ground.

Esmia was about to say that he wouldn't be much use against a scarvhe and that besides, they were not likely to double back here with the mob of people chasing them. But then she understood. Teo wanted to protect the boy and make him feel useful at the same time. She lit the torch for him.

"Where are you hurt?" asked Mender as Esmia was getting to her feet.

"I'm all right," she insisted.

"So am I," Teo said with a wry smile. She was so pale Esmia was afraid she was going to collapse. But she was leaning against the building one of the scarvhes had smashed against. It was lying dead at her feet, and she prodded it tentatively, then grimaced.

"Mostly second-degree burns," Mender was saying. Ne helped Esmia stand. "Can you walk?"

"Yes," she said.

"Then I think we should get both of you back to the infirmary. Adam, will you come and help?"

"No," Teo said. "Arsenio. Would you go to our house and tell him we are all right?"

The boy nodded gravely and ran off, the flame of the torch long and thin next to him. Mender slipped nir arm around Teo's waist to support her.

Esmia closed her eyes for a moment and listened. She could still hear the scarvhes and all the noise the pursuers were making. But the sounds were growing fainter and were going in the right direction, away from the inhabited part of Siena.

"You did well. Thank you," Teo told her as she leaned on Mender.

"You too," Esmia said. And it was true. This was the first time any of them had fought scarvhes, and they had won.

43:

Renn

Sentients never seemed to reach the extreme emotions that humans were susceptible to, but Nanny undoubtedly was experiencing some kind of distress. "There have been complications," she said, then added, "The technology here is remarkable. Not only can the Superiors communicate with one another via thought, but they also are able to keep constant vigilance of a vast number of places to ensure the safety of the humans under their care."

Renn understood the warning and nodded in agreement.

"I have finished the cure, and the Superiors helped me replicate enough to help everybody in Siena." she continued.

"And Luca?" Renn asked, unable to take in the good news before he knew why Luca wasn't present.

"Apparently there was a misunderstanding regarding his intentions and abilities."

The complications, Renn understood when Nanny explained, were actually quite simple. Luca had told someone he could reprogram artificials, and now the Superiors saw him as a threat to their community. It made perfect sense. From what Renn could tell, the artificials were the leaders of the Shelter. Not humans. Encountering someone who so clearly viewed himself as superior to those who were so called would perceived as a danger. "Where is he now?" Renn asked.

Nanny shook her head. "I don't know. I was told only to wait here for you. They have taken Luca into custody."

Renn tried not to scowl. They could see him and hear him. He had to stay calm. "I would like to see Luca to ensure he is unharmed," he said, not only to Nanny, but to the room at large. That Luca had somehow erred, Renn was in no doubt. Luca spoke and acted without thinking, and he sometimes appeared to take delight in being rude. But that could not possibly warrant his incarceration. Could it?

"I as well," Nanny agreed.

"Where is the cure now?" Renn asked.

"Still in the lab," she said.

The Superiors had Luca. They had the trading materials Luca had brought. They had what the Sienans needed. And they had an underground fortress that made escape hard. Even harder than Florence. Renn sighed. He had nothing apart from his actions to help with the broken water tank, and he doubted that would give him the leverage needed.

"He will be fine. We will be fine," Nanny said. Her voice was warm and soothing. Such a contrast to the Superiors. "They asked me a lot of questions," Nanny said quietly, catching Renn's eyes. "It appears that the Superiors here are quite concerned for my well-being. Since Luca's manner is not one they are accustomed to, they worry that he might not treat me satisfactorily," she explained.

Renn was about to reply when the door opened again. It was not a Superior who entered this time, but a pale, dark haired man whose features reminded Renn a little of Mender although his demeanor was vastly different from the sentient's.

"I hope you aren't busy," the man said, glancing around the room. "I've been asked to accompany you to the Supreme."

Renn exchanged glances with Nanny, but she didn't seem to understand either.

"That is what you wanted, isn't it? Your partner is with the Supreme," Giuliano added to Renn.

He took them to the closest elevator, and they went further down than Renn had been before. It seemed to Renn that the depth dictated the use of the stories in the Shelter. The further down something was, the more foreign it seemed to him.

The level they exited on was so deep in the ground that Renn's ears popped several times before they reached it. It was empty of humans and Superiors alike and the hallway led only to a single set of doors that opened as the party approached.

Inside, the strangest being Renn had ever met was seated in the middle of a circular and otherwise unoccupied room. When Giuliano kneeled, Renn and Nanny both followed his example although it irked Renn.

"Rise," the creature said, and the voice came from several directions at once.

"I have brought you the Superior Nanny and the wanderer Renn," Giuliano said smoothly.

The Supreme stood and approached them. Renn was reminded of his first encounter with Mender; something so weird and otherworldly that his words were insufficient. This creature only held the slightest resemblance to a human being. "Well met, Nanny," the Supreme greeted the other artificial first. It was a pattern Renn saw everywhere in the Shelter, and he was not surprised to see it repeated here.

"Supreme," Nanny said, inclining her head before looking straight up into nir face. Seeing her next to that being emphasized the enormous difference between artificials.

The Supreme turned nir suggestion of a face to Renn. "Wanderer."

Renn didn't reply.

"We were told you have Luca here," Nanny said. Renn was grateful to her for getting straight to the point.

"Yes," the Supreme said. "Indeed I do. Thank you, Giuliano, you may leave."

The Supreme beckoned toward a door in the opposite side of the room. "He is in here," ne said.

The door opened, and Renn followed the Supreme with Nanny making up the rear.

Inside, what looked like inert bodies under white sheets lay on tables. The place was as clean as all the public areas of the Shelter, sleek and bright and with no personal touch. Apart from a bag on the floor spilling some of its contents. The long strings Luca and Teo called wires were littering the floor too, some of them unconnected to anything while others tied strange devices to an indentation in the wall. In the middle of this island of purposeful disarray, a familiar figure sat hunched over something.

A sigh of relief clawed its way up Renn's throat.

"Be with you in a minute," Luca called out. He sounded exactly like he would if Renn had approached him while he was working on something in Siena. "Okay," he added after a moment and swiveled around the chair. He grinned. "Hey, guys."

Renn felt an irrational urge to grab his shoulders and shake him, but when Luca approached them, Renn saw everything the wide grin was intended to distract from. The bruises on Luca's face, the purple, swollen wrist, the dark circles around his eyes. There was fright and humiliation and anger behind the grin.

Luca flashed Nanny a smile and then closed the distance to Renn and pulled him into a sudden embrace. "Are you okay?" he muttered into Renn's ear.

Renn was surprised to feel his own arms automatically wrap around Luca's smaller body. "We are fine," he replied. "Did they hurt you?"

"Nah," Luca mumbled. "I've had worse." He rested his forehead against Renn's shoulder for a moment longer. Renn could feel him smile. As he pulled back, Renn thought he briefly saw another question in Luca's gaze.

Luca hugged Nanny too, and she asked careful, sensible questions while Renn and the Supreme stood looking at them.

282

"What have you guys been up to?" Luca continued. He sized Renn up and pursed his lips at the sight of his new footwear. At least his suit was identical to the one he wore before.

Renn decided now was not the time to tell Luca about his recent adventures. "I fulfilled my part of the deal," he said.

"And they were so grateful they gave you a new pair of boots of all things?" Luca asked.

"My boots got wet," Renn explained.

"Did they, now," Luca muttered. "You'll have to tell me about it later." He clapped his hands. "So! I'm glad you could make it. This is my new, very temporary workplace. You've already met the Supreme. These are my patients, busted artificials One, Two, Three and Four."

Nanny held up her hands. "What happened, Luca?"

Luca crossed his arms over his chest. "Could we have a moment in private?" he asked the Supreme.

"As you wish. I am in no hurry," the artificial said.

Renn wished the same could be said for them. The Sienans were waiting for them to return with the cure. If Luca hadn't gotten himself into trouble, they could be well on their way back by now.

Luca picked up something from the work table. Renn thought he recognized the device, but he had no idea what it did. "Nanny, how is the cure coming along?" Luca asked.

"I have finished it, and there should be enough for everybody in Siena," Nanny replied. "It is currently in the Shelter's medical facilities, but I am assured I can return for it at any time."

"Good." Luca's fingers were holding the device too tightly. Renn wondered if it were a weapon. "I want you both to have a look at what I'm working on," he said. "I focus better with music, though. Do you mind?" He didn't wait for a reply. As he touched his thumb to the contraption in his hand, noise began to erupt from it. Instruments Renn couldn't recognize and a distorted voice singing in a language he couldn't understand. "Pretend I'm showing you things on the artificial and keep your heads down when you speak." Luca's voice was barely audible over the noise. "There's surveillance here, and I don't want the Supreme to monitor this."

"Clever," Nanny said. She pointed to a coil of wires on the table next to the artificial. "Are you sure you're okay? We have been extremely worried."

"Yeah, sorry. I swear I didn't do anything to warrant all this crap. Renn, have you been treated all right?" Luca said, making gestures that didn't match what he was saying.

"Yes. What happened to my boots was pure accident," Renn added, quelling the small voice in the back of his head that wasn't so sure. But even given what had happened to Luca, it was too drastic to think that the accident with the water tank was anything but coincidental.

"Good. I'm working as fast as I can," Luca said. "But to be honest, I guess you could take the cure and go back without me."

"No!" Renn said.

"Keep your head down," Luca said. "You could come back for me later. I'm not sacrificing myself here."

"I would not feel comfortable leaving you here," Nanny interjected.

"I could order you to," Luca said. "But the real trouble is I can't do much more here without spare parts. And I need to ask... I want to hear your opinion of the people here, Renn." He pointed to the artificial's expressionless face.

Renn risked glancing up. Luca's face was unusually worried. He was looking for a particular answer, and Renn hoped he could give him what he needed to hear. "They have technology that reminds me of yours more than anything I saw in Florence. I also saw a garden. It was unbelievable. Even underground, they manage to grow plants. And they have water tanks—"

Luca waved his hand dismissively. "I want to know... if they seem... happy? This whole hierarchy deal is rubbing me in all the wrong ways. Sentients are supposed to be like Mender or Nanny and Alfredo. Not like... that." He made a gesture toward the closed door. "And the Supreme is having me repair other artificials because they can't do that

284

here. But I'm not convinced the thing with Superiors and Supremes is such a good idea, and if they can't repair them on their own... I just don't know if I'm doing a bad thing here."

This was the first time Luca sought Renn's advice on anything. "I think," he said, "that the Shelter's occupants live comfortable lives. From what I have learned, no one goes hungry. They are taken care of."

"But are they happy?" Luca insisted, again with incongruous gestures as if he were describing something that had to do with the lifeless artificial's eyes.

"They seem content in their ways," Renn replied.

"But is that enough? I mean... Those artificials act like they are superior. I mean, obviously. They could use a thorough reprogramming, honestly. Should we leave people to believe their Superiors are almighty, infallible beings who never die? It's kind of fucked up."

"Luca," Renn said. He wanted very much to risk another glance at the other. "You cannot start a revolution."

"It worked pretty well last time, though," Luca interrupted.

"Teo and her peers were already working for a change. You only helped them along. This is not Florence. I don't pretend to understand everything about the Shelter, but I don't see atrocities here. Just difference. We have to respect the Shelter's ways. It is not for us to change them."

"Okay. I guess that makes sense. I just don't like that they don't know what they're missing because they're constantly chaperoned by their artificials. I want them to have choices, you know?"

"The best way to give them that without trying to force them to abandon their ways," Renn said slowly, "is to show them that there are other ways of life. Our presence here is already doing that. I have talked to their researchers about the surface."

"Right," Luca murmured. "Yeah. I guess you're right. Thanks, man. Do you concur, Nanny?"

"You know my priorities," she said.

Luca laughed dryly, "Yeah. I do. But—" Whatever he had meant to say was cut short. "That is why it's difficult to get around to the right pathways," he continued, "so I practically have to look at each segment of nir programming individually."

Renn turned to look at the door. Indeed the Supreme had just entered.

"I'll finish up here as quickly as possible and hope it's enough. If they won't let me go, you need to get the cure back regardless, but come see me first. And be safe, okay?" Luca muttered so softly that Renn could barely hear him.

44:

Luca

Luca rubbed his eyes. He felt like he'd been working non-stop for days. In reality, it had been less than a day, and he'd taken one quick nap to clear his head. But the work he did was intense. You needed to be one hundred percent focused when you sifted through code to look for errors, and when physically repairing circuits, a second's lapse of attention could ruin hours of work. Now he was done, though. As done as he could be, at least. The door opened behind him.

"You're just in time for the big reveal," Luca said, not even bothering to turn. He knew the Supreme's sounds, or lack of sounds really, by now.

"You have finished, then?"

Luca stood up, stretched and turned, unable to resist patting the shoulder of the sentient on the table. "This one should work perfectly when booted up again. Ne will have some memory loss. I can't say how much, but nir original programming is intact." He pointed to the next artificial. "The one there should be fine too. All it took was basically a defrag."

"I will have to take your word for it," the Supreme said in a way that suggested ne was a tiny bit dismayed with that. "And the two others?"

Luca made a face. "Like I said, I can't do shit for the one who was shot. I need parts. And that one," he gestured at the last artificial, "is going to need some new hardware too. Nir circuitry is fried, and I couldn't save much."

Luca endured the Supreme's scrutinizing stare. Some artificials working in law enforcement back in the day would be equipped with rudimentary lie detection, and Luca was probably being analyzed for traces of dishonesty right now. "Want to boot the two up?" he asked instead of asking how his heart rate or body temperature looked.

"In a moment," the Supreme replied. "I was relying on you to repair all of them."

"And I told you it was doubtful I would be able to get all of them up and running," Luca retorted, hating the way his voice threatened to break. "I've been working my ass off here, and there's nothing more I can do. I need parts you don't have."

"You, however, do," the artificial said.

It was Luca's turn to study nem. "Well, yes," he said slowly, "but I can't just magically teleport them here, can I?"

"But you can retrieve them."

"Technically. But—"

"I will remind you that your cooperation with me is the only thing keeping you from being interred. A security detail can easily apprehend you again."

Luca gaped. That was dirty play. Who the fucking fuck programmed that robot to be such a shrewd bastard? "You're blackmailing me," he said. "You are actually blackmailing me!"

"I am attempting to find the solution that will be most beneficial to both of us." Nir voice was so smooth and untroubled that Luca almost shivered. It took a lot to freak him out, but this was doing it. For that fact alone, he should not be cooperating. But what choice did he really have? And Renn said it was okay. That the Shelter's people were happy enough with how things were. He still couldn't believe he'd asked the nomad in the first place. He absolutely hated feeling that his own moral

288

compass was so broken he had to rely on someone who believed epilepsy was caused by evil spirits to tell him what was right and wrong.

"We don't have time," he finally said. "We need to get back to Siena with the cure. People could be dying." Shitfuck, he hoped that was an exaggeration. It probably was. Esmia's tribe had suffered losses, but they were primitives without any idea how to treat a fever, right? They definitely didn't have access to modern medicine or artificials who could care for them 24/7.

"You can go there and come back with the parts you need."

Luca smiled. "That is a great idea!" he exclaimed. "Absolutely perfect. Let's boot these guys up, and then I'll get out of here."

"Though I have no guarantee that you are in fact going to return here as you promised."

"You have my word," Luca said, although he had to admit he was entertaining the idea of breaking that promise. He would have to think about it. Being on the Shelter's good side was preferable, of course, but he wasn't so sure it was a good idea to be too chummy with anyone here.

"This is what is going to happen," the Supreme informed him. "Once I have verified that the two artificials are indeed fully functional, you will leave to get the supplies you need and come back with them, at which point your Superior and your partner can then leave with you."

Luca dug his nails into the palms of his hands in the hope that it would keep him from picking up something and physically throwing it at the Supreme. He was denied any sense of pain to distract him from the anger, but at least he managed not to say or do anything stupid. "I think the plan needs a bit of work," he finally replied. "I'm not going to just leave them as hostages here. What guarantee do I have that you will let them go once I return?"

"They are not hostages," the Supreme said smoothly. "They will be guests here."

"Okay," Luca retorted, trying to keep his temper and his breathing under control. "Then I want to take a guest with me too. In the interest of cultural exchange and all that. And," he added before the Supreme had time to form an objection, "I'm not leaving both of them here. Just one."

"As you wish," the Supreme said. "In the interest of cultural exchange. Both will be treated well."

"Of course," Luca agreed.

"May I ask which of your companions will be staying here?"

There was only one logical choice. "Nanny, my sentient," he said. It felt like betrayal. But then, naming Renn would feel as much as betrayal, so that point was moot.

"Very well. As for the person who will go with you..."

Luca was 99 percent sure ne was going to say Giuliano just to annoy him.

"Marco Osei."

"Okay. Will he get a say in that?" Luca added, almost regretting it.

"That won't be necessary. I have analyzed all maintainers who have gone outside for an estimation of who is most suited for the task."

"Of course you have," Luca muttered under his breath. "Well, let's get started, then."

The first sentient booted up flawlessly. Like Luca had expected, some of nir memory was gone, but ne recalled everything that had happened until a few months before ne malfunctioned. If Luca expected a touching reunion, he was pretty disappointed. After verifying that the artificial worked properly, the Supreme simply sent nem away to take up nir duties. But at least ne thanked him before going.

The second sentient was back to basics. Nir data had been too corrupted to save. Luca had hoped there was an untouchable black box backup as was the case with a lot of advanced sentients in sensitive positions to make sure they weren't tampered with, but no such luck. This didn't seem to bother the Supreme too much, though. Ne sent nem on nir way like ne had the first. Ne was probably spending a bit of nir processor capacity giving nem instructions via the handy network the Shelter artificials shared.

"Giuliano will take you to your companions and Marco now," the Supreme said.

Luca nodded. "Well, until we meet again," he said, holding out his hand.

The Supreme took it in a slightly too tight grip and shook. "Indeed," ne said. "I trust you will contact us by radio if anything unexpected happens."

"Of course." He wanted to add something about the Supreme better taking care of Nanny, but it was unnecessary and would only antagonize the sentient he had to trust. "See you later."

45:

Renn

"Hi, guys!" Luca greeted them when Marco, Nanny and Renn entered the so-called briefing room Marco had been asked to take them all to. Renn hoped they were there only to get the cure and be reunited with Luca so they could all leave.

This time Luca didn't embrace him. He looked even more exhausted than last time they met not even a full day ago, but he was eating a sandwich and drinking something out of a big mug.

Renn noticed that Marco took a slightly defensive stance. It was not strange. Although Renn had done his utmost to explain that what happened between Giuliano and Luca was a misunderstanding and that Luca never used his skills to harm Superiors, Marco was still a child of the Shelter. The mere idea that anyone could do something that even the Supreme could not do was startling to him. The suggestion that Luca's work entailed taking Superiors apart, even if it was to help them, was disconcerting.

"Well, then," Luca said, brushing the back of his hand across his mouth. "I've done all I can here and have been sort of pardoned of my crimes, but there's a bit of a catch. Or two catches, depending on your point of view." He glanced at Marco, then stood up and brushed crumbs off his fingers. Some of them landed on the floor.

"A catch?" Nanny repeated.

"I need to go back home and pick up parts so I can fix the artificials I couldn't repair right away. So I get to leave and go to Siena with the cure, and then I come back here to work. Don't worry," he added, "they'll let me go once I've done the job. But... I had to agree to some terms."

Renn tried not to mirror Luca's sharp intake of breath.

"One of you has to stay here until I've done the job."

"I will stay," Renn said.

Luca bit his lip. His gaze shifted from Renn to Nanny and back. "No," he said. "Nanny stays. Don't argue," he added to Renn with an annoyingly dismissive wave of his hand. "I'm sorry, Nanny."

"Don't be. I will be fine," she replied.

"But—" Renn began.

"No buts, nomad," Luca said. "This is the best option. The second thing," he said, turning to Marco, "is that you get to go with us."

Marco's eyes grew huge and round. His dark skin seemed to grow paler, and Renn almost reached out to steady him.

"With you?" he repeated. "Outside?"

"Yes, outside," Luca replied. No sarcasm, thankfully. "With me and Renn to the settlement I contacted the Shelter from. Then I'm picking up supplies from my place. You can stay with Renn in the meantime. After that we're going back here." He paused, then added, "I don't want to force you. If you really don't want to—"

"No!" Marco interrupted. "I do. I want to. Renn has told me all about his people and the settlements. I want to see. I'm not scared if Renn is there." He looked up at Renn as if seeking approval.

Renn nodded. It was a relief that his presence could make up for the apprehension Marco felt around Luca.

"Oh good," Luca said, clipped and without the sympathy he had exhibited seconds before. "I feel super safe with Renn around too."

Renn looked at the ceiling.

"Well," Luca continued, "You might wanna bring your PJs. I don't wanna waste any more time here, but I'm gonna need some sleep soon."

"Are you sure you should be driving?" Nanny asked.

"I'm not going to fall asleep at the wheel," Luca told her. A brilliant grin lit up his face. "I've got caffeine tabs in the glove compartment. And Renn will keep me awake with his riveting tales. Or poke me with his staff. Whichever. Right?"

Less than an hour later, the three of them were walking up the slope of the valley where the Shelter's entrance was located. Getting out of the Shelter had taken considerably less procedure than getting in, and they did not have to go through decontamination before changing into their own clothes.

When they reached the wall of tall masheenery, Marco stopped and turned. Renn studied him. The maintainer was not wearing the suit and the helmet he had donned at their first meeting outside. His clothes were similar to what he wore inside the Shelter, though of a sturdier quality. He was carrying a backpack with, Renn assumed, personal articles, as well as the portion of the cure he was tasked with carrying. Luca had called him morbid when Renn suggested they split up the vials and syringes between all three of them because in case something happened to one of them, there was still a chance the others would reach Siena. It was the logical thing to do, and despite his objection, Luca had agreed.

A canister was strapped to Marco's pack, and from it, a tube ran to the side of a mask dangling from his neck. It looked like an elaborate version of the ones Luca provided, and true to his character, Luca had made a snide comment about it being overkill that Renn was hardly qualified to evaluate. But his focus was not so much Marco's equipment as his mental state. He was glad to see that Marco coped surprisingly well with the situation.

"Get a move on!" Luca called out. He was already on his way over the ridge of the hill. "Or I'll leave without you!"

"I did not think you were in the habit of making empty threats," Renn replied, louder than he meant to.

"Oh ho!" Luca laughed. "Ten points for snarky comeback to the nomad!"

Renn refused to satisfy him by arguing further.

"I'm sorry," Marco said, briskly catching up to Renn. "The view never stops amazing me."

Renn made a non-committal sound in reply. The view was something Teo talked about quite often too, a stark contrast to the comments about the landscape being dead that Luca would make. To Renn, their surroundings were a more trivial matter. Not that he was unable to appreciate seeing a stretch of greenery or a lake or a particularly stunning ancient city, but to those who had lived their lives inside domes or underground, the mere idea of being outside was something extraordinary. "You are not worried about going with us?" Renn asked, hopefully too softly for Luca to overhear.

Marco looked in Luca's direction and frowned. "No," he then said. "I have always wondered what was out here. I didn't expect we would leave the safety of the Shelter in my lifetime, but here I am. With you." His smile was grateful and a little overwhelmed.

"Seriously though," Luca called back at them, "Are you here to admire the scenery or what?"

They caught up to him quickly. Renn kept an eye on Marco. The maintainer felt like his responsibility, although it was Luca who had asked him to come. But Luca was clearly not taking it. For anything at all. Renn berated himself for that thought. It was not fair of him. Luca was taking responsibility, in his own, erratic way. And besides, Marco did not trust Luca.

Renn also found himself watching Luca. Despite his behavior, Luca was clearly fatigued. Nanny would be the logical choice to bring as she too was able to drive the car. She was also the one who had created the cure they were carrying and would know how to use it correctly and to care for the ill in Siena. Renn only had his wandering skills, and since they would be traveling the majority of the trip by car, there was not much need for those.

"Luca," he began after making sure Marco was occupied studying something on the ground a few paces away. "I am not sure I understand why I am here."

"Most of us feel like that," Luca said. "Oh, not in general? Just here now?" He grinned.

"Yes," Renn confirmed. "Just that."

"Because I said so," Luca said. "But if you want reasons, fine. Nanny is a sentient. They wouldn't dream of hurting her. And since Marco is with us, I need you to take care of your new fanboy."

"My..?"

"Have you seen the way he looks at you?" Luca asked, rolling his eyes. "He thinks you're the best thing since algae-based kebab. 'Oh, I'm not afraid if Renn is with me!'" The last bit came out in a high-pitched tone that did not sound like Marco at all.

"He is attracted to the outside." The moment Renn said it, he realized how it sounded.

Luca snorted with laughter as he sized up Renn with his gaze. "Well," he said.

"The world outside," Renn insisted. "I have told him about the life of wanderers, and he is curious to see some of it for himself."

Luca adjusted his backpack. He ran a hand through his hair. "About that," he said, "You aren't doing a lot of wandering these days."

"I have no Covey," Renn replied. It felt like a lifetime ago that he had considered leaving with Esmia if she moved on. He had never reached a decision, and a lot had changed since then. "I am content in Siena for the moment."

"For the moment," Luca echoed. "Okay."

"I haven't forgotten," Renn said. He had promised to tell Luca if he made up his mind to leave.

"Good," Luca replied, understanding the reference without any explanation which in itself spoke volumes.

Renn shot a glance at Marco. The boy was studying something on a boulder now, touching it carefully with his hand. He quickly straightened up and hurried to catch up to the others. "There was a flower coming out of the rock," he explained.

"I'm glad you're enjoying the sightseeing trip," Luca said.

"I know the circumstances are not what any of us would like," Marco said. "But I am, yes. I have never been this far away from the Shelter before."

Even Luca could not ignore the sincerity in his voice. "Yeah," he agreed, "I'm not a nomad, but I would go nuts living underground."

Renn had no doubt that was true. As for himself, he could not imagine a life without the sky.

46:

Marco

Walking through the wilderness was entirely different from going through the long hallways inside the Shelter. The ground was not at all like a smooth floor where the worst thing that could happen was that your feet became sore if you stood and walked for several hours. It quickly turned out that tired feet was only one of the perils of marching through the rocky, dusty hills. Renn had no trouble, did not skid on loose rocks or painfully kick outcrops with his toes. He kept a steady pace and often checked if the others were all right. Well, checked if Marco were. Luca wasn't as used to it as Renn, but Marco could tell he didn't have to concentrate on finding his footing either.

Marco had not forgotten he was essentially here as a hostage or that they were not on a leisure hike, but on their way to a settlement in order to deliver medicine that could save lives.

Even though Renn had reassured him that Luca respected Superiors and never would deactivate them without their consent, Marco found it hard to fully trust him. But the whole thing about Luca being summoned by the Supreme nemself after threatening Giuliano and how this subsequently ended up with Marco traveling with Renn and Luca was quite obscure, and Marco knew a lot of the details were being kept from him.

Despite his reservations, he found himself asking questions. Most of them had to do with the surroundings, but he also asked Luca how he could stand the sunlight when he had such a pale complexion. It turned out that the other boy used certain lotions to keep the sunlight at bay. Renn seemed surprised to hear this.

As they made progress on their trek, Marco took in the landscape in awe. Everything was vast. The world had no end wall and no ceiling. It also did not have clearly defined and marked floors.

Their transportation was waiting for them beyond the hills on the far side of a shallow ravine that they easily crossed. Renn landed with perfect poise, Luca more aggressively and Marco with a pounding heart.

The car was covered in a layer of dust, although it had only been waiting for a few days.

"You ever seen one of these?" Luca asked and patted the roof of the vehicle.

"No," Marco said. "We do have vehicles, but not like this."

"Well, hop on in," Luca said with a grin, opening a hatch in the side of the car.

"It moves very fast," Renn explained as Marco climbed on board, "but Luca is good at steering it. He would not put us in danger."

"Thank you," Luca called out. He was moving around to the other side in order to open a hatch there.

Marco sank into a cushioned seat and listened to Renn's explanation of safety belts. But if it really were safe, there should be no reason to be wear harness. Marco was not going to question it, though. Instead, he investigated the small cabin. Renn and Luca were sitting in front, Renn strapping himself in while Luca retrieved a couple of tablets from a compartment in the front of the car. He stuffed them into his mouth and began to chew. There was a closed box on the floor next to Marco's feet and an empty plastic bottle that was wedged under Renn's seat. The car was hot, but Luca flipped a switch that turned on a ventilation system. Its whir was nothing compared to the sound of the engine coming to life.

"Okay," Luca said, "We're good to go. But kick me if I fall asleep."

"That will not be necessary," Renn said. Only a few hours ago, Marco would have felt the urge to kick their driver in any case, but as the trip had progressed, he was starting to relax a bit more around Luca. It became harder by the hour to imagine him as the dangerous person Giuliano and the Superiors had made him out to be. The Superiors would never lie, but perhaps it really was a misunderstanding, after all.

The landscape began to move as the car rolled in a lazy circle at a slow crawl. Then it accelerated. Marco began to see the sense in being strapped in when his stomach was jolted into his throat as the car bounced over a bumpy stretch time and again. After a while, the terrain evened out, and Marco could concentrate fully on staring out of the window.

He registered that the two others were talking now and then, but he didn't pay attention. He was flying over the landscape, every so often putting a Shelter length between himself and his home. No, not just that. Between himself and his whole world. Because the Shelter was not only a home. It was a world with everything anyone could ever need and with so much more safety and comfort than the inhospitable landscape outside could ever offer.

Marco was glad he went outside on a regular basis, at least. That had prepared him somewhat. Still, the views rushing past his vision were staggering and breathtaking and... Beautiful. The constant presence of the sky and the ever-changing light hitting the ground at an angle, creating shadows and patterns in the whirling dust was utterly incomprehensible. Any words he could think could not do it justice.

For perhaps the first time, he wondered why no one ever went exploring. There was no law against going outside. Only cautionary tales and the comfort of the Shelter to keep them where they were, but although the world was undoubtedly full of perils, it was also full of beauty. He wondered if he were the only maintainer who viewed the outside repair work like a privilege more than a dangerous chore. He wondered what would happen when he told his family and friends and colleagues about this trip and what would become of the information Renn had given the surface research department.

A jolt and raised voices snapped Marco's attention back to the front seat.

"I wasn't!" Luca was saying. "You're worse than Nanny!"

"If you say so," Renn replied. "But you were getting very close to the edge."

Marco stretched to be able to see out of the window on the driver's side of the car. A few paces away, the ground fell away at a steep angle. Whether Luca had been taking them too close and whether it was due to his exhaustion, Marco couldn't determine. But he was glad Renn was with them. He had seen Renn act in a crisis, knew he was capable of keeping his head, thinking fast and taking the actions needed. More so than most human Shelter inhabitants.

"Right where we left it," Luca said after a while.

Marco leaned forward to look out of the front window of the car. From further away, Siena had not looked special at all. But now Marco could clearly see that it was an inhabited town. There was a wall shielding the settlement from the elements. It was odd to say that it looked new when it was clearly made up of old slabs and rocks, but each item had been carefully placed and interlocked with other pieces, and nothing seemed to have slipped out of place or been overgrown with vegetation.

The car went through a gap in the wall and came to rest next to another, bigger car. Renn and Luca opened the hatches and stepped out. Marco fumbled with the mechanism on his until Renn let him out too.

47:
Teo

The moment she heard the car, Teo left Arsenio's side. Her heart had lodged itself in her throat. She had waited for this moment forever, it seemed, although it really had only been a couple of days. She made her way to the door, barely pausing to put on her shoes before hurrying out. She could not move fast enough, and at the same time, she didn't want to move at all. She had waited, putting her trust in Luca's plan so hard that now she was afraid something had gone entirely wrong.

But hanging back would only delay the inevitable, whether it was getting the cure or being handed bad news. So she limped out, trying not to show her concern or her pain.

When she spotted them, Luca was opening the boot of the Rover. Renn was staring down the street. As she watched, his expression changed from observant to alarmed. She had no doubt he spotted the marks left in the dirt by the scarvhes since no one had done anything to cover them and very few people ventured out.

"Welcome back!" Teo called out. "Did you get the cure?"

Renn's head turned and his expression softened. "Yes," he replied. "How is the situation here?"

Teo held back a sudden flash of anger. She wanted to say most people were ill, that Tonino was dead, that scarvhes attacked while

Renn and the others had been dawdling somewhere instead of hurrying back. Probably, Luca had been too caught up in exciting new technology, or Renn had needed to observe some wanderer holiday that he took for granted others knew of. She pushed back the irrationality. They were not to blame for the situation. Like her, they were doing their best. "We were worried that you took so long," she replied instead.

And then she noticed the third person standing on the other side of the car, helping Luca with something. It was not Nanny. It was a lanky, dark skinned boy with short hair and a bewildered look on his face, and she had never seen him before. "Where is Nanny? Who is this?" she asked.

Luca slammed the boot shut. The boy handed him an armful of what appeared to be bundled fabric. "Nanny was super annoying, so I exchanged her for a younger model," Luca said.

"What?"

"Nanny is safe," Renn came to the rescue. "This is Marco. He is from the Shelter. It's a long story."

Teo smiled distractedly at the boy, Marco, by way of greeting. "It will have to wait, then," she said, stepping toward Luca. "The cure?"

"It's right here," Luca replied and handed the bundle to her. He sized her up. "The hell happened to you?"

"I could ask you the same thing," Teo said. He looked like he hadn't slept for days, and one side of his face was bruised. "But I suggest we get this to Mender right away so we can begin distributing the medication."

"Brilliant idea," Luca replied.

"You were attacked by scarvhes," Renn said as he fell into step next to Teo.

"What?" Luca exclaimed.

"Yes," Teo said at the same time. "But we managed."

"Good," Renn replied. He turned to Marco and added, "Wyverns."

The boy nodded, but Teo could tell his attention was drawn by their surroundings. He was staring in what looked like innocent curiosity. But why was he here? Teo hoped it was the beginning of a trading relationship or something similar with the Shelter, but she could not shake the feeling that it was probably more complicated than that. Couldn't Luca and Renn go anywhere without stirring something up?

"We are going to the infirmary now," Renn was telling Marco. "We have three Superiors working there."

Superiors? Teo filed the comment for later enquiry.

"How bad is it?" Luca asked her. His voice had lost its sarcastic edge, which was good because Teo might very well have snapped if not.

"Tonino died," she replied.

"Shit," Luca said. "I'm sorry."

She nodded in acknowledgment, not trusting herself to answer. Blaming Luca because he took so long was entirely as useless as blaming herself. Instead she focused on what they had to do. She wanted to go directly to Arsenio and give him the cure, but that wouldn't do. She had not founded a new society to play favorites. Just like everything was not solely her responsibility, she should not have special privileges just because of her position here.

"Mender!" Teo called out the moment they entered the infirmary. "They are back with the cure!"

The patients on and by the makeshift beds scattered around the waiting area all began to ask questions.

"My daughter needs it now!" one man said urgently.

Two other people had risen, one from a bed and the other from the floor. They began to approach her with outstretched arms, begging.

"Are you an idiot?" Luca hissed at Teo. "Calm the fuck down!" he added loudly. "Mender gets to distribute the medication, and everybody waits their goddamn turn!"

Renn moved swiftly to stand beside Teo. His usually calm presence had turned threatening. He would have been an excellent arbiter.

"It's all right!" Teo said. "Mender knows what to do. Please stay calm. There is enough for everyone."

It was at this point that Mender, thankfully, appeared. Esmia followed nem.

304

"The cavalry has arrived!" Luca called out.

Mender nodded, and Teo was once again amazed that ne looked perfectly serene and not at all exhausted despite the circumstances. Esmia appeared as worn out as Luca. "I will prepare the medication and begin to distribute it as quickly as possible," Mender said, loudly enough for everyone to hear. "Please be patient a little longer." Ne turned to Luca, Renn and Marco. If ne was surprised to see a stranger and the absence of Nanny, ne did not show it. "Please come with me. Esmia and Teo, you too."

Teo was glad to escape the waiting room. Luca was right that announcing the cure to everyone like that wasn't particularly farsighted of her.

Esmia brought up the rear of the group and closed the door behind them. They were in Gabriele's room. Teo loathed that place even more than she hated the rooms full of patients. There was just one bed in here, and Gabriele was asleep or unconscious in it. She hated seeing him like that.

"What if something happens while we are all here?" Renn asked Mender, indicating Esmia with a nod.

"It is better for us to hurry up with the medication," Mender replied. "And Sia and Simon are doing well. Speaking of your artificials, Luca, where is Nanny?"

Luca had wandered over to Gabriele's bed. "Um, she had to stay for a bit," he said. "It's complicated. But I've got everything under control. This is Marco, by the way. Mender, Marco. Marco, Mender."

"Welcome to Siena," Mender said.

"Thank you. You are a Superior, aren't you?" the boy blurted out.

"He means sentient," Luca said.

"I am," Mender confirmed. "Now, let us get started."

Ne examined the syringes and explained to everyone present how to administer them. "I will begin distributing the medication here with Sia. Esmia, will you take Simon and visit those who are still in their homes?"

"Yes," Esmia said. Her mouth was a firm line.

"Teo, can you take one to Arsenio?" Mender continued.

"Yes," Teo promptly said. "I can go to other houses too."

"I would like to help as well," Renn said. He glanced at Marco.

"I can go with Renn," the boy suggested.

"Super. I'm going to be realistic here and opt out," Luca said. "Is there anywhere I can crash?"

Teo was glad he said it because she would have felt obligated to ask him to rest otherwise. "You can come with me," she said. She didn't like leaving Arsenio alone, and even given their relationship, she would feel better knowing Luca was there. Besides, she needed to talk to him about Nanny and what had happened in the Shelter.

And with that, they all went their separate ways. Luca looked like he might collapse from fatigue at any moment, and Teo was still limping after the scarvhe attack. They were a pitiful sight. When they entered her home, she directed him to the cushions in the living room and went to get him a blanket. When she returned, the ancient teenager had arranged the cushions like a mattress and was already curled up and half asleep.

Teo sighed and went back to the bedroom. The smell wasn't as bad as in the infirmary, but even so, there was a sour-sweet scent of sweat and illness. She sat down on the edge of the bed. "Hey."

Arsenio stirred and opened his eyes, blinking up at her. "I wasn't asleep," he said blearily.

"If you say so," she replied. "Let me have your arm."

She could see the implications sink in as Arsenio pushed away the blanket. "They are back?"

"Yes. I have the medication for you here," she replied.

His skin was covered in goosebumps, and he shivered as Teo put a wet cloth to his arm. He was still in better shape than a lot of the other Sienans, possibly thanks to the injection Luca had given him earlier, but he was running a high fever.

"Are you qualified to do that?" Arsenio asked.

"Mender showed me how," Teo said. "Renn is doing it too."

Arsenio's gaze wasn't entirely steady as he watched the needle sink into his arm. "And Luca?" he asked.

Teo breathed out. One down, twelve more to go. She smiled at Arsenio. Injections were supposed to work fast, but it would still take a while. She wouldn't see any effect today. "Actually, Luca is taking a nap in the living room," she said.

"What? Why is—" A coughing fit interrupted him.

Teo reached out for a cup on the floor. It was still half full of lukewarm water. "Drink," she said, "and then rest. I need to go distribute the cure. Luca has been working hard and needed sleep," she added by way of explanation although she still wasn't certain what exactly he had been doing.

She kissed Arsenio's forehead and smiled. "I'll see you soon."

48:

Teo

They worked quickly on distributing the cure. Clara had joined them, and Teo saw her, Esmia and Renn and Marco go from one residence to the next. Someone, Teo suspected it was Renn, had suggested drawing a line in the dirt outside each house they visited so they all could easily tell where the others had been.

Afterward, they regrouped in the infirmary. There was a noticeable change in the atmosphere. There was hope now, Teo thought. Perhaps even confidence. They just had to get through the next few days, and even if more of them should get ill, there was enough medicine for them too.

Luca and Arsenio were both asleep when Teo returned to check up on them. She stood by Arsenio's side for a while. His breathing was labored and shallow, once in a while hitching in a way that had jolted her wide awake with worry in the middle of the night for the past few days. She touched his forehead lightly. He would be better soon.

In the living room, Luca had turned over in his sleep and lay sprawled on his back in a strange tangle of cushions, blankets and limbs. He was snoring lightly. He looked so defenseless. So young. Teo considered waking him up, but decided against it. There would be plenty of time to hear his version of the events later. She would seek out Renn and the boy from the Shelter first.

As it turned out, they were easily found. They stood together in the middle of the dusty street in front of the watchtower, and Renn was explaining something to Marco.

"Hello," Teo greeted them.

"Teo," Renn said. He sounded relieved. "Perhaps you can answer Marco's questions."

"I can certainly try," Teo replied, smiling at them.

"May I leave you for a little while?" Renn asked. "I would like to make certain there are no scarvhe nests left."

"Alone?" Teo said. "We did search the ruins for more scarvhes, but if we missed something, it could be dangerous."

Renn shook his head. "You won't have missed any scarvhes. I'm only looking for eggs. I can easily do that on my own. If you don't mind?" The last part was for Marco.

"I don't mind," the boy said.

"Well, then," Teo started when Renn started walking toward the ruins. "Is there anything you would like to see?"

"Renn said he would take me up there later," Marco replied, nodding at the watchtower. "But I'm curious about your water and food supplies."

Teo made a gesture for him to follow. "Come on. I'll show you our greenhouses and the big well."

"Did the wyverns—I mean, the scarvhes hurt you?" Marco asked.

"Yes," Teo replied, wishing her limp wouldn't be so obvious. "It's not serious." Painful, yes, but not serious. Mender had given the wounds a few stitches, and now they just needed time to heal. It was a small price to pay for what they had achieved.

Marco looked like he didn't quite believe her.

"I have to confess I am not sure why you decided to come with Renn and Luca to Siena," Teo said.

"Well," Marco began. He interrupted himself with a short laugh. "I'm not completely sure why I'm here, either," he said. "The Supreme nemself made the arrangement with Luca. His Superior is in the Shelter while I am here, and Luca needs to take me back with some components he calls hardware. Then his Superior will go with him when he leaves again."

That sounded too much like a hostage situation for Teo's liking. "I hope you are not very upset by it," she offered.

Marco frowned as if he wasn't really certain himself. "I'm not," he said. "I'm a maintainer. I go outside to take care of our communications array. It's like your antenna," he added as if that explained everything. "And Renn has been very kind to me. Luca too."

"I'm glad to hear that," Teo said.

"I was asking Renn about your Superiors. I have only seen four, including Nanny," Marco said before she had time to ask.

Superiors, Supreme. Teo wished she had managed to talk to Luca or Renn about the Shelter. Here she was with someone who appeared to be a willing hostage and who, from the sound of it, had a completely different view on artificials than anyone in Siena. But she would have to deal with it like she did with everything else, plunging into it relying on her intuition and diplomacy and hoping she'd land on her feet. She was not supposed to have all the solutions, she reminded herself. Only do her best. "There are no more Superiors here," she said. "Where I grew up, there was not a single one. But it sounds like the Shelter has more?"

"We do!" Marco exclaimed. "I can't imagine living without them."

"Nanny, Sia and Simon usually all live with Luca," Teo explained, once again wondering about the nature of the latter two. "We are very fortunate to have Mender here with us. Ne is a great assistant to our doctor. Especially now that he is ill."

Something changed in Marco's expression, and Teo was afraid she had offended him somehow. "I assumed Mender is in charge of your medical facilities," he said.

They had reached the well, and it was a welcome interruption. "This is the biggest of our wells," she said. "We have constructed a pulley system to get a bucket to the water."

Marco peered over the clay barrier around the hole. "It's not very deep," he said. "I didn't know there was water this close to the surface."

"The Shelter is much deeper, I imagine," Teo said.

"Yes. By many levels." Marco pushed himself away from the barrier.

"When I met Mender, ne told me ne is a nurse," Teo said, hoping she had decided on the least offensive way to explain matters. "Ne was employed by humans to work for them as an equal before the fall."

Marco was staring at her.

"Our Superiors are not—" She managed to stop herself before she said superior. "They are not in charge of us. They have jobs and functions like humans, but we do not answer to them."

"Then," Marco said, "who looks after you?" His eyes widened as he came to a realization. "Does it mean you have a human Supreme? Are you the Supreme?"

"No." Teo shook her head. "We don't have a Supreme. We all make decisions for ourselves, and we agree on the rules we want to live by."

Marco nodded. He was frowning in concentration, trying to come to terms with this version of a society.

"But," Teo added, surprising herself, "for practical reasons, I am Siena's spokesperson. I am the one who makes sure everybody gets a say, and I do my best to solve problems peacefully when they arise." And she found that she believed it. She could not shoulder all of Siena's problems alone. She could not fix everything and save everyone. But she could organize things. She could take responsibility for herself and ask for help when needed. She found that perhaps the trust her fellow settlers placed in her was not coincidental at best and ill-placed at worst. Everybody did indeed have jobs and functions, and, astonishingly, she discovered that she finally felt at ease with hers.

49:

Esmia

It was still quite strange that, at the end of every day, Esmia's feet were so sore that she pulled off her shoes with a sigh of relief. She was a wanderer. She knew how to walk for hours in tough terrain. But standing still and going back and forth over the same, short distances in the infirmary was not something she was used to.

When the cure started working, there would be less work for her, Teo had said, assuming that Esmia would be staying in Siena. Already, Esmia could tell Gabriele was better. She had coaxed him into eating almost a full meal earlier that day, and although his clothes were too loose on him now and his glasses didn't conceal the dark circles around his eyes, he would be well again.

"Amen," Clara said.

Esmia looked up. They were seated on opposite sides of a small table with a pot of soup and a loaf of bread on the table between them. Clara couldn't eat without first drawing a cross in the air and putting her hands together in front of her to utter a string of words. Esmia understood she was giving thanks, and while being thankful for every meal was second nature to Esmia herself, she was grateful to the land and the animals and the people who gave her something to eat. Clara's thanks were aimed at something else. Someone else. Clara had explained to Esmia that this someone was called God. God was mostly invisible, but his sign was the cross that Clara drew and had put on top of the church. Esmia thought it was a little like the signs wanderers carved into rocks and the ground for others to find their way.

Clara reached across the table and touched Esmia's good hand. The burns on the other one were healing well, but they would probably leave scars.

"We can eat now," Clara said, smiling. She wasn't angry that Esmia didn't know this God person or that Esmia didn't really believe the story about how God had created the world. She might be a little disappointed, though.

"Thank you," Esmia said, finding it quite a bit more relevant to thank Clara for the food than an invisible being who may or may not be listening in.

Clara squeezed her hand and then let go of it. Her touch was warm and comforting, and Esmia was, not for the first time, struck by how almost unbelievable all this was. That after all that had happened, after all that she had done, here she was. She was welcome here, in Siena and in Clara's home. No, it was far more than that. It was also the spirits leaving her alone if only she ate the pills Luca had given her. And...

"Es?" Clara asked. She was tearing a piece off the loaf of bread and stopped mid-motion. "What is wrong?"

"Nothing," Esmia said, quickly blinking away her tears. "Nothing is wrong."

Clara put down the bread, stood up and was at Esmia's side before Esmia could tell her not to worry. Her arms felt steady when they wrapped around Esmia's shoulders. "It's all right," she whispered.

"I'm not sad," Esmia said with the barest hint of a hitch in her voice. The hole in her chest was not gone. She wished her father could be here with her. She wished Tonino were not dead and that the Sienans had not suffered so. But something was growing now, slowly beginning to fill out the emptiness.

"Sometimes you need to cry for other reasons," Clara replied and brushed her lips against the back of Esmia's head, sending a strange thrill down her spine. She wasn't used to being touched like this. She wasn't used to being touched at all, really. Esmia reached up and put her hand on Clara's arm and felt the wonder that was Clara not shirking away from her. She was helping filling that hole.

"But the soup," Esmia said.

"Worse things than cold soup have happened this week," Clara said. "And better things, too," she added.

Esmia couldn't help smiling. Teo and Clara had both told her she was free to stay in Siena if she wanted to. They hadn't told everybody that the illness was her fault. It didn't feel entirely right for the Sienans to thank her for working with Mender, Sia and Simon caring for the ill, not knowing she had brought the suffering on them, but she could live with it for now.

The previous night, Esmia brought it up with Teo. Teo thought for a while, then said that the illness may have spread to them in a different way, or they may have been surprised by another epidemic later and have lost more people to it because they were not prepared. She said something about never really knowing what consequences anything would have and what mattered was being willing to face them. After that, she went on to talk about wanting to go to one of the stagnant towns to trade. She suggested that maybe Esmia could come with her since she knew more about the stagnants' ways. It made Esmia feel... wanted. It was a good feeling.

"I like it," she said. Then, feeling she should clarify, "I like Siena. And the people. I like... this," she added. She didn't quite know what to call it yet.

Clara squeezed her shoulders, then moved to her side. "Does that mean you are staying?" she asked.

Esmia met her eyes. "Yes," she said. "I would like that."

Clara's face lit up in a big smile. "I would like that too," she said.

"But I need to see Renn," Esmia added.

Clara wrinkled her nose. "I know he has certain strong opinions," she said, "and he is an important part of our community, but—"

"We are both wanderers," Esmia said, although she was well on her way to becoming a stagnant, wasn't she? And that was the whole point in talking to him. "There are things I must say."

Clara studied her for a moment. "All right. Let's eat, and then you can find Renn if you want."

The buildings were casting long shadows when Esmia found Renn. He was on his way down from the watchtower. Luca and Marco had left to go back to the Shelter two days ago, and Esmia thought that maybe Renn was keeping an eye out for the car. She was didn't understand the finer points of Luca's dealings with that place, but she could tell Renn was worried. Part of her was wondering why he stayed behind, then, but it was not for her to ask. Especially since he was, as Clara put it, an important part of the community.

"Renn," Esmia called.

Renn stopped and turned.

"May I speak with you?" she asked.

He had taken her in, probably saved her life, only to find out that she was a plaything of the spirits. And even if Luca's little, white pills had driven the spirits away, she had still brought illness to Siena. She couldn't blame him if he wouldn't talk to her. "Yes," he replied. "Will you walk with me?"

"I will," she replied and caught up to him.

Renn led her out of the settlement and turned. He was, Esmia guessed, about to inspect Siena's boundaries, making sure there weren't any scarvhes nesting close to the town.

She glanced at him. The Sienans might be kind to her, but Renn was the most normal, predictable person here. She knew his ways because they were hers too. But he had never told her if he meant to stay in Siena for good, or if he were waiting for an opportunity to leave.

"I should have been honest with you from the beginning," she broke the silence. She didn't want to have this talk, but she had to.

"Yes," Renn agreed, then, reluctantly, "But it appears that your problem has disappeared."

Problem. Not illness, not spirits. Esmia understood his choice of words. It was hard to pull up your ways by the roots and discard them in favor of someone else's. "Unless," she said, swallowing hard.

Renn inclined his head. He wasn't looking at her, but she could tell he knew what she meant. "They believe the illness travels by air and touch. Not that it was brought upon us by the spirits," he said. "Whichever the reason, we have the cure now."

"Yes," Esmia agreed. And she knew they would not tread closer to the subject, not at this time, and perhaps never. But there were still questions that she had to ask.

The protective eastern wall ended, and Renn stopped. He stood staring out into the wilderness beyond the settlement. Esmia followed his gaze. All she saw was sand and dust, ridges in the distance that may be derelict cities or mountains. She saw a vast, desolate world. Something moved out there while they were looking. It looked like a pack of wolves crossing the wasteland, from one ruin to the next or to a haven of greenery and water. Esmia saw loneliness and danger.

She wondered what Renn saw.

He resumed walking, turning to move into the ruins flanking the settlement. There was a lot of materials here and plenty of space to expand, which was something Clara was hoping for and expecting by the sound of it.

"I would like to stay," Esmia said as they weaved their way through the rubble and the sparse vegetation along the lived-in part of Siena. Her heart thumped so loudly Renn might be able to tell.

Esmia was starting to think he wasn't going to reply when finally he turned to face her. "You don't need my permission," he said.

"Maybe not," Esmia heard herself say, "But I would like your acceptance."

"You have it," he promptly replied. And then, unexpectedly, added, "And my respect."

Esmia's heart made a small leap into her throat before it settled back down where it belonged. "Thank you," she said. That was more than she had dared hoping for. She had been feared, but never respected. "And you?" she asked before she lost her courage.

Renn's brow furrowed slightly, and Esmia saw his gaze shift back to the expanse beyond the city before his expression changed back into his usual pleasant demeanor. "I am here now," he replied.

Esmia couldn't decide if she heard a trace of sadness in his voice. And she could definitely not tell whether such a trace could be because he missed his old life or if he longed for more permanence. She did not ask because she had a feeling he didn't know the answer either. "They are grateful for you," she said instead. "Everyone in Siena. And Luca too."

Renn's gaze darted to her, surprised. "I am happy to be of use," he said. And despite the stiffness of that statement, he smiled. And it occurred to Esmia that she had never seen Renn smile so openly and honestly before.

She felt her own expression soften as the fear of Renn's reaction evaporated like rain from a scorched plain. Her lips curved into a big, completely surprisingly happy grin.

Epilogue:
Luca

Clouds were gathering on the horizon. Renn would be able to tell if they were heavy enough to cause a downpour and how fast they were moving. But Renn was not here, and all Luca could do was go full throttle. Which, admittedly, he was perfectly happy with.

Next to him, Nanny glanced more than a little critically at the speedometer. Luca pretended he didn't see. It wasn't like there was a speed limit or anything.

The exchange had gone almost flawlessly. Luca tried not to think of it as a hostage exchange. Marco had been super chatty on the way back to the Shelter, asking Luca about the wonders he'd seen in Siena and going on about how cool Renn was, how nice Teo was, how cool Renn was, how interesting it was to meet Mender and the semis... And a bit about how cool Renn was. In the end, Luca decided to introduce him to the time-honored tradition of blasting out blendpunk while on a roadtrip.

When they had gone through the awful decontamination process, Giuliano met them. He seemed surprised that Luca and Marco had returned which didn't exactly improve Luca's opinion of him. As if he'd have left Nanny there. As if he'd have abducted Marco. As if he wouldn't keep his promise.

At least the Supreme expected Luca to uphold his end of the bargain. Ne left him to work and agreed to let Nanny assist. It only took a couple of days to fix the artificials, and Luca enjoyed a bit more comfort during this stay than the last one. And at the end of the day, the Shelter was an impressive construction, a smoothly run society and full of artificials so gorgeously built, inside and out, that they practically gave him a hard-on working on them. Okay, so the whole thing was a bit of an ethical grey area what with helping the Supreme keeping up the appearance of the godlike artificials and aiding a society run by secret-mongering sentients, but it wasn't like he had much of a choice. And besides...

"You know, I like to think we started something good," Luca said.

Nanny quickly glanced at him before shifting her attention back to the quote-unquote road as if she needed to keep an eye on it for him. "Yes?" she asked.

Luca made a vague gesture with one hand. "Yeah. Contact, first of all. Possibility of trading and exchanging knowledge. And Marco loved Siena. He'll tell people. Maybe more of them will want to climb out of their hole in the ground someday. We could have some kind of student exchange program."

"I'm glad you are happy with the outcome, after all," Nanny said.

Luca grinned and swerved around an outcrop of rocks.

"Do you need to go so fast?" Nanny finally asked with a certain degree of exasperation.

"Yes," Luca replied. "I do. Don't worry, I'm a good driver."

"I know you are," she said. "But you are also an overly confident one."

He shrugged. She was programmed to worry about him and keep him safe. Programming was a funny thing. It could go corrupt over time, but mostly, everyone was following theirs. For advanced sentients, there was a possibility of development as their experiences and inputs multiplied and they learned new tricks. Luca had created and sifted through enough code to know that everything wasn't completely deductible. They weren't that different from human beings, really. And the Shelter artificials were the most advanced of their kind Luca had ever worked on. He couldn't help wondering what they would think of the small army of deactivated, salvaged artificials he kept in his storage unit.

Luca decided to keep it to himself, but he had searched for a few things in the Shelter artificials' priority protocols while he was working on them. He discovered what appeared to be their original orders to keep their humans safe in the Shelter, but he was convinced they had found room for interpretation along the way. The way they ran the Shelter was not entirely in accordance with the base programming. It wasn't exactly data corruption. More like evolution and exploitation of their innate choices. He copied some of what he found to study back home. And it was tempting to leave a tiny suggestion in there that perhaps the humans in their care weren't children who needed their constant surveillance and guidance anymore.

"What?" Luca asked when he realized Nanny was talking to him.

"I said, you don't seem so disappointed that the Shelter wasn't what you had hoped for."

"True." He thought about it while they sped across the open plain. They were going toward the potential rain, but they didn't seem to get closer, so probably whatever those clouds were cooking up wouldn't be a problem.

Truth be told, Luca did feel used by the Shelter. He did feel disappointed that he hadn't found an opportunity to punch Giuliano in the face. He would have liked an agreement about trading. He would have liked for the Supreme to show some gratitude. But he had gotten the cure, and he had managed to leave the place in one piece and not to leave anyone permanently behind. In the end, he and the Supreme had parted on neutral terms. That was all he could ask for at this point, and he refused to mope about all the things he hadn't gotten out of the visit.

"I guess you just have to suck it up and take it for what it is," he said. "And if one Shelter exists, who knows what else is hiding right under our noses? I'm not done looking. But right now, I only want to get back to Siena and see how things are going. What?"

Nanny was smiling. "In a way, it seems like you are getting everything you wanted."

Luca kept his eyes on the not-road ahead. They would be back in Siena in less than an hour. He wondered what Renn was doing right now. If he was in his watchtower, and if so, if he would come down when he spotted the Rover. "Yeah," he agreed, "almost."

Acknowledgements

You have now reached the book equivalent of movie end credits. This is where I tell you about a bunch of amazing people who made Seeking Shelter a reality. And maybe include a small treat. Who knows?

I am grateful to Spaceboy Books and in particular Nate Ragolia and Shaunn Grulkowski for letting me join their awesome spaceship crew. For loving my debut novel so much they let me turn it into a trilogy. How cool is that?

My gratitude to my wonderful, supportive family and friends for having my back and listening to me rant (a lot) about people living in a future with no Moon.

A special thank you to my ass-kicking alpha readers who help me out early in the writing process. And to the beta team and sensitivity readers for providing fantastic feedback and loving my characters. Thank you also to the Fish Climbing Trees community and the *Space Mantis* podcast crew. And gratitude to my patrons Gabe Clark, Kathy Joy, Kosomolski, Ryan Watt, Skjalm, ZombiEdward, and many more. I really appreciate your support on Patreon.

And, of course, lots of scritches and love to the feline trinity who make sure to keep me company, purr at the right moments, and only walk all over my keyboard once in a while.

Renn shielded his eyes with a hand, squinting to better see the slowly moving shapes in the distance.

He was standing on the platform on top of the watchtower to look out for changes in the weather conditions. But it was a clear day with blue skies and specks of dust glittering in the sunlight. It was a perfect day for outdoor work. A perfect day for migration, too. And longer he looked, the more certain he became that the lumps on the horizon were people.

Judging by the direction they were coming from, they were not Florentines or stagnants or even coming from the Shelter. No, these were wanderers. And they were headed for Siena.

About the Author

Marie Howalt was born and raised in a small North European kingdom called Denmark and started writing stories at the age of 11 when the local library ran out of science fiction and fantasy to devour.

After graduating from the University of Copenhagen with a master's degree in English studies and religion, Marie worked as a translator between English and Danish for years before completely changing tracks due to the chronic illness PCS (Post Concussion Syndrome).

Now Marie writes as much as physically possible. The stories are a lot longer and quite a bit more complex than the childhood scribbles, but they still take place in the far future, fantasy worlds or alternate realities.

When not writing, Marie enjoys being a cat perch, voice acting, drawing, reading and arguing with and bribing imaginary people to tell their stories. Sometimes, you can find Marie pushing art supplies in one of Copenhagen's oldest shops.

Marie's first traditionally published novel, *We Lost the Sky*, was published in 2019. *Seeking Shelter* is its sequel and the second part of the *Moonless* trilogy. The third book is currently scheduled for release in 2021.

Drop by and say hello on Twitter or on Instagram @mhowalt, visit www.mhowalt.dk, or support Marie's writing while getting special perks and previews at www.patreon.com/mariehowalt

About the Publishing Team

Nate Ragolia was labeled as "weird" early in elementary school, and it stuck. He's a lifelong lover of science fiction, and a nerd/geek. In 2015 his first book, *There You Feel Free,* was published by 1888's Black Hill Press. He's also the author of *The Retroactivist,* published by Spaceboy Books. He founded and edits BONED, an online literary magazine, has created webcomics, and writes whenever he's not playing video games or petting dogs.

Shaunn Grulkowski has been compared to Warren Ellis and Phillip K. Dick and was once described as what a baby conceived by Kurt Vonnegut and Margaret Atwood would turn out to be. He's at least the fifth best Slavic-Latino-American sci-fi writer in the Baltimore metro area. He's the author of *Retcontinuum,* and the editor of *A Stalled Ox* and *The Goldfish,* among others.

www.ingramcontent.com/pod-product-compliance
Lightning Source LLC
Chambersburg PA
CBHW030415180626
46812CB00005B/2026